FRANCESCO PACIFICO

CLASS

a novel

MELVILLE HOUSE
BROOKLYN • LONDON

Originally published by Mondadori in 2014
Copyright © 2014 by Francesco Pacifico
Translation copyright © 2017 by Francesco Pacifico

Originally written in Italian, this book was rewritten in English, partially rearranged, and heavily edited by the author and his editor, Mark Krotov. The author would like thank Mark for his passion, brilliance, and friendship.

First Melville House Printing: May 2017

Melville House Publishing   8 Blackstock Mews
46 John Street   and   Islington
Brooklyn, NY 11201   London N4 2BT

mhpbooks.com
facebook.com/mhpbooks
@melvillehouse

ISBN: 978-1-61219-593-3

Design by Fritz Metsch

Printed in the United States of America

1 3 5 7 9 10 8 6 4 2

A catalog record for this book is available from the Library of Congress

For Francesca

As for certain lesser faults, we must believe that, before the Final Judgment, there is a purifying fire.   CATECHISM OF THE CATHOLIC CHURCH

CONTENTS

A NOTE FROM THE AUTHOR

This is a novel about Italians, most of whom speak Italian to one another. Dialogue that appears in italics indicates that these Italians have lapsed into English.

PART I

LA SPOSINA

*T*he personal fulfillment of the bourgeois isn't worth the carbon footprint required to sustain it.

You needed your own space, Ludovica. So your parents freed up an apartment they were subletting to a friend and gave it to you—the no-nonsense twenty-one-year-old who looked forward to movie nights at home, made sure the vase on the windowsill always had a fresh flower in it, wore overalls on Sunday mornings. Who was always enmeshed in one or two or three jobs at once, each one more noble and demanding than the next: bartending, dog sitting, tutoring the ungrateful at a private high school (afternoons), assisting the grim, hopeless woman at the university library's circulation desk (weeknights), leading workshops on digital marketing for aging members of endangered industries (weekends).

The family friend who'd been staying at the apartment was divorced and had three daughters: five, seven, and eleven. Your parents gave him three months' notice. You never asked where he ended up. Now you were on your own, had bills you paid yourself, and you were proud. But though you tried to be frugal—you never took baths, you switched the laptop off at night—it was still one more hot water heater, one more refrigerator, one more washing machine, one more TV set, all of them weighing on the earth.

Your apartment was in Nuovo Salario, far from the center. Your parents paid the rent directly to the local council, which owned the building. (Only €300, rent controlled.) You paid your parents late, but you insisted on paying, because you weren't your brother. He was studying management theory then—a good, boring Roman who lived with his parents and had never even tried to get a part-time job to earn himself some pocket money. But maybe he'd been right. What were part-time jobs really good for? What good was life on one's own, really, in the face of European decline and the increasing global irrelevance of your social class?

Still, you could have stayed put in Nuovo Salario, out there beyond the Villa Ada, on the outskirts of the city toward the high-way, near Via Salaria, where the underage hookers huddle near the bus stops. You could have embraced the pain of taking the endless Delle Valli Bridge to cross the railroad tracks, the shortest of the long routes to the center. You could have stayed among them, the others: the mechanics repairing cars on the sidewalks; the old women pushing their carts through the supermarkets; the loud children, whose voices echoed through the preschool playground every morning and afternoon.

You'd grown up among the sycamores and palms and lemons of the Quartiere Trieste. The luscious foliage suffocating the gates, the confident garages that faced the street—these were your childhood. You knew you'd leave behind that bourgeois torpor, and Nuovo Salario was an improvement; it was more truthful. But you had to move closer to the center. You could have stayed put in Nuovo Salario, but it was always going to be a stopgap.

And so the time soon came for you to try to convince your parents that Pigneto was a pretty good investment, no? It was closer to the center and much more lively. You didn't say—you barely thought!—that it was a more fitting place for someone like you.

They sold their share of your grandparents' house near St. Peter's to your uncle and used the €350,000 cash on a *villino* in Mandrione, a *borgata* near Pigneto only a five-minute ride from San Giovanni and Piazza Vittorio. Two stories that overlooked a backyard, a winding street (*"so* Roma," you could hear everyone say), and the ancient Roman aqueduct—right there, ten meters from your window.

They'd taken a guess about market trends, your parents, and they'd been proven right. "You might use it for a while . . ." they said. That *for a while*—the ellipsis embedded in every syllable—was so tactful, so charming. (And *borgata*, too, was delightful. Mandrione was a perfect neighborhood, unworthy of nuance or diminution, so the word was a lie, a sexy Pasolinian cover-up.)

You remodeled the house with your parents' money. You dealt with the workers yourself—the Romanians, the Albanians, the Senegalese, the Ciociari—though you got a little help from Lilla, your architect friend, who was a trainee in her uncle's practice.

And yet . . . what was all this good for? It was gentrification, waste, a redirection of resources within a closed system. Europe was dying.

THE PURSUIT OF the good life—in both its moral and aesthetic guises—takes work. But you had Lorenzo. He was handsome and healthy, his shoulders made for polo shirts, his eyes designed to shine emerald green whenever he took off his aviators. His aunt and uncle were influential philosophy professors, and he was a post-doc, also in philosophy. They helped him score grants, and he, meanwhile, could be found at parties, where he'd say, "I'm a *filmmaker*," in English, to anyone who'd listen.

Your wedding was "low key," you told everyone before and after, but still, it was a whole thing. You had, after all, asked your friends to hop into their cars on a Saturday in the middle of summer and drive to a reception at your great-aunt's house in Versilia. (Did you think about the effect of all that A/C use? Nobody really carpooled, after all.) The caterers served fresh fish and fried vegetables ("deceptively light" everyone joked), and somehow, by the end, there was nothing left on either of your wedding registries. You laughed as you scrolled through them. Could this really be you, you thought, a grown-up with her own designer chairs and her own spare room to put them in?

By this time you were renting a flat in Piazza Bologna, surrounded by the middle classes. They all seemed to carry shopping bags everywhere they went, and whenever you met them in the lobby or in the elevator or at the tobacconist's, they spoke with a strained, uncivil rudeness. You'd flee the neighborhood whenever you could, shuttling to Mandrione every day and urging the workers to hurry up. Still, even this was better than Nuovo Salario.

You moved into the shiny new house before it was ready, in 2009. You unwrapped all your gifts and stared at them and arranged them and rearranged them while construction workers stood you up and dropped your calls. There were still wires to bury, walls to paint. Lorenzo, meanwhile, had stumbled onto another change in scenery: a year at Columbia, paid for by Rome's Sapienza University. He filled out the grant application, and you thought about New York.

You flew to the States in the fall of 2010. Your parents transferred money into your account for the airfare and a year's worth of rent. You'd been thinking out loud about wanting to be a mother, and before you got pregnant, you said, you wanted to satisfy this whim. You were being mature.

But you weren't clueless. You had gumption. You'd always

6

made more than Lorenzo, and though you loved him, you knew that not sharing the money your parents had sent was a choice. Your parents could justify the transfers to themselves ("The kids need our help; they grew up when public debt was so high, and that was all our generation's fault! They really didn't get much of a chance, when you think about it"), but could you justify your own withholding? You felt so beautiful with him.

You rented a large room in a rickety apartment whose mottled hardwood floors slanted gracefully, north to south—no New York apartment had perfectly straight floors, you'd heard. There were large windows that let in pale, Nordic light and a rotten front door with three locks. You had two flatmates, from Rome and Turin, who were in the city shooting documentaries about infrastructure.

As soon as Lorenzo had gotten the grant, you knew there was only one neighborhood where you wanted to be, and here you were. This was Williamsburg—"Willy"—where you could live among the hip and the young and the wealthy. (The non-wealthy were here, too, of course. They came by bus, like in *Midnight Cowboy*, and their disguises could hold for a while, but soon their money would run out, and they'd disappear.) In Williamsburg you could pull off the life you'd dreamed of but couldn't enact in Nuovo Salario. There weren't any record stores in Nuovo Salario. No cheese shops, no bike shops, no sleek taquerias with beautiful, tattooed waiters. You'd finally begun to get a glimpse of this life in Pigneto, but in Willy you were getting the full version. Here were the pool halls lit like Robert Frank photos; the shaved ice carts in the park, pushed by Salvadoran grandmothers; the ironic bowling parties; and Duane Reade's "cold room," with its special section for retro brands. There was the sense that here you were among future icons, that if you stared hard enough, new trends would emerge. You could sit and read Virginia Woolf and look out onto Manhattan, you could walk around and see real stenciled

posters and fake stenciled posters, you could watch as street artists spray-painted a Jack Daniels ad onto the brick wall of a bar,
because there were no billboards in Williamsburg—billboards
were passé.

I DIED JUST a moment ago, but I'm already awake, and I can see
you. You're the one we pranked. We pranked your husband. I was
almost forty then, with faded red hair and a pale crease in my
skin just above my pubic hair.

I KEEP DYING. I keep waking up. And every time I wake up, I see
other people's lives only in words. I see language and nothing
else. I die toward the end of the story, and after every death I'm
awake again. I wake up telling the story of somebody I hurt, but
I have no voice; the story seeps out of me. I'm an hourglass full
of words, and when the last particle of sand has fluttered down,
the hourglass is turned upside down, and I wake up, though I
was dead.

YOUR HUSBAND SHOT that short film we hated.

Why do all these rich kids want to be film directors? And why
do they never stop trying? They make short films until they're in
their early forties. But before that—before life forces them into
resignation—is there no voice in their head, no clarifying moment when they stop and think *I'll never become a director?*

Your character's name was *La Sposina* (the pretty little bride)
according to the closing credits.

The short film was titled *G*. "'G,' for *gangster*," Lorenzo would
tell his Italian audiences. He boasted that he'd sold his car to

finance the production—but it was barely a car and not even his: a tiny little thing, a Fiat 600 that belonged to his mother, and he'd never paid for the insurance. And anyway, he wouldn't and didn't miss it; by then Ludovica had coopted her mother's Yaris; the woman had decided to give up driving.

Everyone in Lorenzo Proietti's generation got a digital camera for graduation. This was the height of the DIY fad, when *Clerks* and *Il Caricatore* had captured the imagination of the untalented. Lorenzo lived with his parents, his allowance 100 euros a week. A cousin at RAI got him an internship at *Porta a Porta*, which turned into a production assistant gig there and at Buona Domenica. These were bullshit shows for the bullshit public. Lorenzo lent a hand on the set of *Boris*, the comedy series/indie sensation. (He was twenty-six.) This was when you first heard the "I'm a *film-maker*" line, and his version of the English word was impossible to replicate—it was affected, exaggerated, nonsensical somehow; he managed to pronounce it without an *r* at the end. *G.* won a prize from the Comune di Roma, which belatedly convinced Lorenzo, at thirty-four, to apply to the New York Film Academy. New York was brimming with the children of the Italian elite—left-wing politicians, journalists, entrepreneurs—and they were all eager to become cineastes. They were at NYU, they were all over Brooklyn and Manhattan. The two of you left for New York, determined to test the waters. Lorenzo's philosophy grant was your excuse, but if connections were made and the vibe was right, Lorenzo would enroll at the Academy.

G. seemed to aspire to complete derivativeness—a work of total imitation. It nodded to *Pulp Fiction* (the gangster's black outfit, dusty and tight), *Lost in Translation* (a woman staring at the city from the window of a villa in Gianicolo, holding her knees to her breasts with her arms), *La Dolce Vita* (conversations from one room to the other via baby monitor). It referenced *The Usual*

Suspects, The Royal Tenenbaums, The Matrix, The Big Lebowski, Breathless. It had a complicated self-kidnapping plot *(Fargo)*—a long list of derivative shit. The jury, even dumber than Lorenzo, called it "ambitious, a bachelor machine of nods and winks."

My opinion back in 2011 was that the vilest, most inauthentic, most revealing part of this vile, inauthentic quasi-narrative were the actors' accents. The accents reeked of a social class—the *borghesia romana*—that was pathologically un-self-aware and didn't have an ear for how they sounded on film. Their Italian was slow and languid—the sound of summer, of cigarettes flicked off window-sills with inherited casualness, of sitting on park benches and leaning over to friends and suggesting a short walk to "go get a *Gelatiiino*, or a *Cremolaaato?*" In Lorenzo's movie, this clueless accent emerged with an awe-inspiring inconsistency: small-time crooks, nasty hoods in shiny blazers, drugged-out waitresses, corrupt priests, aristocratic looking bartenders—all of them stripped of the virtues and vices of their classes, perfected into abstraction thanks to their creator's profound cluelessness. The only way to tell the Albanese mobster apart from the rich lawyer was through one cheesy linguistic flourish or another—fake-ass slang that aped Guy Ritchie's *Snatch*, a stupid movie many Roman cinephiles my age adored. The maid was played by woman with a PhD who grew up near Via del Corso. The kidnapper—supposedly nasty and ominous—was handsome and tall and lithe and thirty, with salt and pepper sideburns and dark, sexy circles around his eyes. The only thing he exuded was real estate; your husband saw him as the Peter Falk to his Cassavetes.

And you. I laughed so hard when I read your name in the credits. In *Kill Bill*, Uma Thurman is a martial arts expert known as The Bride—*La Sposa*—so in *G.*, Lorenzo cast you as *La Sposina*, the kidnapper's wife: less a remake than full literalism. In my favorite scene, you call your husband to complain that he's late for dinner. You use a beautiful, vintage-looking telephone that sits on the counter next to a beautiful, vintage-looking, baby blue Smeg fridge, as if such a blatant upper-middle-class signifier could ever appear in the home of a mobster. In place of Thurman's tracksuit, you wear yellow pajamas in every scene, and instead of her Onitsuka Tigers, you have yellow sock-slippers. At one point, late in the film, you slice onions with a huge knife, which lets the audience know that somewhere, deep inside, you're a blade expert, and in case the point isn't sufficiently clear, Lorenzo gives us a close-up on the brilliantly sharpened weapon. Still, in most scenes, you're just waiting for your husband to come home, sitting next to the long glass windows and rinsing your face over the yellow and white pebbles in the bathroom sink. You are a generically good, generically young wife, the kind of figure who exists only in nostalgic TV ads produced by your Roman friends on behalf of aspirational coffee-machine brands.

That's the reason you came to America—for your husband's personal fulfillment. But the twenty-first-century bourgeoisie tends toward individualism, creating too many conflicts among its members. And so your own individual quest came into conflict with Lorenzo's: this was why he spent hours on the subway traveling back and forth between Brooklyn and Columbia, because you refused to live somewhere convenient, like Harlem or Morningside Heights. It's Willy or bust, you told him.

He had acceded, but the conflicts hadn't ended. He spent too much time networking with other Roman cinephiles, hanging out with his fellow gregarious Italians in the Village. Lorenzo wore shorts in the summer and stone-washed jeans in the winter, and his polo shirts seemed to magnify the tuft of hair above his chest. His hairline was receding, which on him was classy. If he enrolled at the Film Academy, you'd be staying in New York against your father's wishes. (Your father was mad that you'd left the family bookstore—he didn't answer the phone, didn't reply to your emails.) This trip was making our young couple grow apart, and it was—it felt like it was—Lorenzo's fault.

But a tiny part of the fault is mine, too, which is the only reason I'm here discussing your life. I couldn't care less about this fault—it's not the first or the last—but here we are, and since I never really knew you, I'll be here examining what you did and thought and wanted.

You come from a good family: your parents used to vote for the Communist Party; they taught you to make time for the soup kitchen on Sunday mornings, to spend late winter afternoons at nursing homes, at senior citizens' dancing groups. But your progressivism was unanchored from theory, estranged from the Marxism you never even knew you had outgrown. What was once open-mindedness became pure exoticism: culture was for collecting. You're only good for hailing cabs and booking flights that expand your carbon footprint. You refresh ryanair.com while— far from your eyes and farther from your heart—exhausted old ladies crouch on their knees in an industrial Chinese suburb, pulling obsolete cell phones from heaps of waste, from the sewage of techno-capitalism. You watched the Edward Burtynsky documentary that night at the Kino club, the one with the uranium mines and the nickel residue piercing the dark Ontario earth like lava, and those old Chinese ladies, hunched over piles of electric circuits . . .

$\mathcal{J}$anuary 10, a Monday. The sidewalks are covered with snow. The whole city is a uniform shade of blue; there's no air, only color. La Sposina walks out of the secondhand boutique where she works part-time, her laptop in a huge, stylish bag lent to her by her boss, and no fresh underwear. She has just made up her mind: she's going to spend the night out without informing Lorenzo. She walks down Bedford toward the subway station, shivering with cold, alert to ice, her Uggs ready to betray her at any moment.

Yesterday she spoke her mind for the very first time: "I need to go back to Rome and deal with the bookstore. And you're, what, you're going to stick around for this . . . film thing? You're thirty-four. Is any of this going anywhere? Are *you*?"

Her husband made sure to not quite understand. In the moment, he believed his own incomprehension: "I don't get how your father can tell you that you should feel free to go to New York, no problem, and then tell you to come back as soon as he needs you. You're married to me, not him." He was standing on the uneven floor, his eyelids and lashes doing the work of a smile. Ludovica gazed at him from the couch. She was sleepy and unmoored, and she found him attractive.

The Portuguese boyfriend of one of the flatmates—the one from Turin—had come by the shop a few days earlier and hung out for an hour while Ludovica showed him Lorenzo's short film on the shop's computer, on YouTube. He hadn't understood that this was Lorenzo's movie, didn't recognize La Sposina in the two scenes she appeared in. "Oh my god this is so bad," he groaned, laughing meanly but honestly. Ludovica chalked it up to jealousy (would he and the flatmate ever start shooting that documentary about the Macy's on Fulton Street? Of course not), but still, the idea that the movie didn't meet with international critical approval led her to watch it over and over again the following weekend. It seemed well directed and clever, so . . . what was the problem?

Maybe she was jealous of Lorenzo, too. He was out with the Italian movie buffs every night—the haters called them the *cinematografari romani*—spending far too much money at the IFC, at Angelika, at Film Forum. Even in the winter, when his clothes were buried under his horn-buttoned Montgomery coat, he had the air of somebody who'd make the most of his appearance to win the hearts of the daughters of Roman politicians and Milanese publishers—that wealthy, rascally aura. He made his way among them like he knew he was a good fuck, a master of the signals. He left her at home, in bed, on Friday night and Saturday night and Sunday night. She begged him to stay; she was weary from the winter snow, she wanted to make love and laze around in bed. He made fun of her when she told him (gracefully, gently, with an eyebrow lifted the right way, ever willing to blow him) that maybe he shouldn't come on to these women so much, make himself seem less available. In reply he gave her his Latin smile, his unbuttoned white shirt smile, his unlaced Campers smile. He enjoyed the display of jealousy, and he wouldn't change a thing.

But if it turned out that Lorenzo had no talent, the behavior she'd always condoned could no longer be written off as light and careless. It was vain, and she didn't think she deserved a vain, talentless husband. But was he talentless or not? She was consumed with doubt! Which was why she told him to ask himself a question: should he keep calling himself a filmmaker forever if he was really just a philosophy student, a perpetual apprentice in the philosophy of science? But he wouldn't listen. So she'd be spending the night out of the apartment.

Fifty yards from the train station, she's breathless. She fears she might stumble and hurt herself. A few months ago, a doctor found a blood clot in the back of her neck, so every day at five, she swallows blood thinners to avoid an embolism in the right lateral sinus. If she so much as nicks her leg while shaving, it can take an hour to stop the bleeding. She changes her mind and hails a cab, gets into a yellow SUV that stops at the corner of Bedford and Metropolitan.

MAYBE SHE'LL CRASH with Berengo. She hasn't called him, hasn't even run into him since last fall.

The driver is a big African guy in his early forties, Ghanaian. He's Catholic and has many questions for her—all about Rome— which he asks as they drive up the ramp to the Williamsburg Bridge. There's a picture scotch-taped to the dashboard, his three children in their Sunday best: two girls in emerald dresses, a boy in a turquoise suit.

After dark, the bridge is a necklace of white lights, but now, when the sun is weak and the shadows are faint, it's gray and blue and maybe pink, comforting and fatherly. What she'd really like to do is put her earphones in and listen to "Empire State of Mind" and weep as the skyscrapers rush toward her. She sees many

New Yorks at once. The cab driver is eighties Jarmusch, independent film, the world as it was before the Lorenzos of the world found out enough about it to co-opt it. The bridge is something more Hollywood—Woody Allen, maybe, or *Sex and the City*—the New York all Italians celebrate and suck up to. She compromises: the right earphone for "Empire State of Mind," the left ear for the driver. She asks him questions, tracks his answers. He did well in Atlantic City, where he was a croupier in a Trump casino. *(Queste strade ti faranno sentire nuova, le luci forti ti ispireranno.)*

"Where did you learn?"

"Atlantic City croupier school."

"Was it expensive?"

"Very."

"How much?"

"Fifteen hundred dollars."

She feels relieved because that doesn't sound like much.

"So why did you stop?"

"I got asthma. Too much secondhand smoke."

Halfway across the bridge, she puts in the second earphone, the song on repeat, *le luci forti ti ispireranno,* to let the feeling live on. The driver brakes and throttles in sharp bursts, every shift in speed a punch in the stomach. The hot air is on full blast, and it makes the artificial leather feel sticky. Still, she knows that this—the sun, the iron, the skyline, the song—will mold itself into a happy memory. She'll tell her mother and her friends about it, she'll tell Lorenzo. She can imagine the conversations now, they're happening in her mind. By the time she says any of it out loud, she'll have edited this afternoon drive into a perfect scene, free of unhelpful context . . .

The island is rushing toward you. It's dense with blood and drive and contains within it most of the earth's ambition. There are more exciting megalopolises out there—cities like Shanghai and Abu Dhabi, grander versions of Manhattan, the original re-created in the middle of deltas and deserts—but as new rivals emerge, the scale of New York's ambition, its hunger, never dips. From the queers in the Theater District to the Canal Street vendors who shove fishnet stockings into tourists' arms to the jewelry store owners huddled in Midtown, everyone has a raging boner they're so desperate to release that it's like the whole city is an eight-year-old boy writhing in his bed with his first erection (this is Lorenzo's imagery); entering the city via the bridge, in a cab, you're a fresh drop of blood in the world's grand cock (still Lorenzo's imagery). And blood is what the world longs for on, say, a sunny Monday morning, when women who dried their hair too quickly step out of dark lobbies and get hit with wind and headaches, when firemen on gleaming trucks hurry to save office workers trapped in skyscrapers and preserve man-hours, because someone left a scented candle lit last night, working overtime, when the dirty snow near the curb looks to bigger, fresher flakes for cover (another storm is due tomorrow), when the gray pigeons—true city dwellers—fly from one eave to another in twenty-unit gangs, and every neighborhood begins to speak its own language again: the laundromats, the liposuction ads, the satisfied chatter of a businessman from Alabama in town for the week, the girls with their long straight hair, their bangs . . .

On the bridge, caught in the middle of flowing traffic, she can see the city parting its hair on either side of Delancey. The grim, blocky high-rises along Houston remind her of some past she doesn't quite recall, the murals on windowless facades seem knowable. "È un giorno così crisp, mamma, you'd love it," she says to herself in half-English, half-Italian, a made-up language that makes her feel grand.

Cabs assail the city from all sides. They attack from every bridge and tunnel, an army, an endless scroll of cabs whose drivers never seem to stop for naps or lunch or to go to the bathroom. They're a constant, *e se ce l'ho fatta qui ce la posso fare dovunque.*

She blocks the storefronts with her hands and looks up at second floors to discover an essence: New York before Duane Reade. Many of the buildings are in shadow, almost black, but some are clear and bright, more pristine than a sunbeam. The city cycles between darkness and light, unsteady, like something out of a Meyerowitz photograph . . .

A NINETIES-ERA SKYSCRAPER: bland, hazel bricks, less glass than one would expect. The building looks corporate and defensive, but the Latin doorman bows as he opens the door for her, greets her with a smile. La Sposina steps onto the green carpeting, walks toward reception among mirrors and fake art deco. Now another handsome employee—say, Chazz Palminteri in *Bullets over Broadway*—calls up to Berengo's apartment.

He's not in, and his mobile isn't working, so you leave a card for him and walk out. Berengo gave you the card at that party back in October—VALID THRU 2011, it says—as a gesture of hospitality for whenever you found yourself fed up with Lorenzo. There's a Hello Kitty sticker on the back.

Out on the street, you're less afraid that you'll slip and fall in the snow, because everything in Manhattan is more thoroughly maintained. You walk down Eighth Avenue and look for a place where you can wait for Berengo to come back. You pass a couple of ugly and anxious shops so eager to please that they please no one; a one-dollar oyster place packed with bros in puffy jackets; a lurid Italian place on a dead corner, almost hidden under scaffolding. Finally, you find it: the Cosmic Diner, perennial, greasy, half-filled with ugly people sectioned off in green booths. A big, bald Jewish man with a machine-refined beard, stout but crumbling. A black woman with a grim, round face. A white man in a dull, gray jacket eating tomato soup, the melted cheese clinging to his spoon as he stares at his Kindle.

Sometimes, when you squeeze your cheeks together and your cheekbones protrude, you think you look like an Italian actress, Jasmine Trinca, star of popular yet somehow *engagées* films like *La meglio gioventù* and *Romanzo criminale.* Trinca always plays the outraged type, keen and sharp but quick to resolve misunderstandings with her hopeful, empathetic smile. When Trinca was beginning to break out, you were often told you looked like her, so you began to affect her grimace, alternating between discouragement, moral tension, and optimism. Those sexy, streamlined cheekbones helped you cycle between the three emotions, one after the other. You sit at the counter and order coffee and make faces at the mirror. The counter guys all notice you. You take *Mrs. Dalloway* out of your bag.

LUDOVICA LIFTS HER eyes up from the scene where Peter Walsh exchanges a passionate but renunciatory glance with a woman—a stranger—as he drifts around London. She spots Berengo, who's back from a jog in Central Park. He's wearing high-tech black leggings, a sleek windbreaker, and fuchsia Nikes by Jun Takahashi, which she identifies—admiringly—by sight. Berengo is short and fine assed, she thinks. His nose is okay, though maybe slightly too narrow, too simple. There are dark circles under his bright green eyes. He's friends with the waiters, and though he greets her with a big smile, he never gets too close—he keeps checking his phone to avoid shaking her hand or kissing her. He's clean-shaven under his baseball hat, which he rests on the counter. This is the first time she's seeing him this way: as someone connected to her and not to her husband.

How strange for me to see her in the company of my beloved Nico Berengo.

They move to a booth. The benches are uncomfortable, oddly vertical. Berengo seems so sweet to me, so easy, but to her he's an enigma.

"How are you?" he asks. "Have you eaten?" He doesn't listen for her answers. He keeps his iPhone in his left hand, reads the menu, makes small talk with the waiter, orders an Orange Crush, wishes he hadn't. "So, tell me." The phone is still in his hand.

She laughs, kind of. "I don't know where to start."

Nicola catches his breath, frowns. "You've fled home, right? You're out to find yourself a lover." He's baby-faced and wrinkly.

He asks her if she minds if he answers an email or two. Between sentences, he lifts his eyes to glance at her as she eats. Ludovica pulls her phone out and slowly chews her Cobb salad.

The waiter brings Nicola an avocado cheeseburger, though Ludovica didn't see him order. Finally, he rests his iPhone on the table and starts eating. "So, my Hello Kitty card."

"Right."

"My card. You're here for that, right? So, what, you ran away from home? Do you need a new home?"

"Can't we just talk for a minute? Just hang out?"

"You're *blushing*." He wipes his mouth with a napkin, puts it down and strokes her cheek. She withdraws at his touch.

"I didn't leave home. I just came to ask you something."

"So go ahead."

"Do you . . . do you think Lorenzo should actually give the New York Film Academy a shot? Should he go?" If Berengo responds with a simple, straightforward "yes," that might even be enough. She'll walk over to Ninth Avenue, find another cab, go back to Williamsburg as if nothing ever happened.

"Oh, come on . . ."

"I trust your judgment. I don't know if I trust anyone else's."

"You can't ask *me*! It's his decision."

"Just tell me your personal opinion."

"No, no, I can't. It's a big deal, and there's no way I can be involved."

La Sposina can't seem to swallow the croutons in her salad. She takes a sip of water too quickly and stands up to cough.

Berengo wipes his hands and his mouth with the little napkin from under his glass and stands up slowly. He slides out of the booth and faces her, his mouth still full, his gaze absent and clumsy. He takes her hand and brings it to his chest.

"Are you okay?"

"Yes."

"I'm sorry. Please, sit down." He takes a sip of the Orange Crush through a straw. "I was just surprised to hear from you. I get . . . *emotional* when a woman enters my life like this. I start wondering if I'm *ready to give her everything she needs*. Take your time, tell me everything."

Her throat swells.

"You're right, I should have called you first . . . I don't know. I'm mad at Lorenzo."

"Is he flirting too much?"

"Why would you say that?"

"I don't know... From Facebook? I see pictures, and he always looks like he's . . . posing."

This makes her smile.

"Do you want revenge? Want me to buy you a drink and smoke you up and get you to climax?"

She knows that this is how Lorenzo talks to women, so she changes the subject and mentions her blood clot; her mother's constant fear that she'll die suddenly, unpredictably; the way she didn't want her to leave Rome. "Basically, deoxygenated blood flows down through these two arteries once it's supplied the brain," she says, touching the sides of her neck with her hands. This seems to calm him down. "If you have a blood clot, it'll swell, and you'll have a headache that won't ever seem to stop. One time, I noticed something was wrong just because I scratched my eye and had this crazy reaction: the sclera swelled so much, it was pink . . ."

"What's the sclera?"

"The white in your eye. It swallowed my pupil."

He listens, impassive.

"I was seeing all these little snakes swimming around in my eyes. I stayed home with the curtains down, just stuck in bed. I couldn't move, or I guess I *could* move, but I didn't want to try. Whenever I did, the blood would start circulating too quickly and fill my veins."

Even as he returns to his iPhone activities, Nicola lifts his eyes and nods. *"Poverina,"* he says gently.

"With the thinners, I can get a bruise just from you touching me. And then it lasts a month."

"That sounds sexy. Does Lorenzo like it?"

"A little bit. But I need to take some time off."

"Too violent?"

"You mean the bruises?" She laughs. "No."

"Go ahead, *smile.*"

THE DOORMAN GREETS her but not Berengo. On the eighth floor, they emerge onto a beige landing, dull and anonymous. A dog is barking somewhere down the hall.

In the apartment, Nico points toward an L-shaped couch under the L-shaped window. The window takes up most of the south-facing wall and stretches north for a few feet along the building's western side. New Jersey—an inscrutable hill, vague and ominous—looms across the river. Manhattan appears in fragments: slivers of Midtown skyscrapers, the snowy rooftops of nearby brownstones, the vivid, atavistic green of the McGraw-Hill Building next door to the half-dead Port Authority.

Berengo kneels down in front of the couch to pull out the extension, puffing with effort. Physical task accomplished, he pulls some sheets and a towel from the hall closet and drags a bamboo screen in from the bedroom to give La Sposina some privacy. He doesn't smile and doesn't say anything, yet he doesn't seem displeased, either—merely vacant. He shuts himself in the bathroom, and she lies down on the couch, letting her calves unwind.

The apartment is plain and white, well lit and clean. The bookshelves—Ikea Expedits in beech and black—are full of toys: stuffed Angry Birds, tin robots, lunch boxes. There are three posters in the living room: Megadeth, Hannah Montana, and *Stranger Than Paradise*—the latter a positive Jarmuschian omen. The counter that separates the room from the kitchenette is covered in containers half-filled with Mexican food and a tall vase: two withered irises and a sad bunch of baby's breath.

Without Berengo to distract her, she remembers the first time she saw the apartment: during the party where she met him. There were more than a dozen people angled over the furniture and hanging out the window: photographers from the Contrasto agency, a music journalist from Milan. Without the crowd to take up every corner of the place, the apartment looks smaller.

She lies down and angles her head on two pillows for an unobstructed view of the skyline. The winter sun shines on her face.

THE SUN IS a rich yellow when she wakes up from her nap. Her shoulders and cheeks are heavy, and she lifts herself up on her elbows slowly, as if a sharp gesture might pull her back into full consciousness. The walls are covered in splotchy shadows and diamonds of light. The window feels cold to the touch. She kneels to look out, sees limestone stains on the glass.

SHE GOES OUT to buy a toothbrush, underwear, some new clothes. Everyone in the Rite Aid is fat or ugly: eccentric ugly or Asian ugly or post-Soviet ugly. They're buying twelve-packs of toilet paper, shampoo in large, white containers, two-liter bottles of raspberry-flavored ginger ale.

There's a small beauty salon in a quiet corner of the lobby. It's closed for the day, so there's no one around. She finds a stray chair and sits down to call her husband.

"Now I'm the one who wants to be alone," she tells him calmly. "Don't freak out. I'm just going out tonight."

"Great. Thanks for telling me," he says, his voice icy but wounded. "You're a piece of work, you know. I'm going out dancing."

"Think about what I told you, Lo."

"Come back, will you? You have to trust me; I have a plan."

"Come on, Lo."

"If you don't come back, I'll fuck anything I see."

"Come on."

"You're only doing all this because your dad won't let you stay here."

"Lo."

"You do everything for your father, you know? You two have a really fucked-up relationship."

You let him go through the rituals, because he doesn't know

where you are so he's entitled to some freaking out; still, you don't feel like telling him. He likes that you indulge his abuse, and he says:

"I'll give some thought to what you're saying. But if you sleep with someone I'll hang myself."

"No, my love, my legs are shut. Be good tonight, and tomorrow I'll make love to you."

"Okay, love, make love to me tomorrow."

You hang up the phone and think of Gabriele Muccino, the middling Italian director who became a middling American hack. Lorenzo went to Muccino's high school, and you see now that he shares the director's penchant for bourgeois melodrama. "WellmakelovetomorrowMuccinoboy," she texts him.

"I'm in pain. I miss you."

"I miss you, too."

She needs to use the bathroom. She gets up from the chair in the lobby and runs to the elevator. But when she gets to the apartment there are two strangers in the living room, and they've turned her bed back into a couch and completely ruined the beautiful peace that the apartment had before she'd run out. They're both balding, though one of them is young, twenty-five or so, an Italian hipster who introduces himself as Cugino Hitler. The other one is closer to fifty. His name is James. They sit back down on the couch and return to their video game. "Make yourself at Berengo's," says the affected Italian. In the game, a basketball player is doing dunking drills on a floodlit outdoor court.

She doesn't want to rush to the bathroom, so she stays a minute and looks out at the sunset crouching behind the skyscrapers that stand between her and the sun, seven dark shapes in this light, the spaces between them occupied by black clouds. Somewhere between the distant sunset and the clear, lobster-colored sky is a cluster of chunky clouds that resemble nothing so much as pieces of brain. Above Manhattan everything is still white and blue, the outlines of a day that hasn't quite receded, but the clouds closest to her are prone and hollow and heavy, seconds away from discoloration. La Sposina takes in the view with that part of the soul that emerges in men as they fall from cliffs or realize that they're lost at sea.

Cugino Hitler begs her to play. She detests him completely: the Adidas kicks sloppily thrown off to the side, the tight red pants rolled up above the ankles, the black shirt buttoned up and too tight. He looks a lot like her flatmate's Portuguese boyfriend, the guy from the boutique who didn't like G. Ludovica nods and smiles and strains every muscle in her face as she does so, her smile a Jasmine Trinca frown. James, the older man, apologizes for his dumb friend and tells her not to pay attention to either of them, to just do whatever she wants. His vibe is serene.

The windowless bathroom is tiny and has no ventilation of any kind, but there's an iPod dock for music. She sits on the toilet in a complicated bundle of pain and stimuli that send mail via pneumatic tubes from organ to organ, her armpits and her tongue receiving the most messages somehow. She glances at the white panties between her legs.

Later, she showers with a rich coconut soap and spreads it all over body, on her legs and on her stomach. The powerful gush of the showerhead is a pleasure. She ends up touching herself in a corner of the shower, an abandoned body leaning on the wall, cheeks against the cold tiles.

Her blood pressure low, she wraps a towel around her hair and thinks of her brother. He abandoned his engineering management master's almost as soon as he began and instead enrolled at a Catholic university where he's working on a bachelor's degree in theology. He'd met some Opus Dei people, and that was that. She thinks of her mother's cancer, and the pretentious restaurant they opened in the Sabine Hills, and her dad's brief departure from the family, and his heart attack, and his decision to open the bookstore/bistro in a shitty neighborhood with no nightlife to speak of. But none of it pointed to her family's imminent doom quite as much as her brother's decision to study theology. Her father, now a double bypass, didn't want Ludovica to go to New York because it meant neglecting the bookstore. Still, in light of the global recession, a bachelor's degree in theology seems much worse, and her father, she knows, would have to agree—and yield.

She finds two kinds of moisturizer—grape-scented for the face, almond-scented for the body—and applies both as she sits on the toilet lid. These delicate creams, she thinks, must belong to Berengo.

She retreats to Berengo's room and shuts the door. The city is transformed: the twilight is an artificial orange glow, a rebuke to the intensity of the blue darkness. The skyscrapers' lights have been turned on, and Manhattan looks like an intricate scale model of itself: miniature human models in miniature offices posed under miniature fluorescent lights. She abandons herself on the bed, her face buried in the duvet sheet.

SHE WAKES UP suddenly in a bed in a dark room, party noise seeping in through the walls. Her husband might be out there among the guests, and if he sees her he'll make a scene.

I KNOW THE mattress she's lying on—it's thin but comfortable and rests on a large metal frame, and when I'm visiting Berengo, there's always a moment when I stick my hands and arms underneath to take out The Box. By then I'm usually shirtless, wearing only a pink-and-whipped-cream bra with little ribbons. I sit on the bed, open the Box, and take out the edible ink sharpie. Berengo pulls down one of the cups and draws a swirl around my areola and then proceeds to lick it from the outside in until he reaches the nipple. Then we take something else from The Box: the black tape or the dildos or the beads. When I'm there he doesn't go around throwing parties. No bitter throats from MDMA, no Vitamin Water, no Spanish bubblegum dance music.)

Minutes later two very attractive, very young girls enter the room. They switch on the lights and apologize in two languages, though they don't leave. Maybe they imagine La Sposina as one of those background characters in party scenes, the crumpled lover who prefers to stay in bed. They slide the window open, and La Sposina calmly slips her head under the duvet.

"You all right, *zia*, you need anything?"

They don't like the mumbled mmm she gives them in response. *"Minchia, zia, ce la fai?"* one of them says. Literally *"can you make it?"* but in Milan, it's more like "you're so lame." But La Sposina only catches the literal meaning.

"I'll make it, thanks. I'm all right."

The two beauties laugh at her. Their hair is endless, their cheekbones sharp and ruthless; wide mouths, immaculate necks, knuckle and wrist tattoos that emerge from under rolled-up sleeves. They begin a discussion they've clearly had before, about an acquaintance who only talks about work and wants everybody else to be *tranquillo* "when she's so not *tranquilla, la zia*."

"If she keeps it up, I'll kill the bitch."

Coughing as she gets out of bed, less out of need than for momentum, Ludovica walks out into the living room to face her husband. To her surprise, he isn't there. There are a dozen people in the room, and none of them is Lorenzo. She recognizes her own foolishness: La Sposina had convinced herself that Berengo was trying to help the two of them work things out.

There are so many people on the sofa, the sofa that, only hours ago, was briefly hers. They're watching a Ryan Trecartin video on someone's iPhone and babbling indistinctly, mimicking the performances. Someone throws a stuffed Angry Bird halfway across the room. It's Cugino Hitler, of course. He and two friends are playing Angry Birds IRL: one holds a pig head with an outstretched arm, like a conqueror, while the other throws the red bird at the pig, hoping for contact. They laugh, smoke pot, switch places. Berengo is projecting a Kanye West video on the wall, two girls are playing Mario Kart.

(I have never seen the living room that crowded when I've flown over. Perhaps because I always tell Berengo ahead of time that I'm coming, and he's happy to see only me. It's always the same: I get five days off at the travel agency and persuade *Il manifesto*, the pinko newspaper, to let me publish a couple of interviews with American writers or a piece or two about the New York Film Festival or the New Yorker Festival—the cultural coverage left-leaning Italians hunger for.)

A friend of Cugino Hitler has spread peanut butter on his nose, and another boy licks it off. La Sposina wants to fit in, and her best shot is her sleepy air: she looks wasted, maybe. Her Jasmine Trinca grimaces won't work with these people—they're younger and more cynical—so she has to keep her eyelids droopy, her mouth shut. As soon as there's an opening on the couch, she moves in, hoping she doesn't look too clumsy as she does so or perhaps just clumsy enough. She's sitting in the corner under the windows, where the draft is iciest. The bald, mangy fifty-year-old she met earlier sits down next to her and begins to ask her how she's doing, along with other polite questions. She manages, against her nature, to look jaded while staring out at the view outside. She spots *The New York Times* Building, a Renzo Piano joint, and finds herself telling her mom about it in her mind. She tells James she's from Rome and has many weird jobs that she can't be bothered to list.

She's managed to get him to leave, which allows her to stretch her legs. Perhaps it's time to pretend that she's asleep. But as she drifts off she realizes she doesn't have to pretend. She's telling her friends in Rome about how everything here is so obscure: someone is wearing a black t-shirt that reads HATERS GONNA MAKE SOME GOOD POINTS IN HELVETICA, a sentence that riffs on some other sentence, neither of which she understands or maybe half-understands; someone else has an I AM CARLES shirt, barely more understandable, also in Helvetica. No one seems to be talking about New York, about boroughs or neighborhoods or even restaurants. What she hears instead are only brands: Comme des Garçons, Issey Miyake, Miu Miu. There are two guys talking in Brescian dialect, perfectly dressed, rocking grandiose fur sneakers, their slanted mouths almost identical in mutual disgust.

Cugino Hitler wakes her up and suggests a walk. Everyone's leaving, including the two beauties: one of them is putting on a Barbour jacket, the other (whom La Sposina feels she's met before) a coat that's almost certainly Marni.

"No, no, I'm staying."

Cugino Hitler, unpersuasive in his puffy red jacket, grabs her hand to try to force her up, but she resists.

Alone on the couch, she checks Foursquare to see if her husband has checked in somewhere. He hasn't, and neither has she. There are two new texts from him: "You're not in bed with some man please promise me on your mother's life," and "Don't you see what you're doing to me??"

"I want you to think about us and about your choices," she replies. "How would being in bed with somebody help me think? Lol. Trust me, baby."

Berengo still has company. He's with a woman in the kitchenette and is switching off all the living room lights except a dim orb on the shelf. He has arranged the bamboo screen wordlessly, pretending to believe she is asleep. She can't see anything beyond her little corner of the room, not the kitchenette, not even the table.

So this is how the long Monday ends: behind a bamboo screen, low on the couch to avoid the draft from the two windows as the woman in the kitchenette discusses Margiela sneakers and summers in Japan and begins to bake a cake with Nico, right now, at this hour. What she hears: egg yolks and flour being mixed up in a big plastic bowl. *Twok twok twok*. The oven being turned on, the pans pulled out of their drawers. She smells butter. La Sposina follows the sounds and the smells from her perch on the bow of the cold sofa, exposed to the deadly breath of the city and the hot siren breath coming in from the kitchenette.

After a long period of indecision, she gets up and slips out into the other room, unavoidably exposed to the gaze of the two bakers. Nicola's date is so round and tall, her hair so rich and chestnut that she seems to have emerged from the oven herself; her apron is the napkin Berengo will use to eat her. Ludovica crawls inside Nico's room and locks the door: she'll relax on the bed and in time, as they end up unable to reclaim their room, she'll fall asleep. She'll stay put.

She's lying askew in Berengo's bed, tangled up in the duvet with her pants unbuttoned, the slotted light from the venetian blinds giving her a film noir aura. Ritual can save her. She recalls an underlined passage from Mrs. Dalloway that helps her muster the strength to leave the bed: . . . *Ma lei veniva dal diciottesimo secolo. Lei era a posto.* She pulls open the blinds, revealing a tall white sky that's also gray and pink and blue in the corners, almost beyond the window's reach.

Around eight, she looks for the two lovers, but they're nowhere to be seen, so she does the dishes. She scrubs the colanders and strainers they deployed for late-night baking, the cutlery for the Mexican food. She scrapes away the hard and wet strips of nachos, fills the sink with hot water, takes a sponge and tries to ignore the splashes from the faulty faucet, which drips inconsistently.

She walks to Central Park to see the snow, a meandering stroll inspired by a book of architectural walks she found on a shelf at Nico's. It's daylight now, indisputably, the pink filtered out of the sky. The park is pale and readable, its spectrum condensed, its extremes mitigated by crisp, shimmering snowbanks. She's not ambitious enough to follow the walk the book suggests, which would take her all around the park: down the deserted paths, past the bare trees, north into the wilder corners. A paper she picked up in a coffee shop is panicked: snowfalls, subway-service changes, road closings. She finds a bench and leafs through the book with fingerless gloves. Well-equipped joggers run up and down the asphalt and through big white hills, their prework rituals unaffected by the extraordinary landscape. They're wearing every kind of expensive sneaker in every possible color combination, they're wearing Beats and Skullcandy headphones. Lorenzo's texts persist.

Now she's in a crowded, sunlit Starbucks on Broadway just south of the Ed Sullivan Theater, which Italians imagine as some kind of temple, an entertainment mecca. So she tells her friends about it, in English, but instead of opening Skype on either her phone or her laptop, she contents herself with addressing them in her mind. In her mind her accent is perfect, her vowels just lethargic enough. She buys two bananas and a bottle of water in a colorless cylinder tapered like a perfect bullet.

For two hours a day and €300 a month, she works as an administrator on a forum run by a prominent viral marketing website. The forum is purely transactional: customers willing to test products are rewarded with discount offers and corporate junkets. Her first task of the day is to spark debate about a viral video of a man jumping into a hay baler and turning himself into a human bale of hay. "*È un fake?* And what is it advertising??" Conversation started, she has to post a pitch—"You can be paid to blog about herpes. *How cool is that??*"—and track the feedback for a recent Colgate campaign promoting gum health. Next, she launches a forum dedicated to the Opel Young. This means convincing Italians between the ages of twenty-six and forty-two to buy an Opel instead of a VW Golf, an eighties icon whose impact still lingers. She's typing and posting and emptying her mind.

A text from your mother sweeps away all your serenity: "Are

you alive? Call." The ceiling of the Starbucks descends, the pedestrians pick up their pace, the line for Frappuccinos gets longer. The sun is out, it's a kind sun, almost loving, but as more and more city dwellers walk in in a state of snowbound relaxation, you lose yourself wondering if your mother knows (maybe from your in-laws?) that you didn't sleep at home last night. Your throat shrinks. You think: this may not be panic; this is suffering. Yes, you are dying of suffocation. You ate the bananas for potassium, because of your bowel problems, but maybe you've become allergic? It's panic, or it's colitis, or it's suffocation, but in any case you're dying: your fingers feel numb, your sweat is cold; it's definitely an allergic reaction, and it'd be crazy if you minimized this by calling it a panic attack.

You swallow and swallow, trying to relax your throat through sheer effort. You stretch out your shoulders, hoping that this might help you breathe better.

She logs off the admin account and closes her laptop. She's covered in goose bumps, she can feel extra heartbeats: it's as if someone is blowing air directly into her skull, like her heart has been inflated to an unsustainable size, like her body isn't whole but coming apart into many different components, each of them posing its own set of problems.

There are a couple of tourists in their forties, kind-looking Midwesterners in baseball caps, sitting next to her. She decides it's not allergies and turns to them out of desperation: "Excuse me. I'm sorry, but I think I'm having a panic attack. I think I'm choking."

"Oh *dear*," says the woman and grabs her hand. An angel in dyed jeans and a fake YSL bag. Her hand is warm and soothing. The best plan is to return to Rome, since she'd already promised she'd come back soon to handle the bookstore's yearly audit—reason enough. This is a sign. She leaves Lorenzo out of the explanation entirely. She has to find a way to reconnect with her father.

Outside in the open air, she begins to breathe again. She exchanges a few words with the middle-aged black man standing under the *Mamma Mia!* marquee, asking for charitable donations for a group that serves the homeless. Ludovica goes back to Berengo's and opens Skype.

Her mother answers. She looks ten years older than the last time they spoke. Her cheekbones are identical to her daughter's, but there's something yellowed and waxy about her face. Her eyes are cratered, and her hairline seems to have receded, leaving a vast forehead above a shrunken face.

"Hi!" your mother says in her most cheerful tone. "I was on Skype, waiting for you." Her face is so tiny, it's as if it's been curdled. Signs of active life—of bustling, adult life—are invisible.

"Fine, well, here I am. I'm alive. You're not even going to ask me how I'm doing?"

That face—that yellow face framed by a chaos of flyers pinned on the cork board over the cashier's stand. Late afternoon in Rome: your mom's mood is distracted but good. "I'm freezing, love. We're going to get some *coso* . . ."

"*Un coso* what?"

"Tea."

"Don't say *coso*."

"But I want hot chocolate. We're freezing. Fofi is warm, but I'm not."

"And are *you* alive by the way?" La Sposina can't stop. "I can't believe you won't just ask how I'm doing. Does whether or not I'm okay matter at all?"

"What's this nonsense, you silly girl? I just asked if you were okay."

"You *didn't* ask, though. You just sent a text wondering if I was alive or not."

"Will you stop it?"

35

"How's Grandma?"

"Fine. She's fine."

Grandma had had a brain hemorrhage the previous week, after she'd suffered a stroke. So she's fed up with talking to people. She's scared and she's ready. "There's going to be a storm there tonight. Is Lorenzo at the university?"

"He is."

"Good. Don't go out tonight."

"He's fine. You want to know how he's doing? How I'm doing?"

"You're boring, Ludo, you know that?"

"Mom, you don't care about me."

"Stop it."

"I think maybe I should come home and take care of the bookstore." She watches her mother with tremendous concentration. "The three-month visa is expiring, so I was going to have to come back soon anyway . . ."

"I thought you were going to Toronto for that."

"I've changed my mind. As soon as I find cheap tickets, I'm flying back so you won't have an excuse not to visit your mother anymore. I'm taking you to see her."

"You're a pain in the neck."

"Wouldn't you be happy if I came back?"

"Of course I'd be happy."

"Have you talked to Grandma today?"

"No. Is Lorenzo coming back too?"

"Is Grandma maybe dead? Like me? Will you ask her how she's doing?"

"You know," her mother responds without changing her expression, at once jolly and distant, "you can be so unkind. Stop this before you really hurt me."

"You're the one who's forcing me to be like this! You're not asking me how I'm doing!"

"Oh, really . . . Hey, Fofi!" (Ludovica winces as she hears the name.) Come here! Something's wrong with Skype, Fofi, it's not working, there's a mosquito stuck in the screen!"

Fofi has heard the joke before and comes over. He's the same as ever: curly hair, bright red beard, balding, fat but not obese, uptight, upbeat. "Ciao, bella. How are you?" Fofi asks Ludovica.

"Fofi, look, she's neglecting her mother, the selfish little girl. I call her, I care. And she won't even ask me how I'm doing."

He has always wanted you without ever asking. You've never surrendered yourself, but he's not without his skill set: he took your parents instead. He hugs your mother and kisses her on her head. He was the one who solved the problem with the distributors after you'd made that terrible deal with publishers to return unsold art books without charging them for shipping. When he hugs your mother, this old woman in need of affection, Fofi looks like a social worker: a model of charity in an ex-goth's black sweater. You imagine, just then, what it would feel like to have Fofi hug you as an old woman. The second Fofi hugs that old head (your mother's old head, but also your own) you feel your productive life—your allegedly meaningful adult life—evaporate. You see yourself in her: old, careless, unfathomable, unable to run the bookstore your husband bought for you as a pastime, compelled to entrust your duties to an ex-grad student because your son is a mystic and your daughter has dreams. Your mother's fossil cheekbones can no longer testify to the presence of adult life and now neither can yours. You learned the word "adult" from your father, when you were five. "Films with real people in the flesh are for adults, and you're a kid." "What about Mom?" "Mom is an adult." "What about Grandma? Is she an adult?" "Of course she is." "No, Daddy, Grandma can't be an adult; she's old." "Well just be sure not to tell her that; it's rude." Your mother's robust back isn't reacting to Fofi's hug. You know that there are moments, hours, days when you are like her, when you are one and the same. You will become her unless you get what you want, unless life is arranged in some specific way. You don't talk to anyone, you've forgotten your friends, and you only talk to people in your mind. Hugs no longer warm you. It can happen.

"Bye, Ludo. I'm going to see if I can make myself a hot chocolate. I think you look great. I think you're doing fine, even though I had a feeling you weren't when I texted you. Talk to Fofi. I'll see you tomorrow."

"I think you look great, too," Fofi adds too quickly. And: "Bye, honey. When are you coming to rescue us?"

"Soon. Super soon, actually."

"We miss you. I'd love to work on the audit with you."

"Tell Dad not to worry. I'll be back soon."

"Alright, honey."

"I'm hanging up. Ciao."

"Don't have too much fun."

Ten minutes later Ludovica sends her dad a self-portrait from Times Square, *Your square little girl.* She has a feeling that after two months he will finally reply. He'll have been updated with the news of her imminent surrender.

And he replies. "Hi, love, did you talk to Fofi about the audit?"

"Daddy, love, I'm coming back. We'll work it out, promise." She's already in tears, clogged up with mucus, covering her face with a flimsy napkin, recycled brown paper ripping into little pieces.

"Try and be in touch with Fofi daily. Be good."

"Love you, *Pops.*" Your throat tightens for a moment. You lower your head, join hands, weave them together, and wring them like two wet rags.

The purple cloud hasn't lifted from your chest—you'll need more than a few coughs to dislodge it—so you call your brother, who dispenses with you quickly. He doesn't want to talk, and he doesn't switch the camera on, because he can't figure out how or he doesn't want to, so he denies you the chance to see him stern and enervated, judgmental in his pinstriped shirt. Yet you succeed at making him feel judged without any visual aids: your determination not to ask him how theology is working out for him is conspicuous. His fellow students recite the Pater Noster before class, then talk Protagoras.

Now that you've dealt with the whole family, you find yourself deeply affected by a stray piece of news on repubblica.it: "This game-winning touchdown by a boy with Down syndrome has America in tears." One of those little pieces of not-quite news on the right side of the homepage, the only column anyone clicks. You yourself give in to tears and hide your eyes behind the now-shredded napkin. You stalk Facebook for names and faces from yesterday's party, you look up Berengo's profile to check if he posted any pictures of you Lorenzo might see. Nothing.

A STROLL THROUGH a non-neighborhood. The area behind Times Square's cardboard facades, Broadway's backside. Fat white people, democratically nondescript; euphoric black high-school kids; mothers with big butts.

THE HOSPITALIZATION WAS part of Dad's escape. Escape, heart attack, hospitalization: no explanation at all except for that time in the living room before dinner: "Let's all thank God that Dad still has a job, and let's thank our patient Mommy," said mommy. This was ten years ago, and Ludo really didn't want to make her father's life any harder. Yet she'd left anyway. And they're supposed to prepare the audit, which is sure to be a mess.

The store's name, Librici, was La Sposina's idea. After a few months in New York, she's started feeling embarrassed by it, can't bring herself to spell it when asked. She used to dress like a Parisienne—scarves, skirts, coats—but now that she's a new woman in a new world of leggings and red wayfarers and aggressive bangs, that half-Italian, half-French name (*libri* + *ici*) really doesn't fit. It's possible that nobody besides her ever loved the French touch in the first place: employees and friends still pronounce it *lee-bree-tchee*. The store's style is a bit outdated, too. Books are divided according to "whims" ("inner trips," "discoveries," "what's cookin'," "the cosmos and the divine," "on a train," and so on), and the menu features quiche and salads and muffins, a creation of a widow friend of Mother's. Open until midnight, Librici is consistently deserted from eight on, except for those rare nights when friends conjure up some kind of activity: classical guitar concerts, poetry readings, and so on.

If Librici is a failure, Ludovica feels that some of the blame is hers. The industrious precision with which she approaches the viral marketing gig eludes her entirely when, on a long, slow winter afternoon, she has to decide how many copies of a particular novel to stock. During the day she and Fofi are both on bar duty, and she's had one too many hugs behind the back—his plump, shy hand always landing in the same place: on her left hip, just above the curve of her butt—and her mother is sitting at the computer doing inventory with her usual mix of confusion and sloppiness. Moments like this—and their endless iterations—propel Ludovica into an unprecedented state of hallucinatory laziness. Her mistakes are serious but preventable. She has inherited more than a little bit of her mother's allergy to the practical, yet the ambition is still there: she wants to do all the fancy things a bookseller does without first learning the basics. She has decided to buy books directly from the independents, in order to avoid the big distributors, but she's careless and unpracticed: her experience with publishers consists of a year's worth of editorial classes she took at proud indie minimum fax. But that wasn't about tactile knowledge, anyway; she just wanted to find her way into the Roman scene. She made a deal with Sur for their South American fiction, but she forgot that she had promised to pay them up front. Fofi spots her screwups, but it's usually too late, and anyway, he always tells Mr. Vozzi first.

The other category of mistake: she's a compulsive buyer of art books. Before they opened, she insisted that a bourgeois neighborhood needed a place to buy expensive art books. (To Fofi, this has always been about projection rather than market strategy.) La Sposina went all the way to Paris for some Taschen special editions: she spent time in the Saint Germain shop and then had them sent over. Her dumbest whim: too often she takes off the shrink-wrap and puts the huge, excessive books on display. A few customers flip through, but that's the point: once unwrapped, they're impossible to sell.

And then there's the €1,600 rent. They ended 2008 down €3,000, which happened to be the same amount her father "invested" to keep the books balanced. The following year, they lost €10,000, and Mr. Vozzi erased his wife and his daughter from the list of personnel and started settling with Ludovica directly, from his pocket to her wallet. It was awfully close to an allowance—the very transaction she had renounced since university. (The amount her brother receives each month is unknown to her—a secret among men.)

"How far are we willing to go?" Fofi asks with desperation and more than a hint of strategic thinking. "A €40,000 debt? You'll go bankrupt with a bookstore full of books! It's lost inventory, a fatal opportunity cost!" Mr. Vozzi only trusts Fofi now; he's the only one who can talk the talk.

LIBRICI IS A structural mistake with a precedent: the restaurant the family opened in a small village in the Sabine Hills a decade earlier.

You were single, a student, and for two years you spent every weekend sacrificing your free time on behalf of the hills you called Sabinashire, a faux-ironic designation you secretly hoped would catch on, like Chiantishire. The second year you moved to the country and only came back to Rome during exams.

The restaurant your mother had in mind was as inessential to Sabinashire as Librici was to Quartiere Trieste. Even the more refined restaurants in the area offer big portions and aspire toward the easy pleasures: a full belly and a meal shared with family and friends. But her mother and her chef friend favored a different style: small portions, a pretentious menu seasoned with plenty of high-end, mass-cuisine slang, a misguided commitment to slowness.

It was then that her father had left home. His high school–aged son was studying for exams in Rome and was left alone, because his mother never left the countryside. The father's escape lasted less than three weeks; he had a heart attack in Florence, where he was treated. He had been staying at a friend's house; he was on vacation, trying to prevent a breakdown, meeting a lover, or some combination of the three. And so, neither La Sposina nor her brother Fausto saw their father in the hospital. Ludovica, who was hurt by her father's escape, stayed in the countryside, and Fausto was ordered to join her there. Mother spent some time alone with father. They decided that they couldn't live apart, so the restaurant was shut down. Mother fell out with her partner, who found herself jobless due to the tumult. (She eventually recovered and now works for a catering company.)

Ludovica took it all in stride. Months earlier, she had discovered that the restaurant had a bad reputation. A man who worked on her neighbors' vineyard mistook her for a family friend visiting from Rome and told her he had had dinner at the Vozzi restaurant the night before. The country air made you hungry, in his opinion, but the Vozzis' place "won't fill you up, and it's not as if these flavors are, you know, exceptional. It's not like it's some kind of culinary experience . . ." He was a rough man: he'd lost his thumb in a plow accident and had a history of premature deaths in the family, so he didn't mince words about someone else's tragedies. The ingredients weren't as good as they should have been: the *tiramisù scomposto*, in vogue at the time, was served with whipped cream that didn't taste fresh or homemade, and the pieces of marinated zucchini were hard and rubbery and didn't have that true zucchini smell.

And now it's the new generation of Vozzis who are overseeing the big mistakes.

Now that you've reconnected with your father, you spend the afternoon trading emails that are frank but not hostile.

"You promised," Father writes, "that you'd be back in three months, that you'd spend a month here, then three more over there, then back here for good to run the bookstore. Is that still the plan?"

"I don't remember promising that, Dad, but if the priorities are different now, that's fine. I'll look up flights today."

CUGINO HITLER IS back at Berengo's in a checked shirt, and so is his fifty-year-old friend, as well as one of the two patronizing girls from the bedroom and the two Brescians in tight silvery clothes, whose nearly identical hairless faces are lined with dark shadows, neorealist horrors barely concealed by the thin film of an elusive cultural élite. Yes, she'll go back to Rome and find a place behind the counter right where her mother was sitting just a few

43

hours ago, where she sits every day and responds "yes, Fofetto, of course" to every command Fofi issues. A few months ago, it was this reality—the outlook of more of the same—that gave her the cue to escape. It would feel like giving up now, sure. But it would also feel like a relief.

It starts snowing around eight, and as they arrive, the guests pull off their snow-dusted jackets and coats, which soon begin to drip. Berengo has placed a red plastic shower mat under the hangers, and everyone has an in-joke ready. Somebody quotes the Coen brothers: "The mat ties the room together." A friend of Cugino Hitler's, in falsetto: "Don't forget to bring a towel." Counts and cocottes in the salon, they were born to nod to western memes and old-fashioned references. Tonight they fear a snowpocalypse: "We'll all sleep together, Nicolone." The projector is set up, someone calls in an order for Japanese food, a group in the kitchen tries to figure out how to make fudge. That's when La Sposina finds out, via a laptop on the counter, that Nicola's girlfriend hosts a cooking show on TV, and that all the males in the house pine for her. She's not here tonight, only on YouTube, and toward the end of the episode, they begin to make jokes as she pours fudge onto the ice cream and smears her upper lip with caramel and whipped cream as she eats. She must have a father, too, and he must also ration his emails to her, keeping her heart between his fingertips like dough, forming it into a tiny pale ball he idly rolls around the tablecloth for obscure reasons. Or maybe she doesn't, and that's why she's licking fudge off her lips as the whole world watches.

You chat with people. James Murphy,[*] the kind, bald fifty-year-

---

[*]JAMES MURPHY, 52, Pulitzer Prize–winning author of *The Rockwells*, born and raised in Akron, Ohio. After majoring in Economics and minoring in Philosophy at the University of California, Berkeley, he returns home to work at

old, is a novelist. You own one of his books, I Rockwell—it won him the Pulitzer Prize. Berengo is a friend of his. And Berengo thinks Lorenzo has no talent. Even worse: James Murphy tells you he likes Berengo and Cugino Hitler so much he's taking notes on them. It's a book project, but you don't ask for the details. Does this mean, then, that even Cugino Hitler is a more interesting person than Lorenzo? That he's an artist? And does that mean . . .? Every question she doesn't ask makes her want to start cutting her forearms like she used to.

Ludovica recognizes the long-haired girl, not just from last

---

his father's temp job agency and write a novel on capitalism, as seen from inside the private sector as opposed to the academy. He publishes *The Rockwells* in 1996 when he is in his late thirties. While initially viewed as a "cult author" and an "experimentalist," Murphy and his views on literature are de facto popularized by the success of Don DeLillo's *Underworld* and the works of contemporaries like David Foster Wallace, George Saunders, Ralph Moody, Marcus. Since counterculture has been transformed by the Internet into a game of nods, which is also a way to describe Murphy's prose, the new millennium transforms Murphy's cold cerebral non-empathic style into a new empathy. Murphy writes two bestselling books dominated by a helicopter-as-metaphor conceit and tamed by a traditional realism borrowed from Henry James—a slim pseudo-memoir titled *Godspeed* and the novel *The Rockwells*. For Murphy, the obnoxious abundance of helicopters has a real life origin: his younger brother Jonathan died in a helicopter accident in Ohio in 2003. Jonathan had made his money in an online shopping start-up, "perverting the dear American simplicity of our family style," as Murphy writes, and giving in to a tacky, provincial, luxury lifestyle. Jonathan later crashes in a field somewhere in flyover country after the spare car parts he invested part of his money on fail. After Jonathan's death, Murhpy takes three years off from writing. Then, after a burst of a few months' writing and one year of editing, he publishes the pretend memoir *Godspeed* (awfully titled, in the Italian edition, *La ballata degli elicotteri*, "The ballad of the helicopters"), in which a reflection on his difficult relationship with his brother and his reaction to Jonathan's death is complicated, storytelling-wise, by the fact that the parallel reality of the pretend memoir, otherwise identical to our reality, sees all the people in his life dying from helicopter crashes—including his mother and father and wife and daughters. The streak of imaginary tragedies starts with his brother's actual death. The helicopter, in *Godspeed*, ends up identifying with death and the human condition, overwhelming through repetition the original need to mourn his brother, anticipating future deaths.

night but from the boutique; she's come in a few times to sell her old clothes. Her name is Anna. She's entertaining some of the guests with a theatrical deliberation over whether to pose naked for a chic erotic magazine. Anna sits at the end of a chair, then stands up, agitated, and begins to walk back and forth on the parquet floor, her Lacca oxfords making loud clicking noises. A friend of Hitler's is streaming some of the magazine's clips: a big, pale girl with a head of perfectly curly hair rides a bicycle. She's wearing a skirt but no panties, her soft breasts moving gently in the breeze. Everyone agrees that the video is legit. "We'll finally get to see your pussy," Cugino Hitler says thoughtfully. Anna brags that she can't be bothered to accept the job and punches Hitler's puny frame, generating a pitiful shriek. She brags some more, frowning: she'll be forced to accept Terry Richardson's offer after all. Ludovica gathers that Anna also works at a gallery in Chelsea.

Anna pretends not to recognize you; you can tell she'll never talk to you.

Three of the guests are photographers who seem like they're everywhere. There's a gay Italian—a literary scout and former tour manager—who rolls his *r*s in a funny way. (You add him to the list of people you envy, but it's something more potent than envy: he's about to find out, from you of all people, that like him your husband studied philosophy at Villa Mirafiori, but unlike him he's at Columbia for a year on university money. So he'll ask, "Is he *raccomandato*? Has he got family connections with the board?" You'll be forced to lie and say no, and he'll know you're lying. The scout's name is Sergio de Simone—with me he always went by Sergino—and he hates well-connected people with easy access to grant money. He sniffed the odor of your husband's connections on you. He's the one who'll think up the big prank, and ask me to join him.) Sergio de Simone has a smug, fake American accent,

46

his Italian swims in a sea of *"kinda"* and *"sorta."* He's from Via Tiburtina in eastern Rome: shaved head, no beard. He's wearing pistachio-green pants with ridiculous triple-folded hems.

"So," he says with affected bonhomie, "who are his connections? His relatives?"

"Are you kidding me?" She's baffled, as if it were offensive to bring up that particular name.

"So how could he get a grant from Villa Mirafiori to do work abroad, then?"

"I guess he's good?"

They engage in this back-and-forth as they nibble gyoza from a communal plate. She's hungry, but she walks away.

More problems from another guy—"Marcello." Cugino Hitler introduces him and explains that this kid—a wealthy twenty-five-year-old from Parioli, Rome, tall and black haired, in a Ralph Lauren polo with a diagonal stripe, tight red pants, and designer sneakers—only speaks broken English. He's a rapper who's about to make the ultimate *italorap ammericano* record. "I'm doing the artwork."

The playlist is Arab hip-hop, noise, calypso, grind, *Italia anni Sessanta, italodisco*. (When there's just the two of us at the apartment, we use the projector for videos, mostly HD documentaries about wildlife or the solar system, nighttime videos of cities shot from helicopters, Tokyo from the first car of a monorail. The city muffles this apartment, spins a silk around it that lets us out but doesn't let anyone else in. At night, with the lights off, all we see are the videos flickering on the canvas, our phone screens dimmed for darkness, the LEDs from electronic devices. There's no place I'd rather be. Which doesn't mean I'm incapable of living in Rome without him; I have a full life there, and I have other homes I can go to, and even other little boxes under other beds. But they're secondary boxes, they're not The Box.)

You're not okay with his inviting people over two nights in a row. He's not the same when he's around people. When you suggest that "Marcello" is *veramente poco easy*, he dismisses you without looking up from the game on his phone, the one with the frog that tries to eat as much candy as possible. "A young man has to take himself seriously," he says, leaning on the bookshelves, "if he's to achieve anything."

You laugh at his affectation and respond in half-Italian, half-English: *"Sì, Nico, and yet, è poco easy."*

"Don't judge. With all the *velleitari* we have in Italy—they're so content, so savvy, even though they're really no good at anything—'Marcello' produced fucking Gassa. I think that's enough."

When Berengo says *velleitari*—the aspirants who dabble in the arts with little talent or stamina or awareness—does he mean Lorenzo? If so, it's your duty to walk out the door and go back to your husband. Instead you strike back: "But he seems so uptight, he's super intense."

"Look, *bella*, he's a serious person. He's not an *allegrone* who thinks he'll find his place in the world thanks to his congeniality."

This is unambiguously Lorenzo. But how can he say it so openly?

"Well, regardless, your friend is *poco easy*." You're weakened and losing, and you're waiting for this to stop so you can reach the bedroom and lie down, but then the conversation takes a turn.

"You say *'easy'* one more time, and I'll kick your ass."

"You're so boring! That guy talks like an idiot, and I can't say *'easy.'* You're *poco easy* yourself, you know?" You place your hands on his forearm—your form of self-defense.

"I told you. I'll kick your ass." But this time he says it warmly.

"Oh yeah? And what exactly are you going to do?"

"Beat you up, *sweetie pie*."

"I don't think so."

"Come to my room, then. I'll beat you up." You stare at him with a smile—*only connect . . .*—then head for the fridge.

THE LATE EVENING walk is a relief. It's barely snowing now, and the temperature has risen. Nicola stayed home, and La Sposina is tagging along with the other guests, who are on their way to the subway or about to hail cabs. The street and the sidewalk have blurred into each other, the landscape shiny and brittle. La Sposina holds on to Cugino Hitler's arm, afraid she might slip, but the snow lends her steps a grainy friction. The square around the corner from Berengo's is transformed: the big planters with the Japanese maple trees are a bright white, as are the bollards and the metal chairs and the round tables chained to the cobblestones. The doormen are invisible—this weather is beyond their pay grade—but the supers and the janitors are everywhere, shoveling their little sections of the sidewalk. The air hums and crackles. The few parked cars on the street and those stacked like tin cans in expensive lots are glazed over, nearly invisible. La Sposina's crew weaves through the choreography of late-night hard work: polite, uncomplaining slaves with shovels in their hands. The snow begins to fall again as the Italians reach Times Square, where they meet new shovelers illuminated by the bright blur of the place, the snow on the plaza lit up in the green and yellow and red of the unceasing billboards. It's wondrous, this nighttime labor performed by those we don't love? Isn't it, Ludovica?

It's just the three of you now: you and Cugino Hitler and "Marcello," the *poco easy* guy, who entertains the two of you with his weird Italo-English slang: *"niggaz we hate," "hos we wanna bone."* He gesticulates furiously, a monkey in a Loden coat.

"Marcello" and Hitler tell her about their current project: try-

49

ing to sleep with Anna. *"We'll date-rape her pronto. Bright pussy lights."*

She ignores the sexism and tries to play along. "Anna is a talker. She wouldn't act on it is my guess."

"Must be punished. Constantly talking cock." That's Cugino Hitler.

A Fox News cameraman shoots b-roll in the middle of the deserted square: a heavy-duty snow blower and its operator alone with the elements. The sidewalks have been swept clean, but the five o'clock shadow of new snow gives both the shoveled and the neglected parts of the square an uneven texture, like a floor in need of polish.

"So what, then, should we all bang her together?" they ask her.

"Is she game?" she replies. "I doubt it."

"She's all about the cock talk."

"She's not going to do it."

"You don't think so?"

"Talkers aren't doers."

"Which are you?"

"I'm a woman," she points out. The young men hold her arms as they walk through pools of pure color and light.

"Mmm. A woman, Hitler, *capisc'*?"

"Listen, Ludovichina, since you're a woman, would you like to get on your hands and knees and be, like, a slinking woman for our album cover?"

"A slinking woman?" she sniggers.

"We're in love with you. You inspire us. Vuittone inspire us. We inspire Vuittone."

"You think you can play the part of a slinking woman? Our thinking is . . . We've got your imposing beauty, your ankles, and Louis Vuitton. And 'Marcello's' record, his love for a real woman . . ."

50

"You guys are crazy. Are you really making a record? Or are you just shooting the shit? Do you even have a contract, or are you just teasing me? Why don't you ask Anna to do it?"

"Women in Willy, they expect it, Ludovica. They want you to ask them to degrade themselves."

"I'm a woman in Willy."

"*Naaaah.* The Willy women, they're all affected. They're not natural, like you'd be. We'll give you the shoes."

"The concetto of the cover: you be our model, foot model; we buy the shoes, Louis Vuitton; we take the pictures of your feet in shoes Vuittone."

"But do you have a contract?"

"We do! 'Marcello' is with an indie in Rome who could work it out with EMI to get them to distribute it. But this is wicked shit, because it's *broken English rap,* some far-out shit from this rich kid from Parioli, this kid here, who's worse than the toughest Puerto Rican."

"Aiiight."

"He definitely looks like a Parioli kid to me."

"Exactly!" they giggle.

"And you want to take pictures of me kneeling in the Louis Vuitton shoes? They're expensive!"

"We'll find a way to bring them back to the store afterwards. You have to take risks, you know? And if it doesn't work out, you've won a pair of shoes."

"We no pay you; we debase you for glory."

"But you really do have a contract?"

"James Murphy is pushing us, networking-wise. The super-queer guy tonight, Sergio, he works with Gassa, the rapper. 'Marcello' was a producer on one of Gassa's tracks. So in Italy we're covered, and here in New York we have James, Nico, and some guy at *Vice.* Nico says he's talked up our project with people at *XL*

Mag in Rome. And in Milan *Rolling Stone* is on it. And then there are all of Gassa's connections."

"I've never done a photoshoot."

"Oh, come on. It's solid shit. I took portraits of James; I sold one to *New York*."

Every sign resonates in the snow, each logo an imperfection. Sbarro, *Mamma Mia!*, Wonderland, McDonald's, Maxwell House, Barilla, JVC, Coca-Cola, M&Ms, Forever 21: circles, doodles, cheerful puppets, the tabloid news, the Nikkei ticker.

"You have to hold me up or I'll die!" she squeals, laughing, and then tells them about the blood clot. They greet the news as a kind of encouragement and tenderly stroke her back and her hips. They distance themselves from the stragglers and the disoriented tourists and stop to watch the ads. They're silent for a whole minute. Then they escort her back to Berengo's and ask her for her phone number.

SHE UNBUTTONS HER coat in the elevator next to an Asian couple in red slippers on their way back from the laundry room. Their clothing bags give off a pleasant chemical smell.

She tidies up the room a bit, slides the window open, lets the cold air in and the smoke out, picks up the bedspread from the sofa she still hasn't properly slept on. Berengo's door is shut. After closing the window, Ludovica changes into Berengo's tracksuit, which she finds stuffed between cushions, and gazes out at the snowflakes. They're eerily still, or maybe they're floating upward.

"My bed, my fucking bed, at last." She pulls out the extension, takes the sheets and the pillow out of the hall closet. On her way to the bathroom she hears an alarming thud coming from Berengo's room, then a pause, then two more thuds. Nicola and his girlfriend grunt. Silence, more thuds, more grunts. She stands in front of the door, swallowing all her saliva, until the sense of danger recedes; these are consensual grunts, deliberate thuds. *"Oh, nel bel mezzo della festa,"* she says to herself, quoting Woolf, *"ecco la morte."*

Back at her window, she takes off the track pants and places her knees on either side of the A/C window unit, letting the warm air blow between her legs. She's alert to the solitude of the hollow red air, the surfaces receding into a darkness busy with snow. She looks out at the top of the *Times* building, its roof floodlit and ominous. The thuds and grunts go on and then stop as she keeps playing with the warm gust of dusty air, lies down on the bed to climax, to relax, fall into sleep, barely able to pick up the pants and put them on and cover herself with sheets and the duvet cover.

A WAN MORNING, pale and white. Before meeting Cugino Hitler and his rapper friend at Louis Vuitton, La Sposina, book in hand, takes a self-guided architectural tour of the East Side's postmodern skyscrapers. The little round temple at the corner of Lexington and Fifty-Seventh, Acropolis-like; the colorful indoor mall, straight out of the seventies (posted to Facebook mid–coffee break); the pink granite silliness of 550 Madison; Trump Tower, all its surfaces either pink or gilded or both, its lobby open to the public (a beneficial compromise) and overwhelmed with fountains and mosaics and mirrors. She doesn't like what she sees, finds all of it repellent and distasteful, until she gets to the Dior boutique, housed in an angular building faced with teal glass, the work of a French architect. It has the look and tone of a tall woman standing in silhouette, her elegant profile wedged between two nondescript buildings, one from the twenties, the other from the eighties. Perhaps her taste for the French hasn't disappeared entirely.

She meets them in front of the large Vuitton windows on Fifth Avenue, currently an orgy of stuffed animals. Against a quilted velvet background somewhere between jade and moss, the animals pose in impossible shoes, their weirdly colored heels and platforms made of unexpected materials. Some of the animals are composed of scraps of fabric and leather and even metal studs, their grotesque forms imprisoned inside glass reliquaries. Roosters, beavers, deer—all of them not just dressed up in leather that strongly suggests S&M, but manufactured from it: ex-handbags, ripped suspenders, stray tassels. Their golden claws, which protrude from their cute little paws, are made of clips pulled off $150 key rings. Animal cruelty. A stuffed giraffe poses with three enormous scarves—red, black, pink—inside an oversized photo frame. Under the giraffe are two suitcases and one hatbox. On the sidewalk two kids laugh hysterically and point their fingers and jump on top of each other, trying to get a better look at one of the windows. Inside the window that provokes their fascination is a female mannequin in furs and stilettos, arranged in a desperate, kneeling position. She looks out toward Madison Avenue, praying for a lifeline.

They take her by the arm to a Pain Quotidien. They wear identical furry white earflaps under their baseball caps.

"Marcello" is quiet. "What's with him?" she asks.

"He's excited. He thinks today's the day, the shoot and everything. He's superstoked, he's nervous . . ."

"*Marcé*, you could at least speak Italian with me."

"Baby baby baby, it's my drive, it's my ambition."

"See, we've entered the Vuitton orbit, and now we're a little discombobulated. It's just a bunch of Vuittoning in the Vuitton void-a-thon."

"Too much Vuittonné in my blue balls, bae."

"Marcello" asks for tea in his ostentatiously bad English, his order full of words she doesn't understand. The place is packed: tourists, people who work in nice offices, maybe even at Condé Nast.

The three of them eat tartines. Capers and mesclun leaves fall off the paté-smeared crostini onto their plates. The boys, whom La Sposina has christened Chip n' Dale, tell her about their projects and discuss the possibility that her blood clot could become part of the artwork.

"Thin blood. It teach the lesson. But what lesson?"

Chip n' Dale have gotten rid of their protective strata of winter clothes. They're lean and thin and asexual. "Marcello" is intense: big brows, wavy curls, face snobby and unhappy. Cugino Hitler is mousier, more flexible, more welcoming, pensive, bald, fair. La Sposina has forced them to take off their caps with a rhetorical flourish: "We're in France here, not America."

"Are you kidding me?"

"Place is Belgian, bi-atch. Ma we love Parigi, doll, we love Roma, we're from Kansas City and we heart Milano."

La Sposina has stopped seeking out literal meaning in "Marcello"'s words. She hands the book of architectural sights to Cugino Hitler, who is intrigued. The three of them end up in Bryant Park after a cab ride paid for by Chip n' Dale. They're delighted by their nicknames, even more delighted by the chance to walk around and gaze up at art deco buildings while waiting for La Sposina to agree to pose for demeaning pictures. The American Radiator Building, a decadent tower made of black gold, evokes the coal its first owners helped make obsolete. The boys take out their notepads and cameras. She thinks they're cute, concentrating. Chip n' Dale convert to art deco at the corner of Lexington and Forty-Second, the Chrysler Building on one side, the Chanin Building on the other: *"Gay under, cock over," "Pink polo, zio!" "Terracotta and bas reliefs!"*

Then they tackle the Chanin's lobby, shooting until the black doorman asks them to stop. "All gold," they exclaim. *"Elevator, gold,"* *"Gold* newsstand, *gold* letterbox," "that black fucking doorman." And finally: *"Che fascismo! Che fascismo!"* *"Duce duce duce!"* They shout and laugh and punch each other's backs.

"Are you nuts?" La Sposina asks. "What's fascist about it? It's so exotic! It's like a forest." But they can't be convinced. Deco, they insist, is "fascist sublime."

They finally leave the building, and La Sposina is tired; she wants to go home, she's exhausted: now the kids are discussing the new artwork they've just conceived of, inspired, of course, by the Chanin: "Fake mosaics with hip-hop niggers in place of nigger slaves building the Chrysler and the Chanin. Niggers building white popular culture for us to exploit! *Che fascismo!*"

"No Vuitton, then? Can I go?"

"Not at all! You're *pivotal*! We'll find a way to make you kneel in Vuitton shoes in the middle of all the deco niggers."

"Seriously, guys, are you fascists now? Is this a joke?"

"Woman. You degradation o you no degradation?"

"Sure sure, Marce, it's not like you're just saying random shit and I'm so impressed with your intelligence." She hails a cab as Hitler checks his pockets and tries handing her $20, but she refuses.

Hitler: "Well then, call us if you want to pose!"

"Marcello": *"Bi-atch!"*

She climbs into the cab. The driver, a huge Indian guy, is swallowing his last bite of non-Indian food. He places the Tupperware container on the seat next to him and stares at her through the rearview mirror. La Sposina, who hasn't shut the door, catches the stranger's windblown eyes and turns to Cugino Hitler and runs a hand through her hair. "Okay, get inside."

So the three of them head down toward Union Square, to the

apartment where they're staying. They're so excited that she's changed her mind that they start brainstorming what shoes they can use for the test shots, and when to go back to Vuitton.

"Let's first see if I'm even right for it."

The house where they're crashing is another New York fantasyland dreamed up for Italian consumption. It's not Willy, or Midtown, but the Village: fancy little streets, rusty fire escapes. Lorenzo's friends live in places like this, and so does Carrie Bradshaw, leaning on the windowsill after writing down her latest reflections on sex; an old reference, whose relevance weirdly seems to linger. Up the carpeted stairs, through a metal door painted beige, and inside to two rooms: one bedroom and one glorious living room with an exposed brick wall, a long sofa under two large windows. Outside: snow clumped on dead branches, one car drifting by, then another, a row of confident buildings just like this one, under a bright, gray sky.

It's a grown-up's apartment. It's furnished with a big TV and an antique cupboard. Over that, the boys have imposed a layer of their own mess: sweaters everywhere, big sneakers thrown into a corner, grocery store tote bags with cereal boxes.

"It's nice, goddamn it."

"You can come by any time."

"Marcello" sits on a stool at the kitchenette counter, rolling a joint.

"You happy?"

"Ludovica, you bella fica, 'course I'm contento."

"You're two babies. I like you."

"Two babies with humongous cocks."

"Of course, love."

And when, finally, after a couple of puffs, Ludovica kneels on the floor, shoeless, in a skirt that she found in the owner's closet and that she can't zip up all the way, facing away from the windows and from the boys, who shoot her from the couch with a reflex and a mobile, she recites one of her favorite lines to herself, Clarissa Dalloway on Sally Seton: *"Aveva un egoismo così naturale e il desiderio che si pensasse a lei per prima era scoperto."* She brings the novel along on every trip, evidence that women have souls even when they make mistakes.

"The absolute best would be seeing you crawl around on stage like that."

Her panties are yellow and high-waisted, and the skirt is gray, a sad thing a lawyer might wear. Cugino Hitler stands up occasionally to gently pull the skirt around or up or down, not to expose her lingerie but to figure out her legs.

"You're beautiful," he says with real emotion. "These legs you have—they're big but they're not fat. No offense." Tenderly: "You're like this *donna cannone*, you're majestic." He shoots her from the back, then from the front.

"Should I make a face?"

"No, these are for me, for my personal archive. You look good in a white shirt, you know. I'd unbutton it a bit."

"My back hurts. Can I sit down for a minute?"

She sits on the floor. They look at each other, she and Cugino Hitler. "Marcello" keeps his eyes on the ground, aroused and tense. Her husband could never talk to these people, but she can. They know that making Italian movies isn't the answer, not anymore; this is. Maybe Italian cinema is dead. Lorenzo should try to understand these people. She doesn't get them, yet she's here and now she's kneeling again and Cugino Hitler is snapping away. Will she look okay? Will the black stockings hide every last hair?

LATER, IN A cab with Hitler's twenty-dollar bill in her purse, she realizes that what she loved most of all was the way Chip n' Dale

58

were dying to ask her for something more but couldn't. Her husband keeps begging her to come back home, and her texts in response are more composed, more confident. She only loses the confidence when she drafts an email to her father. At Berengo's, she watches YouTube videos of girls sniffing condoms.

*S*he takes the train back to Willy on Thursday, around noon. Rosa, the owner of the boutique, has ordered her to stop by and discuss her new schedule. Rosa is a Neapolitan who moved first to Milan, then to Brooklyn. A spinster with a heart of gold disguised under hip, becoming looks, she must have let Lorenzo convince her to lure Ludovica back to the neighborhood. On the C train, La Sposina examines a ripped gay guy, two unpretentious yuppies, a family of tourists. On the L, she's reunited with men and women dressed exactly the way she likes them to be dressed, their asymmetric faces ravishing. They stand pressed against Hispanic men reading romance novels and black teens in electric-green basketball sneakers.

Outside the Bedford stop she sees the familiar double-breasted SS-style coats; fitted down jackets; blazers with ridiculously large lapels; checkered lumberjack blouses. It's a parade of fresh, elongated, unwrinkled faces that are almost perfect, marred only by buggy eyes and overdetermined glasses. New trash bags are lined up along the curb under a sharp sun and a layer of snow that's alternately gilded and dirty. It's warmer than it was yesterday; the sky is a confident blue. The boutique encounter is obviously a plan hatched by Lorenzo, an ambush plotted with Rosa's not quite witting participation. La Sposina walks warily on the frozen sidewalk.

The boutique's door is unlocked, but the sign apologizes: SORRY WE'RE CLOSED. A long hug with Rosa. She's forty, short, and dense and tough, with close-cut hair dyed red and two creases on her thick neck. She wears a tight white sleeveless T-shirt, a vast knee-length skirt over heavy black stockings, a gold vest with a single button, and a shawl covered in skulls.

"What's going on with those pants, love? Here, go try this on." Her Neapolitan accent has gotten Milanesthetized with the years. She hands La Sposina a light gray skirt, felt with uneven stitching along the edges. "Maybe these stockings, too? I'm doing inventory; the shop's closed all morning. I meant to do it yesterday, but I just couldn't make myself."

"You got yourself a male intern?"

Rosa pretends to miss the joke; that's how she is. Warm and affectionate—less a boss than a member of the family, and indeed, Ludovica got the gig through her cousin, who met Rosa at the Istituto Europeo di Deisgn. Middle age is cruel to her: she wears layers of foundation and has no men in her life, except for the occasional boys in their twenties who develop a crush and offer themselves up and then vanish, leaving her alone at home with her posters, Mad Men and Wong Kar-Wai. She's spent the last few months transforming La Sposina's style, using the boutique's best merchandise. She points a finger toward the back of the shop. A mirror covers the entire back wall like at a ballet school. There are racks of clothes barely illuminated by the dim light of a table lamp and two curtained booths, one of them obviously concealing Lorenzo. So La Sposina ignores the booths and positions herself in front of the mirror; if her husband is really lurking behind the curtain, this is exactly what he wants to see:

his wife with her back to him, undressing and trying on a new skirt.

When she stands in front of a mirror, it's hard to pretend that she's Jasmine Trinca. In a large mirror, she has to accept herself for what she is. She's not a nimble headstrong *moretta* like Trinca; she's too big, a *donnone* who overlaps with contemporary standards of beauty only in a few key respects: no belly, an interesting face with almond-shaped eyes a reasonable distance from each other, a nondescript nose, a full mouth. The rest: a chin so thin that from certain angles it disappears entirely; big, round shoulders; an ass that appeals exclusively to real ass-lovers, too wide and soft; legs that aren't huge but certainly too noticeable, saved only by elegant ankles that tie together what she's always thought was an impossible balancing act. Rosa has spent the last few months making her more attractive: she forced her to get bangs, encircling her face with hair, and persuaded her to abandon the Sorbonne style, which fit neither her body type, nor the neighborhood. This self-effacement was a prerequisite for the job: no more uptight coats; no more Parisian stockings, which gave her *monstre* legs; no more blouses that never closed properly (she has a large, flat chest; her torso is unfortunately wide). Though Willy is full of perfect girls, people appreciate atypical beauties, and Rosa made her into one.

She stands there in black stockings and a man's shirt buttoned up to her neck. Rosa is pumping music from the other room, a confusing mix of trap rap and free jazz. Since Lorenzo hasn't come out yet—she stands still for a second to see if he's in there, playing hide-and-seek—Ludovica puts her skirt on and zips it up high on her waist, over her belly button. This is how Rosa likes her: the vertical and horizontal lines of her body all mixed up so that her facial features stand out. A hipster Mina—and that's how Lorenzo wants her. Now, for him, she pulls the skirt up in the back, so he can see her ass from the room. At least the thick, black stockings make it look smaller.

Lorenzo emerges, slightly discolored, as if transported from some other dimension, and La Sposina feels her sternum snapping.

"Don't move, love."

The wife holds on to the little handrail in front of the mirror. Beloved husband, bourgeois director, she can't find the strength to utter the words: no, no, please, not the *scena madre*, the big scene, the drama. She feels she owes it to him. Which male sexual fantasy is worse, her husband's or Chip 'n' Dale's? In the mirror she sees the husband, the ragazzone from Prati with the nice oval face and the pretty yellow-toothed smile, one horizontal wrinkle on his forehead; curls pressed down by the wool cap he has just pulled off his head; glasses with big tinted lenses and a thick gray frame, a figure out of a 1970s Italian gangster movie; unshaven with sideburns; a horizontal scar on his chin from falling off his bicycle; wool scarf; the black sweater, half unzipped; the striped Muji shirt you can glimpse beneath, a few buttons undone; black jeans, slightly faded, tight but not too tight; and finally, his boots, his boots, his boots. He's begun to look unfamiliar—especially compared to the subtle androgyny of *casa Berengo*—though it's only been three days since she's seen him.

And here's the sceneggiata:

"Careful, I've got stockings on!" she yells as he grabs her.

"Don't turn around."

"*Muccino mio*, my stockings."

"Don't move, silly."

"Rosa's in the other room."

La Sposina wants him, and wanting him comforts her. When he's done she'll be able to ask him the question she's been avoiding. And then she'll fly to Rome. She looks his reflection in the eyes: he is focused and hurt. She lifts her skirt knowing he'll

63

never tire of this scene: a woman lifting her skirt, moaning, caving in. She waits before pulling down her stockings and panties just enough, but then she hears a metallic snip, a pair of scissors. "What are you doing?" she asks, though she knows the answer.

"Don't move. You'll get hurt. Rosa's gone."

"Is this a movie? Fucking scissors?"

No response as he continues to widen the hole in the crotch of her stockings.

"Are you shooting a porno, love? Is this our big break? A porno?"

"I love you."

She feels two wet fingers push past the curtain of stockings and panties. The director and protagonist enters her and moans like a man who's just gotten inside a woman, and she moans like a woman. His hands are warm—he knows she hates cold hands—and she feels him lift her shirt up over her bra like in those American Apparel ads he likes, the ones where the models always have their clothes sexily askew. When she's fully naked she's not as pretty as she used to be, but with clothes on she's different every time. It's like being with a whole bunch of women. He pulls one breast out of her bra.

So here they are, these two, the boy and the girl who landed in JFK after sending a link to the short film and news of the movie award to a couple of émigré acquaintances, including a friend of a friend of Lorenzo's, Elisa, a cockteaser currently in New York, for whom Lorenzo has at times lost interest in Ludovica. The daughter of a producer, the cockteaser has never gone through with anything, but the two friends have talked it all over. Ludovica hasn't been shocked by this stuff; she's practical, and the girl's friend (the daughter of a Center-Left senator) could prove useful. The short film really had seemed good when they were leaving for New York, and at JFK, she'd felt lucky to have this Mastroianni guy by her side: an enthusiastic philosopher/filmmaker—could you ask for more from a husband?

So here they are, in front of Rosa's large mirror, her hands on the bar as if clinging to a ledge. She shuts her eyes the moment she sees a sigh on her mother's face—no, it's Ludovica's, no, her mother's face—as the focused, stern-looking man-child pounds against her through the warm tingle of the shredded stockings, disappearing behind her because they're the same height. Lorenzo's hands cling to her breasts, her hands cling to the bar. They exchange gasps and affected quips:

"Are you giving me an STD, bitch?"

"That's so Little Italy of you, Lorè. Mmm."

"Ciro. Call me Ciro. Mmm."

"I love you so much. Mmm."

"You taking the Coumadin? Mmm."

"Give me bruises. Mmm."

"Mmm. I'm gonna bruise you black and blue. You're not drinking are you?"

"Mmm. No, I'm not drinking."

"You like this? Mmm."

"Mmm. I do."

"My hair's turning white and it's your fault. It's the pain. Oh."

"I love you so much *Muccinomio*. Mmm."

He squeezes her hips and then her ass, and after a minute of painful squeezing and desperate thrusts he comes inside her. (The pill.)

He keeps a hand there as he pulls out to collect what's dripping, holding her belly with the other hand, pulling her back with him. They trip on their pants and stumble, gasping, all the way down into the old, green armchair. Abandoned there, finally, the woman on top of the man, they breathe. Her comment: "What a mess." She's not going to clean herself like this, her hands dirty from the subway. "Clean me up, dummy." she says. Her skirt is up, like a doll's. His hand held humbly under her body, flattened beneath his wife's weight, he manages to wipe, but he ends up staining her stockings as she lets out a goofy, inevitable queef.

Then: "I might be getting the assistant director gig on Wes Anderson's next movie."

La Sposina is still focused on the air coming out of her. "What the fuck?"

"Yeah. Maybe. Keep it to yourself for now. Through a friend of a friend of Elisa's."

"Crazy. No, really. That's crazy. Well done, love."

"It's still just a possibility. To show you what we might be able to accomplish here."

(La Sposina is laboriously trying to recall how high up the food chain an assistant director is; she wants to figure out if her husband's news is important. What's the name for the guy who basically works as a full-time slave for the film crew? Is that the assistant director or the production assistant? There's the one who's the apprentice, who actually learns the craft as he works, and the other one, who brings everyone coffee.)

The phone rings at the bottom of her bag. She stands up, and her husband follows, his hand still between her thighs, his pants still down. They do this contorted, parallel walk across the back of the store, as if inside an invisible camel costume. As La Sposina bends down to pick up the phone, he mimes penetrating her against her will, a childish gesture.

Mother is on the phone.

"So you got some Skype credit, ma?"

"Yes, Fofi helped me with it."

"What did he want for it?"

"Aren't you happy I called?"

"Mommy, I can't really talk now."

"Okay. Tell Lorenzo I say hi."

"Bye . . ." She hangs up. "Mother."

"What did she want?"

"Listen, Lorenzo. I was going to lay out my thoughts very clearly . . . And now you've thrown Wes Anderson into the mix, so what do you want me to say?"

LATER ON, AT a cafe, as the beautiful people walk by on the other side of the glass, they get back to it between sips of orange juice and a shared blueberry muffin.

"So, what did you want to tell me?"

"I had a speech all ready: If I asked you to, would you give up trying to be a director?"

"Who knows what I would have said if I hadn't gotten the Wes Anderson news?"

"Who knows?"

"Since you left home, I've felt like you've been very close to me. Like you're taking me more seriously."

A single tear from Ludovica. "I totally get what you mean." But then, after swallowing and bringing a napkin to the lower eyelid and sniffing softly: "I'm going back to Rome for a month. Let's see how it goes. Let's see what happens with you and this job. It sounds like big news. I don't want to ruin it for you." She flashes a Jasmine Trinca smile, heavy but hopeful. "But I want to tell you exactly what I think."

"So tell me, baby," he says. He's all puffed up right now. La Sposina wants to believe in the Wes Anderson news but she can't. But she doesn't want to treat him badly either, not without evidence.

"This is what I'm thinking. If you don't want an academic career, I'll support you. So let's borrow some money, and you can go look for a different job. You can even work in movies. But you're thirty-four, and you don't have any real connections with any producers, and I think it's too late to think you can still be a director. I'm scared that all this trying is going to screw up our life. You understand how hard it is for me to tell you this, right? I'm saying this because I love you. I don't want us to spend our whole lives waiting for this thing to happen when it's not going to happen. Please consider what I'm saying."

"But it's happening now."

La Sposina suppresses her rage. "Fine. I'll go to Rome, keep my father happy, maybe even turn the bookstore around and keep it from ending up in Fofi's hands. You—"

"You know what I think about this father thing."

"Will you fucking let me finish?"

"I'm sorry. I'm listening."

"You stay here and see if the Wes Anderson thing happens. If it does, fine, I'll go along with the New York Film Academy plan. But I think you should give it some serious thought anyway, figure out if this dream is more important to you than I am. I don't want to ruin my life because you've still got no clue if you're going to make it. It's not like it's a bar exam, where they tell you if you haven't passed, and you can just move on with your life."

"No, you're right."

They clasp hands over the table.

"I'll go back to Rome. I'll behave, I won't fuck anyone, and you won't either. We'll see how it goes with old Wes, and we'll figure it out from there."

YOU'LL SPEND THE rest of Thursday alone at Berengo's. At midnight you'll pull his bedroom door open to suggest the very new idea that you want to spend some time with him. His face is

68

gray in the glare of the iPad, the dumb noises of Angry Birds the room's only soundtrack. He'll say no thanks without raising his eyes from the game.

BUT ON FRIDAY night, Nico Berengo comes in to talk to you. You've spent the day alone. On Skype with your mother, you kept the camera off and went out of your way to pretend you were home in Brooklyn. You followed the results from the referendum over whether to close Mirafiori, the historic Fiat factory in Turin. You read the news about Berlusconi and Ruby Rubacuori, his former underage acquaintance. You complained about Italy. You hear Berengo sneak in around eleven p.m. with another man who seems to be dragging a heavy plastic shopping bag. They whisper inaudibly to each other. You decide not to emerge from behind the bamboo screen, and you don't get a ciao.

To your surprise, Nico comes in after dinner and lies down next to you on the sofa bed. "May I?" He's so smooth, what with his tight, teal acetate tracksuit and the casual way he slips into your bed with you. Under the duvet, you're in panties and a T-shirt. He stays on top of the duvet.

So here he is, smelling of body wash and grape-scented moisturizer. He lies between you and an episode of *American Dad!*

"Well, welcome," you say. "Make yourself at home." You give him room.

Nicola lies on his back and stares at the ceiling. If he turns toward the TV, he'll block your vision, and if he turns toward you, it'll be too intimate too soon. (Right there on the sofa, shrouded in paisley bedspreads, he often falls asleep without brushing his teeth. He's terrified of getting stains on the fabric [it's a phobia], so even now, here, with her lying next to him, he investigates the landscape with his cell phone flashlight. He's rarely seen me

69

asleep, whereas a large part of my relationship with him involves his sleeping as I orbit around him reading or watching muted close-captioned TV.) Then, having resolved the moral conundrum, he slips under the duvet. You were already warm enough, and now you're sweating.

"I can't sleep," he explains. "Can we watch together? Can I try and fall asleep here?"

Your heart is beating fast, but you feel you can remain in bed. For now the only thing you're guilty of is enjoying someone else's smell—the most modest form of guilt there is.

Nico is awake and cheerful. "Or why don't you come into the other room with my friend? He's married with five kids, unhappy with his wife. It'd be cool to let him blow off some steam."

"Married?"

"He spends the night here when he's in New York for work. He's a dear friend, an Italian. *He's super Catholic, so this isn't his idea;* he's already asleep, actually. But I'd love to wake him up with a surprise. *You.*"

Your breaths are short, your heart races. "You're crazy, Nicola. Why are you only talking to me now?" You lean over, resting on the right elbow. "You haven't talked to me since Monday."

"That's not true, not true. I just let you be. *I thought you needed it . . .*"

A lava of fear has climbed up your legs. You shut him up and tell him you're having a panic attack. Nico gives you room. "Oh dear," he says softly, considerately. "We're family. So you get those attacks too, huh?"

You start picturing a forest, the trick you use to calm yourself down. You're sitting naked on the cold, moist soil in the middle of a dark grove. Berengo gets up and comes back with a tray. There's a small glass bottle with a dropper and a glass of water. He starts praising Melissa—the liquid inside the bottle—in a goofy, over-the-top way that's impossible to read. "It's the grass from Serenity Now, the herbal tea. I'll show you how to do it: you just pour drops into the water yourself. I wouldn't want you to think I'm giving you roofies or anything. It's the Serenity Now drug."

"Are you joking?"

"No, I'm not."

"What is it, really? Is it any good?"

"It's natural, not chemical. But you have to sort of accompany it with thoughts; it's not automatic. It relaxes the muscles. So if you're thinking about how your throat is stiff, it'll relax the throat."

You drink it, and you feel like laughing. The fear recedes back down your legs and into your feet until it disappears entirely. Maybe it's the Melissa, or maybe it's his voice.

You stop talking and turn back to the TV. He begins again: "You were fine when I asked you a favor: he's in the other room, *married with kids,* such a fine man, a bit uptight, a great job in Finmeccanica, but *five kids, per-pe-tually tense,* broom up his ass, you know what I mean? *And even if he'd love to,* he could never bring himself to visit whores or get himself a lover. *I know, right?*"

"You're silly, you know? You come to me and talk about bad marriages? To *me?*"

"Oh."

"Come on."

"I need love."

"You do need love, Nico. We all do."

He turns his back toward you and watches *American Dad!* so you have to lean in closer and closer to hear him talk. You place your chin on his shoulder.

"Gustavo, my friend in there, he's tall and he's smart," he insists. "And he's hung! I'd pay to see you two fuck. Huge cock. You can't make that thing go away with Melissa, that huge cock."

She laughs. "Will you shut up? I don't know what's in the air right now. Everybody's getting horny around me. It hasn't happened for a while."

"Must be your desperation."

"Hey!" You punch him on the shoulder.

"So, who wants you?"

You tell him about Chip 'n' Dale, the Louis Vuitton afternoon, and the "demeaning" pictures, though they weren't that demeaning, you say, or you wouldn't have enjoyed the experience. Nico tells you that Cugino Hitler is Gustavo Tullio's cousin, hence the nickname. And Gustavo Tullio is the guy sleeping in the bedroom. And—more confusingly—Cugino Hitler's name is also Marcello.

"It's a nice nickname, Chip 'n' Dale. *Serves them right*. But you can't bang Chip 'n' Dale; they're nothing."

"Oh, really? Then how come you introduce them to all the important people? They're super well connected."

"Well, sure, they're good. They've got drive, and they work their ass off. But they're fascists! You wouldn't bang a fascist, would you?"

He's on a roll. The talk is such pleasure that you find yourself revealing to Berengo that on Thursday you made love to your husband in the back of the boutique where you work. Your chin is still on his shoulder as he watches the ending of the episode. When he hears that you made love in front of the big mirror, he wants details. You tell him about Lorenzo's short film, say that it isn't any good. But Nico doesn't comment. He only wants "the details of the conjugal visit."

"It was so trashy. I expected him to show up like that: Lorenzo has this super-predictable imagination. When he came out of that changing booth, though, I loved him. It was so sweet."

"What a genius Lorenzo is—a real Italian director: he wants

to do drama, maybe even drama with the nasty bits, *sporcaccione*, some nudity, then he shoots postmodern shorts with nods and winks all over the place. He should shoot something that has this exact scene in it. I hope he gets to it sooner or later."

"Isn't it too late to become a director, though?"

"Don't ever tell him you told *me* you call him Muccino."

"No, of course not . . ."

The cartoon ends. It was on a flash drive, and the TV shows a dark blue home screen, files and folders.

He says: "He should shoot ironic, erotic movies where all that's supposed to happen happens, no surprises, and the entire pleasure is the surprise of not having any surprises. You, though, you wouldn't make a good director. You don't give me enough detail. *Did he finish inside you or all over you? Are you on the pill?*"

"You're a perverted child, Berengo."

You're abandoned on his arm, and you're bigger than him, and you're watching the screen and so is he, so that neither of you has to face the other. You describe in detail the scissors cutting through the stockings, he asks if you kept the ripped stockings, you reply that you threw them away, he shrieks, you laugh. He's made you laugh, and now you tell him that you're sleepy. But he transforms the moment. "You're aroused," he says, *"I can tell: it was nice feeling you get aroused while you were talking, I'm so down with these things."* Then he clarifies his intentions: "Now you're going to want to stay alone and finger yourself, and I'll miss your show."

You laugh. He asks you about your climax habits, says he thinks *you like cock.* You laugh.

"So, you only climax by hand or through intercourse, too?"

"Oh, both ways, and plenty," you confess. You want to brag that you're a squirter, but you never tell anyone about this because men like the idea too much. It's so fashionable these days:

all the porn sites have tags and categories, and everybody knows what it means. It's a status symbol. The last person you told was Fofi, but then you stopped when you realized that it's the kind of confession men aren't be able to get out of their system.

But right now, at least, you don't have a mother. Your facial features are yours; they feel disposable and nonhereditary.

"When I heard you wrestling with Edele in there, I touched myself."

"It wasn't Edele, it was another one. Her name's Vera."

"Oh, good for you."

"I like girls so much," he says, as if this were some kind of weird predilection, then turns his head to look at you over his shoulder. You tell him to go back to his previous position, to keep facing the TV. He obeys. You slip your hand inside his track pants, inside his underwear. You order him to remain still, spit on your hand, and put your hand back in his pants. After he shudders and tells you, without disgusting you, that you are good and that you are family, you order him to stay still; you want to come, too, and you will do it alone while he stays put. You wipe your hand against his tracksuit, you lick your fingers out of habit, stick them in your panties. He isn't very manly, and you can tell by how still he is that he's exhilarated by your ways. He's listening to every sound you're making.

IN THE MORNING he's gone. As compensation, La Sposina gets to meet Gustavo Tullio, the other guest. The sunny morning, slabs of light barely concealed by the blinds, wake her up slowly, over the course of two hours. Gustavo Tullio first appears as a slightly affected voice on the other side of the screens: "Good *morning*," his voice is stuffy. "Sorry to dis*turb*."

"No worries."

74

"Are you pre*sen*table? I need to get *break*fast."

La Sposina scratches her eyes under the duvet. She also scratches the corners of her mouth, wipes her index finger on her shirt, licks the back of her hand, and smells it. "Help yourself."

The family man is busying himself in the kitchenette, knocking over pottery and wooden bowls and silverware with total gracelessness. He apologizes for the noise. As he stumbles around, a powerful image of Gustavo Tullio is being manufactured in Ludovica's imagination, someone who's not part of the usual Berengo crowd. She remains behind the bamboo.

"Will you join me at the table?"

"Oh, don't worry, thanks."

Their voices climb over the screens. La Sposina is imagining a middle manager, aloof in a gray suit, a Don Draper.

"I make American breakfast on Saturdays. In Italy. With my children."

"Oh yeah?"

"Bacon and eggs. Are there any?"

"No idea. Pancakes?"

"Sure."

"Want me to go buy anything?"

"No, no problem. All sweet stuff, then."

La Sposina sits down when the table is set. She doesn't go to the bathroom, doesn't change into something less revealing, doesn't even rush to take a quick sip of orange juice to mask her breath. Gustavo Tullio spent the night in a shapeless red tracksuit with a round neck. He's out of shape and looks tired: his eyes droop, and his head is covered in yellow curls. But he's tall and obviously well endowed.

"I'm Gustavo, by the way," he shakes her dirty hand. "Oh, no need to stand up."

He sits down and faces her. The pancakes are good, and they

discuss the weather, the surprisingly sunny days. The tracksuit man's sad appearance is calming. She spreads butter on her pancakes and drenches them in maple syrup. Her head is light.

Suddenly, Gustavo Tullio is preaching: "Ludovica. Well. Now that it's just the two of us here, I must tell you straight away that I'm sincerely uncomfortable being here with you, like this." He continues, encouraged by her shy smile. "I find it immoral." He pours her more orange juice, then some coffee. "I find it immoral that Nicola is hosting married men and women, in this, well, combination."

Ludovica smiles, swallows, spreads more butter on a bite of pancake, just happens to lick the messy knife. "Sorry," she just happens to say.

"You are as much a victim as I am. I hadn't been advised of your presence. Otherwise I would have said no, stayed somewhere else, out of respect for you and your husband." Gustavo licks the wet crumbs from his fingers.

"What do you mean, exactly?"

He sits upright, his arms glued to his body, cutlery again in hand now that he's wiped his drool-covered fingers with a napkin. Chews. Drinks. Talks. "I'm sorry to take the liberty of bringing it up, but, well, I have three daughters, so it's an occupational hazard, no? To raise the issue of how fair it is for a woman to find herself in such a predicament."

"You have three daughters. That's so lovely, I'm jealous."

"If you were my daughter, well, I'd pull you up by the ears."

"Oh, come on."

He's silent for a moment. Ludovica stares at her plate.

"You sound like a real father. You're making me feel ashamed. I feel like I can't look at you," she laughs. "Is it the same for them? For your girls?"

"Forgive me. I shouldn't have."

"May I raise my eyes?"

"Of course you can."

La Sposina slowly lifts her head and knows she's trying to be liked. She looks him in the eyes, sees his embarrassment, sees how he quickly lowers his own head and stares down at his plate.

"How old are your girls?"

"Well, one of them is not so little anymore. She's thirteen. A few weeks ago she wanted to go to a Fabri Fibra concert, but I said no. Her mother loves hip-hop, though, so *she* ended up seeing the show."

"Her mother! Why did you say no?"

"It's vulgar."

"Yes, that's true. And a bit misogynistic."

"I agree. Her mother hasn't told her that she went. She'd go crazy."

"Are there many rules they have to follow?"

"Many," he says with a laugh.

"I can picture you at home. You have authority."

You search his eyes for the smallest shifts. Your dialogue—composed, gentle, mature—reminds you of Ozu: an awkward father, his mannered gestures and his careful way with plates and glasses, the short sentences, the exclamations partially repressed, less spoken than coughed up.

"We don't listen to Fabri Fibra at home. I'm sorry, forgive me for insisting on this, but Nicola is crazy. He left two married people alone in the house—not good manners, I don't think. I have five children, and he's the one who complains about getting panic attacks."

"I have them, too."

"You, though . . . I'm sorry, but I have to say this . . . I don't think Nico slept in my room last night."

"Oh, you're laying it down hard." She tries to make eye contact and manages to hold it for a beat, but he is still very interested in his plate.

"He probably went to visit some lover of his in the building." Tullio must be waiting for his plate to nod at what he just said; that's the only possible explanation for why he keeps staring at it so intently.

"Please, Gustavo . . ."

He continues to bend over the table, and you can't help but smile at the rare curls and endless skin on his head.

"He didn't sleep in my room, anyway. And I must tell you," he tells his plate, with the firmness of a man from another era, "that you should think this over. Does it really do you any good being here? This home is no good."

*S*unday: viral marketing in a coffee shop. It's just after ten, four p.m. in Italy. Right now your mother is napping in the bedroom, right now your father is looking over the bookstore's books and his investments as he listens to football commentary live on the radio in the living room, a blanket between his lap and his laptop.

"It's settled, Daddy," you write. "I'm flying back. I changed my tickets."

"Oh what splendid news. It's a gift, my love." And straight away: "Use my credit card. You still have my information?"

There's a one-way ticket for €630 but via Warsaw, so you scratch it. Then you scratch all the nondirect flights. The cheapest one-way flight today is €950, but you want it to be expensive, you want your father to pay dearly for the privilege. You look at return tickets, so that in case the sadness lifts, you can come back to New York . . . when? Let's say one month from now? You buy a round-trip ticket with a February 20 return date, €1370 euros, nonstop, Alitalia/Delta. You've never dared to pay this much for anything before, and you feel a pang of revenge.

Then you get to work. "We wouldn't want to rob you of the pleasures of your first time," you write in the introductory post on a new forum on women's razors. It's you—yeah you, La Sposina, Ludovica—it's you who writes things like: "A brand-new campaign, straight out of the oven! Yummy!" and "The account? Pfizer. The goal? Testing out their new web community: a laboratory for the study of sexuality." You draft emails for the buzz-marketing forum. "Sex is everywhere; everyone's talking about it," you write with your belly in mind (the belly Berengo got sticky), you write with Lorenzo's hands in mind, enmeshed between your legs after your sad, comic performance. Your eyes squint and your throat hardens, the skin on your face softens and heats up, tears wet your cheeks. You wipe your eyes and your nose with a handkerchief. "There's not much talk of sex education, though. And now's the time. Have fun!"

IN THE AFTERNOON, you stare out the window at a skyscraper. It stands there, posing for you as you take a picture. In the brilliant winter light it seems to contain every hue at once: turquoise, pink, eggplant, tangerine, cobalt, copper. The glass panels seem inconsistent—some are fuchsia, others are green—and the hues and flares pile up, exaggerated and tacky, inspired and affecting. Further south is the wide, brick Belvedere Hotel, its windows pimpled with air conditioners. You snap more photos and apply the essential filters. No frame, no background, just a wall of ACs and tiny windows.

Berengo's not coming home tonight, and you sleep alone, slightly scared.

ON MONDAY, THE sun is beautiful. "When most Italians look for vacation souvenirs, they usually choose local food. Do you fit the description?" This is you, your voice. "Do you buy pesto with capers, or pesto with wild fennel, or anchovies in oil and pepper, or salt-baked sea bass, or jam, or Sicilian chocolate bars, or . . .?" I let you write all this because you are this. You're the woman who jerked off Berengo, the lead actress in that little scene in the boutique directed by your sweet, melodramatic husband. "Now it's your turn! Post your favorite local dish from your region!"

It's late, and Nicola isn't back yet. You haven't even managed to pull the blinds closed, because you think you have to keep watch. You're hypnotized by the hollow tank of air that separates you from the other buildings nearby. You take some weed from Nico's little box, but smoking alone proves a mistake. You have a horrible thought: of the thousands of people you've seen throughout your entire life—on buses, on trains, in restaurants—how many of them died the day you saw them? You don't close your eyes until four in the morning.

TUESDAY. THE SNOW begins to fall before dawn, you feel the harsh pain of PMS. Is it a delayed period due to the distress of the last few days? It begins to drizzle at nine: clouds linger over the top of *The New York Times Building*, its spire lost to gray blankness. It hasn't rained in weeks, and at three p.m., it's still raining. The snow begins to melt.

You work on the Adidas and Colgate campaigns in bed, then fine-tune the copy for Dash Stain Remover: "Bad news, guys— this promo is for girls only." It's you who's writing this. You studied the philosophy of language, *la Societè du Spectacle*, the ability of monkeys to figure out other monkeys' intentions. And then instead of getting your PhD, you began to work for your professor's private enterprise, researching viral marketing and analytics and buzz. Everything seemed to fit. Now, in bed, after a deep but complicated sleep, after an early afternoon nap in the deserted apartment, you work. You write: "There are so many campaigns for boys out there, but with this product, it's the ladies we're targeting first, because they're the ones who do most of the chores." (You are La Sposina. You're the protagonist in a bourgeois story that concerns me only tangentially, which I've been asked to observe. I honor you, I may even like you.)

You take the elevator down to the laundry room in the basement to wash your clothes before tomorrow's flight. Your belly aches. You sit down on the carpeted floor. You take the elevator back up as soon as the fear gets to you. You go back down, put the cold wet clothes in the drier. You go up, wait fifty minutes, go down. The clothes are warm, some of them even hot, and you stick them in the hamper at random, without folding or ironing.

Going up and down in the elevator for hundreds of feet at a time has left you dizzy. Every time you step off, the floor is unsteady under your feet, like a soft earthquake. The windowless space is geometric, abstract, hanging above the earth at an ever-changing distance according to some immutable logic.

Nicola comes home in the evening, but he won't talk to you. He withdraws into his bedroom, and you remain unseen behind the screen, unsure of how to tell him you're leaving. You place two pillows under your belly before you fall asleep.

IN THE MORNING you put away the extension, return the pillow and the eye mask to the hall closet. You brush off the couch and spread two bedspreads over it. This home, you realize, will endure without you, and you wave the view goodbye. You bought a bag at American Apparel that now sits zipped up on the glass coffee table. You admire its fullness, its air of finality. I'm finished here, you think: I won't be coming back to New York.

And now, the trip: the filthy proximity to strangers, your own inescapability, another day without human talk. You couldn't bring yourself to pick up your things from Lorenzo's because it would have seemed too final. It's less fraught this way: you're leaving them behind for him as collateral.

You abandon Manhattan by train, losing what was, until just now, your city. You bury your face in your scarf. You travel through Brooklyn and Queens, through neighborhoods full of unlucky black people—too scarred, you think, or too unhealthy, or too poor, or none of the above, in worn brown suits—who survive in this city without any privileges, this city you're being forced out of.

The Delta terminal at JFK resembles a bus station. Institutional blue carpet, gray wallpaper, ambiguously quiet, quiet children and pacified children and terrified children, the shuffling of pages, the dim yellow light, unsmiling adults drinking coffee from huge paper cups, the smell of hand sanitizer, the narrow aisles no one complains about, bathroom stalls whose metal doors begin twelve inches above the floor—you hide in one at the end of the row and put in a tampon. You drink a caramel frappuccino and think of it as a *"consolino,"* your mother's word for the dessert she'd buy you when you were having a bad day.

When you ask for a glass of water to swallow your Ibuprofen in the middle of the sky, the American flight attendants smile and call you *"honey."* The night is short but uneasy, and the plane isn't one of the newer ones, the ones with individual TV screens. You read *Vanity Fair* and barely sleep. Taking off in the dark was distressing, so the whole flight feels like a long emergency landing. Two hours before landing, you fall asleep for real. You wake up when the flight begins its initial descent to Rome. You fall asleep again, and when the belly of the plane seems to scratch the earth, you wake up with a gulp, convinced you're dying. Then you realize you're home.

PART II

THE UNHAPPY LIVES

OF KEPT ROMANS

IN NEW YORK

*T*hey sleep together on the sofa in the living room, he and Ludovica, with their feet pointing toward the window, the same position he takes whenever his parents come to visit and colonize the bedroom. Nico stares into the void outside the L-shaped window. The buildings look like thin glass reeds floating in a lake of air and light, the landscape disturbed from time to time by private helicopters and planes on their way to Newark.

The night's dusty redness has vanished, the predawn sky clear and still. He turns carefully onto his side to figure out how close she is to waking. She lies facedown, with her mouth agape, her cheek nestled in the sheets, and her forehead against the hem of the pillow. He's convinced that if he could always feel the way he feels at this moment, he'd be a saint. The way he feels toward Ludovica is the way God sees women.

He's sitting like a girl now, his arms around his knees, his legs pointing left, his right foot pointing down. He stares at Ludovica but doesn't touch her: her round shoulders, the generic mass of chestnut hair. Her forehead looks more sloped when she's asleep, a little more aggressive. Over night, the fabric has carved small rivulets into her skin. Her face is serenely inhuman, a little bit of crust around her right eye, her mouth dirty, letting out the occasional wheeze or gust of rank morning breath: his guest is a creature, a living being. Nico recites the Lord's Prayer, gets up and takes a shower without waking her or Gustavo Tullio.

He pulls a razor blade from its little cartridge using the rubberized metal handle, squeezes some shaving gel into his hand, rubs it on his head and his cheeks and starts shaving his scalp to prepare for today's lunch, where he'll introduce James Murphy to Gustavo. As of now, Tullius remains unaware of the project known as *The Happy Life of Nico Berengo*, of the way Murphy is trying to tell his story, of the pages and pages of notes the author's taken about him.**

He rides the elevator down to the gym, an iPad in his hand and a duffel bag with clean clothes hoisted over his shoulder. He runs on the treadmill for half an hour, exchanges friendly glances with the familiar faces, showers again with lemon-scented soap, buys a bag of cookies from the vending machine in the lobby, and finishes it by the time he's standing in line at Starbucks, waiting for his coffee.

Today is a slow day. He needs to check his bank account to see if he can afford presents for Gustavo's children: the €6,000 from his father's last bank transfer, for the fourth quarter of 2010, has gone quickly, and the first payment of the year usually arrives a little late; his father needs time to divest. Checking the account always makes him feel anxious. He sees that the €260 for his Coldplay interview has finally come in, so now all he needs to know is whether Tullius, who has strong opinions about parenting, will bless Nico's desire to buy his children presents. Later that afternoon, he'll sit down and map out his review of Kanye and Jay-Z's upcoming album for *Vice Italy*. He's decided to de-

---

**See "Notes for *The Happy Life of Nico Berengo*," page 291.

scribe it track by track without actually listening to it, to show that the Society of Spectacle doesn't actually need to produce or consume any actual works of art. He texts Tullio and tells him he'll meet him at FAO Schwarz at 11:30.

He strolls through the park to the reservoir, thinking about Jay, Kanye's mentor, then about the woman he's left in the living room. What does it mean for someone to be married? What kind of damage did he do last night? It doesn't seem possible that vague third parties could find themselves in trouble simply because of a soothing, friendly late-night conversation, unconducive to the spread of STDs and utterly lacking in malice. He brings his bag forward to keep his erection hidden. Why does such a sweet, pleasant thing—sex between two people who haven't been formally assigned to each other—feel so destabilizing?

He recaps the sex he's had over the last week with growing arousal: beating up Vera, Edele's breasts, and now Ludovica. His face is stolid and dignified as he walks, his mouth shut tight. He's breathing through his nose but now he's gasping, so he stops, opens his mouth wide, and stretches out his arms to fill his lungs. He's shifting around in his acid-green down jacket, and his mind returns to the scene last night, when Ludovica stuck a hand down his underpants. This is how he loves to do it: no passion, no aggression, and total availability—a circumvention of everything fraught.

YOU LEAD GUSTAVO Tullio—Tullius—through aisles filled with jigsaw puzzles, Lego sets, stuffed animals, board games, toy cars. When I see you there, on the second floor, I see you as a composite image, stitched together across different times and different aisles. In the eighties, your parents would always come here at the end of their trips to buy presents for everyone back home.

You dissuade Tullio from buying a Chicco DJ Guitar for Sara, who is six years old. It's a flimsy piece of plastic with many red, blue, and green keys, appropriate for children between zero and thirty-six months of age. Sara will learn to play guitar like other sisters do: from her older brothers, who are ten and eleven. As you walk along the crowded, colorful aisles, you hear Tullio's detailed account of his children's likes and dislikes. "Sara, she wants to *fare l'americana*: the night before my flight, she asked if we could cook burgers together, just the two of us. She moved the processed cheese *sottiletta* onto the patty after I'd put it on the plate."

"Didn't Elisabetta feel left out?"

"Totally. So then Sara made a burger for Elisabetta—I was giving her instructions the whole time—and as Betta ate it, I could hear Sara talking to herself, saying 'Compliments to the chef!'"

"That's cute."

You tell him that he has to buy Sara the bracelet kit. And for the two girls, the Sit 'n' Play Activity Tray and the plush toy shaped like SpongeBob Square Pants; for *I Maschi*, the Transformers Hot Wheels racetrack with the 360-degree loop and two 3-D puzzles of Chicago and Las Vegas. You drag him—with his green sweater, his black windbreaker, his blue pants, his Timberlands, the sweat accumulating on his balding temples—to every corner of the loud, warm, cheerful store. Tullius lets you take him by the arm, and you almost seem to dance around him, jumping from section to section on the tips of your shoes.

Gustavo Tullio always leaves for New York with a travel bag and an empty suitcase. For his children, the empty suitcase exists as a private myth, a story they tell one another throughout the year. Before every trip, each child inspects the suitcase to confirm that it's actually empty, that it can accommodate as many presents as possible. America is the family myth: Tullio always envied the trips you took with your family after the two of you got back from scout camps. He'd head to Nettuno beach in a station wagon weighed down by suitcases and bikes tied to the roof, but you'd be in a different car, sleepy but jittery, on your way to the long-term parking lot by Fiumicino. The myth endures, though these days you can find all of these toys—these luxurious New York toys—in Italy. Which means that Tullio can never quite reproduce the glamour of the presents Berengo would bring back for him in the nineties: the marshmallows, the Cherry Cokes, the special Transformers sets. He tells you that he's planning an American trip with the entire family, all seven of them. They'll go west, to the National Parks. This is, you know, the kind of family Tullio has always dreamed of.

Your feelings for him are complex, but you do care. You'd love to make music with his two sons; you just can't muster up the courage to ask. You can imagine yourself flying to Rome to show the kids how to use the latest music software, how to make songs using basic samples. Still, you keep your distance: you won't even let yourself introduce I Maschi to music that's cooler and less hopelessly out of date than the stuff they listen to. You know that for Tullio, it's important that the kids not feel too inspired by art, too seduced by it. What he wants them to avoid, above all, is an undefined life, a life like yours.

You feel happy when he tells you that Marco and Luca want to be *"Rockstar americane."*

"Is that their expression or yours?"

"They came up with it. I asked them, 'Not just rock stars?' 'No,' they said. *'Americane.'"*

"That sounds just right. But they're not listening to dub step? Or grime?"

"No, just rock. It's because I told them that Mom is rap, and I am rock."

"Good, clear ideas to live by."

Tullio has ensured that the kids will grow up in a parallel reality: a familiar combination of *piccolo-borghese* vulgarity and a Christianity built on the terror of all desires—theirs as well as other people's. You care for him, so you won't object. It's almost as if it weren't a coincidence that you're short and he's tall and large.

"They want to live in a skyscraper. They want to see your apartment."

"Bring them!"

"They'd have to become famous, first . . ."

"Well, let's go to a guitar shop, then."

"No, it's too early for electric guitars. They already make too much noise as it is, and that's just with classical guitars. God, they'll be horny teenagers in no time. I'm terrified. But what can I do? Esther is already scaring me, and she's not even a boy."

"How old is she?"

"Thirteen. She's into Fabri Fibra." Fabri Fibra's rudeness and vulgarity are a bad influence on a young girl, but worse is his depressiveness. He's a self-proclaimed miserabilist who calls women whores.

You ask for updates on the Eurock, the currency his kids can use to buy sweets and toys. Every chore is worth a certain amount of Eurocks. (*I Maschi* came up with the name.) The family is moving to a new apartment soon, which means more demanding and difficult tasks, which means more Eurocks. You were the one who told him about this system twenty years ago—your mother's family had used it back in the day. "They'll become good people, Papa," you tell him. "I'm happy you stayed with me," you add. "You sleep well?"

Tullio doesn't answer. Instead he talks about how unbelievable it is—how frustrating and unbelievable—that Esther will soon be the same age as his high-school girlfriend Daria (that's me) was when he first sodomized her (fifteen). You listen intently and offer advice.

Tullio blames Esther's hip-hop rebellion on his wife, Maria, and you go out on a limb and defend her: "You have to find a way to care for Maria between now and when Betta and Sara come of age. One day you'll be alone, like you were before Esther was born, and you'll need to love her again." Of course he won't actually be alone; the members of the Neocatecumenali, the Catholic organization Tullio belongs to, tend to still have young kids at home when their older children start to get married and have children, so as the last of the children enter adolescence, there are grandkids to take care of.

"Sometimes . . . sometimes it's hard to love her."

"Do you pray for her?" You know he loves metaphysical talk.

"I have to say it's hard. Praying *with* her is easier because we do it every night before we go to sleep and in the morning when we wake up."

You keep going. "It's important that you pray for her," you say with feeling. You're trying to support him, encourage him, and you want to make him feel that the church roots of your friendship are still alive. You like that he marvels at your faith every time you talk to him, that he knows you're more of a mystic than he is.

"I have too much guilt. It's impossible for me to pray for her."

"That's the devil putting thoughts in your brain."

"You think so?"

You do. You think praying gets you closer to God. This morning you stared at the married woman asleep in your bed and prayed. You think that as long as you keep praying, you're going to be a good man. "Yes. It's the devil trying to convince you that you can't pray for her."

As you talk you pull toys in and out of their little compartments, store shelves that serve as temporary homes that they'll soon abandon for new shelves in the elegant homes of solvent, well-managed families, where their physical forms will matter less than their subtext: once they leave FAO Schwarz, they'll serve as stand-ins for love and warmth.

"The devil exploits your one weakness: you don't respect your wife intellectually. You despise her."

"*Ugh*. That hurts, *ciccio*!"

He called you *ciccio*! He cares about you, even though he's convinced you've slept with a married woman. Maybe he's not being himself.

"You think of her as your inferior. And this is a problem. Hey, what are we buying for Esther?"

"No, no toys for Esther; she'll just throw them at me."

"Isn't it incredible that you can pray for someone you just fucked in the ass, and also for someone you don't respect intellectually?"

"You're crazy," he laughs. "I don't fuck my wife in the ass."

Back in high school, when he and I were together, Gustavo Tullio was a fan of anal sex. It feels like a distant era: rote translations from Ancient Greek; clear-cut duties, all easily dispensed with; and then, during all the stray half hours and half days that weren't accounted for, the grand experiments with smells and underwear, and in summer, the ecstasy of sweaty armpits and fainting with desire.

"That's the problem!" you say with a laugh.

"*Ugh*, Nico, stop it. You're shooting a bullet right through my heart, old man," he says with a laugh, the hair on his knuckles dancing as he mimes his wound. "No sodomy."

You let him pay for the 3-D puzzles you thought you would pay for yourself. The two of you had gathered three big bags' worth of toys, and you were happy when you saw how confidently he pulled the credit card out of his pocket to cover them. He was always so desperate to succeed, and now he seems so content, so proud. And you're so proud that he made it. You hope he'll keep calling you *ciccio* with this kind of intimacy; to you it still sounds like the king inviting the commoners for dinner at his castle. In the scouts, he was the king, and you were the little one, Nicolino, a tiny blond boy with colitis who captured the friendship of the camp king, all thanks to me. I was your friend, and I was one year younger than Gustavo and two years older than you. I had red hair, and I felt soft, so all of you wanted to hug me in the polyester blue sweaters I wore that covered more of my thighs than my daisy dukes.

You two met on those thighs, which were pale and covered with little moles, and the mystery of time transformed them into distinct phenomena: for you, a kid, they were grown-up stuff, but for him they were already sweet and young and tender things.

Tullio was three years older than you and one year older than me. Back then such age differences mattered. At twelve you were a little blond bear, overweight, your arm hair wispy and downy, your skin smooth; a year later, Tullio fucked me in the ass.

You cared for each other. Tullio was a man, a giant, You see him in his short, tight jeans covered in grass stains, drinking from the fiery glass of the river at sunset, hunched over it with cup-shaped hands, his bony ankles protruding from his gym socks, the black hair on his long calves. He always shaved by the river, twenty meters downstream from where he drank his water, his facial hair and his shaving cream dispersing in the stream among the rocks.

You've come a long way: you're about to introduce him to a Pulitzer Prize–winning writer who's taking notes on you.

The two of you take the subway down to SoHo and walk around leisurely, searching for fashion accessories for his older daughter. Now you're on the south side of Houston, and you cross the street and cut through the small park wedged between Houston and First Street.

There's James Murphy pacing back and forth in front of Prune, his hands deep in the pockets of a Loden coat he bought on your recommendation. Tullio quickens his step. "He looks nice, Murphy," he says.

IT'S BEEN LESS than half an hour since the men sat down, and Nicolino is drunk and full of shame. He keeps his eyes down and chats with Edele on WhatsApp, reporting on the turn his lunch has taken: James Murphy and Gustavo Tullio, the two moralists, have judged him and humiliated him: first for talking about yesterday's fling with the married woman, then for the time he made a woman pay him for kisses. *"Edele, I'm being messo in mezzo."* She knows that expression of Berengo's, knows he has a big persecution complex. He always thinks he's *messo in mezzo.* She consoles him, but he can tell she's not especially eager to humor him; he is, after all, talking about another woman.

At the end of Murphy's story, the one about payment for kisses, Nicola stands up. *"Bene,"* he says in Italian. *"Vi auguro un buon pomeriggio."* Before he walks away from the table, he kicks the bags of toys with his left foot, a sad and clumsy gesture. He almost gets tangled in his coat as he tries to put it on while he walks toward the door. It's only when he hits the freezing air that he regains a little bit of composure.

IT'S FUNNY THAT after everything I've been through with Nicolino, I'm now forced to navigate a day in his life as a *bambino adulto.* Even without a body, all this surveillance and scanning

96

of Nicolino's life is tiring and bureaucratic. For this observer, his life, so full of pleasure, is little more than a slog. It's especially annoying that our prior topic was my supposed blame for the Big Prank, and now here we are with him, who didn't even take part.

NICO WALKS BACK to SoHo and enters Miu Miu with an over-whelming sense of anxiety, the cold wind blowing in behind him. He buys an expensive *craquelé* calfskin crocodile-print key-chain for Edele, but she texts to say that she's unavailable this afternoon. Maybe she's just jealous, but in any case, the handoff won't work: he won't be able to give her the present, so he returns to Miu Miu and gets his $200 back. Instead he decides to bring a couple of bottles of Sonoma cabernet to Sergio de Simone's. He knows that Sergio hates Tullio, and he'll be happy to hear his rants. He'll console Nico in his incredible living room on the Williamsburg waterfront, on the twenty-fourth floor, twelve-meter windows looming over the river.

There, Berengo steps out onto the balcony and feels so dizzy that he has to get back inside and hide behind the supporting column in the middle of the living room. He sits down on the couch, but he can still see the terrifying view: the gray river, the skyscrapers thin as matchsticks, the island much longer and wider than it looks on the map, the surprising expanse of the power plant at the east end of Fourteenth Street. Even from here, the view is unencumbered: the balcony has a modest steel and glass railing that leaves no part of the landscape to the imagina-tion. He steps out again. The twenty-fourth floor is so high that Manhattan feels frayed and low and endless, New Jersey's hum-ble skyscrapers visible in the background. He goes back inside.

Berengo doesn't go onto the terrace because he's afraid of

heights. Sergino thinks of Berengo as his savior, the man who got him out of Italy, introduced him to people. So the apartment is su casa: Nico is free to do what he likes, including spending the entire afternoon complaining on the couch and walking around barefoot on Sergio's soft, sheepskin rug, his wallet resting on a bronze Vishnu head, his electric-green down jacket on the chair.

Sergio is proud of the place. The birch wood furniture, the translucent white curtains, the low coffee table surrounded by pillows (for more sophisticated reclining), the huge flat screen TV that takes up most of one wall.

"I can't really tell you what happened. I was *messo in mezzo*. They ganged up on me. So I got up and left. They're such bastards."

"What? What do you mean? What did they tell you?"

There's a dessert plate with a small pile of coke, a video game—"DJ Hero"—on the TV, and audio blasting through a Bang and Olufsen stereo system. They sit on the couch and take turns using the controller: it's a mock-turntable with buttons, levers, and a little rotating black disk to simulate scratching and filtering. They shuffle through Beastie Boys, Jay-Z, Tiësto, Morillo, and Gorillaz, pausing the game every other second to talk and register their outrage, sometimes in falsetto.

"Oh man, Tullius was heavy as fuck. He told James, 'I saw him lead a married woman to commit a mortal sin.' That's what he said! Those exact words! He's such a shit. 'You don't go around sleeping with married women,' he told him, and me. And also: 'You're setting a bad example for the kids hanging out at your place.' There was nothing he wouldn't have said to make me look bad in James's eyes. He doesn't like it that I get to have James."

"Right. So he wants his job in Finmeccanica, with the salary, the five children, and church on Sundays, but he *also* wants to be friends with James Murphy? Mmm." Sergio grabs his phone, tweets, "And he'd love the *messa in culo*," a bit of teenage wordplay shorn of context: *messa*, meaning "Catholic mass," and *messa in culo*, meaning "fucking in the ass." "Exactly! The *messa in culo*. Shall I bend? Shall I? Bend?"

The conversation cracks them up.

"Tullio said, like, 'I work, I come to New York for work, I'm your guest. You have nothing to do all day—it's your choice. You think you're brave for choosing this lifestyle, but you're not ballsy enough to handle other people's judgment, even though you're always showing off your lifestyle choices.'"

"He said this shit to you?"

"Swear to God. He said, 'This is what it comes down to: you do drugs, you're a fucking *mantenuto*, a "trustafarian," and you always act like some kind of philosopher about everything. But you haven't done shit with your life, you've accomplished nothing, so you're going crazy and that's why you get these panic attacks.' Isn't that awful?"

"What did James do?"

"Oh, that asshole finally lost his shit. He basically admitted to being a Puritanical douchebag, so he took Tullius's side. Tullius was like, 'You're empty!' I'm empty? Come on! Am I empty?"

"You're not empty."

Sergio owes him, so he always takes his side. He can now afford to live in corporate Williamsburg, and he's done it—skyscrapers with built-in gyms, the eleventh floor of an apartment building whose units have been up for sale for little more than a year—but he owes it to Berengo who connected him to the right people. I don't know exactly who lent him the apartment, if it was a friend or some kind of formal sugar daddy. From the island, now, a shaft of artificial light as the day dies, from Midtown to the Upper East Side; on the right, blurry and abstract, you can see the Chrysler building.

They laugh and Berengo pauses the videogame and takes Sergio's iPad out. He goes on YouTube and finds the short film shot by the husband of his female guest.

"Oh," Sergino says when he recognizes her, head to toe in yellow. "That's the wife of the *raccomandato*. So *she's* the one who jerked you off."

"Just look at her. She was so good—so sweet, so friendly."

"Yeah, but these people are so lame. It's a lousy, lousy short film. I talked to her at your place, when was that, Tuesday night? She kept insisting that her husband wasn't a *raccomandato* in the philosophy department, that he'd managed to get the year at Columbia totally on his own."

"Poor thing. She's cute, though, isn't she? A neurotic rich Roma Nord girl, you know? I've always dug those, always will."

"Annoying as fuck."

"No, it was sweet."

"The husband—that guy's *raccomandatissimo*."

"For sure. And no talent, zero."

"Well, anyway, you really like these useless rich girls even when they don't dress like rich girls."

"That's right."

"The kind who only jerk you off."

"That's how I like it."

"Bitches."

"Well, I've seen worse bitches than that."

Sergino and Nico don't hang out often. Nico isn't wild about Sergio's passion for cocktails and *barella* and hotel parties in Midtown and the Meatpacking District. Sergio calls cocaine *barella* because he's a social climber and uses Milanese slang.

"I know what you've been through with that asshole, so I'm not surprised about all this." Then, emphatically: "Isn't it wonderful that the two of us are here, you and me? I mean, look at the view, man. Isn't it wonderful that we get to see this? Tullio doesn't get to see it. No view for Tullio. What the fuck does he want? Does he want this view, too? He wants to come here and get the view?" It's a dogged and random performance, very Serginesque, a barrage of insults and compliments that crescendo beautifully: "And what does Gustavo's sexual life really amount to, anyway? Kissing his children on their mouths? It's all wrong, *zi*. You're only trying to right the wrongs, man, *one hand job at a time*." This last part is spoken in a John Rambo voice. "Tullio can't judge you. He's Evil incarnate, that guy."

Whenever it's your turn to play the video game, Sergio's on Twitter. He's tweeting about "Darth Vader Bone Machine," Tullio's old nickname: "Keep your children locked away at home (you don't have children, *pederasti*!)." He's been obsessed with Tullio's dick for ten or fifteen years.

He's gone off and found a fancy paper straw in the cutlery drawer, and now he's snorting coke from the little plate to stave off sleep. The plate reflects the glare from his track lighting. It's gotten dark. He speaks in phrases borrowed from the English language, calques that sound perfect in translation. "You don't deserve this," he says. "You don't deserve the Tullish Inquisition."

"They made me feel evil, man, like I'm the villain."

WHY DOES NICO always fall back on the Catholic paradigm and talk evil and villains? I know he enjoys his life; he likes it. Why is it that he's always into discussing the way other people see him? Why does he do that if he really *loves* the way he lives?

LATER, AT DINNERTIME, he's dozed off at his Irish friend Natalie's house, because Edele keeps snubbing him. Natalie lives a few blocks south of Sergio in a loft with the warmest, whitest interior lighting he's ever seen. The supersized windows face a narrow Brooklyn street and look north toward the Williamsburg Bridge, framing a single, elegant slice of the pale blue structure, its arches a perfect echo of the garlands of Christmas lights that run along Natalie's walls in transparent rubber tubes, a cheerful mess that wends its way up a beautiful plant with big leaves and reaches all the way to the ceiling.

At Natalie's he can pop some Xanax, doze off on the couch's rough upholstery. Natalie wakes him up an hour later with a cup of jasmine tea and listens to the story of the hand job.

". . . So Tullio tells me, 'You shall not sleep with a married woman.'"

Then they go into the guest bedroom and lie down. The bed is perched on a high, wooden base that wobbles with their every movement. Nico repeats the hand-job story—this time with more details about the sex itself—as he caresses first her ankles, then her thighs, her bush, her clit.

You love this home, Nicolino, and she loves to get off on your sex stories, which you always tell in your calmest, most careful voice. She climaxes with an *iiiiiii* sound, a weird noise that seems to lack an *h*. As she rests, you smell your hand. She's with you now, it can't be denied. She keeps her left hand on her belly, the age-old instinct to cover up stretch marks. She's wearing a long vest the color of the apartment's furniture and walls. She owns several of these, each a slightly different combination of white and beige pallor.

"I'm glad I could at least use this whole mess to make you come. It really hurt me."

"Poor Nico, I feel so sorry for you."

"I was *messo in mezzo*."

"You're so sweet, and people are always giving you such a hard time."

"Stop joking around, baby."

"Let me blow you right now."

"No."

"But tonight it'd be so right."

"No, come on. I like our arrangement."

"Okay, but just know that I would love to."

"Baby, you know how much you like to idle."

"Nico, my geisha."

They lie side by side, their fingers woven together after they've brushed each other's hips with studied carelessness. They're pleased and proud of this little thing of theirs, where he tells the story and she climaxes and warmth is generated.

"It'll work out, Nicolino. You'll see. Because you're good, you really are." Nat is whispering benevolent words in his ear, her fingers in his fingers.

"No, my love, no. Just tell me you care for me."

"I care for you."

"I am good."

"You are good."

PART III

BRAINWASH

A half-empty pack of Gocciole ExtraDark on the kitchen island. Tullio sits on a stool, ready to dunk the remaining cookies in a glass of cold milk. His suit is still on, his tie folded over in his jacket pocket. Tullio looks at his wife's ass and her shoulders as she loads the dishwasher. The dishes from the old house look smaller here, in this new, square kitchen, bigger than the original.

The girls—the five-year-old and the six-year-old—were put to bed while he was still out on his TMax scooter, riding down Via Salaria, passing on the right to try to make it home in time. He's still upset by the first thing he saw when he walked in: unwanted toys spread out across the wooden floor by the entrance, abandoned in the dark. It's an intentional act of desertion: the girls have left these toys behind. In the old house, the foyer was a neat rectangle—when Tullio walked in every evening, he felt as if every room and all their occupants were visible, tangible. But in the new house, the foyer extends around the corner, and now he feels a tinge of pain whenever he comes home: it's as if the girls have vanished into the darkness, like a sunset you've just missed. The two buildings are on the same side of the same street, and on a recent Saturday, a very solemn afternoon, the girls loaded their favorite toys into a supermarket shopping cart and moved them into their new home.

I Maschi, the two sons, are playing in their room, and Esther . . . well, she's almost a grown-up. The only babies he has left are the little girls, and Maria puts them to bed right on schedule. She does this on purpose: she knows how much her husband loves rules, how much he fixates on them, and here she's managed to manipulate his predilections to his disadvantage. This afternoon the girls made jackets out of Scotch tape and rags and shreds of tablecloth. These are costumes for a fashion show slated for Saturday at their grandparents' new home, the apartment they inherited from Gustavo. They'll sleep there on Friday night to avoid interfering with the move, which will colonize the third Saturday in a row. Each new box they move reveals forgotten and surprising things: two hair dryers no one remembers buying; a set of matching Hawaiian shirts, ostensibly for weekend outings; battery chargers and extension cords intended for specific sockets, soon to be plugged into new sockets and stored in new containers on new shelves that come in new colors. The family will marvel at these old objects and their new trajectories, looking at them reflected in the new bathroom mirror and through the new kitchen window. Tullio, though, Tullio's not interested in things.

Maria's ass isn't calling to him, not anymore. Right now, the woman it protrudes from is one with the sink. She's all ass and straight, black hair done up in a bun. You can see her olive skin and her tiny, wide body, but you can't see her little nose, not from here. You strangle your mouth and your taste buds with the Gocciole, the extra-dark chocolate luscious and overwhelming. You find it shocking—or something close to shocking—that she insists on keeping her back toward you as she does the washing up. No contact.

Tullio crosses his heart with his thumb. It isn't fair that he has to miss out on the girls' debut as fashion models. His wife puts the detergent capsules into the dishwasher, and as he begins to get up, she tells him about the fashion show. "They saw how Mom worked the sewing machine and started improvising immediately: they found old T-shirts and started putting Scotch tape all over them, singing the whole time. *Ta-ta-ta-ta-ta*, diligent and enthusiastic."

A tear wells up in his left eye, and as he tries his hardest to keep it from sliding down his cheek, the veins in his forehead throb unbearably. Maria has brought Sara and Betta's big day to an early close, and the head of the family has been transformed into a cookie thief. Tomorrow the kids will see that their cookies are all gone, and they'll have to make do with cornflakes.

Though these are the final moments of Sara and Betta's paradisiacal youth—his last chance to smell the brilliant, innocent odor of their young sweat—the Tullios are done with children. Maria's faith isn't strong enough, so now, for the first time, they'll start buying condoms. Will they have to hide their purchase from the vicar? It's either that or he'll need to start pulling out again.

I Maschi play football with their dad, and they're decent at guitar, but they've begun to smell bad, and they'll soon come into contact with desires Gustavo doesn't want any Catholic boy to ever know about. (In his time he was a great French kisser, the hallway at school his base of operations. Out in the park, he'd always manage to sneak a peek at the older girls' tits.) The boys' *formaggia*—his eighth-grade term for the smelly residue between his toes—suggests that I Maschi are about to abandon him. Maybe the older one is already locking himself in the bathroom; Tullio isn't around enough to know for sure. Esther, meanwhile, is a difficult woman, a sharp strategist, and she's already mastered Maria's fierce hand gesture, the one that accompanies the *vafangul,* mouthed but never spoken. The whole display freaks Tullio and his mother out.

I Maschi aren't allowed to play their music too loud, so they have to use headphones, and these must be turned down low. Esther has her new room, with its own closet. She's the only person in the family with her own room, but she's not satisfied: she's coming off three years of proud preadolescence sleeping in the storage closet at the old house, her furniture little more than a mattress on the floor of a non-space. She'd begged them for weeks to let her have her internal exile; her new room is so much more civilized.

Maria scrubs the sink, washes her hands with soap, dries them on her apron, exhales, takes the apron off, dries her hands some more on her sweatpants and her generous ass. "Will you put I Maschi to bed?" she asks.

"Yep."

"If you're going to finish those cookies, write a note on the fridge so I remember to buy more."

"Just buy them."

"No, please write a note. It'll help my peace of mind." She pulls a stray lock of hair back behind her ear and arches her brows—her classic gesture of superiority. Going part-time at work has given her the ultimate moral advantage; he's to blame for asking her to do it in the first place.

"Okay, in bed in twenty. You do I Maschi; I do Esther. It's better that way."

"You don't really need to put her to bed," he murmurs as he looks down at the few Gocciole still left in the pack.

"We'll just chat for a minute," she says, and she's gone.

He picks up three whole Gocciole, dunks them in cold milk, crushes them with a teaspoon, waits, drinks the milk, and picks up the little bits with his hand to get an even mouthful of cookies and milk. Then fills the glass up and starts over. He unfastens his belt and takes a breath. After round two, with four more Gocciole, there are only three left, and he saves these for later, for after the goodnights. He leaves the glass half full on the counter and writes "Gocciole dark" on the magnetic notepad on the refrigerator. He leaves his jacket draped over a stool in his American-style kitchen.

I Maschi's room has no memory, no past, just winter clothes arranged neatly in the new lime-green chest of drawers, the toys they got for Christmas and from New York, the guitars, the old Acer desktop with the HD mic and the MIDI mixer and no internet connection—last year's gift from Berengo, so that the boys could record their "minimal songs" as a "postpunk post-meaning duo," as he put it. The band's name is I Maschi. Their mother dresses them in vests or Cosby sweaters, but when they record or do a *photoshoot* with the computer camera, they put on their dark blue scarves themselves.

Tullius pulls the two boys away from the computer, switches it off after saving the song files, his movements sound-tracked by their little whines. He pushes them into bed.

He sits on the floor with his legs crossed, then lies down and stretches his legs. He lets out a sigh. "Let's do the recap."

"Yessir."

"Homework."

"Yessir." Only the older one is answering; he's responsible for the younger one.

"Teeth brushed?"

"Yessir."

"Did you record any tracks today?"

"Yes!"

"Yes!"

"Good. What about outdoor activities?"

"No."

"No."

"Hmm. I wanted to tell you boys also that there's a problem, a minor problem. It's about the Eurock."

The Eurock system will remain in use until the children begin to need real currency. Esther already has a privileged Euro-Eurock exchange rate, and now Marco is pushing to get the same deal. Tullius would love it if their kids spent their whole lives using only Eurocks. He's had to restrain himself from introducing financial mechanisms into the system, like an interest rate that would increase along with their Eurock savings rate, making it more fun—and more inscrutable. But he wants the system to stay pure. Maybe, though, this is the time to put something into action. I Maschi want to buy an electric guitar, a Fender rip-off, for €400, or 8,000 Eurocks. Tullius and Maria hate saying no to their children without the possibility of redemption or at least ambiguity, but they also hate saying yes. So the rates haven't changed: the reward for clearing the table after lunch is 2 Eurock credits, or 10 cents, meaning that the kids will have to save for an excruciatingly long time without incentives or changes in the underlying financial reality. If Tullio instituted an interest rate, though, unused money would make them more money. Wouldn't it be fun to teach I Maschi something about finance?

"The problem," he says, still lying on the ground, serious but also quietly amused, or at least content, "is that you don't rinse the dishes before putting them into the washing machine."

"No, Dad. It's not like that!"

"Dad, that's not it, exactly!"

"I'm just saying: you have to pay attention. Mom has started to notice. Don't tell her I told you. Just pay attention."

"All right."

"All right."

They always buy milk before dinner: 3 Eurocks. If he's right about what they're up to, what they're longing for, they might end up needing to scrub the toilet—another chore. How much would that be worth?

As he steps into his own bedroom, lit by a dim lightbulb under a pale green lamp shade, Maria tells him that the girl from New York, Ludovica, ended up baby-sitting for a couple hours. "She just helped me run some errands. You know, because she has a car."

"Did you pay her?"

"*Cash,*" Maria says in English.

That word, a residue of her hip-hop lingo, is doubly offensive here: accepting this young woman's ludicrous offer in the first place (a thirty-one-year-old babysitter—the girls from church are fourteen) and then indulging in her own desire to act like a signora with a driver-slash-babysitter.

"*Pff,*" she half-says, trying to keep him from going to the kitchen. "Where are you going? You already finished the cookies."

When Tullio is upset he usually goes to the living room, takes a few deep breaths to try to somehow expel his anger from his body, says a prayer. The room, illuminated by a single floor lamp, hasn't been consolidated yet. The kids' toys have descended like an army, a multitude of mutilated dolls and toy cars and blocks. Their early childhood will take shape here, but something is already lost.

Berengo had ordered him to pray for his wife, and it felt so potent that it's as if Berengo's father, Morelli, the architect, was the one who had given him the advice. Tullio never seems to find the time to pay Morelli a visit; he doesn't want to see him get old, though he always keeps him in his thoughts and his prayers. Nicola is a bad son: he uses the byline Morelli Berengo to trade on his mother's family's name, and in the end everybody ends up calling him Berengo.

There isn't much in the room yet, other than the toys and the cardboard boxes labeled with the different elements of the old living room. What has been unpacked is modest but essential: a few candles, the old Bible open on its carved lectern, the photograph of the founder of the Comunità, the blessed palm hanging outside the door. The classical guitars, to be played during celebrations, will go into the closet. Morelli used to pray at night, both in the living room and as he walked along the corridor, watching over his wife and son. Now he walks in circles in his new apartment with its €1,000 monthly mortgage payment, which he's able to afford because his in-laws sold their garage and gave them money for the down payment. This is the second time Gustavo and Maria have taken out a mortgage; they transferred the first one to his parents. Tullio is trying to pray for his children, but he keeps getting distracted. He prays for his wife: "that poor beast, that pet, please steer her right, Holy Father." He prays for the many objects in his children's world, constantly disassembled and reassembled, atomizing in cardboard boxes and then exploded again in Maria's divine—no, demiurgic—hands in this new, bigger place.

Here, in the middle of the new living room, you find yourself moved: "Thank you God for what you've given me." You think about that breakfast with Ludovica, back in America. You imagine yourself moving her next to Berengo's kitchen counter: you bend her over, and after slipping her pajamas down, you start pressing on her perineum with your index finger and your thumb before you slide these two fingers into the two crevasses on either end. (I'm forced to know this, and I can't not know it. I'm forced to know, though I'd rather not. I remember you pressing on my perineum, your old fixation: the woman's tender zone, where her darkness falls, the place from where you can control her mind, or my mind, or, in the current fantasy, Ludovica's mind—Ludovica, who now comes to your home to beg at the gates of your heaven of cookies, your temple of Bibles and curfews.)

In late January Ludovica called your old landline and talked to Maria, who told you about the call a few minutes later. "Is this really in everyone's best interest?" you asked. Tullio doesn't even want his children to hear Ludovica's name. (She's a confused woman, and he had breakfast with her, and they were both wearing pajamas, which no one must ever know.) "If that's not the case, we'll discuss this later." Later, on the phone with Ludovica Vozzi, Tullio was curt: "Talk to my wife, listen to what she has to say, I'm sorry, I'm going into a meeting . . ." She did. She asked Maria for some baby-sitting work: yes, she said, she had baby-sat for the whole neighborhood as a kid, and even though it felt funny to do it again at thirty-one, she needed *pocket money* due to a family issue she didn't seem especially eager to elaborate on.

So Maria has disobeyed her husband. Babysitters are supposed to be kids, barely teenagers, possibly the children of some Brothers and Sisters at the *Comunità*, or relatives, like Marcello, and they're supposed to be fat or at least homely. Now, back in bed, he has to endure Maria's explanation of the event and the transaction. She gave her €30 *cash cash cash*. (She insists on using the word the way she insists on wearing those old Air Max sneakers whenever she's gardening on the balcony.) Ludovica helped pack the car with boxes of books and kitchen appliances. "We got a shitload done. She was here on time, dressed totally unpretentiously. She said she was ready to help, unlike Marcello. What a preppy douche. We picked up the kids; she helped us unload; and then left. What's the problem?"

"It was unnecessary."

She's content, leaning on two big pillows and holding an old issue of *Marie Claire Casa*, her knees at her chest, the big, white armoire in the background somehow altering her face's complexion.

"And you just put the money in her hand." He wants her to say *cash* again, so that he can hate her even more.

"Thirty."

"No envelope. Just three bills in her hand, like she was a fifteen-year-old."

"She needs it. At the end of the day, it's just money."

"And how did you feel?"

"Oh stop it, will you? *I* needed help, not you. I needed support for my big lazy ass."

"You're not a big lazy ass—you just want to make me fu-ri-ous." (That's how I Maschi say it, with emphasis.) Maria laughs. "You getting a kick out of this? You feel good?"

"It was useful. Yes, I did get a kick out of it, if you mean that I managed to work my ass off in a more efficient way and spare myself the hassle of looking for two parking spots."

"It still doesn't seem like a job for a thirty-year-old. Don't call her again."

"Will you relax? She's a good person. She's married, and she's having some kind of crisis with her dad, which I can totally relate to. Her mother's just lost her own mother—her grandmother—so she needs the distraction."

"She's from Corso Trieste."

"She still needs the money." Maria must have loved the experience of being waited on by a wealthier woman. "Work is work, and it's never lowered anyone's dignity."

"Weren't we going to call Marcello?"

"He stood me up! He left for New York on a whim on December 26, after I kept reminding him all month that he needed to keep some time free for me in January."

Tullio didn't see Marcello in New York, and he's not happy that Berengo has now begun to cultivate his own cousin (and worse, I Maschi!). He's also not happy that Berengo rechristened Marcello

Cugino Hitler. That's what all his friends call him now. But he knows he owes Berengo a makeup call. Berengo is only the last in a line of beggars waiting outside his home, and Tullio can't confront them all without Maria.

This whole moving scheme is a masterpiece, an exquisite set of arrangements orchestrated by his wife, so if she's committed a few provocative faux pas along the way, like hiring Ludovica, he has no choice but to treat them as rational externalities. Maria, after all, was the one who came up with a solution to the problem of Tullio's older brother. He said he could no longer afford the rent on his sixty-square-meter apartment, but he refused to look for a place on the outskirts. So Gustavo Tullio's parents let him and his twenty-year-old girlfriend stay with them. They put him up in the boys' old bedroom and let him store his boxes in the basement. The center held for nearly a year, from September 2009 to June 2010, but everyone was growing miserable, and last March Maria presented Tullio with a visionary plan: they could move the Tullios into their own apartment and get a mortgage for a bigger place on the same street in Prato Rotondo. Prato Rotondo was a small neighborhood, but new buildings were popping up constantly. This was their time. "We won't have to break our necks to visit them. They'll help us out, and then eventually we'll get the apartment back, and then we'll have two apartments in Prato Rotondo, so some of the kids can stay and live near us when we get old."

Tullio's parents' old apartment, on the sixth floor of a building in Porta Pia, belongs to a different Italy: spacious balcony, wooden floors, warm beams of sunlight. Tullio's father was born in 1939 and worked as a clerk for the army. He was awarded the apartment by the Fanfani program, a miracle of the Democrazia Cristiana party that built homes for Italy's many grateful middle-class workers. The apartment sits confidently on the Via Nomentana, where the sycamores carve delicate patterns of light onto the yellow-tinted buildings, where summer is summer and spring is spring, where the groves that loom over embassy walls seduce tired bikers stuck at intersections.

That apartment has now been transferred to Tullio's brother, a man undeserving of the security and certainty that the *regime democristiano* was once able to provide. He spends his time as an inconsistent TV writer, unable to lock down a stable contract at either Rai or Mediaset. Tullio felt bitter about the swap, but for Maria it was transformative: it was both the birth and the fulfillment of their new family project. They still had so many more years left, but she had already managed to confirm which apartment would bear witness to the moment when she and her husband rendered their souls to God. This was her greatness, her triumph. She knew exactly where the mysteries of time would unspool and where the mysteries of blood would reveal themselves, shaping chins, foreheads, small noses, and tight yellow curls and decomposing the bodies that created them. She knew where blood would move back and forth across the elusive line of time. A few months ago, walking along that very street in Prato Rotondo—already her street but now so much more so—she couldn't help but notice the *real estate* office in the one-story prefab trailer, its occupants busy filling up two new buildings quickly emerging at the end of the block. Her street: a street that decades from now will continue to find itself enlivened by a flow of Tullian incarnations. Maria has something of the politician in her, a quality that Italy only encountered in its superior, modern form in the years after World War II. His wife shapes the earth, paves the roads, demarcates the neighborhoods; she lines up the tracks in the valleys of time, she places apartment-shaped locomotives on them and populates them with facial features whose consistency can't help but feel mystical. Ten years ago,

Prato Rotondo was covered in barracks; only recently has it attained the density of all the other neighborhoods in Nuovo Salario. There's been a torrent of construction, and Maria knows what to do with it.

But in spite of it all, her personal satisfaction is in decline: she's paying a woman to drive her own car. This isn't about trying to buy herself a surrogate sister (whom she only talks to once a month, if that). What she wants, instead, are two ugly things: she wants Tullio to hire a Donna Fissa—stable help at home, the old bourgeois myth—and she wants to strip the dignity off a confused woman from Corso Trieste. These are immodest aspirations for a girl from Turin with a Neapolitan mother, a girl who abandoned the hip-hop subculture she loved and has now abandoned herself to the same pettiness her parents loved to indulge in. But Tullio understands; he grew up among people richer than him, and he, too, has a point to make: he was determined to get his salary above €3,000 a month. And it has continued to rise ever since he hit his goal.

HE GOES TO the vicar for confession. Don Luca is also a lawyer at the Sacra Rota, where Catholic weddings are annulled in expensive, arduous proceedings. He is a man, in other words, with whom you can discuss your conjugal problems. His standard joke, when he prepares young parishioners for marriage, is that 80 percent of Catholic weddings should be annulled. But though they have a good relationship—Tullio went out of his way to help Luca invest his inheritance from his father, so that the vicar's mother could retire comfortably in Molise—he doesn't trust him enough to confess that his kids' babysitter and the woman he had breakfast with in his pajamas and the woman whom he fantasized having anal sex with are all the same person. Maria sees

Don Pablo for confession, so no priest can square the couple's accounts. This is liberating, but it also means that Tullio cannot confess the horrible thought he's been nursing about his wife: that she is intentionally treating this woman, the babysitter, in a way that can't help but provoke tenderness and affection in him and that the attraction is thus her fault, her responsibility. "I'm going to use her as a caretaker for my mother-in-law," Maria joked the other day, after mother and babysitter took Sara and Betta to the Cinciaolin, the co-op where the girls take percussion lessons.

As penance for the sins Tullio has managed to confess, Luca orders him to pray the rosary on his way to work and to go a whole week without putting on a tracksuit at home, to facilitate conjugal attraction. Also, the following Saturday, he has to treat his wife to breakfast in bed. Gustavo Tullio doesn't tell his vicar that just then, as they're sitting in confession, the babysitter is somewhere in the parish with Maria. Ludovica, Maria says, is "wrestling with God." Her husband is in the U.S., and she's trying to get him to come back. It's a sorry predicament, a crisis: her brother talks God to her nonstop, and her grandma has just died . . .

You'd nail her to a wall in her husband-less house in Mandrione, wouldn't you? Your thumb stuck in one of her holes and an index finger in the other, the two holes separated by that thin piece of flesh. You've always found your soul adrift in that space between two holes. When you think about her you think about me, and you think about Nicolino, who can still know me, though you can't. You'll be damned, Gustavo Tullio.

LATE MARCH, WEDNESDAY, five p.m. Ludovica drops Marco and Luca off at football practice. Their father will pick them up at seven, so all she has to do is hand the boys off to the coach in the locker room, but she decides to stick around. She sits on the small wooden bleachers that divide the two fields—one for the younger kids, one for the older ones, five boys to a team—and watches the game.

Gustavo Tullio hurries to get to the Futbolclub a little early; they have three PlayStations by the entrance, and he wants to play a few minutes of *Pro Evolution Soccer*. He won't buy a PS3 for his children, even though he'd love to own one himself, so the only time he plays is here, at the club, under the canopied roof that connects the little office structure to the bar, the restaurant, and the gym. The game has evolved radically since the early versions he knew well, back when he let himself have a PlayStation. He isn't able to pick up the kids more than once a week, so he always tries to show up early, to have time for a game.

You saw her well after she saw you, after she'd already descended from the bleachers. She stands at the top of the stairs that lead out to the fields, at the edge of a walkway dimly lit by the glow of TVs in the bar on the other side of the windows.

"Now you know my horrible secret," you joke as you put the controller back in its holder. It falls off immediately and dangles from an antitheft cord.

"Are you any good?" She picks up the controller and hands it back to you, brushing your fingers.

"I was, what, ten years ago? Don't tell I Maschi that I play; it'd make them really fucking mad."

"Right. You won't buy them one."

"I got them the Wii, but it came with all these little kids' games they hate."

"So what are they complaining about? They've got a father who's cool enough to play PS3 games. I Maschi idolize you."

Nobody has called you cool since your senior year of high school. You go back to the game, stand in front of the screen in your trench coat. You've loosened your tie. You're playing to try to forget what you can sense: Ludovica in a skirt, black leggings (you still call them *fuseaux*, the old eighties term), black Clarks, white blouse, cardigan, orange canvas jacket, unbuttoned, hair up, emerald eye shadow. You can't stop playing Barcelona–Man United, you can't tear yourself away from this series of passes you're trying to get Xavi, Iniesta, and Messi to make.

Three statement-like questions, or question-like statements: "You're really getting worked up, aren't you?" "You like football?" "You know sometimes I come really close to calling you 'Mr. Tullio.'"

"Oh yeah?" You use Piqué to escape Rooney's high press and Park's doubling.

"Well, I mean, you're the first person I met in your family, and now I know all of I Maschi's songs by heart, and we never talk anymore. Maria says you love to consider yourself the *capofamiglia*. You're . . . it's not that you're old fashioned but . . . you're an *old soul*."

Piqué has passed the ball to Busquets, who sparks a web of short midfield passes that Scholes and Anderson can't break with shoulder-to-shoulder contact. Messi rushes to catch a pass and frees Villa with a cross on the left. "Which of their songs have you learned?" Villa dribbles around Vidić, gets in the area, squares it to Xavi, who tips it in. To yourself: "Phenomenal."

"Supergol! Bravo!" She slaps your shoulder, but with her whole arm, not just her hand, and for a moment she gives you a squeeze. You want to keep playing, but when she sings "Io sono una star del rock and roll forever . . . forever . . . forever," one of I Maschi's one-chord blues numbers, you're so secretly moved that you abandon the controller and the game and invite her to the bar.

"I only understood what rock and roll really was when I heard I Maschi's songs," you confess. "How can they get it so right when they're just kids?"

At the bar there are many mothers and a few fathers, dressed expensively but not elegantly. One of the latter flirts with a big-breasted waitress. She looks Puerto Rican, but you know she's actually from southern Lazio.

"Since you're taking them home, I'll have a spritz."

"A Coke for me."

"Oh come on, *papo*, have a drink with me."

You carry Ludovica's second spritz and your first to one of the outdoor tables, weaving between the clusters of parents and their little hairless footballers, clad in over-large brand-name shirts. You sit down and face the bleachers. Marco and Luca are playing on different fields, and you see Luca and wave hello. The sun has set. You tell the babysitter about the circumstances of your departure from football over a decade earlier.

"I was a striker. I was always on a team, but when I finished high school I wanted a real job. I didn't want to become, like, a third-division player and screw up my life. No way: small-time tourneys, club level, amateur stuff, till I was thirty. I was ten when Roma won the title, and when we won again twenty years later with Totti and Capello in 2001 . . . I don't know why I'm telling you all this . . ."

"I love listening to you. I know your kids so well . . ."

"You like them?"

"I wish I had my own just like them."

"You have to burn down your life to have children like that."

"You're the most intense man I've ever met, you know? In New York everybody seemed so dumb and tentative to me. If I hadn't met you, I'd still be stuck there."

"Eh..."

"No, it's true. After our breakfast I knew I had to fly back home. I finally found the strength to do it."

You frown as you stare at the sugary dregs of your spritz. You picture Ludovica imploring Go easy on me, Gustavo.

"So, the Roma win?"

"Two-thousand one was the first year I didn't go to a single Roma game. I gave up my season tickets when I got married. Football was an idol, and I'm an idolater."

"*Idolater, idolatress, idol* . . . You and Maria use these words a lot."

"It helps you fuck up less. In two thousand, all at once, I stopped playing football and stopped watching Roma games. There's . . . No, I shouldn't tell you. It's . . . it's dumb shit, but it's dumb shit that's . . . precious."

She stares at you with her woman's eyes, her glass unsteady on the bumpy table. "You've got unlimited credit as far as I'm concerned."

In the summer of 2000, the Catholic Jubilee year, his comunità organized a weeklong prayer retreat at a convent. "The place had a clay football pitch, and we played there every day during our lunch break, baking in the sun. One night, just before dawn, we were summoned to prayer by the deputy vicar. Each of us had to kneel down on the clay, on the dead leaves and the pebbles, and recite the rosary with our backs straight and our arms outstretched. The priest said, 'If your back begins to give, endure. Endure the pain of staying awake waiting for God with wide-open arms. It's one thing to wait for Him at church on a Sunday morning; it's another to stay awake all night, like the wife who waits for her husband, the sailor, to come back from the stormy seas.'"

"You should talk to my brother," she says.

Tullio prays silently: "You know what's on my mind, Lord. But she was a child and before that she was just a thought in Your mind. And one day she asked her mother to let her try on her eye shadow, and now she can use it any way she wants, but Lord, you will make a saint out of me." He finishes telling her the story: how he recited the rosary and hurt his knees; how his back solidified into hard cement; how, by the end of the long fifteen minutes, he was almost shouting his Hail Marys. He says he watched kids and grown-ups praying out loud on the moonlit field, everyone turned toward their own Mecca . . . the temple of God is the human heart . . . everyone bent in increasing effort, some crying. In the midst of this surreal chaos, he had a terrifying insight: God is mighty enough to come down and steal them away with His love, mighty enough to summon them all up into heaven right at that moment, just as they were, in shorts and t-shirts. This image, he says, seeing that she has stopped sipping her spritz, stopped looking away to watch the end of the practice, the boys dragging their small goals to the sidelines and finishing the night with dribbling drills, this image of God's rapture—of the sudden disappearance of the membrane that separates the living from the dead—made it clear to him how vast His might could really be. His reasoning wasn't totally cogent, he knew, but "if I could be that scared by a full moon and a bunch of poor people praying, just think of the fear our actual God might induce, our formidable God who made the heavens and the earth."

Luca comes up to the table. His mother has recently shaved his head, making it look even more like a ball. He has thick eyebrows and a round chin as soft and big as a third cheek. He walks like a boy, without a hint of ease or naturalness, a wholly contrived creature. "Coach is fu-ri-ous."

"You're exactly like your father." A daring statement, as daring as the pat she gives Luca on his butt, or rather his warm-up jacket, which is triple his size.

"Naah," Luca whines amiably. "Ludo, please, I'm begging you, can we go without showering today?" For a moment his father imagines his pubic hair–less child in the shower with her, with her loose, thick hair and her pubic hair of indeterminate shape and color and her areola of unknown width, and what kind of belly button does she have? But the moment passes, and Tullio wonders why Luca is asking his babysitter for permission and not his father.

"You definitely need to shower, kiddo."

"Oh no, dad, *please?*"

"Since they started going to this preppy club," Tullio says, "they've become disgustingly preppy."

"They're not spoiled. Right, Luca? What do you think?"

"Not! At! All! Can I play PlayStation?"

This is when Ludovica winks at Gustavo Tullio.

"Fifteen minutes. Tops. Shower first. And don't rush." Dinner's at half-past seven. They'll be late, but he can't bring himself to say no.

Luca runs away. His father and his babysitter shrug.

Marco plays center back. He is tall, and his hair is a big brown tuft. He hates his jacket, but he's wearing it when he joins them at their table to avoid being ordered to put it on. He sees that Ludovica is still there. "You waited around for us," he says, placing his left hand on her wrist in a silly, affected gesture. "That's nice." And then, to his father, "Hello." He's still gasping for air, while his milky sweat accumulates on the invisible blond mustache he's never shaved. It's at this moment that Tullio realizes that Ludovica, too, has an invisible blond mustache.

"Hi, sweetheart."

"What are we doing? Maybe I'll get a drink," by which he means a Gatorade. He's only a year older than Luca.

"Yeah, go talk to the barkeep, cat," Tullio teases as he hands him a two-euro coin. "Share it with Luca."

"All right, but only if he's fast," he replies, taking the coin from his father's palm with practiced aloofness, unfazed by the transaction. Then to Ludovica, without losing his aplomb: "Are you in a rush, or will I catch you later?"

Ludovica hugs him and ruffles his hair and kisses him on his head, then pushes him away. "They're so cool," she says to his father. "If only they knew that their dad was a PlayStation phenom," punctuating their complicity with a sly wink.

"You think they need to learn the awful truth sooner or later?"

"I think so, yes." She unbuttons her cardigan, and her shirt creases ever so slightly with her breathing and her joking, gentle shifts like a sea at dawn.

"Okay, but you're not allowed to tell them. I get to decide when they find out."

"I wouldn't dare! *Boss.*"

"Good."

"It's so weird that I'm working for you. It feels like a hundred years ago that we first met . . ."

Gustavo Tullio doesn't react. He doesn't even move a muscle, except for his jaw, so instead he glances at her mustache, that new discovery. A moment later she's embarrassed and changes the topic. "So, why exactly did you stop playing football, then?"

"Oh, you know, I just happened to see the way God sees us. I saw mortals on their knees in the position we all occupy when God summons us to heaven, when He separates us from life and from the vanity of all our possessions."

"Whoa. And you couldn't play anymore."

"I told you."

"That's far out."

Tullio laughs. "The day after the prayer, after lunch, seeing all the same people on the same pitch getting ready for another game like nothing had happened, I couldn't bring myself to play. When I looked at them I couldn't see them as footballers, only as the mortal souls they'd been when they were on their knees, their backs nearly broken because of this tremendous need they'd had for God. So I started to realize that human history, culture, all of it is just the effort to ignore that cemetery hidden behind the pitch."

Ludovica is unable to grasp every nuance of Tullio's conversion narrative, but she honors him and his story with silence as a throng of children begins to surround them. The kids exit the pitches to the busy small talk of lawyers; the bankers' cheerful, competitive banter; the vague shouts of rich mothers; the indecision of dusk, gasping in the cool, veiled sky.

Later, as he says goodbye, Tullio knows better than to kiss her on the cheeks. But when he's in the car with his kids he makes the mistake of asking them to sing "Rock and Roll Forever," and he realizes that the song now reminds him of the babysitter. After dinner he will tell his wife that Ludovica has developed a morbid affection for I Maschi. "And we have always been clear about babysitters and their morbid affections. She cannot and will not invade the family sphere."

A MORNING IN spring. Tullio is in his office in Finmeccanica, near Via Veneto, where he has never let anyone seduce him; always chosen the moral path; never allowed himself the leisure of an afternoon coffee in a bar with his female colleagues, even as springtime oozed its magic; never shown favor to one woman or another by taking her to lunch; never sought out an office wife as a recipient of some token or another of platonic love. Ludovica, who hasn't worked for the Tullios since that night at the Futbolclub, texts him:

"Gustavo, I need to talk to someone about a family matter, urgently. Can I stop by for lunch?"

"Is everything all right?"

"Everything is not all right. Please?"

You email your colleagues to say you'll have the revised Power-Point ready by four p.m.

You tell her to meet you at the intersection with Via Veneto and you walk slightly ahead, make sure you don't look at her too closely (lace shirt, hair loose, no makeup, the light blonde mustache that revealed itself as a relative of Marco's preadolescent down), and lead her to a place far enough from work that your colleagues would never wander in: a sleek New York–style place called T-Bone Station on Via Crispi. You walk briskly and realize that a few steps back, she'd asked you how the kids were doing and you gave her some kind of answer, but you have no idea what it was. Your strides are long: you're trying to put as much distance as you can between yourself and Ludovica and the office while she apologizes and thanks you and tells you over and over again that she owes you big time. "I'd love to come visit I Maschi," she says, "but these weeks have been a mess . . . I'll tell you right away when things calm down . . ."

"Oh, don't bother, our weeks are full right now, too . . . Maybe when we get closer to spring . . ."

"But it's already here, thank God."

"Let's not thank God for Christmas . . ."

"But don't you smell the air? It's so sweet."

Sweet, healthy, cozy air—perfect for fucking in the park (a devilish memory, a flicker from a past Tullio and I once shared).

Ludovica orders a cheeseburger, Tullio a bacon cheeseburger. The restaurant looks like the Wild West cleaned up for general consumption: leather booths, brown wood, brushed-steel lamps, black-and-white photos in tasteful frames. Her shirt is buttoned to the top; the round collar forming a kind of white mustache on her neck, an echo of the invisible mustache that laces her gorgeous upper lip. She thanks him again for agreeing to see her. "You shouldn't thank me or apologize to me," he says sternly. "Just tell me what's the matter. Start by keeping both feet on the ground. If you have a serious matter, you should be serious and try to avoid a half hour's worth of small talk."

Tiny tears appear in her eyes. "It's embarrassing."

"What is? Talking to me?"

"No, no. Talking to you is calming. It really is. The embarrassing thing is what I'm about to say. It's nothing, it's . . ."

"Don't say 'it's nothing.' If it's nothing, how can I help you? How can I take your side?"

She smiles gratefully, her eyes gleaming with the faintest trace of tears, her neck tilted down and to the right. "You're right. I know. It's a bad habit."

"So?"

"I have to tell you about Fofi, the guy who works in my bookstore. Or, well it's my father's bookstore, really . . ."

"Don't do that."

More gratitude and submission in her clear eyes, eyes slightly darker than her face, eyes that haven't slept much, that may have spent most of the last few days crying. "Anyhow, Fofi—I don't know what Fofi thinks of me at this point, but when I was in the U.S. he turned against me, and now I've come back and he's been so rude. It's like I've lost all my rights, all my liberties."

"Look at me. Don't cry. Just tell me what's going on."

"Sorry. No, no sorrys. The bookstore was my family's business— my business—and now it feels like it's his."

You ask her to tell you more about her year abroad, and you quickly hear enough to come to a decisive conclusion: "It's your fault. The first thing you have to do is accept that immediately."

"What?"

"It's very likely that it's your fault."

She lowers her gaze. "But . . ." She lets you hear her sighs and then a "why?" so soft it barely leaves her lips.

"Ask your father to lay you off, to let you go. You shouldn't have gone to New York."

"Why . . . what? What about Lorenzo? And his grant?"

"No. You two didn't think this through from the very beginning. Your husband should have found a European university and then just traveled back and forth . . ."

You eat the cheeseburgers with your hands, and the conversation gets buried in drool and pork fat and melted cheese, in grease and oil that shimmers in the glare of the restaurant's silver lamps. You stare at the grease that coats her lips and think of the stark smells you wish you could smell, smells that this lunch only modestly alludes to, her mouth and her mustache drenched in kisses, your head between her legs, your mouth glinting wet in the shadow . . . So when Ludovica sighs and hiccups and swallows her food in a messy, emotional burst and snot spurts from her nose too quickly for her to blow it back in, you grab a napkin to help her clean her face. It's a father's instinct. You pet her nose and her wet mustache through the napkin. She has my face—my shy, soft face—and you're reminded of me. When you feel the cartilage of her nose through the napkin, you bend it.

"Listen," you say, handing her the napkin and leaning back in your chair, your hands under the table. "The only thing I can tell you is this: think about your responsibilities. Start there. How much did you make before leaving for the U.S.?"

"Depends on the hours."

"Right, but it's your family's bookstore, not Fofi's. So you should figure out how much it was, exactly, and how many hours were involved, and you have to decide if you're willing to commit to the job, given those numbers."

"You know I really needed somebody to talk to me like this, openly and honestly." And a few moments later: "Gustavo, I needed you, needed to hear you." She starts weeping again. The burgers are gone. You drain the last of your Coke, put down the glass, and look at her.

"So what is Fofi actually doing to you, specifically?"

"I don't know if it's anything specific. It's little things. The way he asks questions. He's really demeaning. He always tells me not to let the espresso percolate too much and checks if I'm rinsing stuff before putting it in the washing machine. It's hard to explain."

And it's at this moment, as you order two espressos from the waitress, that you understand what Fofi sees in this immature, mustached girl, this girl who won't do what she's supposed to while he tries to run the store and has no choice but to want to treat her badly. Because Ludovica looks like someone who was designed to be mistreated.

"What am I supposed to ask my father to do, Gustavo? To let him go?"

"You should walk."

"And who would benefit from that? What happens when my husband gets to the end of his grant and we have no idea where his next grant is supposed to come from or what we'll do next?"

"You're right. I don't know. Listen to me." The coffee arrives, and you both pour two sugar packets in—white for you, brown for her. "You're in pain. You're not doing well, and you're feeling lost. I don't know if I can give you any advice. I think that many of the things you've done are wrong, starting from . . . how can I put it, starting from where and how we met: why that apartment, why New York . . . What's your rationale for any of this? How do you make decisions?"

"Oh that was just a mistake, that's all. It was . . ."

"Okay, but it's one mistake after another. They're all linked. But I guess you've decided that I can tell you what things are really like."

This last bit, *I can tell you what things are really like,* is the same thing you used to say to me whenever you tried to convince me that I had to study harder in school, be better at one thing or another, pay more attention to my translations from the ancient Greek so that they'd actually make sense in Italian, "cultivate myself," "become less ignorant." "Sometimes you sound illiterate," you'd say. "You have this cow face, you don't understand anything, you ask the wrong questions," but you'd say that only after you'd fucked me in the ass in the single bed you and your brother shared, though he was never home. It was always in silence: you'd muffle my face with your hand because your mother was in the living room, and I couldn't climax, but you could. All this came back to you with total clarity, in vivid colors, when you told Ludovica that you could tell what things are really like, and so you find yourself saying something totally different from what you'd planned to say. When you remember me and us you feel weak, and instead of saying to Ludovica "You should make your father understand that Fofi is a douche bag and he's taking advantage of the family," the sentence you had planned, you come up with something totally different: "You remember what I said about giving up football? You want to know the really ludicrous thing? And then we can change the subject?"

"What?"

"I didn't even want to get Sky Calcio on TV at home."

She's laughing, relieved.

"But then, at night, after I put the children to bed, when everyone is asleep"—by "everyone" you mean your wife, but you're too embarrassed to mention her—"I sneak into the kitchen to stream games from pirate sites ... Anything: football, South American football, basketball, American football. I'm disgusting."

For a minute you feel free. She smiles and with a warm roll of her eyes confirms that this habit you deem so unacceptable is of course anything but. "Lorenzo streams games, too."

"Is he back in Rome?"

She lowers her head, and your posture changes. Your fingers tense when you pick up the credit card receipt. She thanks you again, and you both get up from the table. You don't say anything until you're holding the door for her: "Sure," coldly, through clenched teeth. Then you step out into the day's unforgiving warmth, into the sweet odor of armpits flowing through the city center and the thwack of tourists' flip-flops and the invisible smolder of their naked shoulders.

BETTA SITS IN her father's arms. She's wearing a teal dress, and after gazing at her father's face for a while, gives him a kiss on the lips. Sara walks in circles around the living room, snorting and pointing at her wrist because Betta is late, though it's unclear for what. I Maschi are in their room getting ready for an afternoon performance for their father, who has just returned from Brussels, where last night he had his first online chat with Ludovica.

Esther is out in the city, shopping with Maria. Spring makes its way into the house through the open windows and carries the scent of Maria's new garden. Betta's fresh legs under her dress push up against Gustavo Tullio's big thighs, clad in Bermuda shorts. Betta is the only one who hasn't yet abandoned the paradise of total childhood. Sara has already changed. She stands by the chair and addresses her father: "Dad, I don't think it's appropriate for you to keep kissing Betta when you don't kiss the other kids."

"Aw, you're such a drag."

"Drag!" Betta echoes her father.

Gustavo Tullio dangles his youngest child on his knees. "My sister's such a drag," she says, laughing.

"Which one? Esther? Sara?"

"Ob-viously Sa-ra!"

"But I thought that you and Sara were BFFs."

"Naaah."

"Nope," Sara says. She's back in the living room after delivering a roll of Scotch tape to her brothers. "If she messes up our afternoon performance, that's it. We're not BFFs anymore."

Gustavo Tullio can't stand the thought that soon these girls will lose their spirit, just like Esther did, hates that the cost of entering adolescence is the dimming of their infectious liveliness.

Betta moves close to her father, her lips prone, her eyes puffy, ready to cry. But before she can feel hurt, he kisses the curls on her forehead, then buries his face in her hair and the top of her neck as he pats her shoulder with a single finger.

Sara watches them from below. She snorts and turns sharply, 360 degrees instead of 180, leaving her stuck in place despite her frustration. Gustavo Tullio begins to pity her, the second-youngest child, the little girl who only got to experience the joy of being the youngest for a single year, who is jealous of these kisses because she no longer has access to them: there's a rule in the house that the parents will only kiss their children's mouths until they're in kindergarten. So Gustavo Tullio gives Betta a hug and one last kiss on her cheek, then puts her down and tells her to prepare for the performance.

A quiet Saturday: no one has the flu, no one's pollen allergies are acting up. Alone in the living room, Tullius lies down on the floor. Unusually for him, he's not hungry: no cookie cravings, no desperate longings for ice cream. The smell of basil and mint is wafting through the open windows. Last night in Brussels, around eleven, he searched for Ludovica's name on Skype. LudovicaVozzi8o was online. Since the first lunch in Via Crispi, they've had more lunches, all clandestine but totally chaste, the only topic of conversation Ludovica's troubles. Kissing Betta has made him feel open and free, and he wants to make the most of this sense of possibility: what he wants is to stare at the ceiling and think of Ludovica. *Have I behaved?* he asks himself. While Ludovica vented angrily about Fofi's most recent act of rudeness ("Sure, Ludo, remind me to explain to you how warehousing works one day," he said, in the presence of a client friend of her mother's), Tullio was lying in bed in his hotel room in his underwear. In one corner of his laptop screen: a live stream of a Botafogo match; in another corner: a white couple *going all-anal* for half an hour in a seaside resort, with a view out onto the swimming pool. He hopes his presence gave Ludovica some solace, even though he was distracted by the porn, the game, and his own cock, which he held erect in front of the laptop and brandished from time to time when Ludovica's whining made him think to himself that what she really needed was to spend some time with *this*.

Luca steps out of his room to tell his father to please come take his place, then changes his mind because Betta and Sara aren't ready yet.

"Yessir," says Tullius. He feels every muscle, bone, and tendon as he pulls himself up onto his knees. He ignores his own heaviness and his quickening heartbeat as he lifts his leg, secures his foot, and stands up.

"No, turn around! Wait, *papo*, they're calling me."

"Go, go." Tullius is delighted by this sternness, by his children's beautiful lack of irony.

"Sorry, *papo*, Betta's just going to the bathroom."

He sits on the floor with his legs crossed, just in front of the door to I Maschi's room, under the open window. Luca and Marco are inside. They wear scarves over their mouths, and their ears are covered by headphones, the pose held emphatically, a perfect imitation of the photos of DJs they've seen online. The computer screen has been moved to a table overwhelmed by toys. The classical guitar is on its perch. Sara and Betta are clad in old white tablecloths draped over them like tunics, taped together with fluorescent yellow tape.

He stays silent, touches his aching back, waits for the music, nods, changes his posture. He's no longer able to cross his legs for more than a few seconds at a time, the way he used to when he'd sit in a circle with the other scouts. He switches to a triclinium position, leaning on his side. Sara and Betta stand next to each other. They kneel down and lean forward, arms stretched along the floor.

The beat starts: a loud hip-hop track. Tullius refrains from asking them to lower the volume; he wants them to have fun. Sara and Betta wiggle their hips and lean forward while the keyboard plays a lone chord—first a drone, then a rhythmic *na na naaa, na-na na naaa.*

At lunch, Ludovica and Tullio eat bacon cheeseburgers or pork ribs with their hands. He usually eats as she vents and he doesn't say much, but recently a new topic of conversation has emerged: his job.

She loves the grand words you use to describe it.

You watch the girls dance to the beat and hear the prerecorded guitar arpeggios come in, one chord and two interweaving arpeggios, free and weird and euphonic, but all you can think about are the lunches, where her armpits sweat under a light pink shirt as she bites into the bone, rips the meat off with her teeth, and asks you to tell her about your work: "So, the key thing you need to understand to get what I do is the idea of the commercial *offset* . . . It's an international thing: when you get a big contract, let's say from India, you can't just send the goods and take the money. Because the money you're earning basically comes from the Indian state, from India's land, you are in effect taking stuff from them, so you have to give something back, something that will contribute to the technological growth of the country. And the amount and type of thing you give back is proportional to your contract. So, if you're selling airplanes, you have to give back a certain percentage of the value of the jets you're pushing to India." Big words from the adult world get her excited: *technological, development.* "So let's say we decide to bring over a technology that measures pollution. Now, I handle a project where we find drones and retrofit them for agricultural use . . . We might use them to spray herbicides or control production. So that there's value in it."

"You should totally come to Librici and do a presentation about your job, it's so interesting."

"Is it?"

"Totally. It's amazing. And you're basically turning evil into good."

You tell her you've flown on a private Falcon jet. "There was a sexy flight attendant on board—she had a nose ring. It was like a lightning flash, this flight: just a hop from Rome to Trento. I could feel the sun burning through the windows. And when we landed, it was straight into the limo . . . to go develop Sustainable Valley . . ." You are, you admit to yourself, punishing her for leaving her husband back in America.

You allot a special pocket for the receipts, keep them separate from the gum and the candy and the gum and candy wrappers. When the two of you part ways, you always throw the receipts in the same place: the first trash can on the north side of Via Sicilia. (You tell Don Luca that a colleague is proving to be a distraction: she admires and flatters you, and you can't avoid talking to her because you're working together on a project.) Oh, her stupid questions:

"How does it feel wearing a tie to work?"

"When do you button the top button, before or after you put the tie on?"

"Are these tailor-made? I mean for your neck, it's so big."

And the way she sucks the fat from her teeth and then swallows . . .

After a couple of minutes of guitar and keyboard arpeggios, Sara and Betta try out a few splits, then stand back up and press their fists into their hips and push their elbows forward in an extravagant swagger. They nod their heads up and down, gasp for air with an unguarded inelegance, count to four. A prerecorded voice starts rapping: Esther, with a heavy Roman accent.

> *Che m'importa se c'avete il cash.*
> *Voi siete trash, c'avete le meches,*
> *io rappo come un flash,*
> *sul red carpet mi coprono di flash,*
> *prima o poi c'avrò io più cash.*

> *I don't care if you've got* cash.
> *You're* trash, *you have* mèches,
> *I rap like a* flash,
> *on the red carpet they cover me with* flash
> *sooner or later I'll have more* cash.

You're shocked, but you can't help but laugh at what you're hearing. "What is this?"

Luca shushes you.

You weren't expecting Esther's voice. Did she record it for you?

139

Or is this an act of rebellion, a protest *against* you? And does she know that they were planning on playing it? Luca and Marco only repeat the endings in *-ash*. More rhymes:

> *Sei ridicolo.*
> *Il tuo flow è da cavernicolo.*
> *Il mio flow*
> *mette su uno show*
> *che fa sembrare il tuo un ammennicolo.*
> *Faccio rime che ti mandano in clinica,*
> *non puoi dirmi che so' cinica,*
> *il rap è la palestra del successo,*
> *col rap ti faccio fesso,*
> *ci rimani di sasso,*
> *ma io al tuo livello non mi abbasso"*

> *"You're ridiculous.*
> *You have the flow of a caveman.*
> *My flow*
> *puts on a show*
> *makes your flow look trifling.*
> *I make rhymes that send you to the clinic,*
> *don't tell me I'm a cynic,*
> *rap is the gym of success,*
> *I fool you with rap,*
> *you're shell-shocked,*
> *but I won't lower myself to your level.*

Does her mother know about this? Does she know Esther is writing rhymes? That she knows obscure words like *ammenni-colo*? When the chorus starts—"cash cash cash, / lo faccio in un flash, / cash cash cash, / io sono queen tu sei trash"—Tullio stands up and begins to clap. "So much talent in one house!" he says with persuasive enthusiasm, towering over his children.

"Wait!" shouts Luca as Tullius picks up the girls and carries them away. "Gelato!" he shouts back to I Maschi.

After Maria and Esther return home, the scheme is revealed: the entire performance, including Esther's guest appearance, was a special surprise, choreographed just for him. Mother and daughter went out so that the four younger children could show off without the powerful constraint of Esther's embarrassment. She's offended whenever anyone likes what she does. Everything was arranged yesterday while Tullio was in Brussels—an epic welcome-back gift. While he was out of town, Maria bought Esther a rhyming dictionary. Tullio's disgust spikes as husband and wife stand on the balcony. Maria tries to defend their oldest child's "choices," but he isn't having any of it. "Don't call them 'choices.' You liked hip-hop, and you forced it on her. Why should Esther listen to fucking hip-hop just because you do?"

"Well, maybe if you didn't give *me* such a hard time about listening to what I want to, I'd be less interested in my daughter's freedoms."

"So that's where we're at, huh?"

"We're at: you don't let me listen to rap, and then you secretly stream football and God knows what else, and then, because you're a hypocrite, you won't buy your sons a PlayStation. You're such an asshole."

"God knows what else," you ape her with a sneer. "I won't even dignify that with a response. If I ever turned against you, I know that I'd end up sleeping on the street."

She finds this satisfying or satisfying enough. "That's right," she says with a laugh.

The two of you start talking about the garden, and you feel such a violent sense of relief that a half hour later, you've got a painful headache.

ONLINE CHATS HAVE put an end to lunches. They are so intimate that meeting her in person again would be fatal. Ludovica's husband sleeps in the living room most of the time—a man with no control over his household. Ludovica chats with Gustavo from the bedroom, alone in a bed denied to her husband. He was such a fool for not coming back to Rome when they first began to argue. He stayed in New York because he was supposed to be interning for this famous director, helping him out on set and bringing him coffee. But then the director said he didn't want a thirty-year-old doing the kinds of lowly tasks more suited to someone a decade younger. So now Lorenzo has lost his wife's respect. Ludovica and Gustavo discuss all of this online. Now that he knows that his wife knows about his secret football watching, Gustavo retreats into the kitchen at night without fear, making it seem like he's hiding to stream games or to look at porn, which his wife thinks he's doing, too.

Tullio has started going to a gym. One evening, he's leaving the office on the way to his workout when he orders a female intern not to leave for the night before she finishes translating a document. He ends up scolding her, and he watches her sulk at her desk without saying anything. No response, no push back— she just takes it. Tullio suddenly imagines that right at that moment, Fofi is at the bookstore mistreating Ludovica. Tullio told her recently that they should come up with some kind of practical joke to ridicule him in front of the customers.

He arrives at Librici before sundown, his pale blue tie tight and his gym bag thrown carelessly over his left shoulder. His bathrobe is dry inside the bag. The sudden appearance of Fofi and Mrs. Vozzi, two people who have come to exist as literary characters in his online chats, transforms reality into a vague mist. Mrs. Vozzi sits behind the counter, like in her daughter's stories. Fofi is in the middle of the dining area, between the tables and the bar. Tullio enters like the Lord, without attracting any attention. He knows that Ludovica, whom he's ignoring, is standing behind the bar, startled and frozen, her spirit and her body jerked upward into a position of intense focus. He knows, too, that his skin looks better after three weeks of exercise. He sits at a table that lets him avoid eye contact with Ludovica, so she'll know he's not planning on saying hi. Two students sit at another table, drinking iced tea. Ladies browse books along the shelves closest to the entrance.

Fofi's hair is curly, like Tullio's, and red, with a matching beard that creases beneath his double chin and suggests animal fur and a kind of creepy dignity. He looks disheveled, with his argyle pants and his shabby sneakers deformed by his fat. But his body language is confident: he holds his ground as if the place were his. He rearranges books compulsively, but with a manic elegance. He calls some of the female customers by their first names, though with others he's more formal.

Tullio, the stranger, is greeted by Fofi but not by Mrs. Vozzi, who is absorbed by the computer on the counter. She's not as old as her daughter made her out to be. They must hate each other, like Maria and her mother, but she doesn't look especially angry or reactive, at least not from this perspective, where she's mostly hidden from sight by the counter and a support column in the middle of the store.

From the bar, Ludovica can see the knot of the tie, the sucked in stomach, the carriage of a real man. And yet Berengo is right when he says that losing your faith doesn't happen easily or simply. A fair and good God looks upon him here, keeps him from doing irreversible things, melts his heart a little. The pity he feels for Ludovica has endowed him with pity for his own mother. He lets her invite him over for lunch once a week when his father has his postural regimen at the physiotherapist, the only time mother and son can be alone. Sometimes Tullio doesn't even tell Maria that he's there, even though she's just nearby, cooking for the children in their new kitchen. As he races back to the office, he prays for his mother, a prayer provoked by Ludovica. How horrible it is to be a mother, thrown atop society's waste heap. Please, have mercy on her, Lord. Please bless her, be by her side. And the Lord is there that evening, at Librici, because wherever there's an aging mother, God is there, too.

Ludovica takes his order, and Tullius asks for a Coke Zero without raising his gaze. She retreats to the bar, her stride tentative and unnatural. Gustavo heads to the bathroom; he wants to know if this place resembles the vision he's concocted in the midst of his erotic fantasies, but it's breathtakingly mundane: spacious, handicapped accessible.

His Coke arrives as he sits down, and he pulls out a legal pad and a day planner from his briefcase to take some notes for an upcoming meeting. He needs to figure out what he can say to upset Fofi. He tries to relax and glean the man's personality.

A middle-aged woman: "I'm looking for a book that's like *The Name of the Rose*? Could you suggest something similar? It's my favorite book!"

"Ma'am, if there were other books as good as *The Name of the Rose*, you'd know about them already, and their authors would be super famous and super popular."

To a young father, clean-shaven with a fanny pack over a Korean shirt: "We're obviously not France, you know. Children's books aren't an art form here . . ."

It's not hard to find reasons to despise this hairy little bear and his scratchy, prickly voice. He must have the saddest, tiniest cock. It probably hungers for that part of Ludovica's belly where the flesh sinks down and flips over like plowed earth. Ludovica is the only valuable thing in this entire bookstore, this ridiculous place with its orange walls and its overlapping identity crises. Fofi's petty, high-pitched voice is bad enough, but the fact that he keeps the music this loud is truly detestable; it's impossible to take any notes when you're being bombarded by Italian prog rock from the seventies.

Gustavo Tullio glances at Mrs. Vozzi, still at the counter, and at Ludovica, who stands at the bar looking miserable, chewing a carrot and returning his eye contact with a kind of half-smile/half-frown. She looks captive, broken down. And then Gustavo Tullio's off: "Excuse me, sir, are you the manager . . ."

"Beg your pardon?" Fofi is ready for combat. "No, sir, I'm not in charge. That'd be the lady over there." He rearranges a few books on the shelves without turning away from him, the whole exercise performed in a single, fluid motion.

"Well, you seem like you might be the owner, if I may . . ." Gustavo Tullio feels his eye sockets turning to marble and tries to tone down the decorous language, but now he finds himself unable to look Fofi in the eyes or to look at anything in particular. "You've got the music turned all the way up here, and you're yapping away, and well, you know, some customers come here to kind of, collect their thoughts and, how do I put it, be among books, but then there's this guy here, this guy who's acting like he's at home by himself . . . I don't know, I think it's pretty weird . . ."

He gets up, grabs his gym bag and puts the legal pad and the planner back into the briefcase, a gesture born of confusion. "You want to collect your thoughts, sir?" Fofi says without missing a beat. "Go to a church, then. This is a café."

The reference to a church, random but potent, makes Tullio feel dumb and exposed. He heads toward the exit, thinking that Fofi must know about the two of them somehow, like Jesus predicting Peter's denial. He's almost out the door, and he hasn't looked back to figure out how Ludovica has reacted to this exchange. He hopes that this, here and now, will finally terminate their relationship. Praise the Lord! But before he can make his escape, Fofi nails it a second time: "Your coffee's on the house, sir," he says with cold politeness, forcing Tullio to respond with a whimpering, Pavlovian "Thanks!" Back on the street, he feels uncomfortable, sliced in half, reset, restored, saved. "My nonsense will make me a saint!" he moans as he unlocks the handlebars of his bike.

HE BLOCKS HER on Skype. He tries to spend more time talking to his children. He trips over their neglected guitar, knocks on Esther's door, and tells her to turn down her music. He's ashamed he hasn't been able to yield, hasn't told her that he liked her rap. Without the online chats, he feels that the life he's allotted between work and sleep amounts to driving around in circles near the church, looking for a parking spot after he's dropped off Maria, or Maria and the children. He survives these half-hour-long challenges, these feats of strength, by listening to contrarian radio shows whose commentators discuss racist politicians in northern Italy or the latest skirmish with Gaddafi, or some starlet's new leaked sex tape, or a sadder starlet's full-on career move into porn.

But then one day, after work, he's surprised to see her at his gym, on the step machine. She grips the padded handles tightly, moving them in sync with her steps. In a haze, he realizes that her presence here is a miracle: her back and her precious ass, finely contoured in her tight track pants, her back sweating under a white t-shirt that dangles just above the two cheeks of her ass, which take turns flexing. All he can do is accept this prophesy, this prophesy in the shape of her grand head of hair tied up with a black hair band he recognizes. He concludes without a doubt that it's her when he sees her jaw move, a generic gesture that nonetheless feels intimate, and he decides that he won't approach. Tullius in shorts is not a great spectacle, with his white wristband and his new white sneakers. Going over to her means accepting what she's chosen for them both.

Tullio climbs onto a stationary bike at the opposite end of the room. He aims a thought in her direction, hoping, somehow, that it will reach her. "You won't do my family any harm."

You see her reflection in the mirrored wall. You see her back, the black sports bra under her t-shirt, her sweaty hands on the handlebars, submissive, resentful, explicit. You go over and apologize for making a fool of yourself at Librici.

Ludovica looks down at the hand you've just placed on her shoulder, and you begin talking before you can make eye contact. "I have to apologize. I looked like such an idiot," you say.

"No, not at all."

"I'm such a dumb ass."

"No, not at all. My mother called you 'that gentleman'—you really looked the part!"

They don't talk about the Skype block.

"No, really, I was pathetic."

"No, honestly, it worked wonders. Basically, I haven't said anything, and neither has my mom, but she talked to my father, she told me, and now Fofi has stopped blasting all that Italian seventies music in the café. Mom definitely talked to Dad."

"What about you?"

"Well, I'm supposed to just stay at the bar, but when it's a *slow day* I help him out with the books. Being a woman is heavy shit; there's always, you know, there's this thing in the way—the fact that he wants to sleep with me."

"Being a man is heavy shit, too," you add for no reason.

"Being a woman is worse, though."

"Well but are they paying you? Have they started paying you again?"

"Not yet."

"What about your father?"

The two of you sit on a padded bench near the swimming pool, drowning in the romantic smell of chlorine.

"I know it's the most ridiculous thing ever to have joined your gym, but . . . It's impossible, everything is impossible. I don't have anything anymore. Lorenzo left for New York again, and when he comes back . . . I've changed the locks."

And it's here, Gustavo Tullio, damned Gustavo Tullio, that you enter the darkness, and it's here that I abandon you, if I can, because I can't stand this: I don't know why I have to know these things. I don't know what notion of truth this is.

*G*ustavo Tullio claimed me as his at scout camp the summer I turned fourteen. He took me the way the hacendero takes a farmer's daughter—through the recommendation of a man he trusts.

He was the king of our reparto, the twelve- to fifteen-year-old scouts. His animal name was Resourceful Lion Cub. He was the chief of the Hawks, he played guitar. He even managed to make morning prayer look cool with his earnest, heartfelt style—*very sessuale*. Tullio signed his letters "Gusty72," spoke to teachers and counselors with a confidence and an intimacy that seemed impossible, was an expert in tying knots. He wore a trendy red Moncler vest that had been passed down to him from his brother, lilac sweaters from Best Company, ripped jeans with Naj Oleari flower patches on the sides. He was a *gran gallo*: he'd already *dunked his cookie*, as the boys used to say back then, with a girl who was two years older than him, a legendary feat accomplished the previous summer, when he'd stayed in Rome while his parents were down by the shore.

Keen Porcupine, aka Franchino, deputy chief of Tullio's squadron, was the one who made the recommendation. He spent his first day dragging logs over to the wide field in the middle of the camp, where every squadron—the two all-male ones and the two all-female ones—was to build a pile dwelling topped with a large tent. But this was just a pretext for his real mission: an inspection of the two female squadrons. We watched him as he approached with his Esprit sweatpants cut off at the thighs, watched him press down on his stomach to keep it from showing through his London U t-shirt with the anxiety of the former fat kid he was.

He was doing reconnaissance for the Black Feet Tribe. The news was that a new third-year had joined the group the previous fall—the second deputy of the Ducks squadron—a coy, modest girl with a good singing voice who had visited and befriended popular Silvia when she'd been hospitalized with Ewing's sarcoma. Silvia had called this girl—Daria, me—a nun, though she also claimed that I'd been caught fingering myself in the bathroom: an odd but compelling diptych. So here I was, a red-haired beauty in the making, or as one of the boys had put it, *una sfitinzia arrapation*, a chick worthy of a boner, in the Milanese/English-inflected *paninari* slang of the time. Very original, they'd said, *e con davanzale doc*, a certified rack.

That summer, I was one of the campers who would get to take part in the totem ceremony and I would have to endure the night rites, a mysterious and esoteric set of rituals. Franchino told everybody in the Black Feet Tribe, who organized the trials, that any trials I faced would have to have the effect of making me feel more slutty—*bottana*—so that I could change *[my] life forever, and hopefully end up blowing someone.*

The totem ceremony was an orgy of trials—some of them violent, some of them sleazy, some of them truly disgusting—at the end of which the third-years would get their own animal names, their own special nicknames, and membership in the Black Feet Tribe. Some of the trials involved stripping and cold showers; in others, campers had to face their fears (spiders, hours alone in the woods) or cover themselves in mud or garbage.

The Black Feet, who supervised the trials, were an informal organization whose hierarchy paralleled that of the counselors and who ranged in age from fifteen-year-old fourth-years to teachers in their twenties. The faux- or quasi-torture that defined the totem nights had little to do with the educational principles espoused by Catholic *scautismo*—they were in fact opposite tendencies, impossible to reconcile—so the outcome was an authentically Fascist education, an echo of the old days of castor oil and public humiliation. But it was hardly aberrant: the counselors who ruled the camp were Black Feet members, too, which meant that none of this was an aberration. It was almost an official event . . . it would have been, but for the camp priest, who stayed in his tent so as not to give the proceedings his blessing. He tried his best to sleep as the children's screams echoed through the forest.

My parents had pulled me out of my previous group after it was revealed that the thirty-five-year-old leader had been spending a lot of his time hugging seventeen-year-old girls in their sleep. No one knew if he'd had sex with any of these girls (as it turned out, he hadn't), but still, this was too much. The new group's headquarters were in Viale Regina Margherita, a rich neighborhood near the Policlinico Hospital. This group had retained its links with the right-wing terrorism of the late seventies, and its vibe was distinctly Fascist.

We bestowed fake nicknames on one another before the real ones were announced—I later learned that the fake name Keen Porcupine had chosen for me was Sorca Madonna. *Sorca* literally meant "rat," and also "an extremely sexy woman." Some implications were more risqué: as a play on words, the name sounded even worse if you substituted *P* for *S*, turning it into *Porca*, as the combination of Pig and Mary was a typical and forbidden slur word. The fake nickname was the first thing about me that got Tullio's attention. "You're right," Gusty said with great deliberation "She has appeared here just like a Madonna."

(Tullius was morally complex. He dressed the part of the *paninaro*, and he watched *Drive In*, the dumb, trendy comedy show that everyone was into, where they all got their English/ Milanese slang, their *paninaro* style. The right-wing comedians on the show popularized that look of preppy leisure. But Tullius also had a spiritual streak. When he joined up he began to conform at once to the scout group's Fascist style and started using the Roman salute as a form of camaraderie. Soon enough, he'd shapeshift again and become a leftist, though this also only lasted a few years.)

Me, I had blossomed that summer. In the city I was all about Closed capris and Superga sneakers, like all the other girls. And like all the other girls, I looked bland and repressed, pristine in my fuchsia sweaters. I was a church girl, even though my mother hadn't been one. I never disobeyed orders—I was always boring—but when I showed up to camp I had Silvia's clothes with me. She was in recovery and wouldn't be coming at all that summer, and she didn't want the clothes to go unused. So I made them my own: the short cutoffs rolled up at the top of the thighs, the baggy white tees that made me look bountiful and tender and softened my features. I kept the sleeves rolled up, too, and revealed my gentle shoulders, which gave way to arms scratched up from helping out with construction in the neighborhood, from carrying wood and rope during long afternoons. My knees were grazed, my shins were bruised, and I had scabs and small burns from spilling boiling water on myself. I'd tie back my red hair with a thin piece of rope, and someone would usually stick in a flower or a blade of grass. Right after I got to camp, a female counselor (the girlfriend of the brother of a Fascist who died in prison) offered me a hazy omen: "This summer at camp, you'll rock their world."

I was always ashamed of my round face, here, but now it was finally in fashion. On the third day, Gusty and Franchino showed up together at the site of the Ducks squadron's new home, then still under construction. They said they'd come to help us build the pile dwelling. The smell of burnt grass, which appeared around this time every year, wasn't there that summer. It rained almost every day. Nature was pregnant and green, and our shorts were always smudged and wet. The first couple nights we'd slept in a damp tent; our kidneys hurt and our eyes were heavy. Everyone wore shorts: the homely girls and the cute girls, the fat girls and the thin girls. Keen Porcupine and Resourceful Lion Cub, guitar around his shoulder, entertained us by making fun of the wet spots on our butt cheeks. "You're soaked through, girls. For Pete's sake, *reghiuleit*"—an English-sounding thing that meant "get your shit together." "Did you sleep in a swamp," Franchino added, "or are you just happy to see us?"

"Why the Christopher are you out here turkeying us instead of building your own pile dwellings?" said our squadron leader in that weird slang, which makes less and less sense as time goes by. Chesty, with thin eyes and long, straight chestnut hair, she was the only girl who could put up with them. (She helped take care of Silvia, her ill friend, but she's the one who will die first, in her thirties, from a disease similar to the one she helped Silvia conquer.)

"You mean you don't appreciate our *prezijon* knots? No? Should we take off, Tullius?"

"*Ingratitiud,*" said Tullio. He was a sensitive *paninaro*. His dark leg hair protruded from under his short, pale jeans and commanded respect, even if the legs themselves weren't quite straight. He was tall and brawny enough that he was a little too big to be considered slim (his stomach bulged out after meals), his hair was dirty blond and curly, and he had an adorable flat nose, which had inspired the Lion Cub name. The ends of our ropes were all frayed, so he pulled open his Opinel clasp knife, trimmed each end with a sharp cut, burned the ends with his Zippo. He cleaned his knife on the soles of his Timberlands before folding it up in his pocket. Franchino kept joking as I watched Tullio, the Lion Cub, stack the logs in neat groups of three.

Franchino wasn't trying to pretend not to stare at my round shoulders, my large-ish thighs, my big and pointy breasts. My ass had just taken shape, suddenly. I was fourteen and hadn't done more than kiss a boy. I touched myself, though not often, and only climaxed in my sleep. I wore Sylvia's Stan Smiths with short socks, the white of the sneakers smudged green and brown. I longed to be a *sfitinzia*.

That morning I'd gotten another burn on my shin when I slammed into a pot of boiling water. My white t-shirt looked like milk pouring out from under my freckled neck. I wore a light green bra and had big green froglike eyes that people had finally started to notice under my bulging forehead. I had my hair in a ponytail to keep my face exposed.

I now knew everything about my looks, and I was starting to accept that people liked me. When Franchino had had enough of staring at me, he helped Tullio tie up the first three logs, the triangular structure of the first tepee. They raised it with great exaggeration.

They teased us as they finished the knot for the second tepee. At morning assembly, the camp counselors had announced that someone had taken a dump behind a bush near the fire pit, instead of in the wooden latrines. This person had cleaned him- or herself up using wax paper from a pack of prosciutto. The counselors had mocked the unknown perpetrator, invited the person responsible to turn him- or herself in.

Franco: "You ask me, it's a woman."

Gustavo: "No, please, get that thought out of my head. Girls, please tell me it wasn't any of you."

Franco: "'My dear,' the man said while they were in the middle of anal, 'where's that prosciutto smell coming from?'"

Our squadron leader laughed.

We watched them lift the four tepee structures, one after another, with great skill. We couldn't have done it ourselves, and thanks to them, we got two weeks of dry sleep and pain-free kidneys.

Architecture was the camp's real lesson, its presiding force. Architecture helped us make sense of what would otherwise have been a virgin green field and a spring and a stream. Instead the landscapes were quickly organized, mapped, regulated: the sleeping area for the kids; the service area where the counselors handed us food from the pantry tent and equipment from the equipment tent; the counselors' sleeping area, with small single tents; and the huge wooden structure where every morning the associations' flags were raised. That year, architecture was more crucial than ever: because it was always raining, the tents and the wooden structures had to be perfect. The sporting events were canceled as were the craft workshops, so we spent a lot of time in our pile dwellings three meters above the earth, which meant that everything had to be tight and secure: the wooden base, the ropes, the log ladder that led up to where we slept. We spent hours chatting in tents three meters above the earth, mostly in ours, and sometimes in the big group tent where we discussed our individual moral goals for the camp and for the upcoming school year.

After the pile dwelling structure was set, with the three teepees connected by four long logs, the boys added more logs and then mounted the structure and laid down the floorboards, which they also secured with rope. They then mounted the tent on top and threw the ropes down to the ground, so that we could nail them into the earth with pegs. Finally they picked up the guitar and began to sing a Vasco Rossi song.

One of us dunked tea bags in metal mugs; another played the cymbals. As Gustavo sang he made eye contact with me. "Sing a harmony to the refrain," he told me before the refrain started. When he sang the lyrics "I love you, don't change the subject," he glanced at my tits. I touched my belly.

IN THE DAYS that followed, we would meet to practice harmonies for other songs. We'd meet after lunch during the afternoon break. He wanted to teach me some guitar, too, to figure out harmonies for the songs we'd sing around the fire in the evenings. "When two voices harmonize . . . on thirds and fifths, let's say, it's like one of them is vibrating in the other." When he was alone with me there was no English slang, no Milanese accent. Four days after we first sang together, we were sitting on a rock in a hidden recess by the stream. He began to sniff my neck. "This is good sweat," he explained. "At camp you produce a ton of good smells. City sweat stinks; it's neurotic sweat, ugly sweat." The next afternoon, it was pouring, and we were sitting in some squadron's tent with a group of cool kids, discussing sex stuff. I was sitting with my legs crossed, very rigid, and he must have guessed that I was tense. "You've got bad sweat today. Are you nervous?" I wasn't letting him touch me, and I wasn't letting him kiss me, but we both knew that he was circling around the subject.

ON THE NIGHT of the totem ceremony, Nicolino Morelli, a twelve-year-old first-year from Gustavo's squadron, encounters the otherworldly roar of pots beaten by wooden sticks. *Shtang! Shtang!*

Shtang! "Wake uuuup!" The Black Feet have been gathering under every squadron's pile dwelling because their strange, muezzin stadium chant has to be performed in sync. They sing their ghostly, nonsense song at the top of their lungs: "Brama-pu-tra! Him-a-la-ya! Chin-chu! Chin-chu-ay! Born-fag! Dead-stiff!"

It's two a.m., and the earth is drenched from a downpour that cut the after-dinner campfire short. The fourth-years and the counselors wear artfully ripped shirts, their hands covered in soot from holding pots blackened by fire. Their cheeks are painted black, they wear bandannas on their foreheads, and they scream at everyone to exit their tents. The instructions are brutal, delivered with a snarl: "Wake up, idiot!" They climb in and look inside the Hawks' tents, stomping on a couple of feet that scramble inside the sleeping bags, warning that the punishment for being late includes mandatory consumption of The Beverage.

The younger kids, like Nicolino, are terrified and still half-asleep as they get pushed toward the flames. On a hill on the outer edges of the camp, the Black Feet have built a fire that's much more powerful and far taller than what the kids see every evening.

As the third-years gathered at the top of the hill, I looked down toward the artificial lake down below, eerie and rectangular. One of the Black Feet hid under a poncho and explained the trials to us in the voice of the goddess Kalì. The first- and second-years were in the hands of the fourth-years—Keen Porcupine and Gianki, or Thoughtful Antelope—who immediately began to impose their reign of terror on the preadolescents.

"Your lives are worth nothing!" they shouted, their spittle raining down on the campers, their voices hoarse. The kids couldn't have imagined anything like this: they lived easy lives in rich neighborhoods; they were accustomed to the softness and good cheer of the *Jungle Book*–themed cub scout camps or the day camps that were set up at convents during the summer.

Nicolino was a little lord with careful manners—hairless, potbellied, his straight hair gelled back carefully, his features and posture feminine. It was his first time at the camp, and when he reached the promontory and kneeled down in front of the fire, he was accused of displaying inadequate submission to the goddess Kalì. "You haven't mastered the art of submission!" Franchino shouted. "What's wrong with your back? You're not kneeling down enough," said the other. "There's too much pride in that back!" They beat the jugs right by his ears, deafening and, it seemed to him, blinding him.

The Beverage was poured into his mouth from a cold ladle. An oregano twig got stuck in his throat as he drank the vile combination of water, tea, coffee, salt, soup, celery, beans, watermelon, cocoa, chicken bones, and a drop of piss from someone who couldn't help himself (as well as, according to rumor, a used tampon, more likely a pristine one).

"This isn't fair! You told me to kneel, and I did it! Look, my face is on the ground! I submit! What else do you want?"

"It's not enough!"

"Drink again, you worthless shit! How dare you challenge the almighty power of the Black Feet?"

And after they made him drink more, they pressed him back down against the earth with their rods. He felt the rods piercing his back and experienced a grand feeling of outrage over what was happening, a feeling he'd always recall with equal parts affection and scorn. Their persistent focus on Nicolino was partly my fault. Nobody could remember where the tradition came from, but every year, for the duration of the session, the popular third- and fourth-year girls would pick first-years to coddle and keep around. For a certain kind of well-regarded girl, it seemed utterly natural to keep a darling little featherless kid nearby—to position him between your legs while sitting around the fire or to place him in the crook of your arm while lying in the grass. They were babies, these little boys: they had just a hint of down on their upper lip and were still in middle school, they had un-muscled bodies that we covered with hugs and kisses on their necks and foreheads and shoulders and arms. They sat with us and abandoned their weight against our breasts, and it felt so warm for them, so comforting; they knew they couldn't find these feelings anywhere else in the camp. And it made us feel warm, too, and also powerful and possessive. The boys regulated our horniness—we could touch and play and carry on without hindering any of the sentimental things that were happening with kids our age or older. Nobody saw these hugs as sex, or even as anything sexual, but we gave ourselves over to the feeling, and as a result we had less time to spend with the older guys. It wasn't unnoticed, of course: all this hugging and kissing with our little guys would necessarily provoke questions like "Did you jerk him off?" or "Have you two made love?"

Gustavo Tullio, in particular, didn't like how much time I was spending with Nicola, because it meant I wasn't kissing the Lion Cub. At night, when the campfire was done and the singing and dancing were over, before I returned to my squadron in the tent, I'd grab Nicolino instead of talking to the kids my age or to Tullio. He was as tall as I was, but he looked like he could have been my son. We'd hug from the front, both of us stinking of fire and fried cheese, and we'd kiss each other's necks and cheek-bones and foreheads as we whispered Edoardo Bennato songs. "You are a wonderful person," he'd say, "I really care for you." I could always feel his hard-on: he didn't move as he held me, but I could feel his coiled passion, his ecstatic energy. He'd sniff my dirty hair.

I never asked Nicolino if he was being bullied by Franchino, Gianki, or Tullius, but it turned out that Franchino and Gianki were subjecting him to a light but steady torture: they farted on his face while he slept, stuck his toothbrush in among the dirty dishes, peed on his sneakers. They'd force him to go get water from the spring right after lunch, the two jugs weighing almost as much as he did, and they'd laugh when his digestion got the best of him and he had to stop what he was doing and run back into the woods ("Don't forget the wax paper!").

Nicolino was a delicate drama queen, a delicate boy full of artful complaints: he'd tell the second deputy in the squadron that he'd "almost fainted due to the farts" or that carrying two full jugs every day after lunch was "altering his posture." The squadron reveled in the precision of his formulations.

I accepted the reality of this bullying, this *nonnismo*, the way any Italian perceives the existence of the mafia. The girls discussed it among ourselves, but we ignored the best stories, like the time Franchino took a dump, wrapped it in paper towels and aluminum foil, and handed it to Nicolino, passing it off as a chocolate salami. "We smuggled some *Ciòcoleit Salàmi* from the pantry, now go set the table for teatime." Nico only figured it out when he unwrapped the package.

So,

ON THE NIGHT of the ceremony, as Nicolino drank ladlefuls of the Beverage, the six of us began the trials that would lead to our initiations. Someone was sent into the woods to look for specific kinds of leaves, while someone else had to figure out what certain objects were while blindfolded, the older boys screaming in their ears the entire time. The Black Feet filled a small, inflatable pool with cold, dirty water, and we had to bob for apples with our teeth. Nicolino didn't get to enjoy this particular spectacle;

the two Black Feet were still on him full time. "You've broken my back!" he moaned as they shoved their muddy boots deeper into his spine—a loud and futile expression of paranoia. He was still gagging from the disgusting taste of the Beverage, which lingered in his mouth.

They made him drink more Beverage, though he was still gagging from the last portion, and this time he understood that there was no point in keeping anything down: he spit onto his right thumb, wiped it on his t-shirt as best as he could, stuck it in his throat and, as soon as he could feel the acids gurgling in his esophagus, directed his mouth toward Gianki's sock-less sneaker. The fourth-year madman responded with a rageful shriek and started to wave his arms around.

Nicolino stared down at the earth, a few steps away from the pool of his own vomit. He waited for Thoughtful Antelope to be carried away by the wiser Black Feet. He had lost interest in the ceremony and was relieved when one of the counselors, a woman, came over to him and told him to go back to the tent. She escorted the limping victim back to the pile dwelling, her hand on his shoulder. When they were outside, he told her that he was too dirty to go to sleep, and she suggested that he take off his clothes and leave them outside the tent. So he stripped down to his underwear in front of her, right under the pile dwelling. She had large, saggy cheeks that made her look a little like a beaver. "Please," he sobbed, "please come up to the tent." She didn't respond for a while, but he kept begging, kept sobbing, and at last she agreed. He went first, a master of the rope ladder, and when he slid inside his sleeping bag, still in his underwear, he uttered a strange sentence: "I feel so deprived" he said quietly. He found a way to rest his head on her crossed legs, and she began to stroke his hair to calm him down. Then the counselor (unemployed, gourmand, big-bellied, *mantenuta*, twenty-seven years old, soft pink complexion, unmarried) gently suggested that he put some toothpaste in his mouth and lean over the edge of the pile dwelling and spit it out onto the ground.

THERE WAS ONE other time when Nicolino rebelled against the *nonnismo* at camp. We were sitting around in a circle one afternoon, drinking tea and reading the newspapers. He was sitting to my right, facing me, his posture somehow both cherubic and lecherous, his kerchief as dirty as his hair. Gustavo was sitting to my left, his cock visible through his tight jean shorts. The wind was cool, the sky huge and flecked with scattered clouds. At one point, Gustavo put his arm around my shoulder and thought he'd grabbed my hand. He caressed the small, delicate hand distractedly but intensely. It was a firm and friendly gesture at first, but as he went on he dug his thumb deeper and deeper into the palm—a sign, according to the era's code, that he was hungry for sex. I shifted around in my seat to get a pebble out from under my ass, using both hands to shift my weight around, and it was at that point that Tullio realized that it wasn't my hand he was holding but Nicolino's.

The whole thing made Tullio feel loathsome, like a tyrant who'd discovered evidence of the people's disgust in him, and right at that moment he realized that he would have to choose between *nonnismo* and mysticism; there was no middle ground.

Still, he couldn't help but tell Franchino about what had happened. Franco was known by some in the camp as "Gusty's puppy," and the incident with the hand was what provoked the chocolate salami prank he implemented the following day. Unwrapping the gift, Nicolino saw that moist, human thing, its smell overpowering all its other physical qualities, and he felt hopelessly lost. When Tullius got news of the prank later that afternoon, after an all-male jerk-off session in the woods, he didn't protest, but he made sure not to thank Franchino, either.

AFTER THAT, GUSTAVO came to feel a connection with Nicolino. He'd witnessed the Beverage scene from a distance, and during the rest of the night he recused himself from overseeing the trials. One day, after everyone had had their showers, he took one of the warm water jugs out of the pantry and brought it out into the woods without being seen. He left it where another girl and I were supposed to be subjected to a new trial.

At a Black Feet meeting prior to the next ceremony, the group agreed that a girl known as Fat Lorella and I would be sent into the woods half-naked to pick up carrots with our mouths from a plastic poncho laid out on the ground. The counselors rejected the proposal that we do this in front of the younger kids—too provocative—but they'd approved the concept. We would also have to put some green peas in our underwear, mostly because *piselli*, peas, also meant wieners. The field where we were meeting was a thousand meters above sea level, and the nights were cold. There was another element of psychological torture for fatty Lorella, who would have to walk half-naked next to me, the camp's anointed new beauty. And Tullio would be sticking the green peas inside our underwear himself, and he'd be the one to escort us back after the trial.

We arrived at the meeting point in bras and panties, muddy, our hands tied behind our backs. We walked toward the faint light we saw flickering in the woods. Tullio was waiting for us with a camping lantern. He wore a t-shirt with a single rip that revealed his left nipple. He came forward and said, "This stays between us." We'd been instructed to wash ourselves with cold water from a jug only after we'd picked up five carrots each, tied up and clumsy. Tullio showed us a clean rag, wetted it with warm water and proceeded to wipe the mud off our bodies, First Lorella, then me. He delicately stroked us with the rag and washed everything, bra included, except for our panties, which we cleaned ourselves after he untied us. Lorella and I were silent. He didn't tell us to pick up the carrots. "Lori," he said to Lorella, "if you need to go to the woods, go now." She got the message and ran off into the darkness, pretending that she needed to go. Tullio gently pushed me against a tree, made me rest my back against it, then pulled down my underwear a few inches. (My period was almost over. I'd worn dark colored panties and had thrown my sanitary napkin into the bushes outside our squadron's pile dwelling; I was afraid of being made fun of.)

Tullio squeezed me against the tree and slid his long right arm behind me, absorbing the uneven bark into his skin. His arm kept sliding, first into my crack, then out to my butt cheek, which he grabbed with a burst of force. The arm seemed to stretch farther and farther, surprising me with its reach, until his finger rubbed the wet folds of my pussy, peeked in, emerged, then suddenly shifted toward the rim of my asshole and then, even more surprisingly, entered it. I had experienced this before, but only with my own finger. I could tell that he had washed his hands with soap, but I was often constipated and was worried that something would go wrong. I didn't know how deep he wanted to go.

He turned me so I'd face the tree. We were both standing there facing it, and I wanted to fall apart, to crumble into pieces. Then he pulled out his finger, and after a moment I felt his index finger enter my pussy and his thumb enter my anus. I froze.

"Do you see how perfect this feels?"

When his fingers were settled inside me, he seemed to want them to touch each other *through* me. Only a membrane kept the two fingers apart. (We'd discuss that membrane in the years that followed. If only there were no membrane under the perineum, that sweet zone he loved and pressed every time before entering my two holes with his two fingers, "I'd make a ring through it so I could cling to you." When he met my parents and was welcomed into my family, they were smitten, but he urged me to hate them. He highlighted the unfairness of their behavior toward me: the way my mother would physically shove me when we argued, which meant, he said, that she didn't love me. As to my father, he said that while he thought he did love me, he was cowardly because he never distanced himself from my mother's behavior. With his two fingers inside me he'd say, "I'm your real father, so you have to listen to me.")

After shouting a shy "May I?" and receiving an okay, Lorella returned. Gustavo strained some canned green peas through his hand, rinsed them, strained them again, and told us to put them in our panties ourselves. Lorella nodded silently, and I didn't say anything either; I was listening to the night's cool air. What he'd done lingered, as if his thumb were swelling inside me. We walked back to the fire, where everyone thought we'd washed ourselves in cold water. We pretended that our limbs were numb.

After the trials, the six of us were blindfolded and our hands were tied behind our backs. Our feet were tied together, too, so we had to walk perfectly straight, very close to one another. We were still in our bras and our underwear, suddenly exhausted now that we'd finished the trial. A thin strip of ground separated the artificial lake from a small precipice, and we walked in rigid formation, hyperaware of our surroundings. (The next morning we'd be told that our slow, careful walk, illuminated by the fire and the moon, had been a formidable sight.) The goddess Kalì taught us our new names, and each of us was supposed to scream them as we took turns jumping over the fire, which was now only about a meter tall. When they untied me, I felt the green peas jammed inside my panties. I jumped over the fire and shouted "Generous Frog!"

*Y*ou always tell me, Sergino mio (here we're in our early twenties), that respectable long-term relationships between respectable young people like Tullio and me are a dream longed for far more by parents than by their children. These relationships tame us and rob us of life during these dangerous years, and the damage caused by giving in to the wishes of one's peers puts us in a category with the broken, the war veterans, the cultists. You always tell me that you'll never be fooled. You love to preach, just like Tullio does, just like all my men do.

YOU'RE BALDING ALREADY, and you have a beer belly. You hide your nose in my neck. You're wearing a black t-shirt and baggy jeans; you're not photogenic; your complexion is pale; your sweaty forehead, like mine, is shaped like a bomb; your beard is patchy and your head clean shaven; your eyes are little and nondescript; your face is well meaning, bordering on dumb; you have flat nostrils and a clueless little nose that turns out a bit at the end, a perfect way to underline your critical stares, which are really barely critical at all but tender, gentle, cartoonlike.

YOUR COCK TILTS left. It's pale, neither small nor big, and you always keep it clean, like you're washing it throughout the day.

YOU'RE AN INTIMIST *Fascist*. You have a few eccentric friends from university whose reading list tends toward the futurist; you go to mod nights, but you stay off the dance floor. You wear a black bomber jacket, just like the Fascists in your neighborhood do. You say that Rome is a Fascist city and that for anyone to try to build an imaginary non-Fascist city on top of Fascist Rome, for anyone to go—as I do—to Via Tasso every April 25 or to San Giovanni every May 1 is to indulge in ahistorical cultural nonsense. You say we should be *niche everymen*—straightforward, commonsensical people—because otherwise we'll end up bourgeois like Tullius, and it's people like him who are the real *fasci*: "I mean, the only way not to be Fascists is to be Fascists." You play Sonic Youth covers with left-wing rockers who treat your words as the whole truth, as sheer punk Geist.

"I THINK WHAT you had with Tullio was a case of intermittent, low-frequency sexual violence that began with brainwashing."
You call Tullio Bone Machine, Brainwash Machine, The Big Cocker, Satan, The Anticock.

ONE DAY WHEN the school year had just started, my mother and I were on our way to buy textbooks. She was a cold woman. "Pleasure," she explained, "is not frowned upon in our home. You have to learn to know yourself. No one will think it's a tragedy if you lock yourself in your room; they won't panic. In our house the only intolerable things are AIDS and drug addiction. We don't like mothers like mine, mothers who make their children's lives impossible." Thus my mother saved me from the quintessentially Italian fear of parents suddenly opening a bedroom door and discovering the naked bodies of their child and their child's lover. Unlike so many other children of Italian parents, I never had to keep my door open at all times, never had to subject myself to the stuffy smell of the hallway. My mother allowed me countless hours of undisturbed sexual intercourse with Tullio. But my orgasm has disappeared, and it has never returned.

your r sounds French, but whenever you start preaching at me, you end up leaning on your bad-ass Roman accent, which makes your French *r* sound funny, so you conceal it in subtle ways because you don't want to sound too much like the child of aristocrats slumming it with the general population. It's weird: it's just a matter of phonetics, outside your control, but you're ashamed of the sound, and it ends up dulling your speeches, seeping them of power.

"Boy scouts are fucking bourgeois hypocrites. This fucking totem ceremony—it's scandalous but crucial to the whole project. Greasy, conformist Catholic values during the day, right? And abuse and power at night. You don't get it. Same as with the UN and secret societies: officially you support UNICEF, but deep down you long for a superstrict order, for ritual. Man, I hate the bourgeoisie. I fucking hate them. Really, Daria, I raise my arm in Roman salute against the bourgeoisie, and long live Mussolini. Duce Duce Duce!"

"Oh but my scouts, you know, they were Fascists. You would have liked them."

"I'm focused on Tulliooooo. Tullio thinks he's reached a cross-roads in his life. He plays the part of the man with a struggle. He thinks he'll be a saint and stop harassing people, and then what does he do? He inaugurates his holy period with an act that I don't think anyone could call selfless. He thinks he's saving the two of you from scout torture. Ha! But what he really wanted was to fuck you. Tell me, what does any of this have to do with holiness? *I won't abuse people anymore—no, no, never ever—but I'll head into the woods to finger you.* Is that holy behavior? He spins it exactly the way he wants to. Again. First he's sensitive enough to realize that the very idea of your trials, your tortures, is perverse, because the whole thing is designed to shame the other girl, the fat one. Then, he ends up fingering you while the fat girl is forced to watch. Those losers—they roam around the countryside in their dark blue argyle shorts as if there weren't a Tangentopoli, as if the lira hadn't collapsed, as if we still lived in an age when Baden-Powell was fighting and winning his little wars against lesser cultures . . ."

And throughout all this, Sergino makes sure to keep his *rs* hidden between consonants, so that he doesn't sound lame.

"But listen, Sergino, this was all *before* Tangentopoli."

So you yell at me, and then I humor you by going down on you. Then you go home and finish in your bathroom.

I MET YOU in line at the Italian department, two years after breaking up with Tullio. You were coming from Political Science and you needed information about an exam you were going to take in the building. Ten minutes later you were lecturing me—in straight Italian, without a trace of the Roman accent—about the "guilty homogeneity of grunge music—a Baedeker of counterculture for the bourgeois." You were forcing this stranger, me, to listen to the Pixies, Sonic Youth, Dino-saur Jr, Suicide, Battisti, Ivan Graziani, Battiato, Miles Davis, Ornette Coleman, Coltrane. We sat on the dirty steps outside the bar, and I told you that my ex listened to grunge bands. By sundown you knew everything about me: that I was nice, that I was fun, that I couldn't climax. You were already beginning to take my side when I told you that my mother wished I were still dating straight-A Tullio.

Three days later, I got the knees of my overalls wet in the hard grass in the park, behind a pine tree near the pond. It was a bleak, cold day—Rome in November—and after fifteen minutes, you announced you weren't going to climax until the day I did (so delusional). Hands and mouths forever, no climaxes, and God forbid, no coitus.

"SEE, TULLIO DOESN'T think with his cock, only his colonial thirst. I mean, think about the very act by which this bourgeois douche bag attained his holiness: it's a sham, a total quid pro quo, just like invading a country to bring it religion. These nasty feats of charity, they're classic bourgeois moves: they're holy, righteous, no, *self*-righteous ass-wipes. It's freemasonry, it's the boy scouts. Tullio is the Andreotti of the boy scouts, and he's fucking us all in the ass with his big cock."

WE WERE TOGETHER for three months at an age when three months amounted to something: a whole era of tastes and quirks and bus or car routes never tried before and never attempted later.

I try to make you come, but you've developed a technique to avoid it: you breathe deeply, regularly, and after a while I give up because my back aches. You're lying on my bed, in my room, legs protruding, feet touching the ground. Your breathing allows you to absorb any spikes in pleasure that occur when I shift my position or change my rhythm (which was always the excuse Tullio used whenever he came on my face—"Sorry! You caught me off guard"), and you refuse to fly among the weightless clouds preceding climax.

I TAKE YOU to the hall in Piazza Fiume where your band rehearses, then I blow you in my car outside the Villa Ada, on the charming hilly roads that run among the *villini* and in my locked room, especially in my locked room.

MY BELOVED SERGIO, you preach about my engagement to Tullio and my junior role in it. "Come on," I say, "you're exaggerating," and you freak out. "Oh yeah? *I'm* exaggerating? You were brainwashed! He ruined your life!"

"You know you really take gender roles too seriously, as if I were just a woman and nothing else. But don't you see, I'm not a woman; I don't behave like a woman. It's like you think my womanhood alone makes me a victim." I read aloud from Judith Butler's *Gender Trouble*, try to trip you up. "And you're not an alpha male; you're a brainwasher, like Tullius."

"The ugliest thing"—you don't even pretend to listen, you're off on a tangent— "is that you think of him as just this high school sweetheart, but you'll pay for it your entire life. I'm 100 percent positive about this. I know it; I can feel that you don't belong to me, not really."

BUT SERGINO, ALL this scrutiny, all this obsessive analysis make the time we spend together feel thin and fragile. They open up a door to the past, and as a result the present feels dull, unpolished. Tullio lingers like an old recording on a worn-out tape. I try to stay with you, but I'm constantly plunged back into my high school years, into long afternoons and homework. The room is the same, though the posters are different. In Tullio's era it was tidier, a sliver of a room right next to Marzio's, a mirror image. (When we were younger it was one big room for the two of us, but the drywall went up as soon I got my first period.) I'd put the stereo on to mask the sound of sex while my brother strummed his electric guitar with his headphones in. After Tullio dumped me, I painted one entire wall light green, *verde speranza*, his favorite color. The two eras now discolor each other, and the posthumous green wall weaves itself into Tullio's high-pitched moaning: different eras, inseparable.

I KNEEL IN front of you on the carpeted floor. I close my eyes and return to the tidier room with fewer posters, with a different bedspread. After a light meal—arugula, robiola cheese, boiled zucchini, Rosetta bread straight from the oven—he lays me down on my bed and proceeds to massage my butt cheeks, then plays his favorite game: the imaginary ring that circles the perineum. After this, he stops and waits for me to finish my homework, so that he can stick it in my backside.

THE ROOM PULSES and breathes one year in and the other year out. Then it breathes the latter in and the first one out.

WHOLE AFTERNOONS ARE spent locked up in this tropical room, the wash of rain in the fall, sweating in the springtime and sneezing on the bed till we pass out. Then he scolds me: "What do you think you'll accomplish in life if you don't do your homework properly? Do you want your children to have a mediocre mother?"

WE HAVE SEX at my apartment because we can't lock our doors at yours; you're both the children of Italian mothers, Roman mothers. All I see are your tiny children's rooms in that elusive city, a city made up only of parking spots, university bars, two pubs in San Lorenzo, the rehearsal space, car rides and bus rides, a political rally through the city center. And we always end up in my room to have sex. Rome has no history, no future. There are no drastic changes ahead: no new influx of poor immigrants from the south to make the city poor and sad but no onslaught of rich foreigners with coke, either. My father moonlights as a private Latin tutor, my mother does the same at home, after school. In town there are very few of the Romanians and the Chinese you'll become so obsessed with, Sergino, only Africans lining up their trinkets on canvas sheets on the sidewalks, and even then they're only in the center; they haven't reached your neighborhood, where in fifteen years they'll sell acrylic socks, a new merchant every seventy meters. The Calabrians haven't shown up yet—you can't smell them, you don't hate them yet.

YOUR ROOM, WHERE I never blew you, was once your father's office. Your mother is not to be disturbed, but she's a lively, passionate woman who asks me about my life and my interests.

She always wears a skirt and has a classic Roman face, scrappy and round, her nose a straight line between the five circles of forehead, cheekbones, and cheeks. When she's tired, her face tends to sag instead of hardening. It has more dark spots than my mother's, but it feels freer somehow, unsealed.

TULLIUS SHARES A room with his brother. Their house isn't very big, and his father needs one of the rooms as his private office—he's a clerk, but he also builds model cars in his spare time. He glues little doors to convertibles and carefully hangs the wheels on the axles, displaying the results on an ever-expanding series of pedestals.

Tullio treats my room as though it were his. He goes out to the kitchen to make coffee and returns with a tray, and from then on I'm not allowed to do anything until I finish my homework. If I try to touch his pants or anything else, he starts preaching in cold, curt sentences that seem to emanate directly from his nose.

He calls his room the "sperm room" in English. It has a windowless bathroom, a cramped space—an illegal addition. I don't visit him because I want to get my homework done. When I'm there he throws me against a closet built into the wall, spits on his hand and slips it into the back of my panties, plays the ring game, then slips inside me in a state of desperation.

But by the time we start having sex at his place, we're no longer a couple. We keep having sex for years without telling anyone. Why do we lock ourselves away in his room? Frantic booty calls, uncontrollable urges, mournful itches that have to be scratched. By then his mother isn't troubled by whatever it is we are anymore.

My parents allow me to install my own phone number, though I can only receive calls. Which is why my mother is unaware that Tullio is still a part of my life, even though we broke off the engagement she was so fond of. When Tullius calls, I take a bus down Via Tiburtina, get off at Via Morgagni, a half-hour–long trip to spend less than that at his apartment and go back home with wobbly legs and a bottle of water in my hand.

HE DOES IT in silence, suppressing his high-pitched moans as they form. I no longer love the music he chooses, and I'm frustrated enough to order him to change it. But I don't find an adequate replacement on the vertical CD shelf. When we finish, I always pass by the living room, where Tullio's mother watches TV amid the smells of old fabric and meatballs and tomato sauce and coffee and cigarettes. It's an old-fashioned Roman home, cozy and neat, a little group of Chinese statuettes on a round table in the corner, a copy of *Il Tempo*, the right-wing paper, folded over on a small glass coffee table. She sits in her kingdom of certainty and sees me as I walk out staring down at the floor. She guesses, but she doesn't acknowledge me.

WHEN SERGIO LEAVES my room to rush home and unload, my mother sees me close the door and never smiles. When she's done working in the living room she says: "You let your life pass you by without even thinking about it. If you're happy like that . . ."

"But I'm studying for my exams. What else should I be doing?"

"You used to bring people home who had a spark in their eyes."

"By people you mean Tullio."

"If I mean Tullio, I say Tullio."

"If I *meant* Tullio, I *would have said* Tullio."

"No, I can say it that way, too."

"Yes but still, you meant Tullio."

"You're so difficult, Daria, I don't know how you'll ever find a new boyfriend."

"Who told you Sergio wasn't my boyfriend?"

"Or a husband."

"Who told you I want a husband?"

"Leave me alone. A mother isn't allowed to be alone with her disappointment even for a second."

"Disappointment? With what! With what! With what!"

"You keep shouting, and I'll show you the door."

YOU CALL ME on my private line and ask me what my mother said about you. I don't keep anything from you because I love hearing you say that my mother is evil. My father defends her: "Mom had grown fond of Gustavo; you should try not to mind it too much."

"You haven't, though, right?"

"No I haven't, love—there's only you."

YOU AND I discuss corruption scandals or the mafia's links to terrorism. We lie in bed naked and listen to music.

TULLIO WANTS ME to have at least an 8/10 average. We stop working at seven p.m.: he comes inside me, preferably from behind and with no condom. The Greek ideal: "Socrates is the synonym of man." Gustavo never uses Roman slang, doesn't have a Roman accent. Sometimes when he leaves the room I weep; I'm tired, and I try to understand why I don't climax anymore. Tullio stays in the kitchen or the living room to chat with my mom. He leaves before my father gets home.

WHEN I KNEEL in front of Sergio, my memory is a ghost that tingles at the bottom of my numb back. Afterward, Sergio and I hug naked on the bed, a fetid cloud between our mouths.

TULLIO BREAKS UP with me on the sidewalk in front of my apartment building. "We're not equal; there's no parity between us. And I know that you're not someone who could ever bear my children." I stop being a good student overnight. My homework feels like it belongs to him, and I want him gone from my life completely. I score 52/60 on my final exams, the "maturità," though I was expected to get 60/60.

TIME CIRCLES AROUND and travels through both holes, piercing the membrane.

MY MOTHER'S ALWAYS considered me dull compared to Marzio. He's beautiful and cheerful and busy with music and a friend to everyone. With Tullio, she says, I'd finally "found" myself after a "pretty lackluster adolescence," and now I was "lost." "Again."

AFTERNOON AT SERGINO'S grandmother's apartment in the wealthy Parioli neighborhood, for a paper I'm writing about everyday fascism inspired by the French Annales School. Buttery biscuits, tea from old teapots, triumphantly ancient furniture, paintings of weak smiles in heavy frames, hunting scenes, oranges with moldy skin. Grandma and her sister, who Sergino also calls Grandma, regale us with tales of their Fascist youth in houses Il Duce built for wounded soldiers. I brought a recorder and am pumped.

"Here on the piazza you had several houses for the war wounded, two here and two there. The road in the back had the less beautiful houses—let's just say smaller, they were still very nice. The soldiers injured during World War I built a cooperative here: they expropriated land that belonged to the Felicetti, and the Felicetti owned everything here. I believe it was 1,000 lire per square meter—nothing, really. They were all basically tramps; they couldn't afford anything. Here you had the wealthier ones, the ones who bought houses for 3,000 lire, like my father. The poorest of the injured got the smallest houses, which you can see on Via Eleonora Duse. They were nice, though, and well built. And this house—it has strong walls. We clean it thoroughly, of course, but it's never needed major repairs—never."

I record the stories they share, then the two of us move to Piazza delle Muse to eat ice cream: two scoops of vanilla with shots of whipped cream both at the top and buried at the bottom of the cone. We laugh as we listen to the tape—the old ladies' thin voices fill the dusty air.

"We used to walk to Piazza Ungheria, and we'd leave our boots there, at the coal merchant's, and that's where we'd slip on our city shoes.

"Before the war, Dad was a colonel. He liked fighting in wars—see, he also fought the war in Tripoli, right before World War I—but he majored in Italian. After a while, after the war, he left the army and entered Confindustria because he had a degree." We kick the pebbles around with our Doc Martens and create a dust storm. "One of Mussolini's children lived here, Bruno Mussolini, in that house you see over there, the one that's so close to us, and we could all see Il Mussolini very clearly when he came to visit his son. He came twice, no more than that, and we were all Fascists, of course, so we all stretched out the windows as far as we could to see him. Bruno was a jet pilot, and he did some movies, too. But then he died."

And now, on a bench in the piazza, Sergino lets out a single, sudden hiccup and begins to cry.

"What's wrong, Sergino?" I say to him as I hug him. I look for the STOP button, rewind the tape, wrap my arms around his hips. "Let me go," he says, wiggling out of my grasp.

Piazza delle Muse is quiet and dirty, the smell of dog shit a permanent ingredient, an unforgettable memory for the many lovers strolling through the park. A bus line terminates behind our backs, and the buses seem to shiver with great volume as they reach their final stop. The noise is something like *haah*, the sound of a soldier dying.

"Bruno Mussolini," the recording continued, "had married a high-school friend of my sister's, so we went and visited them. She'd invited us over, this lady, and we were in the gift room—she'd just married Bruno—and the room, well, it was a bit smaller than the room we're in right now, but it had all these gifts spread out across the floor, gifts from all over the country, Italy's gifts to Mussolini's son."

He switches the Walkman off. "Viva il Duce!" he says in a high voice. In response he gets two laughs from a far corner of the piazza and an "Oh my" from an old woman sitting right behind us. Nannies and babysitters stare at him. He switches the tape back on and lets out a melancholy sound through his teeth: "Duce, Duce, Duce."

"Plenty of silver plates, a waterfall of plates—that's what I recall: a lot of things. I wasn't a kid anymore. I was fifteen, sixteen. Mussolini's wife must have been twenty-two, twenty-three, my sister's age. They'd been in school together, in the same class with the same teacher. When we visited, Il Mussolini wasn't there. We'd seen him from our windows: we leaned too far out the window and saw him going down the stairs. The building had this little armor-plated door that gave out onto the stoop. He came out in civilian clothes, wearing that crooked hat he often wore, and his car was there. We saw him get in. We saw him once, I'm sure. I remember him well, but I think he came a second time to visit his son, yes, the son who died. He died in a plane crash in Africa, his son. And then the daughter-in-law moved out."

Sergio lowers the volume without switching off the tape. "What a life," he says. "These were the Fascists—these good people were the Fascists, and little shits like my father had the guts to renounce them. What a jerk. Think of the shitty life my father leads now. And you, you're shit, too. You've renounced me. And I loved you. I loved you with my entire being."

My voice was as sweet as sugar: "But you're not a Fascist, Sergino."

"I am a Fascist. I hate the bourgeoisie and its vices. And you're my Badoglio; you've betrayed me. Now that I've gotten to know you I'm even more of a Fascist."

"Sergino, I hate the bourgeoisie and its vices, too."

"No, you love the bourgeoisie."

"Come on, Sergino, calm down. It's not true. I don't love the bourgeoisie."

"You do love the bourgeoisie. Daria, you're ruining your life, and you'll have to pay for it. You call yourself a communist, but your cult is the bourgeoisie. You pray to the bourgeois god, you kneel down and worship the gigantic cock of the bourgeoisie." He glides a hand over his face: "You won't ever know real love, and you'll remain a slave, because you love being a slave. You'll never live free. You'll be a slave, a slave to the bourgeoisie."

I stand up. I smash my foot down on the pebbles. "All right, Sergio. Ciao."

As I left the park, I understood that he had found out I was fucking Gustavo Tullio again. Sergino stayed on the bench and yelled, "You deserve the center left!" as I walked away.

I leave but I don't go anywhere. I just sit in my car on Via Eleonora Duse. I try to force myself to cry, but the only thing I feel is a thick Plexiglas casting congealing around me. It becomes a transparent shrine where I'm on display, where my own thoughts try but cannot grasp me, they cannot know me.

I THREW THE tape out the driver's side window.

BACK HOME, MY mother was sitting at the writing desk in the living room, as if on a throne. "You know," she said when she saw me, "there aren't many mothers lucky enough to have daughters who make faces like the one you're making now when they come home."

AN AFTERNOON ONE week earlier: Sergio walks toward Via Morgagni, where Tullio lives.

This must be Sergio's head. To see it I have to push myself through the thin membrane that keeps his conscience in that moment in space and time separate from me.

His Doc Martens are worn down on the sides and at his toes. He walks toward Tullio's apartment building, and he has bad news for me. He's just spoken to his mother, who needs chemotherapy.

If he can spot me from the sidewalk, if he can see me coming down the stairs through the glass door, it'll mean that I'm still seeing Tullio, and he won't break the news to me. If he doesn't spot me, he'll go back home, and he'll call me to tell me what his mother just told him. Which means that he's only in Via Morgagni to not give me the piece of news.

AN HOUR EARLIER, Sergio's mother: I see her preparing an afternoon snack, bread and butter and anchovies. I hear her start to say something and stop. She opens her mouth again, her eyebrows the shape of a pagoda roof.

SERGIO CAN SENSE when something is happening behind his back, when it's not just his imagination. Years earlier, he realized that his father had a daughter he never talked about. His mother had scolded him: "Don't be dumb," she said persuasively. But a few months later his father confessed: it was true. Sergino's paranoia and the fabric of the cosmos were in perfect harmony. The right hemisphere gathers all the necessary information, which it transmits to the conscience through misplaced thoughts, through insights that seem weird and absurd until they turn out to be true.

THEN HE CALLED both my home numbers to give me the catastrophic news. I didn't pick up the phone, then my mother told him I wasn't home: did she know I was at Tullio's? Did she somewhat enjoy hearing Sergino's disappointment? Anyway, he decided that my absence at that time meant I *had* to be at Tullio's.

I DON'T WANT to see the moment when Sergino spots me from his hiding place behind a car, walking out of Tullio's apartment building.

I SLIP THROUGH the membrane of words that carries me backward and end up inside Sergio's eyes. He's about to see me come down the stairs, ashamed, my ass broken in half. You can see the stairs from outside the glass door, from the sidewalk. I shouldn't have told him so much about what went on inside Gustavo Tullio's home when we had been a couple: for now Sergino could picture what must have just happened in torturous detail.

A LATE AFTERNOON in my youth: I emerge from that glass door onto the street, and I don't want to find out that Sergino is hiding behind a car and keeping an eye on me.

DRIPPING DROPS OF Tullio between my legs while being watched from behind a car. Please take me out of here.

A BALDER VERSION of Sergino parks the scooter his friend has lent him by the building where he lived with his mother until her death. It's what, fifteen years later? It's after he met La Sposina at a party in New York; it's in Rome. He gets off, hooks the helmet under the seat, and ends up sitting where he has often sat, on the marble base of the iron fence. The apartment building is yellow and bulky, healthy like a beloved son. Il Duce built it and his brother's for the middle class. Now the neighborhood teems with Calabresi, the bourgeoisie from Crotone who have come all the way to Rome for a degree in law or Italian. He picks up his phone, tweets *Roma ti amo ma mi butti giù* as he listens to LCD Soundsystem's sad song. Tears fill his eyes, and as he scrolls through his friends' posts he hears his mother's voice: "Are you a weepy pea, my love? Then weep." He's shaken, broken, and after he swallows the feeling he takes a stroll among the crippled ladies with their mall store shopping bags, the girls in their unhip jackets. The streets form a pentagon around the piazza Bologna and its elegant, rationalist post office. The springtime air is warm; the cars are double-parked; the slightest conflict provokes a salvo of horns. He wishes he could postpone his meeting with his father indefinitely, because even though Piazza Bologna is a source of discomfort, he'd gladly stay here and remember. Then Zio Gino appears to him outside the bar.

How can it be him? How can he still be there, in his usual pose, sitting in his idling car with his usual look of concentration? Zio Gino (not his uncle): a shabby, pudgy old man who continues to park his faded little car in front of the repair shop or in the handicapped parking spot just off to the right. He always appears early in the morning and opens the gate before anyone else is around, which leaves him sweaty and panting. (Sergio saw him do this a couple of times when he was rushing for an early train to Milan or heading back after a long night that didn't end until dawn.) He spends the rest of his day either at the bar or sitting in his car without saying a word to anyone. And here he is, across the street. Sergino can see the back of his head. The man is proof that the neighborhood is in the hands of the 'Ndrangheta. Sergio never says hello, and since he sold the apartment he has stopped coming to the bar where he used to drink uneven cappuccinos, the ever-changing levels of frothiness wholly dependent on who happened to be at the bar. Sergino's apartment faced a smaller street that intersects this hermetic boulevard. He's at his old corner now, hiding without putting in any effort, and he can see the *alimentari* shop, which used to change owners every two or three years. One time, on his way out of the store, the owner told him he was leaving, going back home to Calabria.

"So what are you going to do for work back home?"

"Oh, I don't know. They'll fix me up." That *they* still haunts him.

There isn't an obvious connection between the death of Sergio's mother and the continued influence of the *malavita*, the mob, though as a loyal reader of Roberto Saviano's books and articles, he finds it natural to link his emotional life to the drama and the tragedy of the tentacular hold the mafiosi have on Italy. He gave his friends and acquaintances several different reasons for his selling his apartment but never more than one at a time. The explanations all depended on his mood, but none of them was the truth: that his mother had died there.

He wanted a neighborhood—and a city—where he wouldn't feel embarrassed whenever he took a man home, which he had started doing more and more when he was left alone.

Or the apartment was stifling hot in the summer and freezing in the winter. It was built in 1941 and lacked any kind of sound-proofing. His great-grandmother Plinia, the widow of a railroad man, had lived there for years. She saved money on phone bills and received few visitors—a Fascist, aural panopticon.

Or when Sergino already had a job in Milan, a tenant of his once showed him some dead larvae he'd found on a high shelf in the kitchen. There it was, among the sawdust and the canned food, a whole society of white larvae in fetal position: deformed creatures, born dead, imagined into life out of nothingness and soon sent back into the void from which they'd come.

Or everyone in the neighborhood was depressed. One morning, he nearly ran over a thirty-year-old man in a tracksuit who was crossing the street looking the other way. Sergino managed to stop the scooter just in time. He stood in the middle of the solitary street and demanded an explanation. "Hey, no problem, man," said the young man. "I'm sorry." Then he left. The way Sergino put it to his American friends, in French or English, during their cocaine- or Five Hour Energy- or cosmopolitan-fueled conversations was that "For Romans, it's like it isn't even worth putting on clothes anymore." The guy had almost died right there, in his tracksuit, and to Sergio his fatalistic attitude seemed like a terrible disease.

Or the traffic, which was as valid a reason as any other to leave Rome altogether. This afternoon he was riding his scooter through the area under the railroad bridges and the overpasses, between Via Prenestina and Via Tiburtina. And—this still bothers him—right in front of the big French mall, an SUV driver cut him off without signaling his left turn. A Chinese guy in a suit. At the intersection with Via Tiburtina, Sergio tweeted, "Kick the Italians out of China" and also "I'm lucky I've stopped arguing with people at traffic lights like I used to, otherwise this Chinese mafioso would have done me in." And then, "Money is my only consolation."

He ended up selling the apartment to a Calabrese family who bought it for their children, who were in Rome for school. He left his job at Universal in Milan and moved to New York for an unpaid internship at a literary agency. (Berengo had made the introduction.) He was traveling at his mother's expense, investing his inheritance into his plan to change professions. He became a literary scout—a consultant to publishers in Brazil, Ukraine, Indonesia . . . He advised them on which books to acquire: pop psychology, cookbooks, literary novels, vampire novels. Fourteen parallel salaries ranging from $200 to $1,400 a month, which he spent on first-class airfare and $3,000-a-month rent for the

East River apartment he split with an older friend who was never home.

He used part of the inheritance on the down payment on a house in Pigneto, which he rented out to a gay couple. On the way over, as he rode from his old neighborhood to his father's, he felt anguish at the thought that his father might tell him that the house in Pigneto was gradually losing value. Sergino is staying nearby, with a girlfriend who lets him use her scooter and her car. She lives in a cozy two-story house that faces a communal courtyard. It's an enchanted kingdom, and he's happy to be staying there, though his Americanized eye sees that she's paid too much for it. Then again, there are all the pedestrians on the street to contend with, and the house keeps its distance from them with two gates and a short driveway in between. At dawn the gutter punks piss onto the outer gate before they retreat into the daylight: the rich ones, who will eventually return home to their families; and the poor ones, who will die young because they didn't have money for their dental hygiene, forgot to file their hardening skin.

There's a pedestrian street in the neighborhood: a small *rambla* for readers of Artaud and Jodorowsky, trust fund cheapskates who refuse to give any change to the mime who panhandles by the sidewalk tables. "Bro," they tell him, "I'm worse off than you are." The gentrification of Pigneto was never completed, even after years of real estate speculation that pushed out the local stores and replaced them with bars. There are a few fancy restaurants in the area, with the occasional actor or politician or cluster of drug dealers stationed in front, the second-rate aperitivo bars with prix-fixe menus dispersed nearby. Sergio's girlfriend's house is depreciating, and his father might tell him that the ninety square meters he bought from a taxi driver are, too.

The thought distracted him earlier this morning as he tried

to read book proposals slipped to him by literary agents and publishers. The *inspiring memoir* of a vegan marathon runner who ran the Gold Rush trails of the Sierra Nevada. From "his Midwestern childhood hunting and fishing to his gradual immersion in the worlds of *ultrarunning* and veganism . . ." The advance a big American publisher had offered felt more ridiculous than usual. Time had passed unsteadily as he waited for his meeting with his dad. *Confessions of a Guidette* by Nicole "Snooki" Polizzi from *Jersey Shore*: "Can she help it if she was born to love fake tans and juiceheads?" During a break from reading he went to the bathroom and found some bright crimson blood on the toilet paper: his hemorrhoids flare up every time he comes back to Italy. Blood settled in the grooves of his middle fingertip. Sergio comes to Italy once a year: he went to London in the middle of April and came to Rome for two weeks. After Rome, Turin, and Milan. His immune system is so weakened that a mosquito bite on his elbow filled with pus just from resting his arm on the armrest on the train. There's also the Sichuan food he ate in London and the stress of having to see his father. Bruno collects rent on his son's behalf, pays his son's mortgage, checks on his son's investments. Sergio didn't have to choose him as his accountant and he knows it.

He rides from piazza Bologna to Quartiere Tiburtino. The sun begins to set over the off-ramps that lure traffic off the Tangenziale Freeway, over the sleepy, dusty construction site that will one day reveal a more refined, more perfect Tiburtina Station. Quartiere Tiburtino sits just south of the station, beyond the bridge over the Tiburtina railroad. In low light, the massive bridge is blinding and disorienting. Sergino thinks about his father's abasement. His divorce has declassed Bruno, and he has no choice but to live near the station on the wrong side of the tracks. The roadway is a threshold, a drawbridge that shuts down at night, leaving Bruno out in the cold. Sergio's grandma is alive and healthy, so her Communist son can't move to Parioli and take over her villa. Grandma can't move and she barely speaks, but she pays the Filipino couple who take care of her a good wage, and she never sends her son any money. A few weeks ago she was diagnosed with ischemia, but after three days at the Quisisana clinic, she had the couple bring her home.

The two men meet in their usual spot, a bar with pounding artificial light and mirrors on every surface. Bruno's hand is clammy and slick, like a raw fish. They gulp down two Fernets each.

"So, *bello*," Bruno says. "How's New York treating you?" He's wearing linen in May, a rumpled suit the color of dirty doves, no tie. He's bald but doesn't shave his head, and there are sad white wisps of hair on his neck. He has the air of a man who still talks to women with great passion.

Sergio is unaware of his own affectations when the two of them are together. "Well, Bru"—this is what he calls him—"I'm thirty-eight and I'm still not bankrupt, so I can actually afford to party and fly first class."

"You're just like Grandma. She loves parties."

"You do, too; you just can't hold your liquor like we can. Grandma and I, we know what we're doing."

"Better that than being a happy man with a sad son and a sad mother."

"I really hope you mean that. Otherwise it's just depressing."

Sergio studies himself in the mirror. His father is breathing long yoga breaths. Sergio tells him he's stressed out: first London, then Milan, now Rome. "These trips really fuck up my immune system."

"You're drinking Fernet, though."

"That's the great Italian tradition. You don't mess with that."

"All right, but just two for me, at least before dinner. Let's go upstairs," he says even though his office is on the ground floor. He and his second family have always lived in this building on the fourth floor. His two daughters, undergrads who live with their parents, live just two ceilings from where Sergio and his father are now sitting facing each other. Sergio has met them fewer than ten times in his life.

I can't understand why I'm seeing this, this encounter between father and son. It appears that I'm experiencing it just from Sergio's point of view. I read his tweets through his eyes: *"Small-time fathers"* and "The only justice is money" and "You bet you'd love to be wealthier than your father if you had my father."

In the meantime, his father is pulling his son's papers out of a binder and arranging them on his desk. He uses a bulky gray PC to pull up spreadsheets for the last six months' worth of transactions. He speaks lightly but briskly, like someone who's trying to hurry things along. But I can't understand whether this is what's actually happening, or whether it's just what Sergio's seeing. Bruno manages his son's Italian investments (Sergio doesn't trust American banks; he pays taxes there, but he won't invest) and the interest rate on his home mortgage. Sergio usually loves to hate on Bruno's generic homilies about the recession, but he's annoyed by their implication now: "You knew it when you sold the apartment—you knew where the market was going."

"Listen, Bru, all anyone talks about in New York is money. I don't want that kind of vulgarity here." I realize how difficult it is for my dear Sergino to know that what he felt just moments earlier as he was riding over the bridge has to be suppressed and suffocated. Here, in front of his father, he has to stick to his pose—the pose he has no choice but to deploy anytime he doesn't feel free enough to be himself.

"Sure, but I'm your accountant, so we have to talk money."

A tweet: *"I expected less vulgarity from Rome."*

"But the real losses are over . . . And I'd say that Mommy's money"—which is how he's always talked about the €700,000 Sergio got for the apartment and the €50,000 thousand he inherited, so he could imagine that his mother loved him even from the great beyond—"is still relatively safe."

Tweet: "It's great to have more money than your father, yes it is."

Sergio checks the cuff of his pants, smooths it out, folds it over again. His father leans forward in his chair, his forehead the most visible part of him, his flimsy reading glasses lit up by the hot glow of the lamp.

"Listen, Bru, I have to ask . . . You haven't been forging the double signature, have you? Maybe snatching a few bucks here and there? If you're in trouble I can understand, but I hope you're not doing it behind my back."

I'm inside Sergino, I have to be, or else I'd know how his father is reacting. Sergio has no idea, and I'm not getting anything from Bruno, which can't be right. Sergio flaunting his earnings over the last fiscal year. He's asking how high the *tassa sulla casa* has climbed. He's bragging about how much money he's bringing in under the table by subletting a room in Williamsburg to some Italian acquaintances.

Sergio begins to notice his father's state only when Bruno starts one of his yoga breathing exercises again. He places a finger on his right nostril and breathes in through the left, then puts his finger on the left nostril, breaths in through the right, and starts over. His son is offended and changes the subject. "I'm flying back on the BA001."

"What?" says Bruno, a finger still on one nostril.

"BA001. BA's special New York flight."

His father seems unimpressed, but he finally removes his finger from his nose and places it on the desk. Now he's hunched over the little gray mouse he uses to slowly click through the spreadsheets.

"BA. British Airways, zio, the airline."

His father is silent. He hunches forward even farther, as if he were trying to pick something up from the floor. He pushes his office chair backward, rests his forehead on his knees, disappears below the desk.

"No, listen," his son says, increasingly animated. "We fly out of London City Airport, in Canary Wharf, the financial center—the Manhattan of London. The airport is really small—it only has one runway. It's a small plane: it used to have like a hundred seats, but it's been remodeled, so it only has thirty, and they all fold down into beds. The whole plane is business class, so you leave from this tiny-ass airport, this ridiculous strip of land right on the water, and you have to stop in Shannon, this airport in Ireland, where you can clear U.S. customs because of this agreement they have with the U.S. government."

His father hasn't lifted his head or his back. He's continuing with his antipanic breathing technique.

"The flight from London to Shannon is supershort. You get an *aperitivo* in-flight, and then you're basically there. You get off the plane and clear customs in less than twenty minutes in this, like, shit hole of an airport while they fill the tank. You get back on board and do Shannon–JFK, and they give you the entire package: you get wined, dined, champagned, napped, iPadded, blanketed. You're barefoot, totally comfortable, lying down, and then you walk off the plane and go straight to a cab because you already cleared customs."

And here's Bruno. He finishes his yoga exercises and resurfaces with red cheeks, his hands pressed against the mahogany desk. He speaks in a way that's utterly his: "If I may speak my mind . . ."

"Please do."

"I think the real luxury on a trip to America is a nonstop flight."

The pores of Sergio's bald head start prickling at the same time. "Oh, *Madonna*! You're so fucking provincial! Nonstop? Yeah, sure, and then you have to stand in line for an hour at passport control. You spend as much time there as you would on a fucking *domestic flight*. Instead I get this leisurely hour in Shannon among other people who are also into traveling well and have three grand to spend. And then I'm on this little plane, the least-populated little plane on earth, watching Jason Bourne on an iPad. The real luxury is a nonstop flight? *Tiburtina State of Mind, man.*"

His father resumes his yoga position under the desk as his son pontificates. "How can you even think that a nonstop flight is luxury? All that means is that you never listen. Never."

Bruno reemerges and begins putting his son's papers in order as the young man gets up, says "ciao," turns, and leaves. His father calls after him, tries to stop him: "Sergio!" But he has to know that at this point in the relationship, one goodbye is as good as any other.

Sergio crosses the road, goes back to the bar, his legs weak. He fires off a couple of tweets complaining about his father. He looks at himself in the mirror under the bottles of amara, orders a negroni. While he examines the shiny yellow color of his own forehead, of his bloodless cheeks, he gets the idea to convince Marzio, my brother, to fuck Tullio's wife.

Maria Tullio, Marzio, and I all went to the same high school, and she was there around the same time as us. In those years, Marzio was considered the most beautiful boy in our high school. He had a gorgeous nose, straight and long like Louis Garrel's, and like Garrel he had hair that was messy and curly, though paler. He always wore a jacket in the nouvelle vague style.

Like me, he got a down payment on a two-room, seven-hundred-square-foot apartment as a gift from our parents, but he can't make the monthly €700 he owes on the mortgage. So he rents the place out to three female friends of his, students, who pay €800 a month and lives with my parents. He sleeps there, or with whoever will take him home. He's lost jobs in music shops and small publishing houses, and now he works as a waiter at Bar Necci in Pigneto. He's still beautiful, according to Sergio, who every so often consoles himself with the thought of Marzio trading blow jobs for a set at the Circolo degli Artisti nightclub. Marzio only plays in little San Lorenzo pubs that barely register on Rome's indie scene, and if he's kept up a friendship with Sergio, it's certainly not because he likes him: Sergio is friends with Gassa and worked for him as a road manager, and he told my brother that there was a chance that Gassa might sample one of his songs.

And then there he is in the bar with Sergio, as if summoned, in a black linen jacket, a white shirt tucked into tight black pants. He has the crooked posture of a seasoned Bob Dylan/Rino Gaetano impersonator, a grizzled *Jewfro*, a sweet little double chin that gives him an air of innocence, and a minuscule belly under a faint smile. He retains the gestures of the boy who conquered the school by singing quirky love songs in the age of rage rock, and who's continued to seduce new generations of students.

"What are you drinking, honey?" Sergio says. "I have an idea that's so dumb that I need you to be super *wasted* before you hear it."

"What are you having?"

"Negroni."

"Negroni, then. I'm broke."

"On me, bro."

"All right, bring it on."

"Would you be willing to bang a high school classmate of ours? Someone who's desperate for cock and doesn't even know it yet?"

"Well that depends! What are her tits like? Does she have kids?"

"Tons. So just imagine how much she'd love to fuck a handsome, carefree man like yourself?"

Sergio is asking Cugino Hitler for Maria's mobile number via Whatsapp. He gets an answer and a bit of extra information: "Gossip. Ludovica (the Berengo hand job) is babysitting at Tullio's."

"That's lame."

THREE DAYS LATER, Sergio picks up Maria and takes her to a bar in San Lorenzo where Marzio's playing a set. She looks older, but she still dresses like a tomboy: Air Max and a hoodie over her old, round hairdo. He kisses her and tweets "the unbangables."

"It's crazy, I was just thinking about how much I want to go out, and then you called me—it's like ESP!"

Sergio keeps tweeting: *"Random," "matchmaking," "Fixing up dates for money."* This is the same Sergio who only three days ago was weeping in his old neighborhood. If I'd known that his father was having such a bad effect on him, I would have told him to find himself a new accountant; he's been unbearable since he crossed the Tiburtino Bridge.

"This is so fun, Marzietto! I haven't seen you in, what, ten years?"

"Make it twenty."

"Twenty!"

The rest of the evening is live-tweeted in two languages.

"Hope I don't crash my car in #pratifiscali"

"In shock after visit to #pratifiscali. Still lame after all these years. Rome, grow up"

"Back to zone decenti. Talking to milf. Will the milf fuck the singer?"

"Your #pratifiscali pussy has delivered five children. Will singer's cock be big enough?"

"Back to San Lorenzo with old schoolmate turned milf for big concert by big Marzione. Emotions"

"San Lorenzo bar, always a sad state. I arranged mikes and speakers there for years and it's still the same shit"

"You were a great cocksucker, milf. What's the story *with Christianity? Do you still EAT COCK?"*

"You still rock the Air Max and the Public Enemy sweater. Your pussy is all used up"

"You say, justifiably. Okay, he's cute, what does he do for a living? He does nothing, love. And I like men"

"Milf, I just told you there's this rapper whose career I once managed—you're impressed—wanna come to his show. Milf's in heat."

"Milf, your pick: either Marzione or the rapper. Both? Naughty girl!" (Cugino Hitler's reply: *"They're all bitches"*)

"Don't shoot the Marzione"

"Leaving Milf to singer. Not much hope in a happy ending. Singer kinda outta steam."

Sergino left the bar halfway through Marzio's act when he realized that his prank didn't make any sense. He told Maria he was going to go have a cigarette.

In the next twenty-four hours, messages go back and forth in preparation for the second prank. Sergio texts Gassa to say he'll bring him this wild-ass milf he can bang. Meanwhile he calls the milf on the phone and apologizes for stranding her there the night before, leaving her to hitch a ride from Marzio. She felt embarrassed, she says, but he resolves all the bad feelings and misunderstandings by renewing his invitation to take her backstage to meet the rapper.

So Sergio and Maria go out together again. They go backstage as soon as Gassa's show is over. Betani, the "Negro Hipster," lets them inside, and they get cozy with the others in the little room, a three-couched, smoky closet.

Sergio is dozing off, doesn't feel like partying. Maria is talking to the rapper and his dreadlocked Sicilian hype man, who insists that all Neapolitan girls are game.

At one point somebody starts trying to get backstage, begging on the other side of the door behind two girls with straight black hair. "Marzietto, listen, I'm sorry man; I can't let you in." Betani has known my brother for years. "Come on, *zio*, we're working."

Sergio is struck by this, by the fact that it's Betani who closes the door—Betani, the decent, funny, depressed, African-Italian former web series actor-turned-roadie. So he walks out and goes to look for my Marzio in the garden. Kids smoke pot under the trees and stand in line for pizza. Marzio sees him and looks at him with mournful eyes. "Why didn't you call me tonight? I could have met Gassa. Is my sample still happening?"

"Well, first of all, it's Gassa's the one who calls the shots, not me." Now he's defensive. He tweets: *"A long line of beggars backstage after show."*

Marzio tries to cover the screen of Sergio's phone with his hand. "Hey, I'm talking to you."

Sergio pushes my brother's hand away and keeps staring at the screen.

198

"Why did you leave me with the *bocchinara* yesterday?"

"Did she blow you?"

"You wish. She took it badly when you left: hailed a cab and left on her own."

"That's awkward. Damn. She didn't tell me."

"She said you were going to take her to see Gassa. That's what she told me."

"So you two did get along. Did you have a chance to bang her? Was there even a remote possibility, at all?"

"No."

"But she left her husband at home with the kids for two nights in a row. It has to mean something."

"Sure. But to bang somebody, that's a whole different story."

"Fair enough."

"You make me feel like shit."

Facebook status: "Never trust me ever."

"Stop writing on that fucking thing, man. Don't I look miserable?"

"Yes, Marzio, yes."

They're interrupted by a sophisticated-looking kid in a buttoned-up army jacket on his way to drunk: "Hey, everything all right over here?"

Marzio: "We're talking."

But Sergio takes the cue. "My bad, champ. We were arguing."

"Then you should apologize." The kid wraps himself around Sergio, hugs him from the side, like a girlfriend. Marzio lets out a sigh and pulls a pack of cigarettes out of his pocket. Puts one in his mouth and rolls it back and forth with his lips.

Marzio pulls the cigarette out of his mouth without lighting it. "Sergio," he begs, "Come on, man . . ."

"Let's talk on email, OK?"

Sergio leaves with the boy still attached to him. They end up by a trellis in a corner of the garden, a vine enveloping them on all sides. "Do you need to go figure things out with that guy?" the boy asks. "Is he a writer? A musician?"

"I'm sorry, do you know me?"

"I do." The words send shivers of pleasure down Sergio's spine. The two-bit pranks he organized to make the bad feelings from Via Tiburtina go away have brought him this: a good-looking boy who knows who he is and is trying to hit on him.

"I'm a detective," the boy says.

"Oh, yeah?" Sergio laughs. "What, Instagram got too boring? You got sick of taking pictures of food at restaurants? Now it's detectives?"

"It's detectives."

The boy with the pink, poorly shaved lips is interning for an agency that tails the lovers of jealous, wealthy men. He also does background research on reality TV characters, helping writers anticipate whether an unbalanced lover or a criminal relative will pop up in a given season. It's an unusual job for this grad-school boy, but for this generation, Sergio thinks, fame and eccentricity are everything.

"So how do you dress when you're out spying on people?"

"Like this. Normal. If I'm trying to figure out where a lady's off to every day, if she has a lover other than our client, I have to spend a few days in a row standing in front of her building starting at like eight a.m. So then I have to dress differently every day."

"You like getting dressed and getting undressed."

"I do."

"Good fun. Good fun."

"You don't come back from New York very often."

"You know how much I like this thing where you know me and I have no idea who you are?"

"I wish I could go without telling you my name, but then how could you write to me when you fall in love with my manuscript?"

"I don't mean to sound old"—what an *anglismo*! The words sound stupid in Italian, but the sentence makes perfect sense translated into English—"but I find your generation endearingly shameless."

The boy replies, *"I guess,"* which gives Sergio a hard-on. He ditches Maria for the second night in a row and goes off to tail Marzio with the detective. At a traffic light near the bus depot he writes, "Btwn hipsters and the unemployed I always choose hipsters." He checks Marzio's wall and sees that he's unfriended him.

"Does he have a smartphone?"

"No. He's broke."

"Then he's back home?"

"And that's where we're headed." Sergio drives all the way to Via Tiburtina to avoid giving him the impression that what he really wants is to park the car immediately in leafy, hidden Via di Pietralata.

They park in a nearby street, reach Marzio's building, and crouch behind a car in a spot that's not visible from Marzio's window.

You know the apartment well, Sergino. It's where you used to stay in my room for hours and hours, forever. And now, in the future, a wealthier and more diverse future, you're leaning on a car door, smoking a joint with a boy detective. After a while they spot Marzio, who has come downstairs to smoke a cigarette by the entrance to the building. Sergio's knees hurt, he's fidgeting, he's puffing smoke, his eyes are watering, he's happy. He reads a text from Gassa: "So you leave me with the load and leave? I'm not banging her; she's old." He's not going to reply. Nothing and no one can distract him from his detective. He's placed his forehead on the boy's shoulder in order to better read his phone. The detective observes Marzio's movements through the car's windows. "He's out to buy cigarettes," he whispers. Five minutes later: "He's smoking another cigarette downstairs. Poor guy."

When Marzio goes back up to his parents' apartment, they stay crouched near the ground and slowly begin to laugh. "I shouldn't be smoking on duty."

"You're not on duty. Can I touch you?"

They're facing each other, on their knees, touching each other's foreheads.

"No, come on."

"Can I kiss you?"

"I wish."

The little darling, so easy and light, keeps his balance by holding his open palms pressed against the door of the car. He pulls his forehead away from Sergio's and gifts him a kiss.

THE UNEASE HIS meeting with his father gave him follows him to Milan, where he's watching a piece of video art projected onto an enormous cloth. I slide from membrane to membrane, from the two-man stakeout in front of my parents' building to the final day of Sergio's Italian tour. He sits against the wall in a gallery-studio run by photographers from Maurizio Cattelan's crew. The spare, empty room oozes with street cred, an environment so brilliantly modest that in its past life it had to have been a mom-and-pop store. Art-clique girls in glasses and all-black outfits crouch down under the half-closed gate when they enter and throw their arms around everyone they recognize. There's a dim glow from a single blue lightbulb hanging from the ceiling, and a keyboard player from one of the biggest, hippest pop acts in the city is playing music on a laptop he rests on a coffee table. He slouches in his chair, his posture a sign of either endless leisure or endless work. Big pictures printed on king-size sheets hang from the walls. If it weren't for the video he's following distractedly, it'd be a night of joints and networking. There's this fashion victim talking to him, one of those straight guys who enjoys flirting with gays, who's telling him about a Tumblr called *Balenciaga Did It First*. But he keeps coming back to the video in the next room, which he can see from where he's sitting if he looks over the straight guy's shoulder out through the open door. The video fills him up again with that old competitive desire for compensation, as if the kiss from the detective never even happened. It's such an instant feeling that it's not until hours later that he registers why the vision of a yellow electric guitar, the Steve Vai Ibañez, had the impact that it did. Until the guitar appears, the video chronicles the 1985 Heysel Stadium disaster, when thirty-nine Juventus fans were crushed to death after the stands collapsed an hour before the European Cup Final kickoff. Three hours later I find Sergino lying on the couch in the living room of his Milanese host, Tim Small. It's here that he finally recalls why the yellow Ibañez, the grotesque instrument made famous by a grotesque virtuoso, drove him to drink four vodka lemons, and now that the buzz is subsiding, he can't bring himself to sleep. His cab to Malpensa will be here in just a few hours. Milan to London, then the BA001 flight.

If you put aside the ashtray smell, Tim's living room provides a number of anti- or pro-insomnia remedies: box sets of TV shows piled up under the flat screen, movies, a number of American literary magazines, and a PlayStation 3. Sergio lies on his back, his eyes fixed on the ceiling, and he feels that awful drive to just do something, fast, to quell the sense of injustice the vision of the yellow Ibanez has unleashed. It's the same kind of feeling that nearly strangled him back at his father's office.

The story of the owner of the Ibañez—a fellow scholar of philosophy—is one of Sergino's favorite Roman anecdotes. I've heard him tell it many times, and at this very moment I can see him at a party at the *n+1* office, in Dumbo, where he's recounting it to Sheila Heti and Marco Roth. He's stoned and adorable, the gesticulating Italian brought in to spice up intellectual parties; *"Rome is a city of parasites, you see? Miserable people."*

The man was his age, late twenties, a volunteer assistant to the department's graduate student coordinator. It was rumored that the two men were having an affair. The coordinator was a tall, attractive, unlikable middle-aged man. They looked a lot alike: they were both gym buffs and wore black turtlenecks, their aesthetic a combination of the handsome, brooding existentialist and the virile Roman hick. The PhD students complained about the professor's elusiveness and his arbitrariness, and their antipathy was transferred to the duo, or couple, an attitude that had a classist hue. A man who played Dream Theater covers with his band didn't deserve a position in a philosophy department. This was how Sergino felt. The young man had received a grant, whereas he, Sergino, hadn't. He'd had to do his work with no funding.

The privileges awarded to the program coordinator's pupil were of the impalpable sort typical of the informal feudalism that reigns in so many Italian institutions.

For example: the day of their thesis defense, the grad students had to sit and wait outside the faculty room in the late July heat, except for the favored pupil, who was free to come and go between the hall and the air-conditioned room. He'd emerge and deliver some meaningless information to his colleagues, the sole purpose of the exchanges being the opportunity to show off his strolling privileges, which his fellow students found maliciously tautological. "The atmosphere seems optimal." "We're about to start." "The professors are in good spirits."

This is the story Sergio would always tell: the small abuse of power that occurred that day and was, for him, the most compelling evidence that Rome was doomed and had to be deserted by all good people.

After all the PhD candidates defended their dissertations in front of the committee, standing under the unnecessary fluorescent lights that hung from the ceiling of the cool, sunlit room, the coordinator gathered the young scholars in the reading room. "Some of your theses have disappointed us," he said distractedly, casually. "We're not going to tell you which. Our assessments have been noted in the registry and will not be made public."

His words had thrown them all into anguish just as the long day was winding down, just as this crucial phase of their career was drawing to a close, just as they were about to begin a far more difficult path: hunting for grants, waiting for a tenure that might never emerge.

When the professor went to get a coffee at the bar in the garden, the star pupil shared a secret: there was a way to see the confidential assessments, though they had to sneak into the faculty room to do it. The assistant knew that everyone on the faculty was a hopeless technophobe, so none of them wanted to risk saving their files on the old, beige computer. Instead they printed each report separately and then retyped the new information in the same formatted file. They were using the PC as a typewriter.

If you pressed Ctrl+Z, he said, you could look through what they'd written in the final assessment and then go backward all the way to the first defense. This magic trick, which allowed the faculty's largely unimpressed comments to appear one by one, a few words at a time, provoked disgust and even nausea among the men and women standing around the pupil, who sat at his chair in front of the computer. After they'd gone through just four assessments—out of more than a dozen—they asked him to stop.

When Sergio told this story to Americans he'd sum it up this way: "First my mother gets cancer, and now this?" They had let a moron debase them—a gym rat, for crying out loud! A body-builder-philosopher! With a crew cut! With gel in his hair! A guy who read Ruiz Zafón novels and was a fan of Dream Theater! Who took heavy-metal guitar lessons! When he was talking to you, he'd make this gesture of rehearsing pentatonic scales on an invisible guitar, his left hand's fingers all spiderlike. His yellow Ibáñez was the thing he was most proud of. He kept a picture of it on the desk informally awarded to him by the coordinator.

I'm so happy to hear more about this truly happy phase in Sergio's life. I love to provide accounts of his Roman discomfort as much as I love to recap his languid, satisfied sleep on couches next to Pulitzer winners and their editors, the abandonment with which he inhabits his fully realized dreams, the sense of balance, of justice that he feels when he lets reality redeem his Roman blues.

Sergio had good reason to be angry at the assistant and his yellow Ibanez. Two years earlier, he had met a French professor in Grenoble who had heard about his work on Foucault and offered him €10,000 to cover a year of work. Sergio gave his coordinator the news, so that everything could be made official. But the coordinator took it personally that he hadn't been involved, and he let the arrangement fall through.

Sergino abandoned his academic career after the defense. While he was in the faculty room staring at the beige computer, his mom had a final relapse. She would be dead four months later.

The way he'd describe it to Americans at parties, Sergio had no money and a living mother and was looking at everything from the *"entirely wrong* perspective". He soon found himself with no mother and a lot of money. He'd hoped his fate would lead to knowing the feeling of having his own money—maybe in the form of grants—while he still had a mother, but it hadn't been possible. The first money he got, the first money with which he could do what he wanted, was the €50,000 that he'd used to pay his bills and cover airfare while he moved around looking for work.

What he told people was that death had unleashed a series of "celestial forces and psychic fields," and the orphan had managed to find, in incredible circumstances (incredible, "though entirely deserved," he'd said once when he was so high that he actually disclosed the real reason he'd left Rome, *"I mean, I lost a mother and got some money . . . I sort of killed my mom to get some money, isn't that enough of a sacrifice, for fuck's sake?"*), a perfect job: tour manager for Universal in Milan.

"I left before all this crap started making me ill," he dared to say once, and I see it now, I see the effect of "all that stress and all the cars and the traffic . . ." With this perennial confusion about which plane of reality he's on, which tense he's living in—and with the stoned condensation of his sweat on his big, bald head, which heats up whenever he's in the midst of conversation—Sergio is the rare instance of a person who manages to be endearing even when he's bragging about flying first class.

THIS IS THE way I'm seeing all of this, and I return to him sleepless on the couch, overwhelmed by his own thoughts as he waits for the alarm to go off and for the cab to pull up downstairs. Once he recalls the program coordinator at the PhD program, he can't stop thinking about the anger and frustration the entire department has caused him over the years. The memories are physical: his back itches. Sergino hasn't learned how to deal with his demons, which is why he reenters the frenzied mode of plan making: he stalks the pupil's Facebook profile, his Twitter, his Instagram. He's impatient for inspiration, and this is why he can't calm down.

But at one point in the midst of his fevered reflections on the vermin that ruined the entire department, he remembers that the husband of the girl Berengo had sex with last winter— the *raccomandato* scholar who got that lucky grant to study at Columbia for a year, the guy who wants to be a director—is a Villa Mirafiori alum. He's an easier person to prank; there are so many things he and the pupil have in common. A prank could certainly be arranged. And if the two dumb pranks he came up with for Tullio didn't work out because the Tullios are a solid, close-knit family, the aspiring director's world of fantasies and *velleità* would lend itself perfectly to something very outrageous. He thinks about this and begins to feel exhilarated. He bursts into laughter.

The air in the room smells so stale it's as if the air itself has a sore throat. Sergino gets up. He walks in a circle, pumps his arms up and down, tries to release some tension. Then he remembers that la Sposina is back in Rome and babysitting for Tullio, which is weird and sounds promising. Either the young couple is back in Rome, or the husband has stayed behind in New York and is finishing things up at Columbia. The idea of la Sposina working for the Tullios is so exciting. What could it mean? But now he has his idea, and he's so discombobulated that he has to sit down at the table. There are three full ashtrays in front of him. He shivers, sweats, shivers, as if he's in the midst of a bad fever. Then he goes to the kitchen, using his phone as a flashlight, and drinks small sips of cold water. He's so drenched in sweat that he has to keep the refrigerator door closed. He sits at the kitchen table, which is attached to the wall, and that's where he does his research: finds the short film on YouTube, reads the credits, finds Lorenzo Proietti on Facebook, sends him a message:

Are you a Gassa fan? We're interested in you shooting a video. Directing and everything. What about a meeting in Williamsburg, totally informal, just a chat? My place, next week?

SERGINO READS LORENZO'S enthusiastic reply while sitting in the business-class lounge: "Williamsburg next week is ok! *Exited!*" (No *c*). Sergio accepts his friend's request and puts him on the *restricted* list, so that he can post whatever he wants about him.

So Sergino calls the detective and asks him to find out if Lorenzo is in Rome. "I don't know the address. It's fine if you can't find him." As he gives him instructions, he sends an email with the victim's Facebook profile link.

"So what do I get in return?"

"Love," Sergio whispers.

BEFORE TURNING OFF his phone for the Milan–London flight, Sergio stares out at the runway and tweets, "First class."

AFTER CLEARING CUSTOMS in Ireland, he pulls the curtains closed, stretches his legs in his pod with his wine and his iPad film selection and his thirty drops of Xanax, and surrenders himself to the sky. He thinks of his mother, feels his blood warm up, smacks a kiss with his thin lips, and if the sun is bright and the clouds are dark on the bottom and golden on top, he sheds a tear while the drug kicks in.

PART IV

THE BIG PRANK

*T*he train to the airport. Romanians, retired women, and Africans get on at the smallest, shabbiest stops. The parenthetical spaces around Rome's remote bridges are covered in green and brown vines. They look like habitats for sad, sickly gnomes who sleep under decaying walls among abandoned water heaters and half-broken cabinets. It looks like *Stalker*, but here the branches are dry. Tuscolana, then Trastevere. "I'm in pain," Lorenzo texts his closest friend. "But I'm all in. Haven't slept, haven't eaten. The whole car can smell my breath." Bland, symmetrical high-rises organized around a gigantic shopping mall complex give way to the airport.

Rome–New York via London, with a big duffel bag he stole from his father ten years ago. In all the photos of their family vacations, Dad looks tall and happy and always has that bad-ass bag on his shoulder. It's the middle of June, and his skin is already peeling from the sunbathing he's been doing on the beach in Ostia, but all he can think about are the twigs and spiderwebs in his stomach, punishment for not sleeping or eating all night. He's going back to New York after leaving it for his wife's sake.

He walks through the yellow arches of the covered bridge between the last stop and the airport.

The producer—Ludovica's connection—summoned him to New York to shoot a video. "Totally," he replied. "I'm in New York. I'll catch you next week."

In line for the security checkpoint, he keeps getting long, appraising stares from a kid in shorts and a Lacoste polo. He can feel the kid admiring his *fumé* shades and his red scarf. Lorenzo slips off his belt, lets the clerk feel him up, retrieves his phone and bag after they've been scanned, and leaves the area, flooded by endorphins, an undertow of pleasure beating down on his temples.

The duty-free aisles are warm and sweaty, barely air conditioned. The sun outside the windows dries his mouth and moistens his forehead, the natural light making the glass seem thicker and dustier than it really is.

He sweats against the window on the Rome-London flight.

This morning's journey, the awakening—that's the story he should try to tell in the video, with Gassa playing Lorenzo. Up from the couch at dawn to chase his dreams. He wants his wife back, but he knows he has to take the long route, so he hops on the train in multiracial Rome: the dirt, the old women, the graffiti, the liminal spaces. Gassa playing Lorenzo: he'd feel so triumphant showing her the video, getting her back.

At Heathrow Terminal 5, he waits for the second leg of the trip, takes off his shoes at security, then goes up the escalators to the corporate landscape of international brands on the second floor, where he opts for a BLT at Pret, its big flavors and precise smells carefully engineered, either naturally or artificially. He pictures Gassa as himself, asleep and hungover: it's the story of a rapper—a filmmaker—who's sleeping on the couch because his woman won't let him in the bedroom, and he has to go all the way to America to win her over.

New Russian money looks like bouncers and hookers, speaks English to its kids, and sleeps all the way to its destinations. He's taking notes on his phone.

The plane touches down early on a windy afternoon after displaying Manhattan off to the left—lovely to see her again. What a blast this is, queuing up among the families on vacation; what a blast lying to the guard and telling him he's also here on vacation; what a blast taking the train and being able to see the city in the distance, the buildings so weirdly thin that their height seems irresponsible.

HIS HOST IS Elly Parenzo, a twenty-five-year-old Jewish Milanese woman who works for Pixar. She was the only acquaintance who could put him up. (Even Berengo said he couldn't.) The lobby of her high-rise near Ground Zero, where they're building the Freedom Tower, is retrodecadent: brown, black, blood red, charcoal gray flecked with orange. Lorenzo gives his name to the doorman, whose outfit is elegant and intimidating.

The man checks his passport and hands him the keys. He's only been here once before, when he was out with three girlfriends after a movie on Canal Street and a cold stroll in Battery Park. He was looking for refuge; it was snowing that night, and Ludovica had been gone for three days by then, God knows where. You could see nothing in the whiteout, the soft snow had leveled off every surface. The ramps coming off West Street looked like private driveways or front porches. The white exaggerated the magic trick of Wall Street, of Lower Manhattan, where the streets' straight lines are forced into increasing contortions and strange angles, piercing one another to form a delirious spiderweb.

Elly comes home before dinner. She pours him some peach juice and offers him a plate of cookies. They're watching Jon

Stewart on Hulu, and he's impressed by the scale and grandeur of the streaming service—and the way that Elly seems perfectly in sync with it. She quotes old episodes, speaks the fast, hybrid English-Italian that defines this future breed of hyper-accomplished Italian émigrés. She still gets a high from actually living in New York. Her parents bought her the apartment when she started her first job as an assistant copywriter after an internship at Pixar she got right out of NYU. Her parents had allowed her to apply to American universities and skip the *cursus honorum* of Italian academic life. Her half-English/half-Italian doesn't even sound affected. Lorenzo doesn't like to feel envious of others, and he likes her a lot; she's smart and has her shit together. He's trying not to compensate by saying that he's here to shoot a video, but he can't help but feel that this time around, they're almost on the same level.

He drags her up to the twenty-third floor to stare down through a window in the shared lounge at the construction site where the Freedom Tower is taking shape. If she were his wife, he could be a director. But she's a child, and he doesn't find her attractive anyway. She wears a high-waisted skirt and a white shirt, but she looks modest. There's a more attractive young woman sitting on the couch in front of the TV, carefully arranging her curls behind her ears, her legs askew. She makes the couch look so comfortable that it seems to exude an almost spiritual quality. On the balcony they look out onto the illuminated scaffolding against the red light of the city, dark matter in the humid air. "So tell me about this video," she says, flattering him. "It's *so cool, sono troppo excited.* I like Gassa a lot!"

Lorenzo grabs her wrist. "Quite a compliment, coming from you, Elly!"

"What does that mean?"

"You are the Italian-American dream!"

"You're sweet, Lorenzo. I wish you luck, davvero."

It's drizzling, so they go back inside and then downstairs. The apartment itself is spare. She isn't adult enough to see the swanky communal spaces as a challenge, to match them with her own decorative choices. She's a wholesome girl who has everything, and she doesn't brag, isn't lofty. She was the only one among his friends who didn't pretend to be *impicciata, incasinata, strippatissima*—all those hateful, slangy words they used instead of just saying they were too busy—and she let him crash. She makes him a cup of coffee to counter the jet lag.

Later, they take a fifteen-minute walk on the wet sidewalk. It starts pouring, so they give up looking out at the river and retreat into the lounge downstairs, play pool on the tangerine-colored table, warm and wet from the thick raindrops.

Two yuppies sit quietly on two plush chairs, watching a late-night show whose host is the same age as them.

AT NIGHT THE exhilarating haze of success turns dark. He thinks about his host, about the fact that she gets to lead this life every single day. The thought becomes unbearable. Elly is in her room, preparing for another perfect day in the life her parents dreamt up for her. She's from a renowned family of Milanese intellectuals, distant relatives of the Berengos. They're not much wealthier than his own family: real estate, long trips in the summers. He's awake on the bare sofa, which sits between the front door and the kitchenette. He travels back to his parents' American-style kitchen. It was there, sitting on their stools, that he asked them for the money for the airfare.

His parents have always supplemented the grants he's gotten from school. This year he was supposed to get €1,200 a month from his alma mater for the *borsa di perfezionamento all'estero*, but he lost his right to the money in February, when he flew back to Rome. (The entire sum was supposed to be paid out in three installments, but he got the first one in advance and had never really counted on the other two to cover his life in New York.) His parents were sad about their daughter-in-law's change of heart and felt for their kid, so they transferred an extra €10,000 into his account to help him through the rest of the year. And they still contributed to his private pension, €5,000 a year. This is why it's hard for him to ask for more. Ludovica isn't getting a salary for her work in the bookstore, and she asked him to pay for her part of the mortgage installments through the end of the year. He couldn't help but agree, even though he's been sleeping on the couch on the ground floor. And since he's also been network-ing—going out to dinner, buying drinks—he knows he won't be able to pay for the plane tickets. So he goes to his parents and asks for an extra €2,000: he describes the extraordinary circum-stances and promises to pay back the €2,000 when the video money comes in. To which they respond: "Don't be silly! There's so little money going around these days. You earn it, you keep it." Sitting there in their kitchen, his parents promised him as much support as he needed.

Lorenzo has now seen the results of Elly's parents' self-abnegation. They decided to part with their daughter and send her to America instead of spending tens of thousands of Euros on monthly allowances to supplement many underemployed years in Italy, and they were wise to buy her an apartment in New York (which is a great investment, isn't it? Right now it's cheaper than Italy, and they'll be able to rent it out forever). And so Lorenzo has to wonder how two sane and free people like his own folks—a manager in a dog food corporation and a housewife, a reader and a lover of the outdoors—never suggested that Lorenzo and his brother study abroad. His mind wanders and he moans with greed until he stumbles onto a detail from his last visit to his parents. His mother—the eternal dyed ponytail, the olive complexion, the fine and compact lines of her face—can no longer sit on the stools in the kitchen. These stools were the centerpiece of the renovation they undertook in 1986, but now she's tired, and the stools are uncomfortable. The kitchen is at the center of an amazing fifth-floor apartment in Parioli, a maze of rivulets and a fugue of rooms, inlets of intimate angles, islands, hiding spots, storage units hidden under stairwells. Everything pivots around the kitchen: from there you turn in for the night, or head out to the salon and its covered balcony, or leave through the main entrance or the servants' entrance. Before the cancer three years ago, this was his mother's throne. She dominated the apartment from her perch on the stool. Her cordless phone wedged between her jaw and shoulder, she'd sort out deliveries and doctors' appointments for the whole family. In his tired daze, it has now hit him abruptly: his mother isn't using the stool anymore. The stool was a piece of furniture imbued with her personality, but now she sits on the bench at the low wooden table that faces the kitchen counter. During his American winter, Lorenzo's memory had repositioned his mother: she was back on the stool, back on the phone near the buzzer. But that image has disappeared, and all he has is what he's just seen: she's drained, physically and morally, by the removal of her left breast and the death of her younger sister, zia Gianna. She sits at the low Italian table. These thoughts flood his lymphatic system with black rain. Maybe, he thinks, maybe his mother had been waiting for the cancer to appear ever since that day, sixteen years ago, when her sister had found a lump in her breast. Maybe this is why she never brought up the idea of the brothers studying abroad. Maybe she wanted them near her, or worse, near their dad, so that he wouldn't be left alone. In the middle of the night, he feels horror at his own ingratitude.

EIGHTEEN HOURS LATER he's out on the street in a linen shirt and linen pants. He takes the train under the river to East Williamsburg. Grand Street—Laundromats, 99-cent stores, fried food, pizza places—the low center of gravity of wide American roads under an open sky. It's nearly dusk, though not quite yet: everything is brilliantly visible.

Grand Billiards is a big, rickety place half a flight of stairs up from an empty gym. He can sense the three people staring in his direction: Sergio, myself, and Anna—a model/gallerist/producer. (Anna: one of the two girls who were talking in Berengo's room that first night when La Sposina fell asleep. Also the one who announced the following evening that she couldn't decide whether or not to undress for the *Jacques* photo shoot.) The pool bar is a Puerto Rican hangout. Here, tacky is the new exotic: glass and metal and couches and a digital jukebox. Italian, Hispanic, and American hipsters have begun to colonize this place and use it to throw cheap parties. There's an Italian DJ-ing tonight, so Lorenzo's professional meeting is underscored by Mina, Rettore, and Robert Miles's *Children*, and then at the end, a turn toward hard core. The three of us are a reality effect for Lorenzo. Sergino's pants are huge and outrageous, the legs rolled up over thin, gnarled ankles that poke out from his bulky legs. He wears his Church's loafers without laces. Anna stands by his side, a black jacket over a checkered shirt, long hair relatively untangled. Lorenzo—whose point of view I keep evoking here—thinks she's one of the most attractive women he's ever talked to, including during his TV days. Her strong features are almost disquieting. They're kept in check by perfect makeup and bright red lipstick over a full mouth. Her gaze is dark, euphoric, fake fun, tense, frantic. (Later, Sergio tells Lorenzo that she collects star fucks: "indie singer-songwriters you've listened to, artists your wife knows, rappers you know, journalists your wife knows, photographers your wife knows." He also tells you that she's talented: she isn't too well versed in basic Italian grammar, but she manages to hang out with Massimiliano Gioni and Cattelan. You learn that she's prone to anxiety attacks that deform her face, make her cry in fear for her life. She comes from somewhere outside Bergamo, and she wants the world.) As they shake hands, she kisses Lorenzo near his mouth.

Then there's me. The role I'm playing here is that of the middle-aged, redheaded, wrinkled bisexual—Daria, the veteran of counterculture. Sergio dressed me up in bright red stockings and a miniskirt, and now he's leading us to a pool table. There are games going on on either side of us: a group of Puerto Ricans from the neighborhood at one table, some black writer friends of Anna's at the other. The music is loud. Anna leans over to get all the balls into the triangle, then comes over to me and hugs me for no reason.

"What's your name again?" Lorenzo asks midhug.

"Daria."

"I heard D'Aria," he laughs. "I was thinking that that's such an exotic name."

I grab the cue and break.

Lorenzo and Sergio step outside for a smoke, leaving just us women to keep playing. Lorenzo's hands are clammy. Sergio is bleary eyed.

"She's cool, Anna is."

"Anna, yeah, interesting, totally. I'm worthless, by the way. She's the producer; it all goes through her."

"Really? I thought she was the actress."

"Maybe, yeah, maybe. But you know, she's . . . she's like a feminist from the future, I mean, she does everything. She wants to produce, mostly, you know, and she also works at a gallery, she wants to curate—she's the total curator, very modern. She's the curator of bellezza: produce, create, produce, curate. *Self-curate or die*, right?"

"She's a piece of ass."

"Oh, she fucks everybody. If you don't fuck her you're crazy."

Back inside, Lorenzo watches Anna with new eyes: her power, her mouth, the lipstick she slowly sucks on and chews. She and her jacket are both perfectly rumpled, worn out, and she's always touching everybody, jumping around the pool table, shit talking, kissing every black guy who comes over. Then she comes over to Lorenzo, gets close to him, and whispers conspiratorially: "That guy's a douche, a world-class douche. You stay with me, okay?"

The city softens up. Elly's job seems like just a minor brick in this monumental building that he, too, can be a part of. Anna's all over him, and she offers a running commentary on the game, and life is simple and perfect. It's Anna and Lorenzo against Lamar, this big, dapper black guy. "Don't let this *bel negraccio* fool us with his cue," she whispers to Lorenzo. "We're better." And as soon as Lamar gets his first ball in the hole, Anna grabs Lorenzo by his elbow, pretends to slap Lamar's face, and says, *"No more, Lamar, we win."* She puts her cue down in the middle of the table, and the game is over. Lamar seems to expect as much from her. He gathers the balls and goes in search of a new opponent. Now Anna and Lorenzo are walking side by side, almost hugging, and he can feel her braless breasts bouncing against his linen shirt, fresh and warm.

Then, on a couch: "So I understand you're producing my video."

They're sitting very close to each other, staring straight ahead. "Yes."

"And you've seen my shorts."

"Yeah, *zio*, yeah."

"And you like them?"

"Of course, don't be such a loser!"

"You're so young."

"If you don't quit being such a loser, I'll have to kick your ass!"

"You're a weird kid. You're awesome."

"Thank you."

Suddenly she's quiet, all mouth, just front teeth and cheekbones, a little pagan statue.

"You're welcome. It's true, though. And what would the schedule be? Should I send you the script?"

"You're such a Roman."

"What do you mean?"

"You're not talking money."

"Money is not the priority for me."

"Don't say stupid shit. You don't understand anything."

"Oh, I'm sorry. Well then how much is it?"

"I'm not sure I want to be in the video. Do you want me in it? Do you have ideas already?"

"Well, you could play Gassa's girlfriend, the one he's fighting with?"

"No way. He's already after me."

"You mean . . . "

"You really don't understand anything."

"It's the slang from Milan."

"He's on me."

"Is he hitting on you?"

"I was dumb enough to schlong him and now I can't get rid of him."

"Schlong him?"

"Bang him."

"Well, you're the producer, you get to choose."

"Thank you. You dress like shit, though."

"Don't make fun of me! Maybe I want to dress this way."

"*Zio*, I feel bad for you, you know? Wait here, don't move . . ."

SHE COMES BACK with a pretty girl, not model-pretty, nor-mal-pretty. Her name is Chiara, and she's from Milan: petite, red haired, with the confident-unconfident face of a woman who comes from wealth. Chiara and Anna look him up and down, and Chiara jokes to Anna that they should strip everything off of him and start from scratch: a pair of Dockers, a white tee, or a pale blue cotton button-down. "Man, those Campers are in-credible," Anna says. "He should be in Madame Tussaud's. This should go up on a *fashion blog*!"

Chiara works as an image consultant. "We're only teasing you, okay?" she reassures him. "Just some professional advice."

Anna: "Okay, *zia*, give me your keys."

Chiara obeys. "Don't use his room, though, just his clothes!" she says.

SHE TAKES HIM to an apartment just a couple of blocks away from the billiard place. Chiara lives there with a gay German. The place is much more real than Elly's: you can feel it in the warm wind brushing the street, in the two bodegas at the intersection, in the absence of all but a small handful of people on the side-walk, in the carpeted staircase, in the stale smell that ascends behind an ass that's three quarters smaller than Ludo's, in the flimsy wooden door with three locks, in the shrill *clack* sound, in the three-room apartment itself, with its sloping floor and the grim metal bars on the windows.

"CHIARA'S HOMO ROOMMATE has a real-ass closet. Let's see if any of this fits you. Maybe the nonskinny shit will."

Lorenzo's answers are unavailable to me. He's all eyes and smells: wood, dust, a woman's scent, mint tea. They take a break and eat American cookies. Suddenly I see a girl's fingers dirty with chocolate chips, and she's sticking them in her mouth while he goes in and out of the German's messy room and tries on four button-down shirts, two polos, three pairs of long pants, two pairs of shorts, four bomber jackets, all of which Anna has laid out on top of the mattress.

Lorenzo is overwhelmed by the intimacy, and he keeps changing outfits. In his shorts he looks like a queer, in his skinny jeans he's moody, in the buttoned-up polo he's clownish and ridiculous.

Anna finishes up her snacking and wipes her dirty, chocolate-covered fingers on her neck as she scolds, "Chill out, *zio!* You gotta relax." Then she starts dressing herself in Chiara's clothes. She disappears into her friend's room, and when she reappears to him (he's wearing weird elastic black pants and a black polo: he doesn't look like himself; he's tapered and streamlined), she's dressed like a woman, a pale dress that looks like Cape Cod curtains, with a zipper in front that runs from her sternum to her vagina and a flat Tudor neck. She's put on black thigh-highs, and he can imagine how the fabric recedes softly whenever she undresses, how it falls down the leg, mortally sweet.

"Okay, maybe something less skinny?" She's still giving advice. "The buttoned-up polo sort of suits you, yeah?"

They change and reconvene in the living room, on top of the cracked wooden floors. The wind blows against the windows. Anna is wearing a long skirt and a very light white shirt, again with no bra.

I can't hear Lorenzo's words, but I can hear Anna's. "Do you like *me?*"

I hear nothing and then, "I've met your wife. I brought some of my clothes to her shop. Don't talk to me about your wife, *zio*."

From Lorenzo, I only detect the feeling of his ass pressing down on the surface of a wooden chair, his thighs filling up some guy's pants, his moist breath traveling through the smallest passage in his breast, the oxygen not reaching his legs.

Anna is drinking some lukewarm herbal tea. "I know all that, yeah, and I won't tell you shit, it's your fucking business. You might wanna ask Berengo, though, whether he necked her. What I mean is that you are allowed to tell me you like me, considering what your wife is doing behind your back."

Lorenzo is speaking without listening to himself.

She talks in an unintelligible, slangy Italian, which literally translates: "If I tell you, *will you shoot me a lemon? 'Cause dressed like that you're half-behaving*," which means "will you make out with me? You're sort of sexy with those clothes on," though of course he doesn't understand a word.

Before she climbs on top of him, Anna shoots a video of his erect cock. He's lying on the naked mattress, perched on two elbows. Then she hands him her iPhone, gets on top, and lets him shoot a few minutes of intercourse. She's clean-shaven, except for a brown strip of hair. Two waxed, lean thighs. Her knees look pummeled. She's small in the frame, an actress, a star, suddenly unreachable while he's still inside her with no condom ("you're a bad boy," she scolds him, "no condom"), her tattooed bust stretched to the sky, her young breasts, both soft and full, her slightly crooked spine, the shoulders of a former swimmer, her capillaries . . .

She climaxes. The redness of those capillaries smudges her face, her neck stretches, the muscles on her shoulders flex, her face is deformed, grimacing, a look of disgust. (Lorenzo has stopped filming. He puts the phone down next to him.) The grimace leaves vertical shadows on her jaws, her cheeks, her temples.

Her lips are curled up, and her skin looks like it's covered with red spots. It's a terrible, ominous spectacle, and it's still there as Lorenzo begins to come onto her neck, his dick in her hands, which she lubed up with drool.

You're sitting on the edge of the bed, and Anna is still kneeling over, frantic and naked, gasping for air but not yet ready to let go of you.

AFTERWARD, THE TWO of you are in the bathroom. She's pissing, talking to you, scratching her head, still breathing heavily, smelling her sweaty armpit. Then you're in the kitchen splitting a piece of toast. You're famished, and you hope you'll get to do it all over again this very evening, but it's not going to happen. "*Zio*, you better leave; if Sergio finds out I schlonged you, he'll fucking lose it. You can get a cab on Grand." You ask if you can maybe take a shower before you go, and she points to the bathroom. The water is boiling hot, and you sigh and squirm the whole time. You dry yourself off, put on the linen shirt and the rest of the clothes you had on before the masquerade, and slowly return to your old self. Before you leave, you go back to the kitchen and say, "Then we won't say anything to anyone. It's ours."

You wake up feeling blessed by the sun. You have breakfast with Elly, who's late for work and speaking full-on English: *gotta run, gotta run, take your time, enjoy the city!* You're sleepy, but the smell of the toaster and the taste of the mango juice wake you up, enliven you. "You want any bacon?" she asks. You tell her that the meeting yesterday was very promising, and she graces you with her cosmopolitan Jewish gaze. You get the sense that she's treating you like a peer.

You check Facebook on your Mac, and Sergio's profile seems to have vanished. Did he block you?

You want to call him, but you realize he didn't give you his number. As you get dressed, you think about taking a cab to Williamsburg to talk to Anna. You can't stand the idea of an entire train ride, not right now. You slip on the same clothes you were wearing yesterday, only today they suddenly look bad. It's been half an hour since you sent Anna a Facebook message, no reply. Heartburn tightens a fist in your stomach.

You go downstairs, hail a cab, and twenty dollars later you're in front of the building where you had sex last night. A long ride through the morning sun and the warm wind and the smell of garbage. The street is tough and austere, and it feels less like New York than an unfriendly village, invisible eyes staring down at you from every angle. You press a buzzer next to a label with two names—Italian and German—but no one responds. You're nervous, confused. Long minutes go by, and you spit on the sidewalk. Two handsome men walk out of a bodega eating big chocolate chip cookies. Two other men ride by on their bikes, slower than slow.

Another cab. Anna's Facebook profile includes the name of the gallery where she works. In her profile picture she stares into a mirror with her big, hungry eyes. She's taking off her makeup with a white cotton swab, at once adrift and focused.

In the cab your hand vibrates with your phone. A text from Ludovica: "Don't come back." As you call her, you think mostly about your arrhythmia and the bile bubbling in your throat. You don't get through. Her phone is off, and now you're gasping for air. You try forty more times.

There are very few details to go on, almost none. First stop: a Madison Avenue gallery. She's not there. A new cab: the sister gallery in Chelsea, way out on the fringe of the island, near the West Side Highway. What you see: casual visitors, idle collectors, curators, interns, huge works of art hanging clumsily off the walls. Anna talks to everyone in the room for a few seconds at a time, making her way between groups with utter effortlessness. Her black-clad legs look Gothic and unreal.

She spots him, excuses herself from her conversations, and hugs him hard as soon as she reaches him. She presses her face into his collarbone affectionately but avoids eye contact. Her body is warm. I can't make out what you are saying, Lorenzo. She steps back and stares down at the floor. "I don't think Sergio's on Facebook, no . . . Just call him on his mobile."

Again, I can't hear you.

Anna: "Oh, I'm all right, I guess. I have a ton of work, can't really talk right now, well . . ."

I can't hear you.

Anna: "No, lunch is impossible for me."

And then: "No, no, I'm not gonna talk to him. You do it."

And then: "I told you I'm not talking to him. If you want to talk to Sergio, call him and ask him why he blocked you. Don't let him treat you like a child, okay?"

And then: "So go ahead and think that I know some shit and won't tell you. Go ahead, think that, what difference does it make?"

She turns her head and moves away without ever having made eye contact, tightening her fists as she walks. She walks toward a white wall and through a white door you hadn't noticed until now. She closes herself in, and the wall reverts to pure white.

You stay in the gallery. You reach the wall, push open the knobless door, and see her sitting on the ground, her face red like it was yesterday, during climax, but here, in the light of a mid-century modern lamp, the effect is starker and more ominous. She looks scared: her face seems dilated; her cheekbones look like the rearview mirror of a sports car; her eyes are closed. The room has three couches and a desk, all white. It's a formal space set up for meetings. She's sitting with her legs crossed, her back against the wall, her strange long fingers laid out carefully on her thighs. *"Call Laura,"* she whispers in English. *"I'm scared, call Laura."* You leave the room and ask the busy-looking people if they know a Laura. She rushes over quickly; she must be the gallerist. She's dressed in a gorgeous white tunic and asks you: *"The usual? Panic attack? Man, every other fucking day!"*

You walk toward Eleventh Avenue to hail a cab.

Now you're inside Cosmic Diner, in Berengo's neighborhood. And here's Berengo, buying you breakfast. He's wearing his short jogging pants, and he's slimmer than he was in winter. He places a blister pack of Xanax on the table.

"Absolutely. Ask me anything."

I can't hear your words, but I can taste the pancake and the syrup and the butter on your tongue.

Berengo's answers:

"Because I put her up when she left your apartment."

"Because Ludo didn't want to see you and asked me not to tell you. I even untagged myself from all the Facebook pics everyone took at my parties."

"I promise: nothing at all. No way was I going to have sex with her."

Chewing, butter, amber colors, hunger.

All Berengo:

"Lore, I don't like what you're saying. I think I can help you. But you have to be honest. If you're honest, I'll be honest."

"Nothing much. Just that, and I'm sorry to say this, but your short film isn't going to make you a director. You have to let it go. You have to do me a personal favor and let it go."

"No, it's not an obsession. It's a fixation."

"Sergio and Anna are difficult people. They're complicated, *and you may not want to trust them."*

"Well then you should have asked me before you bought the ticket."

"You're right. I didn't tell you because I try not to talk about work I don't like. *I don't want to be that kind of person.*"

"That's the way it is. The short isn't good. You know that the only way is for us to talk this honestly; otherwise I can't help you."

"Of course. All the time in the world."

"Shouldn't be a problem changing it. British Airways?"

"I don't know the details, Lore, but yeah, 'prank' seems like the right word to me."

"Come on. Think. How can this be Ludovica's prank? With Sergio? Maybe she's pissed about something else entirely. Go home, and by the time you land, she'll have already forgotten."

I CAN'T FEEL you, but I feel the Xanax. The Xanax and the drizzle as the two of you walk to Berengo's house. The Xanax and Berengo's sofa, where you lie down in your underwear, pull the soft sheets over your face, feel the air conditioning blasting from the old unit.

THEN I FEEL the moment when you wake up: those thick, round moments of pure pleasure, when you're still high and still big on Xanax. Then the thoughts that try to break through: no news from Ludovica, a few texts from her girlfriends, who say she knows you've been with someone else.

AND THEN I'M lucky enough to not hear your mind anymore. I can't hear your thoughts, your words, your wishes, your desires. It's as if someone has given *me* Xanax. But here, now, I do see you:

A red-eye flight. You sit in the window seat, and there's no one next to you in the aisle. You're in the last row, right by the bathrooms. The crew have dimmed the cabin lights but you can see the shape of the plane, this cylinder that keeps you oxygenated and warm in the inhospitable hollow in the sky. At JFK you bought €200 noise-canceling headphones. You had two hours to kill at the airport. There was a Milanese family sitting across from you by the gate, youthful parents and their two sons, both in their early twenties, wearing Superga shoes. They all went on and on about Madison Square Garden, how cool it looked from outside, and how cool it'd be to see a Knicks game next time they were in New York: "Well, that's just an excuse to come back!" In their conversation you hear the entire epic romance Italian middle-class families have with this city, and from now on, until the day you die, you'll feel hurt whenever someone mentions it, whenever you overhear a happy couple planning a trip to stroll along the High Line, and take pictures with a hot dog vendor at a traffic light under a classic green street sign, and sprawl out on the grass in Central Park. You bought two AAA batteries for the headphones, and you've kept them on ever since, though you haven't played any music. They cancel the annoying frequencies from every kind of noise. You still hear the noise, but it's flattened, like a wildflower pressed in a book. When the plane took off it was unreal, the pure sound of matter making an effort to unglue itself from earth unaccompanied by the roar of the engine. So now, without all that acoustic trauma, you feel flying as more of an abstraction. And the benzodiazepine in your thighs, your knuckles, the soles of your feet, your cheeks, in the softest spot of your forearms, in the nerves of your scalp collaborates with the loss in frequency to make you feel like little more than a tiny marble being flicked into the jelly of time. So you let yourself go. You feel loved by the force pushing the marble through the jelly, enough to tell that force a secret that has just been revealed to you:

I'm technically not a movie director. There are some lucky men out there who get woken up at dawn by a text message from their producer and hop on a bike and ride to Cinecittà, or to the fields of Formello, where they find trailers with makeup artists and actors already inside, and strong young men carrying rolls of wire. I don't, because that's not my life. I wake up and go to the philosophy department, where I talk to students who are committing their lecture notes to memory, who ask what their current credit count is. All the beauty in those wake-up texts, those bonafide directors, their eyes rimmed with dark circles, the way they'll be in a bar one moment and then have to break off in the middle of a conversation to go solve some kind of problem. Never again will I save money by selling my mother's car; never again will I go out of my way to raise €3,000–€5,000 for a short film; never again will I go to those evenings at Kino, where producers talk shop and field questions and I spend the whole time thinking that tonight, finally, this producer will be struck by my smile and feel the need to talk to me, pick my brains. Should I lose my hair trying to learn the trade on some TV series, some Endemol reality TV show? Work my way up to directing a TV movie? No, no. We should always be like this, every organ smoothed out by the benzodiazepine, listening to the sound of the world without its roar. Here, I am stronger, I can take my phone, open the video directory, delete G., which I've kept all this time so I can show it when networking. "You know, we won a prize from the Comune di Roma." Deleted. And maybe delete the idea people have of me. Maybe they

*should never ask me again if I love cinema, if I've ever had
the bright idea to turn this love of cinema into a creative act.
I've never wanted that, and you don't want to ask me, which,
by the way, wouldn't serve any purpose anyway—asking me.
What if I wanted it . . . Mom, come on, you sit right there,
comfortably, pick the seat you're most comfortable in, and
don't ever ask me, and I will pay you as many visits as I can,
and we won't talk money. We'll talk about something else,
about Ludovica, about carnal love, about how beautiful it is
to stroll around my childhood neighborhood, run errands for
you, how happy I am when you need me to go to the hardware
store, to the drugstore. Just ask me, Mom, ask me, all right?*

Then I feel your footsteps on the sidewalk near your house
in Via del Mandrione, four meters away from the Roman aqueduct. It's midmorning, 26°C. You're rested and sad, your phone
is dead, and the last thing I feel is the metal of the key making
contact with the metal of the keyhole in the small gate. You expect to hear the slow *clack*, but your key doesn't work; you can't
get in. You lean in to take a closer look: no sign of tampering, it's
a perfect new keyhole without a single scratch. I can still feel the
Xanax: I feel something obstructing your chest and your tears,
keeping your temples muffled in wool. You try, by force of will, to
change the fate of that key against the new keyhole, but you don't
succeed. Then I feel you sitting on the steps, and then, at last, the
membrane detaches, and I stop feeling you.

*S*hall we be honest about the effect of the prank? Should we admit that Lorenzo Proietti and his wife were hurt by it? Maybe, but still, I'm not responsible.

I want to clarify the extent to which I was involved. I have to reiterate that the personal fulfillment of the bourgeois isn't worth the carbon footprint required to sustain it, particularly when you board a plane because you *think* you've been offered a chance to shoot a music video. I paid for my plane tickets with my money. I have a real job at a travel agency, and I write on the side for *il manifesto*, the Communist paper, and I do it for free. I do it out of pure love for literature and for the people. I buy any tickets I want, and I buy them to go fuck Berengo. My aim is true; I don't go there in pursuit of success or status.

My involvement in the prank was close to zero, and what was happening between Berengo and me at the time was much more important. Maybe I will be woken up again to revisit *that*, to revisit my responsibility for the amount of hurt Nico and I brought onto each other. It'll happen before I die for good, unless it has already happened, and I'm being forced to forget.

so yeah, after my flight to New York (via Amsterdam), I didn't see Nico at the airport. I took the subway to Midtown and had his doorman buzz him while I tried to dry my t-shirt. A downpour had begun while I was underground. Nico let me up, but he didn't rush down to grab my suitcase, didn't take me to the Cosmic Diner like he normally did. When I got upstairs, he was in the shower; he'd propped the front door open with one side of a cardboard box from Amazon. He was listening to Spanish bubblegum pop. The locked bathroom door saddened me, and though I knocked hard, I got no response. I sat down on the couch to look out at the view. I pulled off my shoes. Because we've been discussing other people's lives in detail, please pay attention to the image of a thirty-eight-year-old woman who pulls off her shoes after traveling across the ocean. It's hot, it's raining, my t-shirt is soaked. I pull it off and look out onto the shards of June light bursting through the window. This is me. Do you feel my tired ass cheeks? It's been months since I last saw him in the flesh.

This is what matters, not my involvement in a prank set into motion in a billiard hall: my swollen feet, liberated from my sneakers, resting on the warm wood in the afternoon; the pleasure I get from the cotton clouds as they move past the sun and out of the city, dark and gray in one corner of the window, glorious in the other.

And then, yes, of course we fucked. It was nice. We had fun: we used The Box, almost every gadget in the Box. And it's not as if I usually ask Berengo how he's doing. We've both made choices; we don't ask each other much.

that very first night, we met Sergino at a bar on the Lower East Side, and he explained the prank and asked us to take part.

So this is the moment of my supposed responsibility, when I agreed to participate. The other patrons slouched and spread their legs on random chairs and couches, irony or hostility thick in the air, half-closed eyelids or bulging eyeballs. It was the kind of night that put Anna in a bad mood because they were playing the Smiths, and for Anna, those songs gave off the wrong kind of nonchalance. Because it was the kind of environment where everyone was obsessed with perfecting and differentiating their own brands of nonchalance. Sergino and Berengo slipped the stems of some carnations into their pants and sang along. Vodka tonics; a stray, grandiose reference to doing coke in the bathrooms; the joint I'd smoked before sex; the MDMA Berengo and I had taken before going out, though just a hint, because he got paranoid whenever he thought he'd had too much booze for the combination to be safe, so we weren't as high as we'd hoped.

Is this the exact moment when the prank becomes my fault, too? Sergino has finished singing "Heaven Knows I'm Miserable Now," and he sits on the arm rest of the couch. Berengo and I are slouched next to each other, our arms and legs interlaced (though he keeps his mouth away from mine). Sergio is telling us about this guy—a friend of Nico's—he wants to play this prank on, *uno scherzone*. He has led this guy to believe he's going to let him shoot a video. At the time I'm not aware of the short film and its creator's good connections at a department of philosophy in Rome. I have no idea that he's a *raccomandato*. So my fault here, technically, is laughing when Sergino tells me this guy pretended he was in New York so as not to miss the opportunity to discuss shooting a rap video. Is that the reason I'm now telling the whole story? Is it my fault that instead of scolding Sergino, I laughed when he said he'd hired a "hipster detective" to verify whether the guy was actually in Rome when he accepted the meeting? How could I not laugh with delight as I watched a coked-up Sergino tell the story with his fingers stretched out like the spokes of bike wheels? I couldn't help but laugh, so I did.

In that case, okay, I'm guilty of saying I wanted to be there when this guy showed up, pretending like he hadn't just flown in.

Nicolino begs me to go home. I humor him: "It's all right, we're going in a minute." I wipe the sweat from his forehead. "And in the meantime just relax on the couch, you're going to be all right in a second, drink some water." (He's the only person I know who gets paranoid on MDMA.) I wipe his face with a paper napkin and get him a couple cups of tap water. After a while, he gets up very slowly, like an old man, picks up his sweater, and walks out. I chase him out into the warm stench of garbage. I could never live here, not in the summer or the winter. Tonight the cloudy skies, the wind from the south, a mass of cold air—all of them make their way through the smells that rise from the river.

Nico stops halfway, pulls out his phone, starts playing Candy Crush.

"What's up with you?"

"Don't make me mad. You're bad. We're bad. Sergio is bad. I want a Xanax and I need some sleep."

"Totally. No need to get mad; we're going to sleep."

"Yeah, sure, go ahead and humor me like you always do. I know you think you're right anyway, *babba di minchia*."

"That's not your slang, *ciccio* . . ."

We walk to Houston, where we raise our voices. The street is yellow, cabs everywhere. Berengo's utter lack of tenderness toward me makes me think that he's against the prank out of solidarity with a fellow well-connected bourgeois. I follow him down Houston through the clusters of people standing in line outside bars and waiting for the traffic lights to change. Firemen blast horns on passing fire trucks. Berengo is a child with a receding hairline, hunched over his phone, nearsighted.

I get close and I scream at him. "You're such a *pariolino di merda*"—a spoiled rich kid from Parioli—"and you're making such a dumb-ass fuss, I can't stand you, you're bringing me the fuck down. You should get a job and try to find a way to show me a little respect. I used my vacation days to come here."

He responds robotically. "Sorry, you're scaring me. Go."

"What? You fucking sociopath!" I start punching his back, and I find myself crying, sobbing, shaking. He slips his phone into his pocket, turns, hugs me. I slap his chest, and he says, "Oh we're all bourgeois, all of us, but you, *Pina Broz*, you like soap operas."

I lean back. "You idiot," I say as I sniffle and wipe my nose on his sweater. "Can we make peace? Can we not argue?"

"I'm going home."

"Okay, let's go home."

"No, stay with Sergino. Don't worry. You should do the prank. He's already pranking himself, the poor guy; he thinks he's got it."

"But I don't give a shit about the prank!"

"Oh, yes you do, and I don't want you not to do it. I know you're thinking I went too far, that I overreacted, so it's much better if you do it."

"Why would I care about a fucking prank? I flew here for you, not for Sergio."

"I'm out."

And here I may go after him, but that would mean becoming his babysitter. When he's ten meters away and I realize he's not stopping, I scream, "Hey, fuck you, Berengo! Why don't you just fuck the fuck off!"

I watch him extend a hand into traffic. A cab slows down, but then it speeds up again. I catch up and stare at him as he stretches his arm out horizontally, his fingers also outstretched, as if testing the water of the busy road. He looks like a page in his striped sweater, solemn and dark. I get lost whenever I see him in person, away from the webcam. I remember him: he looks old in his sweaters, even as he tweaks them to fit new trends, changes the way the hoods cover his hair, welcomes fashions without a sweat, thirty years of sweaters, stripes, hoodies, zippers . . .

Another cab slows down and stops. He climbs in and I follow, try to calm him down. "Are you tired, Nico? What's up with you? You on your period?"

His clammy hand lies dead in my hand on the fake leather seat. "Hey," I say. "It's fine if you're weirded out because it's been a few months since the last time. I know you, it's okay." His clammy hand. "We're rolling."

We're on East Eighth. I try to spot a sign to orient myself, but all I know is that it's our third red light. A few minutes later, as we sit at another red light, Nico gets out of the car and tosses his keys onto my lap. I hurl them back on instinct and get out of the car. "Pay," he says, but I don't, so he walks around the car while the light is still red and goes to talk to the driver, who pulls over to the curb in protest and accepts the fare. I escort him as he walks among the horns and screeches. The sidewalk is busy. I can see Madison Square Garden. We step inside a McDonald's and order two meals. I sit next to him, bewildered by the light.

"Are you okay?"

He doesn't answer. When we've finished our burgers—he leaves a half-moon of bread, but I've wolfed mine down; all that's left are pieces of lettuce and lukewarm fries scattered around open ketchup and mayo containers—I try again: "Why are you this mad? Do you want to talk?"

"I can't talk. I can't tell you shit. I can't do shit. I'm your prisoner." He says this with a fry in the corner of his mouth.

"Come on, *ciccio,* you're a big boy now," I joke. "Don't talk like that."

"I'm paralyzed. I don't know where to go from here."

"Okay, but don't make me feel like I'm imposing; you're the one who invited me. If you hadn't wanted me here, I wouldn't have come."

"I must." He stares at the table and eats more fries, one at a time. I feel calm. "I can't help it." His voice is climbing up to a falsetto. "You don't really know what you mean to me."

"Well, say it then. Maybe it'll be something nice?"

In falsetto: "You are God."

"What does that even mean, *ciccio*?"

With a baritone, after swallowing hard: "You are God."

"Nico," I laugh. "Nico, listen to yourself, Nicuzzo."

"Please."

"I'm Daria."

"No, you're not Daria. You are God."

I lower my head toward the tray, and my elbow is on the table. I'm tired, and he's finishing his fries in a McDonald's in a neighborhood I'm not familiar with. "I may be God, but I'm here, I'm here with you."

"I don't want to be here."

"Let's leave then."

He eats the last fry, gets up, and walks out. I follow him outside, where he's waiting for a cab with the same horizontal arm.

We hop in. "So you won't even talk to me?"

"I don't want to make a scene in front of the driver."

"Of course, but take my hand. It'll be all right, no scenes."

"But I'm not all right." He gives me his hand. It's still dead.

"I'm not doing the prank." I squeeze his hand, try to bring it back to life.

"Don't do it."

"Where are we going?"

"Why are you always trying to control everything?"

241

"Oh listen to yourself . . . Me, controlling? I see you four times a year. I'm not controlling shit!"

"See, you're not even *aware* you're controlling everything."

"Are you shitting me? Where are we going?"

He stops talking to me again. I sweat as I hold his hand. We reach the traffic light at the entrance to the Williamsburg Bridge. He asks the driver to pull up to the side, and we pay and leave. We're at the entrance ramp in front of a vacant lot, surrounded by the smell and roar of traffic.

"The difference," I begin, "is that this is a vacation for me, while for you, you're always on vacation."

Berengo is typing on his phone. He reaches out with his phone-holding arm, then starts typing again. He stops, waves to a new batch of busy cabs.

"I wish," I start again, "I wish that at some point you could try to do a week of office work. The whole thing: one-hour commute in the morning, one-hour commute in the evening. And then after you got home you'd have to indulge your love of books not by walking to McNally and hearing some imperialist novelist like James Murphy talk shit, but by sitting at home until four, reading and reviewing a book for free, for *Alias* or *Nazione Indiana*, totally out of love, just because you care. Only love keeps you up until four. I only wish I could see you do that."

Now he has his back to me. The phone is in his left arm, the right arm is stretched out in that dark exaggerated gesture I've seen him do all evening.

"Nico, would you stop it?"

"If you ask me to stop one more time I'll throw my keys off the bridge."

"But I only told you once."

"I'm throwing the keys off the bridge."

"Berengo, what the fuck, you're forty!"

"I'll throw them."

"The doormen have spare keys."

"I'll throw myself in, then."

"Can we just stop this scene? I've come to see you. I'm not taking any other holidays this summer."

"So what. What?" He still has his back to me and is hailing cabs. "You're saying you made sacrifices for me? What were they? You have a shitty job, but you can't be bothered leaving it to come live here?"

"You want me to?"

"No! You should have done it earlier! Leave me alone!" He's swaying as he speaks, still not facing me.

"But I *am* . . . leaving you . . . alone . . ."

In times like this I'm incapable of caring for myself, so I just wait for Nicolino to calm down. His harsh words change nothing. I can never know the outer limits of his insults, so it feels like he hasn't yet said anything to me that he has to apologize for. I don't know how I feel. It never seems like the moment requires me to know. He stops another cab, bargains with the driver over where to go and how to get there. When he's seated, he pauses to watch me standing out on the street, where I've stayed because he hasn't slid across the backseat to make room for me. "Get in," he says. "Will you? We always end up doing what you want."

I obey. This car's roof is lower than the previous ones, and I have a hard time finding a comfortable position. I cough. All this getting in and out of cabs has made me nauseous. This one has narrow armrests on the doors, and my elbow keeps falling off. I keep it on with the help of my left hand, and I realize that both my arms are in pain. Relaxing feels worse than being tense. It's my first night here; it's been a long one. I would settle for something unexpected, like a surprise sex party, but then I'd probably fall asleep.

After driving down Bedford, the cab pulls up in front of the glass entrance to a fancy, pale blue building on the river. The driveway faces the water and leads out to a pedestrian area and a pier. I open the door and feel the cool breeze rising from the water. As I get out of the car, Berengo stays inside, talking to the cab driver. So I wait in the wind. His eyes have mellowed, turned sad. "This is Sergino's place. He's on his way home. He says there's no problem with you staying here, and you can pick up his spare keys from the front desk. He'll be back in a bit. Just tell the doorman you need the spare keys, and he'll hand them over." A barrage of antic hand gestures, staring at his fingers. "I need to be alone tonight. I'm not okay."

The cab pulls out in reverse and leaves, and it's as if there's no one around. I sigh—the sound I always make whenever I'm at a loss for words. What emerges from my nostrils is a gentle, high-pitched *eeeeh* sound, and it's always a surprise, as if the shy ghost of Michael Jackson were skulking about.

The doorman and the guy at the desk are supernice.

FROM THE TWENTY-FOURTH-FLOOR window, the island looks like it's lying on its side, more horizontal than vertical. The effect is strange. I find an iPad and curl up to watch an alternative medicine video that shows viewers how to figure out exactly when they'll get cancer. I have thyroid problems, I smoke bad hashish, and I eat sugar and carbs. I scratch my left breast, a Roman charm against the thought of Death, and I feel It.

AN HOUR LATER, in the couch perpendicular to the window, Sergino lets me suck his dick until he comes. I keep my hand tilted and, exhausted, I breathe through my nose. My eyes can't stop looking out onto the luminous, scaly metal skin of the monster lying across the river.

A COOL NON-AIR-CONDITIONED night. Under the sheets, Sergio shows me the short film on his iPad. He wears bizarre black silk pajamas, we're illuminated by the film in the dark.

"IT'S SO UGLY it's good," I humor him. "It's so irritating. Let's do the prank." (Is *this* the moment when it becomes my fault?) Each of us lies on our own side of the king-size bed, and as I fall asleep, I realize I haven't been asked a single question about Berengo.

I WAKE UP early on Sunday morning and read *JR*, which I find on a shelf. The wind and the violent haze distract me, and I think about the many acres of glass that haven't yet been hit by direct sunlight. I wait for Berengo to call me. By noon, the temperature has risen to 74 degrees. Sergio is working in bed with his e-reader. Around lunchtime, the doorman buzzes up. There's a suitcase for me, Sergio says, adding that I can take the bedroom and he'll sleep on the couch. A young man in an elegant uniform hands me my compact lemon-yellow suitcase. I leave it near the door and go look for five dollars, which I hand to the bellhop. Then I put my bag in a corner of the bedroom. We play DJ Hero, smoke some pot, and discuss with affection how much of a nut job Berengo is, without pushing the argument too far.

AT FOUR I decide that I want to shower and change my underwear, but what I see when I open my suitcase makes my head spin. I slump backward. Sergino finds me lying on the shiny wooden floor a few minutes later, and he helps me to the bedroom, where I spend the next two hours with a sweet, mysterious flavor in my mouth. Its name is a whisper from Sergino's lips to my ears. "EN,

245

it's EN, E-N. I only have Xanax pills, and I don't want you to choke on them, take these drops." I wake up around seven p.m. and feel a presence at my bedside. Sergino is on his knees, his hand on the bedspread with which he's covered me. He's asking if I want him to order us any food. "Make the suitcase go away," I reply. "I don't ever want to see it again."

SERGINO STILL HASN'T said a single word against Berengo, but he has been kind to me. After taking a look at the clothes, which Berengo cut into little pieces and packed up and sent via UPS, Sergino reacted like a volunteer at the site of a natural disaster: he was tactful and calm and never once pointed out the obvious, never said a word about the house that had just burned down. He didn't try to argue that it wasn't bad, that I was overreacting, but the next morning he woke me up and ordered me to go outside with him. I complied, and when we got back the suitcase was gone. We haven't discussed the horrific salad of panties, with its shreds of light yellow and white and pink fabric and the thicker strips and the long filaments that used to be the stockings I'd bought for him to pull off of me. His ugly decision to include the black vibrator hasn't been brought up, nor has the fact that he ripped off its battery cover and pulled out one of its springs. Sergio hasn't said anything about my sneakers with the cut off tongues, about familiar things and their new shapes. I don't have enough money saved up to buy new clothes.

After a pancake breakfast at a flashy new diner whose attractive Scandinavian waiters we discuss while licking our fingers, Sergino takes me to a thrift store and to American Apparel to buy one or two items for the rest of my stay, on the pretext that I'll need to look the part in the prank. "Something modern but not distracting," he says. I'll be the producer, or the fixer. I've accepted reluctantly, but if it hadn't been for Sergio, I would have had to max out my credit card and wait for my next paycheck. Sergio didn't rub my face in the situation, didn't ask for anything in return. He just kept throwing pairs of stockings or pants into the shopping cart, while continuing to talk about the prank. It's good that it's warm out, or else he would have had to spend a fortune.

THERE'S NO WAY I'm skipping the Oneida Show at Secret Project Robot on Saturday night, especially because it's always Berengo who goes into hiding whenever we have our arguments. The warehouse is overshadowed by one of the new buildings near Sergio's. The river is across the street, beyond a tangle of wires, nets, metal cylinders, and danger signs. The members of Oneida are all forty. They wear jeans and t-shirts adorned with Beavis and Butthead's grimaces. Some of the band members have beer bellies; the others are wiry and slim. They've been playing psychedelic jams since lunch. At dawn, they'll play the new record, entirely electronic.

They've also cooked dinner for everyone using two pressure cookers with timers, some kind of Asian-style rice meal. There's a purple strobe light positioned near a column. There are a few hipsters; many fat, long-haired dudes; lesbians; a man and a woman asleep on chairs. James Murphy is there, too, a plate of rice in one hand, under a different strobe light.

I recognize James Murphy's face from the Internet, and I know he came to see me. He has the air of one of those priests too cool to wear the garb. He's not aware of the band, but he fits in, chewing with his mouth closed and staring into space.

He has recognized me from pictures, I guess, and maybe from Berengo's sex videos—I enjoy thinking he showed them to him. He leaves his plate on a shelf and walks over to me through the sparse crowd.

"Did Berengo send you?" I shout, kissing him on the cheeks.

"I wanted to meet you. He and I aren't on speaking terms. Didn't he tell you?"

"No?"

We spend the evening discussing Berengo in the dark, screaming to be heard. He doesn't know about my suitcase, so I can pretend it never happened, and here I am talking about Nico the way I like best—as if he were just a harmless kid who happened to snap. Luminous paint bleeds through the darkness in nondescript stoner paintings. We're Stalin and Roosevelt in Yalta.

He says Nico isn't doing well because one of his lovers passed away recently.

"Why are you telling me about his lovers?"

He's talking about this woman photographer who was shot and killed in a mortar attack while she was photographing a rebel group somewhere. I think I've read about her in the paper . . . so she was banging Nicolino. I make eye contact; he looks down but keeps talking: Berengo wants to break up with me. He tried to start a relationship with another woman, but they stopped seeing each other, and she's already in another relationship, so he sort of had a breakdown.

"You think," I say, "that if you tell me all of this I'll feel less guilty when I end up sucking your dick?"

Our strong opinions are swallowed up by the sound of the band. He keeps interjecting phrases like "So, we finally meet," and "Wow, Daria in the flesh." He says this even though he's seen pictures of me. ("Have you watched our videos?" "No, not those." "You can tell me, no problem." He sneezes in amazement.) In his mind I've always been an IRL version of Daria—

the MTV cartoon—the snobby, literate girl who functions as a kind of nineties compendium: sloppy, simple, well-read, partial to mix tapes. A fan of drab colors in unfortunate combinations—purple, green, fuschia, yellow. In 1997, he was thirty-five, if not older, whereas I was twenty-two. He says he likes my red hair and my round face.

At night, when the jam is over, we get Hanoi Jane, the guitar player, to fix us rum-and-tonics with lime. A DJ spins some dry, early reggae. We talk to him, too, then go down to the basement to smoke Sergino's pot. I want to take him beyond a screen at the end of the dark room downstairs. He stops me, and he says he'd rather not. We go back upstairs and fall asleep on two giant chairs some couple just deserted. We feel dizzy from climbing the stairs, and as I drift off I see cylindrical shapes pulsing red and orange pulled out of the darkness.

I OPEN MY eyes, take a look around. Now the hall is jammed with people. Many arrived just before dawn to hear the electronic set. The keyboard drones and somehow echoes the ventilation fan toward the back of the room. We have a hard time getting up, and as soon as we're awake enough to make a move, we leave.

I HAVE FOUR days left in New York, and James texts me to hang out. We spend Monday afternoon in Union Square staring at crackheads, a small society that occupies a semicircle of benches under the watchful eyes of the Parks & Recreation employees. I keep putting my sweater on and taking it off. Murphy says there's going to be a heat wave.

Squirrels and pigeons; a white crackhead with a spangled, purple cap; a black pusher in shorts, a fat guy in Timberlands trying hard to find a solution to some problem encountered by the group. Maybe he's just speaking slowly.

We talk about books. I argue that his is a fake, hollow empathy, tell him that I wrote about this very thing for the Communist paper. He laughs, says he knows about the review, and quips that he cares deeply about his Italian Communist fanbase, so would I please try to avoid alienating his readership? The crackheads are busy, affectionate. A guy in baggy nü-metal clothes comes over to ask for a cigarette. "I didn't want to bother you before, when I was eating my sandwich," he says.

Two afternoons later, the heat has receded. My armpits are still sweaty, and my period has started, but it's still light. We take a walk around the Financial District, then he takes me to the mall on the pier by the East River. We lie limply on the wooden beach chairs on the upper balcony. We watch barges and water taxis float by, and a boat with a midday dance party. Beyond Red Hook, a cruise ship, and right in front of us, the tips of the masts of the old sailing ships sway in the air, beacons for tourists.

"So if you're actually an empathic person, how come no one ever feels real pleasure in any of your books? *No one.* You force readers to follow some predetermined path to redemption, but you never actually portray their quest for pleasure, for well-being, for a happy, moderate, Pagan well-being."

"Berengo says nobody ever enjoys sex in my books."

"It's because you've only had disappointing sex in your life, and very little of it."

"That's right."

"And you want to have better sex."

"That's also right."

"See? I'm empathetic; I feel you. I've got you, I know what you want."

I'm holding onto the back of my neck with my hands, and my legs are stretched out and crossed at the ankles. I'm wearing a sleeveless shirt and sandals.

James stares at my neck, then pulls *To the Lighthouse* out of his backpack. He has brought it for me, and he offers it with trembling hands. I open it, but he takes it back and begins to read it aloud himself. On second thought, I'm not really sure he's trembling at the touch of my fingers.

Ma come funzionano le cose? In che modo giudichiamo la gente, o ce ne formiamo un'impressione? Su che base, sommando una cosa all'altra, concludiamo che proviamo simpatia o antipatia? E, in ogni caso, qual è il significato di queste parole?

"Well, you know, it *is* sexy to hear you read aloud like this, because I know you're trying to make up your mind about whether you want to take me home or not. The truth is I like you because you're a big-time author, and I want you to take me like you take your female students."

"I don't sleep with my students. Is this something Berengo told you?"

"Virginia Woolf always comes in handy when you need to get laid."

It stops there, and we move on to Jonathan Franzen and his awkward relationship with Murphy. And the whole time James Murphy is thinking, *well, it's happened again. As soon as I knew this woman wanted me, it killed my appetite. I won't take her back to NYU, to the Soviet high rise. I will never know what Berengo gets to experience with Daria.*

AFTER I LEFT, we stayed in touch via email to discuss books we were reading and reviewing. He told me about "Marcello" and the problem of ambition. Something he'd seen in Times Square late June had reminded Murphy of him: at Seventh and Broadway, there was a man perched at the top of a streetlamp and a crowd had gathered around him, everyone filming the scene with their phones. "He was up high, sitting on the lamp, crouching like Spider-Man. You couldn't tell if he was going to jump. He wasn't high enough to really get himself hurt, but the police were still trying to get him to climb down. The next day, I pick up a tabloid and read a short piece about him—there's even a little picture of him. Turns out he's a Jersey guy in his early thirties who wanted to be a rapper and wanted to attract the public's attention by climbing that streetlamp."

"MARCELLO" DIED IN a car crash in Rome's Prati Fiscali while driving his father's Saab. James heard about it from Cugino Hitler, bought a plane ticket for a flight the following day, and flew there with Sergio. (He never mentioned Berengo, and I didn't ask.) He arrived the day of the funeral, just in time for afternoon mass. Berengo didn't attend, even though he's been back living in Rome for a while. (Again, when Berengo and I don't speak, he vanishes.)

*T*here isn't a single octopus carpaccio my American lover fails to describe in his notebook. No island view can pass without his note taking—no trapezoidal moon reflected on the black, cobbled surface of the quiet nighttime sea; no vines creeping along ancient stucco; no choreography of children playing football in a courtyard. My lover is shabby and gray haired, thin and weak and pale. We have come to Ventotene to commit adultery after the funeral, and he never takes off his baseball cap, never varies his outfit: a short-sleeved shirt and and blue shorts. There are a few black hairs on his arms and legs. He wishes he had a hundred eyes with which to take notes, but he keeps dozing off—at the bar in the piazza, under the pergola, on the rocks by the sea, back in our room. He's upset by his first extramarital affair and by the death of the Italian young man whose voice remains an eternal presence on his phone and on his laptop. "Marcello" used to scare him, he says, and now he's dead. He's American, so in a way he has to be a boor: he's polite and professional, but he treats beauty like a parasite. He's a speculative moralist, and his notetaking gets on my nerves. He refrains from mentioning his wife, yet his discretion is a symbol of some kind of masculine vanity. He sits on the rocks and stares out at the sea, sighing and holding my little finger, dozes off sitting, wakes up and asks me if he was asleep. He's going to take notes on everything, and he'll process it all rapidly. He draws major moral conclusions from the posture of a modest seagull that observes a group of children playing in the water. The seagull's rock is two meters away from the one we're sitting on. Between our two rocks is a small canal where the kids show off their diving skills.

The chubby kids with their love handles get in line and take turns jumping. We keep our distance and look down at them from our perch.

Everything has to mean something for James Murphy, who holds his pen with tremendous concentration. Is the sea green like jade, or is it turquoise blue? Two girls dive in and splash his notebook. I stand behind him, whispering in his ear, spying on his work. He wants to describe these eternal kids as ineffably Southern, somehow—he loves the South, for him the image of the Magical Negro is too deep seated to fully quell. He writes: black fish and striped fish. He ignores their names because he never liked going fishing with his father. The small fish swimming through the canal, indifferent to the divers lined up on the rocks.

Beyond the seagull we see the island of Santo Stefano, the hollow ruin of the prison towering over it. He tries to find a metaphor in order to commit the prison to memory, but he fails. The seagull, with its satisfied, feathery belly, looks lost in thought. When the bird speaks it speaks with a man's voice: *"Aaaah."* In James Murphy's notes, the seagull becomes a prison's guardian, depressed and worn down by his unrewarding job. Damned metaphors.

I translate the kids' tussle for him. The girl who dove in first declares, "The women are more brave."

A thin, savvy-looking boy is afraid to jump. "So are there jelly-fish in there or not?"

Now another girl who dove in teases him. She's fat and confident: "Cinderella, the carriage is waiting for you." She crushes the *s* in *aspetta! (wait!)* in an adorable way that I'm not able to translate into English.

I try to help James with dialogue, but I can't translate it all.

The cowardly kid has a new problem. "There's a chunk of poop in there!"

"It's a pebble!"

The girls float in the water and make fun of him.

The first girl: "I've been playing with them in the water! They're just pebbles!"

The fat one: "Hurry up! The carriage is on its way!"

"Is there really a piece of crap in there, though?" And also, "Is it crap or is it a pebble?"

James jots down the conversation in English, annotating my explanations.

"Hey!" the kid asks the girls who swim away. "Is the carriage already gone?"

"Of course it is! It's not for babies!"

The seagull takes it all in, safe on his comically straight legs.

James knows nothing, and he'd love to know everything. At dinner I insult him. You're just an MFA student, I say, like all American authors. He sweats and argues. He's fifty years old and his face is decomposing. He can't eat or drink because of acid reflux that wakes him up at night with coughing fits that are Bruegelian in scale, a sequence of grimaces and anguished pauses. He avoids the lentils, the *paccheri*, and the prawns because he's afraid of death.

I KNOW FROM his notes that James loves the way I smile in bed. *Should I feel lonely? I don't know the meaning of her smile; it might just be that she's able to godere.* He himself is incapable of *godere* (he's mesmerized by the Italian verb): he may find himself content, but nothing more, he cannot experience true enjoyment, *godere*. When he's actually pleased by something he feels too schmaltzy. Still, he is the Author, and people rely on him to provide descriptions of emotion for them to inhabit.

I CALL HIM provinciale all the time. He's from the Midwest, and I'm from Rome. He speaks at a Roman auditorium designed by Renzo Piano and he's invited to the summer festival in Capri, whereas I'm a secretary who works for the owner of a travel agency and I write literary criticism for free. James has always dreamt of making a sex video, and I've told him he can ask me to do whatever he wants. It feels reckless—he has the vague feeling that I might ruin him by sharing it. His fear puts some fear in me too, which makes things interesting—ordinarily I wouldn't care too much. I tease him until he finds the courage to shoot his penis and my vagina.

A GANG OF kids runs right by us and dives into the water, then jumps onto the rock in front of us and claims it, forcing the seagull into a corner. They try to imitate the seagull's voice, but they do it all wrong. I translate what follows for James:

"Regalini (little gifts) is just another way to say *merdate* (crap-dumps)."

"Le merdate are escrementi (droppings)."

"Piss is *escrementi*, too."

"The fish always piss *cacarella* (the trots)."

The cowardly kid stays behind on our rock. He screams to the fat girl, who's now far away at sea. "Carriage! Come on! You have to help me!"

She swims over.

"But how do I hop over you?" he asks.

"Just come in! I'll catch you!"

"Here I come!"

"You're such a scaredy cat! Worse than a girl!"

"Manina!" he begs. He wants the girl to hold his hand.

A lady with dyed hair and electric blue rubber shoes swims by slow and passionless.

JAMES MURPHY, MY seagull, sighs and stays quiet. He wants me to take his cheating seriously, but all I can see is his power. I tell him that's the reason he can have me. His frown grows deeper until he dozes off in the cool air-conditioned air, leaving me alone to watch our latest video. I see my tired face, my belly with its horizontal line, yet when I fuck him I look young.

He can't understand what's happening to us. James is the champion of literary empathy; these modern Americans are so good at making the reader feel human—they think literature connects us all. They became important under George W. Bush, these writers, emerging as an antidote to his regime, so now they feel obligated to provide a model of absolute virtue at all times to suppress every individual interest, to avoid every class vice. Thus they convince themselves and their readers they have no class vices at all, even as they get big grants from billionaires who indulge them with one hand and take from the poor with the other.

My intolerance spikes during our visit to Santo Stefano. A

guide who seems to know every detail and factoid entertains a few dozen tourists in the old prison. For James Murphy the place is a symbolic heaven. He sleeps through half of the ninety-minute-long lecture in a shadowed corner of the courtyard, yet he still manages to note down most of the things I'm able to translate. He writes about the "Rousseau Experiment," when crooks and prostitutes were sent to the pristine island so they could redeem themselves as noble savages, but ended up falling into greater vice. He's fascinated by the premise and the design of the prison, which is organized like Jeremy Bentham's Panopticon but based on the blueprints for Naples's Teatro San Carlo. He tries hard, says that I'm Bentham and he's the Teatro San Carlo, so if we had a child, blah blah blah. I reply that I'm Bentham and that I'm also the Teatro San Carlo, and he's just an American, an imperialist.

What rubs me the wrong way is how he obsesses over the seagull or the blueprints when he can't even grasp crucial details directly in front of his face, such as the wealth of things that one can learn from the short pants and the accent of the forty-year-old guide. The man's relationship with the prison fills me with great melancholy. He tells us tourists that since none of the convicts liked hanging out *con le mani in mano*, idling, an old convict was recruited to stand watch. "He smoked his pipe and *a domanda rispondeva*"—which is untranslatable. It means "he'd answer when asked," but it means so much more than that. It means he did what he was supposed to do and let the time pass, a way, perhaps, to wait for death to come? No, no—the guide would deny death as a motive. And that is why it's untranslatable. It's a way of saying something that, if it were it to be read and restated explicitly, you'd quickly deny having said it.

James will never be able to grasp all the meanings of *"a domanda rispondeva,"* and I will never love him.

And as he explains the difference between windowless cells and normal cells, the guide uses the expression *riscontro d'aria*, which means that there's a double passage for air that creates a pleasant flow between interior and exterior. James is sitting on the dusty ground with his legs crossed, hatless in the shadow. I am struck by a feeling of grief: he cannot possibly know how important *riscontro d'aria* is for us and how mysterious and familiar the word *riscontro* really is. We usually use it to mean "double-check," and it makes the breeze feel vital and alive—an entire institution.

James is a Dostoevskian, so he's completely won over when I translate Luigi Settembrini's descriptions of the corporal punishments that occurred at the center of the Panopticon, surrounded by thousands of people screaming, of the rope that was used to whip the prisoners being soaked in tar in the presence of the doctor and the priest. *Il battuto chiama la Vergine e i Santi, che poc'anzi bestemmiava.* (The beaten calling the Virgin and the Saints, whom he's been cursing.) *Bestemmiava* is so much more than "cursing." James's constant search for depth makes him look so shallow to me. He doesn't even know how much he doesn't know. And if he's using a funeral as a pretext for running away with me, he shouldn't get too carried away with an anecdote about torture, he who doesn't understand *a domanda rispondeva* or *a riscontro d'aria*.

I WAS STARTING to wonder if I was making a point about Americans or about men—he was definitely both a white American and a man: so used to winning that he didn't need to be aware of who he was in order to keep winning.

ONE NIGHT ON the beach, he tells me that he finds me cold. If this were a James Murphy story, this would be the moment when something opens up and reveals the humanity of the characters, their need to be redeemed.

My take is: "Nicola talked to you about me. You thought you needed me. You used a funeral as an excuse, and now I'm here entirely because of you."

"Not entirely . . ."

"And you're waiting for something to be revealed."

There is a group of teenagers fifty meters from us. They're good at fighting and at arguing, and I can't translate their language—the friendly, threatening quips they throw back and forth, a way to kill time before night swimming.

"But I won't reveal anything, James. You don't deserve it."

"I'm frustrated, Daria. I like you a lot. This is good."

The teenagers head toward the water. The sand is hard with pebbles, so they have to be cautious; they can't even take a running start. They continue to talk, and I still can't translate. James is free to move around on the island and learn every trick of the language and maybe even begin to lose his own, the evil English language, which simplifies everything and also seeks to own it all. Most likely, almost certainly, he'll go back to Cleveland. He'll begin a new novel, write fifty pages about me, and then he'll throw it all in the garbage. It'll be discovered posthumously and included in a collection of unpublished work. The editor will slip my review of *The Rockwells* into a footnote to try to make sense of my influence on the author. I'll be alive, an old lady, living in a commune of women.

He leaves his laptop open when he goes to sleep, no password is required, so he wants me to meddle, to find the emails from his family where they beg him to come back. I'm at the desk looking up information on ferries and trains, but instead I find his daughters' pleas:

"Where did you go, Dad? I'll be back soon, after exams are

over. Will you be back? Mom says she doesn't know. Why doesn't she know?"

"I don't really know what's going on, but you should come home, Dad."

"Dad, I'm not trying to be disrespectful, but this thing with the funeral in Rome is ridiculous. Come back. I don't want Mom to start thinking this poor guy who died was your boyfriend."

"I'm sorry. Don't be mad at me; I'm just worried."

"Mom will never say any of this because she's too proud and she's already upset about New York. If you want to get a divorce, you can tell me; I'm grown up enough. Kit isn't, but I am. So be a grown-up, too."

"Papà, there's ants at home. Mamma says we have to tell you because if she tells you you won't believe her. Yesterday we didn't go to mass so we could stay and get rid of all the ants in the apartment."

"Mamma thinks the ants came from the balcony because one of the plants is sick. We're spraying it with this white spray; hopefully it'll get better."

"Papo, if you're in America again, we need American guitar picks. Mamma won't tell us where you went for work."

"Pa' I don't know how to write yet, but I love you. Esther is writing for me."

"Papo if you don't come back we're taking the PLANE to come get you!!!"

I should feel terribly guilty, but I don't. I started reading these emails as I crouched, then kneeled, in front of the sideboard, this classic Danish piece from the fifties, where Gustavo left his laptop open. No password. His children are precocious, but the emails were clearly written by their mother. Now I'm sitting on an Eames Herman Miller chair, Gustavo's ugly office laptop on my lap. I can hear him snoring. My legs are stretched out on the black ottoman.

I was lucky to have had the idea to ask my parents for furniture money; I'll get to keep everything.

Since I've never really made such a big choice before, I can't gauge my own courage. I'm figuring it out as I go, and I'll see where it gets me. For three days—evenings, nights, mornings—we've stayed in bed together through the wet summer rain. My friends, I haven't called you to tell you what's been happening, but I'm speaking to you now as if you were here in our spare room at four a.m., your backs against the other sideboard—a British model from 1968—the napes of your necks reflected in the horizontal glass. I never invite you over, I never see you; you are just my mother's clerks.

Gustavo has opened me up, and I feel lonely and exposed. I've felt too superior to you over the last few years. I'm speaking to you now, though I haven't got the courage to call you. I didn't even call you about Lorenzo and the whore and the GIF she sent.

TONIGHT IT'S NOT as hot as it's been over the last few days, but I haven't stopped sweating. It's still raining. The digital barometer Lorenzo hung next to his desk on the other side of the room reads 18°C. I don't know what to make of the children's emails. I'm weary and thirsty. I'm being drained of liquids. The unthinkable is happening, and I wish I were sleepy so I could lie in his arms. The children have no idea that their mother is writing those emails.

I go downstairs to have some water and maybe a chamomile tea. I open the fridge and pull out a pitcher of cold water and pour it into a fancy Coca-Cola glass. I add a pack of Polase potassium powder, which I found in the bathroom. I close the refrigerator door and find myself in the calm, moonlit darkness.

I haven't lowered the electric shade that covers the illegal balcony window, the one that takes up the entire wall that faces my yard. I love looking out at the train depot, at the tracks where the trains coming from Via Prenestina stop before the split that leads them to Naples or to central Rome.

Should this dream continue? Should Gustavo remain in my life and bring me peace? With time, would the kids adapt to this house?

I pour boiling water into a mug with a chamomile tea bag and carry it out of the kitchenette. I sit at the seventies-looking table, the one Lorenzo never liked. I picture it covered in soggy cookies and drops of warm milk. I picture the children sitting at this round table, everyone except Esther, who surely prefers to have breakfast alone on the grass while reading one of my Jane Austen novels. I Maschi would surely start hitting their mugs with their spoons the way they saw someone do it in a movie about a jailbreak . . .

The citrusy powder lingers in my mouth, and with the chamomile tea in hand, I sit down on the Fritz Hansen egg chair. I tell my friends about Lorenzo's work trip, the GIF. The whore's name on Facebook is *Chissei Miyake—Whoareyou Miyake*—and she's sent me this GIF of a woman's gorgeous, sinewy hands grabbing my Lorenzo's dick. I recognize the little dark spot and the way it bends right.

I get up and try the raw silk chair with the gilded, padded armrests. I've picked out some great furniture for this house. I sit down at the round table, my elbows pressing down on the glass as I weep. I feel a dim pain in my chest. Me, a stepmother to five children, it's like something out of a Grimms' fairy tale, the only fate for a woman who hadn't found what she needed until now. Where was I? I love him.

I loved him before we went back to my house straight from the gym, before I did something I'd never done before: signed up for a gym membership knowing that I would trap him there. I loved him before the online chats, before he told me he was scared about the fact that soon his kids would have to start making their own choices in football, in hip-hop, in everything else. I loved him before I saw Lorenzo's cock in a black-and-white loop. I loved him before we left the gym and rode into the rainy evening, both of us getting wet before we'd made it a hundred meters. I had nothing on over the t-shirt I'd worn to the gym, and though he had a K-Way, he didn't even have time to insist that I put it on. I loved him before he said, "So what are we going to do now" while I was on the stationary machine, before he waited outside, under an awning, while I showered, before I dared to hug him for the first time as he sat there on his bike. I loved him before we cut through the stale traffic of Porta Maggiore on our respective bikes and I couldn't even look at him when he stopped at traffic lights a safe distance away from me. And I loved him long before I frantically rummaged through my gym bag for my keys while he stood on the sidewalk shaking with fear, fidgeting, and doing his best not to press me to hurry up there, on the sidewalk, in front of the many gloomy eye sockets of the Roman aqueduct. I loved him before he undressed me and before he sobbed and shook as he fucked me, before I laughed as he squeezed my ass and left bruises, before he climaxed in an XL condom and sobbed again, then shut himself in the bathroom for ten minutes. He was embarrassed by the horrific stench he'd left for me, but he shouldn't have been. That stench was a kind of scary confession, and the next day he spanked me again, and I laughed again, and he spanked me where I already had bruises—small, raised, red ones and hazier purple ones. He's the only person to have entered my house since I changed the locks two eternal days ago. I spent the day waiting for him to come back from work. I cleaned the house, tidied it up, raked the grass in the backyard and in the smaller front yard.

After the chamomile tea I stop by the bathroom, sit on the bidet, and wash thoroughly with cool soap and lukewarm water. I don't use a towel, letting the water trickle down. I'm naked when I walk into the room, and I dry myself on the clean sheets I've placed atop the turquoise Scandinavian love seat. I take a good look at him.

He sleeps naked under the sheet, which covers his whole body. We haven't lowered the shutters or pulled the curtains closed, and the light from the moon and Quartiere Tuscolano gives the white sheet a warm pallor. I touch a wet part of the bed.

Through the sheet I see his many dark hairs, the curls that fall onto his temple, his bulging dick, which feels so different from Lorenzo's. He lies there with his hands entwined behind his head. He's regal: his face is more tired than baggy, and he has the wide eyelids of a lion, a large mouth, a flat nose. He sleeps with his mouth shut. What a king.

I sit on him with the sheet between us, and I feel the puddle forming, my usual puddle, against the sheet. I shut my eyes and feel him get hard. I stroke his damp, bristly cheeks with both hands.

His need is infinite. He won't even open his eyes as he grabs my hips, feels them. He knows I've barely eaten in three days, and he moves me away to touch his dick, pats me on my hips as a way to order me to pull the sheet away, but though I do what he wants, he suddenly sits up, puts me on my knees, and with an unceremonious gesture slides the tip of his thumb into my anus. I don't complain or tell him what to do. He also puts his index finger in my vagina. I love pressing down with my third eye against the mattress: I'm stuck in a yoga pose. A car passes by, then another with a bigger motor. I let him hold me there up until we hear someone passing by on a bike.

He's sitting on his side and we're not talking. He kneels, gets behind me, and takes me, first in the normal way, sweet and intimate, two bodies melting perfectly into each. Then the other way, and I'm glad it isn't too painful, that it isn't impossible. When he tries to get inside me, I feel a wall forming, the sheer unthinkability of something getting through. Then, suddenly, a thaw: the body caves in, skin against skin no longer violent, everything climbs up to the heart.

I shake and spill as I come. Gustavo wets his hand and puts it inside me for added pleasure. He tells me to sit under the window, and after popping some Maalox, puts his dick in my hand and stands there, watching the trains circle the depot. He puts his elbows on the windowsill. I hold his dick with two hands. Sucking it feels electric. I cling to it and close my eyes.

FOR BREAKFAST THE next morning, I squeeze oranges, slice bread, lay out fig jam, and pour American coffee. I can tell that he loves eating breakfast in the nude. We sit at the round table, the cool breeze flowing from the window, desire seizing the air. He touches the new bruises on my legs and shoulders, studies them every morning the way I study new flowers and buds in the garden. Our talk is silly.

"You have to take care of me. Give me sex all the time," he says, scattering crumbs everywhere, pressing his fingertips onto them to pull them into his mouth.

"You have to take care of me," I say. "You're mine. I'll choke you, and I'll drown you. I'm Niagara Falls."

I don't eat. I drink Polase with one hand and use the other to rub his big thigh.

"Still?"

"Totally. Just order me around."

"Go drown yourself. It's an order."

"Don't talk like that, or I'll overflow and pass out."

266

"I want you to overflow and pass out, and then you'll wake up all sticky while I'm in the office."

"Bad boy."

"Stop drinking Polase. I want to see you faint."

I rest my glass. I'm weak and electric.

"Are you drenched?" He swallows some bread and jam, licks his lips, grabs me, takes my shirt off, and though he's still chewing he drags me to the illegal door and the illegal window and presses me against the unbreakable glass, against the strong frame.

"I belong to you."

"You have to faint."

"I took vitamins."

"I'm stronger than you."

Which makes me so slippery inside that afterwards I'll lie on the cool wood floor, glued to it, sweating against the dust, as he rushes to shower and not be late to work. At some point he's laughing and shouting from upstairs, "And you have to wash the shirt I used yesterday . . . and iron it!"

We've bought three shirts and three pairs of socks and underwear. He uses the same suit every day. I hang it in the backyard at night, under the awning. The same *blu di Prussia* tie.

I tilt my head as far back as it will go. Outside the sky is pale and white, clouds and air becoming hot. I stare at the ceiling so long it turns into a floor. I crawl over the window frame and lie on the grass to dry. The sun is warm but the air is still cool, and nobody can see me here except for an old lady next door, whose single window looks out onto the yard. I sneer, weak and smitten, and doze off.

I WAKE UP to the urgent trill of the buzzer along with a few distant knocks on the door. They sound rude, and I get scared, pull myself together, and rush upstairs to get dressed and see if my guess is right, which it is: it's Lorenzo.

I appear at the window. He knew that's what I would do, and he's retreated across the street, under the aqueduct. He's never looked this serious. He joins his hands in prayer and says, "Let me in. Please."

I signal to him that he needs to leave, and I'm surprised by how vulgar the gesture feels. Who is this man? What does it mean that he is my husband?

He's stuck there, frozen and dumb, ruined, out of ideas. I turn my back to him and look at the things in the room. I want to give them all back. I pick up his Leica in its padded case, open the window, and hurl it as far as I can with both hands. "No!" he shouts, jumping. The two-handed effort throws me off balance, and I feel like I'm falling off the ledge. I don't know whether he saved the camera or not. I have left the room. I go downstairs and realize that I smell of sex, so I roll down the shutter that faces the front yard and lock the door. I'm afraid he might climb over the gate, I'm picturing him pierced by its iron spikes.

When I try to go back upstairs, my knee falters, and I have to rest on the steps for a moment.

Lying on the bed, I write him an email from my mobile.

"If you don't stop now you'll have to pay my alimony."

"Forgive me."

THE NEXT MORNING, I get up even earlier to make orange juice, and the rest of the spread is ready by the time he wakes up. He examines my new bruises. "I took it easy on you last night, but these are becoming darker." We're back against the door that he loves, and as we do it standing up, facing each other, him holding my leg up, I feel my inside tingling, and he's tingling, too. He tells me that this makes it even more pleasurable than usual, this tickle, and I realize my yeast infection has returned. The tingling makes for a decadent torture. You shouldn't have fasted like that, I think. I've screwed up my balance and all my defenses. I won't explain this now, though; I will when he's back from work, after I've bought the medication. For the moment I let him finish fast in my hands while I'm on my knees, then I watch him go upstairs for a shower.

I walk to the pharmacy against traffic. I have the feeling I'm being followed as I check the other gardens to see if their jasmine is richer and whiter than mine—my jasmine's petals are starting to brown. After the underpass I walk up to Via Casilina and cross the boulevard under a gloriously feathery sky. The railroad and the road are parallel with the aqueduct, and I see old shacks, strange gazebos, and mysterious random buildings leaning against the Roman ruin. The yellow and white trolley heads to Termini Station, its rough pantograph combing the air.

I enter Pigneto, go to a pharmacy I've never been to before. I buy Sporanox, a vaginal douche, fungicidal soap, ointment with an applicator, blueberry aloe vera, and vitamin C tablets. I'll rinse and lather Gustavo's cock, which I'm sure will soon be covered in blotches, if it isn't already. He's going to freak out.

I can't bring myself to go farther into Pigneto, beyond the train tracks, to buy greens at the farmers' market. I'm annoyed that Lorenzo might be following me without making himself visible. I return to Via Casilina, cross the underpass, and stop there, looking over my shoulder. I hold my pharmacy bag in plain sight, though I don't want Lorenzo and Gustavo's wife—who I have a feeling is following me with Lorenzo—to guess its contents. So I hold it against my hip, trying to conceal everything other than the aloe bottle.

I open the metal door to my yard, and when I shut it behind

me I feel relief. As if I've escaped danger at the last possible moment. I spend the day catching up on all my viral marketing responsibilities.

At dinner I tell him about the yeast infection. He panics and only then realizes that there's swelling under his foreskin. I calm him down, but he keeps saying that he hadn't noticed. I take him to the bathroom, promise it'll pass quickly; it's nothing, just stress related. He refuses medication at first, then enjoys it. He sits on the bidet, where I soap him up. "So, if you put cream on, then we're not going to do anything tonight?" I laugh and tell him that he's gotten over his fears in no time, that I'll put my cream on just before sleep. We take a shower, and I pee on his shoulder, my first time. He's down on his knees and squints and spits with a big smile.

Later, I tell him that it's a harmless disease, totally straightforward. I apply the cream with three fingers, get him hard, make him come, wash him again, then unscrew the applicator and stick it inside me.

I NOTICE SOMETHING over the weekend: Lorenzo and Gustavo's wife, Maria, have been outside the house. My street is carrying the unmistakable air of having been brushed with danger. The ruffled jasmine, two cars I've never seen, long minutes without anyone walking or driving by, a window in the shack under the aqueduct opened and closed twice in succession.

I jerked Gustavo off earlier in the morning, and now I watch him asleep in bed. I've just used the douche, and I'm sore from the penetration of the cold plastic. My hair is wet; I have a towel around my waist. I have to store Lorenzo's equipment in a corner of our spare room. I pull the wires from the desktop Mac, the printer, the projector, and the Sony HDR-FX1. They're all against the window now, and I'm crouching by them, trying to detect any hints of their secret operations. I should really move them to the toolshed outside, so that if he freaks out and wants them back I can buzz the metal door open and let him collect what he needs. I guess if I left the metal door open, he could come by himself with no need to make an appointment. I keep staring out the window, and I see more circumstantial evidence of his presence: the rake against the wall, the fact the metal door, though it's shut, doesn't seem to be hanging perfectly straight, as if it's been warped.

I move his things into the toolshed one by one. I can hardly keep myself from opening every device's battery case to take out the long-term memory batteries. They're recording, but I don't think they can do much now that they're in the toolshed. They must have already recorded what they needed. It doesn't matter. Lorenzo's cheating has been documented also, and it can be proven that it happened before I got together with Gustavo. So from a legal standpoint, I should be safe.

I start a wash cycle in the backyard, barefoot on the Cotto tile floor and on the grass, and I realize I need more Polase—I'm soaked in sweat and I'm shivering. I run the hot, smooth, steamy tip of the iron around the buttons of Gustavo's shirts. I smooth the creases on the pale blue hue that is so new to my home. I iron his ties delicately, then leave the iron in the vertical position on top of the washing machine to cool off. I go upstairs holding two shirts on hangers. I'm getting good at this. I hang them in the closet while he's waking up, a hand on his crotch.

"I'd like to."

"All right. It hurts, though."

"Backdoor, then."

I smile, even though it's unpleasant with a condom.

We stay in all weekend. I persuade him to not vote on the referendum on water and nuclear energy. We don't agree on the nuclear question, so after arguing for a while, we decide that our votes would cancel each other out and we might as well stay home. He still wants me to go out for groceries on Monday. It's too hot for proteins, we need more greens, a couple of peaches maybe, and what about some fruit for the juicer?

OUR SECOND WEEK of love begins, and his blisters are diminishing. His glans looks wrinklier. I keep it white with soap and ointments, and the antibiotic seems to be working, though it gives us both stomachaches. He begs me to buy an antacid. All I'm doing these days is running errands.

My only problem is Maria: by now she knows that Gustavo is cheating on her; Lorenzo has told her everything. It'll fall on Gustavo to support the kids, and it won't be a consensual separation. It will dent our resources, and I have to be ready. Maria is outside on the street, I'm certain of this: the street is hers; I see it when I'm at the window upstairs. I can't even go out to check Lorenzo's devices for signs that they've started recording again.

I have two garlic bulbs in my refrigerator, an onion, some ricotta that smells questionable, and my stomach hurts. Some prosciutto di Parma that dates back to Wednesday. I lower the refrigerator's temperature by two notches. There are anchovies covered in mold and some leftover Philadelphia cream cheese that's hardened over the last few weeks. The milk smells. Some Aperol plus flat tonic water. I have cod for two in the freezer, with spinach and a few green peas. I don't want to ask Gustavo to buy food for me; he doesn't know that his wife has stopped by several times, and I want to spare him the anxiety. Also I'm almost out of Polase.

This evening we're back to regular sex—with a condom. Gustavo is itching deliriously, and we laugh: love, the apex of love.

He lets himself go and starts talking like a kid. He starts using a Milanese accent, laughing, *"doppia libidine!"*—some weird old slang. He seems so cheerful as he spanks his shiny wet belly while he lies next to me, and I feel more comfortable. "Running errands has become a bit of a problem," I say. "The thing is that your wife is following us."

He starts drumming on his belly with both hands and makes a squishy sound with his mouth, then stops. "No." Then another pause. "She is not following you, Ludovica."

"Believe me, she is."

Some more drumming, and then, "Don't talk. Don't talk."

I put some reggae on the Tivoli on the nightstand. It's Lorenzo's, so the next morning I go downstairs and put it in the toolshed with all the other devices.

I GO BACK to work on Tuesday after Fofi calls me and tells me I've been gone for a whole week.

"You're not paying me, so what do you expect me to do?" I tell him when I get there.

"Don't give me that. Your father told me that he wants to pay you, that he's unhappy he has to do it like this."

"Let's see how it goes."

"Will you come back, honey? We miss you."

In my absence he's reverted to the old *Fofetto* caricature. He treats me like a flower, abandons his patronizing tone and his insistence on talking to my father about everything—his deference to authority.

My mother spends the day not asking me about Lorenzo. It's the first time this has ever happened, so it's clear everyone knows what's going on: Maria, my mother, and also Fofi, I guess. I wait all day for Lorenzo to show up like he did last winter in the boutique, when we were in New York and all of this was just beginning. But he seems to have vanished. Perhaps he has an elaborate plan to avoid being discovered. He's not asking for his stuff back, so maybe he's not working, or maybe he's bought new equipment or borrowed it from friends. My mother, though, what does she want from me? Why hasn't she hugged me?

I gather the courage to water the bougainvillea and the jasmine, though I can practically hear Maria's breathing on the other side of the metal door. Gustavo gave me the courage with his example. He came to pick me up at work, the daredevil, so I left my Vespa at the store, looking all Lorenzian, as if Lorenzo had spent the day sitting on it, waiting for me, and only left at the last possible minute. I'll pick it up tomorrow when Gustavo brings me back on his bike, even though it's not on his way to work. He says, "Spend some time at the bookstore; it's good for you. Otherwise you'll just spend the day waiting around for me to come back, and you'll get all funny in the head."

ON WEDNESDAY MY mother leaves Librici early in the afternoon to go cook minestrone, leaving me and Fofi alone—deliberately, it seems. There aren't many customers around, and the ones who are there order iced coffee and juice—the two things it takes us the longest to prepare. Regulars know never to ask for either item.

How can I describe my mother's behavior these days? She must have talked to Gustavo's wife, and she must have stopped by my house with them. I'm lucky I've changed the locks, lucky that I haven't handed out my spare keys to anyone yet. Suddenly she's gone without saying goodbye. This is how my parents are: they vanish when things get rough.

I wear an empire-waist dress, which has a bit of a maternity look to it. The cotton rustles and feels a little see-through. I haven't had anything to eat, and I spend most of the day sitting on a stool I've dragged behind the bar, which gives Fofi an excuse to try to squeeze by. "You won't let me through!" says the teddy bear behind me, his stomach against the short back of the stool, his sweat a prickly whiff. He places his hands on my shoulders, and I let him kiss me silently on my head, but then he hugs me, and his heavy intertwined arms slide down around my shoulders. What is he doing?

"Fofetto-or-treat? It's hot in here, I need breathing room."

"I've missed you."

"I've missed you too, Fofettopolis."

"Want me to fix you a juice? You look pale."

"Don't bother, really."

"Something light and fresh? Apple, carrot, and ginger."

"Will you finish it for me if I leave it?"

Up to this point it's smooth sailing: I know how to handle him, and I hope they start paying me again. I'm not sure I want to be a kept woman. I've almost quit the marketing job, which always slows down in the summers, anyway.

After closing time, almost all the lights are switched off, and we're in the storage area. There's a stack of fresh t-shirts; he's just changed into a new one, a Polo that gives him some shape.

"You look good in polos. I can tell you can't stand button-downs, but polos make you look very distinguished."

"We're all nice and friendly tonight. You trying to butter me up so you can get your paycheck back?"

He sits on a chair, and I've never seen him this tired, or maybe I've never noticed. His five o'clock shadow makes him look younger. It's possible that he knows everything and is taking my side. "Fofetto, would you ever go and work for my dad, I mean in the company?"

He strokes his reddish cheeks with two symmetrical palms,

from top to bottom, finishing at the chin where the two middle fingers touch. What to make of this gesture? I'm in the other chair watching him out of the corner of my eye while I flip through the pages of a big book, one of those art books I'll have to buy back with my own money, eventually. I have the strange feeling that this place is an extension of my parents' house. And my house, too, is an extension of the same spirit. The windowless room has a vent, but it's off. A faint breeze finds its way inside from the bookstore.

I don't hear his reply, as I become distracted by the genital deformities portrayed in the big square art book on my lap, and suddenly I find Fofi kneeling in front of me like a beggar, looking at the genitals upside down, not looking at me. These balls that seem to be made of brownish dough.

"Sorry, Fofetto, what did you say?"

"Why did you ask?"

"What?"

"If I'd work for your father."

"I'm just wondering."

I blow air on my bangs and pout my upper lip. He is staring at it—at my mouth.

"It's just, I don't know, it's like you totally forgot that you were ever a PhD student, that you've accepted the way things are."

"And do you—do you look down on me for that?"

"Oh no, exactly the opposite."

"Working makes me happy."

"I can tell."

"But was there a reason why you asked that? Does your father want me there?"

"I don't know, but I could see it—in the long run."

"I like working with you, while it lasts. You shouldn't have left Rome."

"I had a dream. I'm happy I did it."

He rests a hand on my thigh and tries to balance himself. He's too heavy and unathletic for this kneeling, sumo-like position. The unforgiving fluorescent lights are off, and the room is lit by nothing but my old floor lamp, a metal thing from the seventies with two round spotlights that face in different directions. I know how beautiful I look right now—the neckline of my dress sags as I lean toward him—and I want to untangle myself from this bubble we're in now. "Fofi," I try, "you know you're quite the catch these days. You'll find a pretty girlfriend. I can show you around if you'll let me."

"You'll . . ." he falters, fidgeting in his place, standing up for a second to stretch his legs and sinking down again. He searches my dress with his eyes, angry now. "No to me, but yes to someone?"

The book falls on the floor, and my breast is under his palm and my mouth is covered by his other hand, which keeps me from screaming. The chair is sturdy, it's fake leather, uncomfortable even after I've covered it with a large linen scarf. Fofi is heavy on top of me, and he fumbles against my body. I'm not screaming, and I'm still on the chair, slouched but tense, with open legs, frozen. He is kissing my neck and squeezing my breast painfully hard under the thin cups of my bra. He is too heavy to be able to pivot on one hand on the chair's arm rest while unbuttoning his pants, so he's not undressing at all anymore. All he's doing is rubbing against me, which is using up his energy. He has ruined my dress by ripping the collar to grab my breast. I have platform sandals on, with my toes exposed, and he wears broken Chuck Taylors that kick my pinky toe because of his clumsy wriggling. "Ouch!" I scream. This unfreezes me, and I press three nails into his forehead and scratch.

So there, it's over. I was lucky, and now he's sitting on the floor. I look at my dress, hold up the hem. "Go get me a t-shirt."

"Take one of mine."

He resembles a dog when he tries to get up on his feet. He huffs as he slowly regains a vertical position, and I see an invisible knife entering his back. Even as I see him walking, shaken, toward the second closet, I imagine him facedown on the tile floor, dead, this knife going in and out of his big, chubby back.

I HAVE A panic attack that night, which makes me look bad in front of Gustavo, who didn't know I suffer from them. I try to drink the water he brings me, but my throat feels damaged, paralyzed, so I can't swallow. All the water I pour carefully into my mouth just drips out onto me and onto the sheets.

We have breakfast very early. Again: orange juice, fig jam on sliced bread, American coffee. I can still see how much he likes having breakfast naked at the round table, a cool, Godly breeze coming in from the window, sexual desire seizing the air, but we don't mention it, don't act on it. We say silly things that lead us to the window he loves.

I wish every day were the same, but then Gustavo doesn't come back in the evening. He leaves behind two blue shirts.

I HAVE SOME gingerroot left, which I didn't even notice when there was other food in the fridge, a handful of organic bouillon cubes. For carbs: 600 grams of pasta, assembled from different packs. I have some of it everyday. I have one meal a day. After the cramps, which usually last no longer than an hour, there's a period of exhausted bliss. I linger in it on the bed upstairs or the couch on the ground floor. The shutters are down, and a bit of light filters in from the lamps and the sun. Once, after an early lunch, it was so hot and humid that I was certain nobody would be lurking around outside. I went out to the front yard, opened the toolshed, took a hammer out of the toolbox, placed every piece of Lorenzo's equipment on the concrete and struck each piece. To keep them from forcing me to reimburse him, it is crucial that none of them—Maria, Lorenzo, my mother— ever gets past the metal door. Coming back inside, I bang my hip against the window frame and get a bruise. This last bruise joins a company of bruises Gustavo has given me. I take blood thinners in the afternoon, and I've stopped trying to cure my yeast infection, though it seems to have healed on its own. At night I close the shutters all the way because that's when they stop by and spy on me. I take Xanax to help me sleep, pull out the wi-fi router cord. I don't reply to phone calls or to Fofi's messages. I've written one text to my mother: "I'm down with the flu. I'm not working this week."

I get a reply from my dad's phone, not my mom's: "Okay."

My brother texts: "Are you okay?"

"You know how I am, brother."

"I love you. Can I drop by for a quick visit?"

"No need."

Gustavo doesn't reply to my occasional texts—"What did I do?" or "I've stopped eating," or "I am the one who can give you what you want," or "I sleep in your blue shirts."

I take baths and let the water boil my skin. I eat the skin around the nails on my fingers, and if they bleed I run cold water over them. The blood dissolves in the foam. Then I get scared, pull myself out of the tub, and put toilet paper strips on the little cuts for hours. If I'm not bleeding, I doze off in the bath. I jolt awake in the evening from the water, which has gotten so cold it feels like it's slamming me in the face.

If I've spent many hours locked in my room or in the bathroom, then they'll muster the courage to enter the house, to lock themselves in the spare room. They say:

"I knew she'd smash the cameras. I had insurance on everything, so I just need to take pictures of the damage, and they'll give me new ones."

"So basically no harm done. Gustavo has come home, and he's killed the ants. The girls greeted him like a hero who'd just come back from war, and I knew everything would be all right. All that's left now is to figure out what she's doing in that other room."

"The game changer was Gustavo making copies of the keys."

"How did he get the code?"

"He knows his stuff. He has five children."

I spend long hours listening to these tedious conversations, which show me that they're successful because they're organized. And it's true: I'm confined to my bedroom, and whenever I'm about to use the bathroom, I lock the bedroom and take the key with me. I'm halfway through the Xanax bottle, and when it's done I won't be able to get any sleep. They are simply waiting for me to go through all the pills.

I'm tired. I can't get up from the bedroom to stick my left arm under the cold water, so I stay in bed. I cut my skin with the tip of the nail file. The cuts itch, but they're just surface cuts. The sheet is wet, which is annoying, but I can't move all that easily. The sheet is covered in bloodstains. I press it against my left arm because I remember that it won't heal on its own. I'm fighting blood clots with blood thinners. So I grab the phone and dial my brother, say, "Fausto, I can't get out of my room; Lorenzo and Maria and mom are outside, but I can't stop my arm from bleeding, and I'm not in good shape. Could you maybe come over and bring Band-Aids? Gauze?"

I WAKE UP to the voice of my brother reassuring me. "Don't worry about the door—it's nothing. It's just that nobody had your new keys, and you were resting." He kisses my wet temple. "I'm taking care of everything".

"So you didn't come with them?"

"No, of course I didn't come with them."

After talking to me, Fausto goes to the other room and talks to a man who has looked in for a second.

"I don't mind staying," he tells the man.

"What's your schedule like?"

"I'm a student."

"You go to class?"

"I do. How long will it be?"

"I can't tell. It depends."

I'm listening in bed as a mosquito flutters around me. It lands on my forearm, and I wave it away. My legs twinge with mosquito stings.

Mom is sedated in the other room. She won't call me, so I don't hear her voice, but I seem to be hearing her whisper all the time. "Sergio, Sergio, come here a second." It's not her, the nurse reassures me. I don't allow my father to visit, and I never go out. After the last surgery she made up her mind not to overdo it, so she asked me to lend her €15,000 of my future money for palliative care at home. She was joking. This was one of the last exchanges we had while she was still alert. I don't know when exactly she accepted her fate, but I hated when she made that joke. It's not as if I burst into tears—I was sitting "at her bedside"—but some tears fell from my eyes, hidden by my eyelashes. Just a light jolt of tears, and then I collected myself. Since then, I've been looking for the perfect retort, and I've finally found it, though it requires a lot of guts and perfect timing: "Make sure you give it back, though."

The nurses, both men, take turns working twelve-hour shifts. The one on the night shift speaks with Roman slang and a Roman accent, and I'm happy that he only comes at night because he is a white-trash *coatto*, and I hate talking to him, with his rough, savvy, entitled manners and his curls and his bald patch. The one on the day shift is from le Marche, has great manners, and almost makes me feel happy. My mother lets them sedate her most of the time. She has asked if I would be annoyed if she left slowly; she wants to reach death as sweetly as possible, with plenty of rest on her way there. She's said she likes it when I watch her, likes that she doesn't feel alone. She hoped, she said, that things were going the right speed for me. Near her night table is the morphine pump, and the rubber tube connected to her arm. These have been ugly years. I can only lie on my bed and keep her company through the wall while she sleeps.

I cannot stay in her room for long. I can't bring myself to watch the basin with the sponges or the adult diaper. I can't be around the house, as the nurses' stuff tends to spill over into the second bathroom and into my mother's study, where they're supposed to keep it all. They have two cots in the study: they sleep here, among the diapers and the special soaps and the white coats. They frequently change coats, and they're tidy, but it's hot, and we don't have AC. They treat her carefully. They're waiting for her to enter a coma. She'll die due to respiratory complications, pneumonia, heart failure, pulmonary embolism. One day I'll know what it'll be (the third one), but for now she dies from all of them every night.

I lie on my bed to keep her company. Yesterday I watched *Midnight Express*. I remember when I was a child, being a convict in a movie was a basic existential condition, a metaphor that kept on giving, like sailors or soldiers. I hadn't watched a prison movie in years. So yesterday I was all *piangiolino*, weepy, and I felt so close to my mother's cell. I knock on the door sometimes. When she goes, I'll leave prison.

I wake up and go to the kitchen. I'm still sleepy. My mother is waiting there for me. She just got back from the supermarket, the bags are still on the table, and she's making me slices of toast. She is the usual healthy mom, and then her mouth opens to talk and she's suddenly not healthy anymore; she never will be again. "My love, I have to tell you something bad. They've found a little thing, I have to do chemotherapy." Two jolts of water from my eyes, warped by eyelashes.

Afterward, in my room, still warm from her hug, miserable, I wonder how I could have forgotten about "Marcello"'s death so quickly. When I'm not thinking of him, of his car crash, of his ugly death on Via dei Prati Fiscali on that easy bend, long and well paved, it's as if he's still alive. He's only alive when I'm not thinking of him. When I do think of him he's suddenly dead. More dead than his career, which had been dead for a while, in my opinion, though I didn't want to let him know because I liked his smugness, and I was wrong to tell him he was wasting his success so far with his determination to rap in English. I fall asleep with this ugly thought.

I WAKE TO the sound of Ludovica gasping for air. She sits up, she isn't breathing. This creature, daughter of man and daughter of God, is sleeping naked. Her skin smells like plastic, and it's an unbecoming smell. I've always thought that, ever since the first time, when we had breakfast at Berengo's, when I was only a father of five, a bigot, and she was the girl who'd lost her way. The plastic smell of her skin blends with the smell of bodily fluids drenching the sheets. I sit up to help, and she's rattling on: "Help me, I don't feel well, I can't breathe."

"Allergies?" I ask, now alert, maybe a little wary, too used to the way one has to navigate a child's nightly crises, calmly but with determination. Sara's convulsions, the ambulance, the car ride the second time. Esther shoving one of I Maschi against the corner of a night stand right before bedtime. And now, Ludovica. I'm sleeping here, I'm not at my children's, at night I fuck an ex-child with an awful father. Am I an awful father?

"No, it's a panic attack," she answers spitting on her lap, panting.

Has she been possessed by the devil? She keeps drooling on the sheet, her back stooped over, the *rrrrhaaaaah* voice, some coughing. It's scary.

Once I rode in a helicopter with a man from work—he was a Milanese— who told me about the time he was possessed. One night, coked out of his mind, he was in a field outside a country mansion. Suddenly he had the feeling that he was being watched by the coldest eyes in the world. He didn't know what it was, what it had been, but from then on, he totally lost it, would just do blow and fuck and work his ass off, argue with people. He came down with serious digestion problems and had a fever all the time. Three months later, when medical reports failed to explain why he'd stopped sleeping and why his skin was starting to glow gray, he decided to have an exorcism, and then everything went away.

I need to leave. The Devil has prepared this drifting ship for me; he has given me this poor, possessed creature. He leaves me with it all night, so I do as I like and he comes back to inhabit her as soon as I'm asleep. The poor thing is suffocating. The hand I place on her back won't save her. The Devil, the Lord of this world, is looking at us with his cold stare and penetrating Ludovica. Don't take me. Get behind me, I tell him. Oh Lord, take his stare away from me; I'm scared.

I get up—"stay, please"—go downstairs, take a glass into the kitchen and fill it with water, go back up and see her try to drink from my hand. She thanks me and lets go of the glass. She trusts me, though what I really am is a buyer, and Satan is the seller, and she's the trinket.

She's having a hard time swallowing, she's spitting out the water, making terrible noises. She irons my shirts during the day, and I have blisters from her yeast infection. I feel it pulsing in my underwear, painless, but it's as if there were a copper wire inside it. She spits water onto the back of my hand. We've continued to do it, with a condom, and the itching is driving me crazy. The pleasure I begged for was awarded to me. Lord, I wanted her; it was me. I wanted the creature's body against mine.

She spits water onto the drenched, filthy sheets again.

"I can't swallow the water down. I'm scared." She pushes two fingers against her neck, apparently to activate manual swallowing. "I'm scared." She pushes with her hand, it contracts, the neck is a monster with a hump on its back, and it contains the muscle.

"You can breathe, right?"

"Yeah, but I can't swallow and I'm scared."

She's gagging: this is the work of Satan, whose eye looks over this sophisticated house, its valuable furniture. Oh Lord, please forgive me for attracting Satan's eye to this creature you put on this earth so that she could love and be loved. I was the one who made her stumble.

When she was born, Maria carried her out of the delivery room on her own two feet. At the time I loved her more than anything. She was my first child. I hadn't been able to stay in the room—I had left halfway through labor—admitted it was too much for me, and Maria had agreed; she didn't want any anxiety around her. Maria is so strong that she came out of the room by herself in a fresh nightgown only moments after screaming the most awful sounds I'd ever heard. Her hair was stuck to her forehead.

Maria lay on the bed and put Esther next to her. She started chatting with my mother and a friend and seemed to forget our child altogether. She was snubbing her: she'd left her there like a little, self-sufficient thing. And so Estherina, so small, the size of an old phone, she was there, newly minted, lying against Maria, while Maria faced the other side of the room. Esther's tininess broke me in half. When everyone finally left us alone, I bit and sucked on Maria's neck, and then I stuck my firstborn's foot in my mouth.

I went to the bathroom and sat on the toilet bowl, which was sweaty and warm from my mother using it. I came back and stuck Esther's little foot in my mouth again. It was salty and delicious, a foot that hadn't touched the earth yet. Its toes were pink peas in invisible pods. On the walls of the corridor, there were pictures of babies with heartfelt acknowledgments to the obstetricians: "I will always be grateful to you for the life you gave me."

Maria's mother was forced to stay home through the whole delivery, and now she can't muster the courage to join us. She's too melancholy, too hurt and panicked. My mother puts a flower behind Maria's ear and presses another against Esther's cheek. In a few hours, Maria's mother will tell her "Maybe your milk isn't good," and in a year, "You're going to make her ill," because Maria lets her pick things off the floor and put them in her mouth, especially the remote control. Maria will cry, daughter and mother. At age three, Esther will be healthy and more than good-looking, and she'll make friends with everybody and complain when kids don't play with her. She'll scream to the other preschoolers, "Friends! Why won't you play with me?" She has the same amusing, round face as her mother. When she's three, she has black hair and is flirty. She looks at men with her wide eyes, blushes, and tosses them a coy "ciao," and when the boys refuse to play hide-and-seek with her she calls them *mascanzoncelli*—the cutest possible way to call someone a rascal—an old word she got from my mother. And now here she is, all grown up and possessed, unable to swallow, naked in bed next to me. I have sodomized her, and she's scared to death.

The Devil's stare can paralyze, but I beseech You, Lord, don't let it swallow us. I think he's watching me, but I have faith in You, Lord. I want Maria because that's your will. I'll go back to my family. Like the saint who ate the lepers' phlegm, I'll get Maria back in Your name, in charity. Ludovica has calmed down and is resting. "It's passed, thank you, my love."

I get up, go downstairs. I look at the wall where we fuck, and I touch the glass in an effort to figure out whether You've given me the strength to leave. You have, thank You. The window watches over the blackness of the garden, the lamps by the train depot. I climb up the stairs, stop at the toilet, where I wash my ass, which I didn't do earlier because I was afraid of making too much noise in the bathroom. I brush my teeth. Then I go back downstairs and stand between the table and the window and wait for dawn. I'll have breakfast and leave for good. Tears from lack of sleep gather under the elastic skin of my eyelids.

Mom and Dad also wake early and, since I've left New York and come to live with them and have stopped seeing Daria, we end up having early breakfast together every morning, the three of us. I have acid reflux now, like James Murphy, so I've stopped drinking coffee. They haven't touched coffee in fifteen years. We drink barley water. They swallow down pills, and I do, too. At night we'd rather skip dinner, so we just have a few *fette biscottate* with herbal tea. Then I go out, but I'm not using recreational drugs these days, so at the end of the concerts I go home.

The wood floor is warm. I crush a mosquito against my knee

and listen to my mother explain the plan in her robe: Berlusconi's legal woes will cripple him, but the international élites still don't trust a left-wing government to stabilize the market, since "the Left believes in the market only when it's convenient to." It's stuff the papers don't discuss, and she comes from the left-wing élite, but now she's into Realpolitik, maybe to please her husband. I crush another mosquito with the hand I just used to caress my mother's shoulder. I get up and wash the tiny black-rimmed flower of blood from the palm of my hand.

I live with them now. I'm not far away; I'm right there. New York has evaporated like a dream or a fairy tale. Was the person who lived there—that person who placed orders on his phone while reading from folded menus, who tipped extravagantly, who was so moved by the view across the river—was that me?

I retreat to my room and pray a rosary for the dead, for Vera and for "Marcello." I scorned her when she talked about her injured friends, her dead comrades. She's gone. "Marcello," Marcellino. I bring milk and cookies to my room, and I place them on the bedside table next to my iPad, three books, and an issue of *Wired*. I lie down, my bones soften, my head dries out. I take a nap and then start working on a *GQ* piece about *Breaking Bad*.

I don't have much time left, though. I'm dying now. My body is lost in a bed that feels so vast I can't reach the edges. Only when someone comes in to visit me and sits on one of the three chairs at my bedside does the distance seem manageable, only once the person holds my hand.

I realize that Sergio has come in and taken a seat, and I ask, "Sergino, do you promise I will die for real?"

"I have no belief in anything, Darietta, but I will stay and make sure you're really dead, okay?"

I haven't got enough strength left in my body to laugh. I touch my face, trying to figure out why it's not moving. It's wrinkled and cool. Sergio has clothes on, a face, an age. I see him from the corner of my eye and feel the strength of his hand holding mine.

"You've never held my hand like this."

"Like how?"

"This decisively, *Sergino mio*. It feels like you have grown."

"Now?"

"Now the hand has changed."

"It's Tullius's hand."

"Oh! Did you two make peace?"

"We did." It's Tullius's voice. He too has a face, an age. "Daria, I'm sorry for being late, but you see, I still came."

"I'm surprised."

"Can I sing a few psalms?"

"Oh, come on."

"They are *spagnoleggianti*; you'll like them. They're sweet, and they suit the moment, what it means to us."

"I can't go telling people I let you sing me flamenco psalms, Gusty, *Reghiuleit*."

The three of them laugh good-heartedly.

"Berengo, my love, you're here, and you made peace with Tullio, too?"

"Does the light bother you? Want me to turn it down a bit? This room has these switches that blend in with the walls."

"What are they like?"

"I can't tell. The walls radiate too much light, and I can't find the switches."

"It's the thought that counts, isn't it?"

"Yes, love."

"I'm pretty tired now. Let me rest. Promise me I'm going to die for real."

As the silence settles, I notice the light, the almost sandy light, which isn't harsh but is still somehow bright. I don't know what corner of the room I'm looking at exactly; my eyes are dazed, I can't hear my friends, I'm scared that I might wake up again after I'm dead.

"And yet," Ludovica says, having been here for a while, delicately holding my hand over the bed, "it's something everyone does. Remind yourself of that; it might cheer you up."

We laugh. Her laughter feels old and wise.

"It's surreal for me, too."

"I can't see you, but I'm happy you came to visit. Are you sad I can't see you?"

"No. I see you."

"Do I have a sheet on?"

"Yes, just one sheet. It's summer."

"That's why there's so much light. Did it rain sand?"

"No, no . . ." she reassures me.

"Are you just passing by?"

"I just stopped by to visit you, but I feel awkward."

"Why? There's no need."

"There is."

"No, really, I'm glad you came."

"But I wanted to ask you to forgive me."

"Of course I forgive you, Ludovica."

"Thank God."

"It's all forgotten."

"Thank you."

She lets go of my hand, and it falls back on the sheet. It's a white silk sheet, or maybe it's a silklike fabric that absorbs sweat and never gets wet. My skeleton sinks into the mattress, but I'm so light that there's no heat and no sweat at all between my back and the bed. I feel funny, as if I were capable of holding everything in: pee, fear, yawns. I feel that I have effortless control over myself, which gives me a strange buzz behind my eyes, the sense of cruising or stroking the membrane of time.

Daria has sat down next to me, and now she's the one holding my hand. Her hand and mine are identical, so holding it feels like stroking my own numb arm. I'm so curious to see her face for the first time, and I try to open my eyes, but I can't because the light that filters through my eyelids is too bright, I'm forced to keep them shut. "Daria, are you moved?" I ask her. "I don't want you to be unsettled, but I'm happy you paid me a visit."

"Darietta, yes," she says, barely audible, and my eyelids still keep me from seeing her.

"Don't be scared. I hope this time's the one."

"Let's hope," still barely audible.

"Do you love me, though?"

"I do, my beloved Daria." It's as though she's spoken to me from inside my chest, it's that faint.

"Let's be like this for a while, I'm tired. You know who stopped by earlier?"

"Ludovica—I saw her when I came in."

"Isn't that really weird?"

"It is. I'd have never imagined. It's weird."

We sneer, but I'm tired and she's in pain. I know her thoughts and I know what she will say, and here she says it: "Do you forgive me?"

When I reply, this will end.

NOTES FOR THE HAPPY LIFE

OF NICO BERENGO

*To identify oneself absolutely with oneself, to identify one's "I" with the "I"
that I tell, is as impossible as to lift oneself up by one's hair.*

MIKAIL BAKHTIN

*What made me stop considering novels in my literary criticism is the
success of that American literary Restoration by which every work must be
dedicated to the moral elevation of the reader by means of the
superstructural device of empathy towards characters. That empathy is
always cheap and yet it's considered the only moral compass of storytelling.
The purpose of the literary American novel seems to have become the
"increment in humanity" of a "human being." In my opinion, what is
perceived as an educated reader is in fact a bourgeois, not a Mensch, but
s/he convinces her-/himself of the contrary: that s/he's a Mensch and not a
bourgeois, that s/he's a Person and not the vessel of class values. Which is
completely absurd if we think of the importance that twentieth-century
French theory has in the American universities where contemporary
authors were educated. With the pretext of teaching their readers to be
more human, the American novelist plunges American literature in the
abyss of the Religious and the Pedagogical.* FLORENCE MATHIEU

*What is Catholic purgatory according to our catechism? A purifying fire.
Before going back to inhabit a body now glorious in contemplation of God,
the soul cleanses itself with the only instrument she has: words. Words are
the purifying fire. That fire is the immaterial that cleanses. That fire is
pure language, the impalpable residue of the soul after it abandons the
body. Purgatory is an area of pure language in which the dead examine,
alone but guided by the invisible force of the angels, the shortcomings of
their life. The history of the novel in Christian Europe and its cultural
offshoots, the ex-colonies, clearly foretells what purgatory is for Christians:
it uses language to cleanse sins; and it confirms in the most unexpected
place—the house of novelists, prostitutes of the Positivistic era, whom Jesus
wouldn't have minded being seen in public with—the marvelous love story
God and Man have lived by means of Logos.* FATHER KACZMAREK

LOTTA DI CLASSE

According to Daria, Berengo is the only member of the bourgeoisie—the left-wing, upper-middle-class bourgeoisie—ever to overcome the problem of personal fulfillment, the obsession with individual accomplishments. He is the philosophe of the bourgeoisie, its great reformer. And according to Berengo, who takes Daria's opinions very seriously, Daria—a Marxist—loves that he is comfortable exactly where he is: on the wrong side of class conflict. (I have yet to get in touch with Daria to ask her for her opinion on the matter; I'm afraid to do so.)

Berengo has, for example, come to terms with the fact that his Hispanic doorman never greets him when he returns home, that he responds with nothing more than a glare every time he walks in. Berengo lives in an apartment building the color of hazelnuts. The place is very much of its time: it was built in the early nineties, and its lobby smells overwhelmingly of carpeting. An entire squad of ushers and concierges keep it running, and according to Berengo, only the youngest among them—the twenty-something students on the night shift—acknowledge him. The middle-aged men—or those the same age as him, just under forty—stare at him with quiet disdain from the reception desk at the end of the mirrored lobby, or they bow their head slightly, imperceptibly, when they stand next to the glass entryway. The Hispanic guy with the salt-and-pepper hair, the round goatee, and the calculated, languid look never says hello. He can't be older than forty. He makes a point of greeting Berengo's female guests when they stroll in at night, arm in arm with the short, slim, balding Italian—the young master who seems to abide by no schedule and seems to have no job to speak of. But even then, he never greets Berengo.

"He hates me, and I get that. I'm fine with it. You couldn't be him and not hate me." Some of his female friends tease him about his antagonist: they tell him that one night they'll run off and marry the Hispanic doorman. "He totally hates you!" they say. "But he always smiles at me."

Nico comes from a liberal, democratic family—"*de sinistra*," he says in Italian, with what I think is a Roman accent. Like all progressive, upper-class Romans, he seems at once good-natured and somewhat simple, both spoiled and naïve. Since childhood he's been taught to respect all social classes, all of which happen to fall below his own. When he first moved to New York, he would always greet ushers, concierges, doormen, but for them, responding to his greetings was a hassle, an activity unworthy of their time. Bob, the head doorman, is a handsome man, white-haired and blue-eyed. He has a third-generation New York accent, Italian or Jewish, and he always sits with his legs crossed as he looks down the hall, tracing its hardwood floor and turquoise carpet accents through his gold-rimmed glasses. He loves to stare at Berengo without acknowledging his presence, like a Buddha. It drives Berengo crazy that this is still happening, years after he first moved in, and it's gotten so bad that for a while now he's been unable to look the doorman in the eye.

If an Amazon shipment comes in for Nico, Bob lets him walk right past, and only as he turns the corner for the elevator does he call out: "Berengo? 8D? Package for you." The thought that a man who doesn't acknowledge his presence actually knows his name is deeply upsetting to Berengo. "It's humiliating. Everything I buy—a new pair of pants, a jacket, comics, posters, PlayStation games—all of it has to pass through those hands. I feel ashamed every time."

Berengo is convinced that all the concierges and porters and doormen are acting out of hostility, that they're talking about him behind his back and discussing his reactions, that of the hundreds of Americans and foreigners that live in this skyscraper near Times Square, they find him to be the most amusing, the most worthy of their mockery. "Their hostility is a weapon," says Berengo. "It's an instrument of class warfare."

CORTE AMOROSA

This is the name Berengo uses for his circle of lovers and female friends. The people around him seem to genuinely love him and care for him. He doesn't come across as a cynic or a nihilist, though I don't quite know how he manages to put up with himself—I like spending time with him, but I can't imagine doing it all the time. How does he do it?

"Corte Amorosa" isn't an elision or a joke, nor is it another word for *harem*. Nico sees himself as an idealist, and each relationship he has he embeds within a philosophical framework he has named Corte Amorosa, in honor of its medieval antecedent. Like the noblemen who came together to compose love poetry and recite it and discuss amongst themselves the mysteries of attraction and romance, Berengo thinks of eroticism as a complex experience: partly an act; partly a conversation about this ongoing, or imminent, act; partly a recollection that takes place after said act. Each amorous encounter is thus related to all the others, and everyone participates in the collective experience of passion. His lovers' stories are passed along to other lovers, forming a Boccaccioesque narrative cycle of which Berengo is very proud. The exception is Daria, his main lover, who is never told about his other experiences.

NEWSPAPERS

He doesn't read the newspapers, and he doesn't follow Italian politics. He doesn't vote. When he picks up an American newspaper he flips through it quickly, the fingers on his right hand ever ready to turn the page. He skips to the sports section and the arts and culture section and throws away the rest. Whenever he deigns to read about politics, he lifts his brow and curls his lip upward, as if the corner of his mouth is hanging from pegs on a clothesline. "All you ever need to read are the titles," he tells me one day.

THE VIEW FROM HIS WINDOW
[FROM BERENGO'S PERSONAL AUDIO RECORDINGS]

Daytime: "The skyscraper they're building 200 meters from my window at four o'clock is orange on the inside—you can see it in the parts that haven't been covered up with dark charcoal glass. Orange inside, with vertical strips of yellow light. When the sunlight comes in from the east, the charcoal glass is more of a . . .

a turquoise-black. There's a tower on top with a little red light. I see four planes and a helicopter. Another plane cuts from south to north. Another building has four lit-up penthouses slotted into one another across two floors, like a puzzle. Small clouds hover over New Jersey. A plane, high up in the clouds. When all the plane routes disappear and the buildings stand empty like abandoned husks, humanity will still remain great."

NIGHTTIME: "A CITY built up of many levels. What stands out to me is the colossal effort everyone has put in, and the fact that all of it has been in vain makes me feel nothing but tenderness toward everyone and everything."

DAYTIME: "I WOKE up with that usual feeling: we are spirits who wear flesh, and both the fact that we inhabit a body now and the fact that we won't in the future, both of these things are absurd . . . I have this tremendous desire that life after death be wholly pleasurable, a place where your wishes and the actual experiences themselves are one."

NIGHTTIME: "IT'S TERRIBLE that Michael Jackson has left the realm of the living. I hope the sound of the air conditioner is coming through. It's the dominant sound here. Let me get away from the window. I don't seem to be capable of thinking outside this idea I have of God. He is the best possible thing, the most pleasant, but I can't think about Him for too long because of the desperate hope that overcomes me when I start thinking about the fact that one day I will have to leave my mortal body forever."

Photojournalist, American citizen. Israeli father. Travels to war zones and follows international drug traffickers along their supply routes. One of Berengo's favorites in the months between the summer of 2010 and the winter of 2011.

THE DEAL

Berengo met her at a dinner party. Everyone there was a photographer except for him. Vera didn't help with the cooking; she sat at the table and behaved like a man, he said, sprawled out on her chair. Lazy, prone to temper tantrums, not a lesbian. Long, frizzy blonde hair. Not pretty, a little too chunky, but not ugly either, thanks to her more uncommon qualities: she's tall and blonde and her skin had a rare brightness. She was dressed in a white caftan! Was she a poser? A little bit, yes, but then again, so were most of the photographers at the dinner, according to Berengo. Vera: "Yeah, dude—I mean, I had to leave LA; they were just spaced out all the time. I like the New York vibes more, you know?" During dinner, Vera's answers to Berengo's questions are all condescending, as if were annoying her. But the next day she messages him on Facebook and asks him to meet her in Greenpoint. He accepts. They take a short walk around the neighborhood at sunset, strolling among the shops and the hotels, the marquees all in Polish. Vera found him very pleasant, she says, because he asked her personal questions. According to him, he was sure she couldn't stand him. A couple of hours into the walk, as things start to get intimate—at some point in the conversation she had said, "You're funny," a sign—Nico begins to tell Vera about his sexual idiosyncrasies. He is trying to determine if she has what it takes to become a part of the Corte. He speaks to her in his calmest, most informative voice, a light baritone neither sleazy nor brash. Then, finally: "Look, I've been holding back for over half an hour. All I want to say is: I'm here to be abused. I'm fully at the mercy of your psychic power. I think you're a tremendous woman"—Vera is taller than him, steadier—"and I want you to use me as you wish, to use me and then discard me. But we have to remain friends." This is when the "deal" is made—it's the moment Berengo is careful to stage at the beginning of each of his relationships. He believes that he is always acting in nothing less than good faith, but he is careful to stipulate an agreement: the boundaries of the exchange have to be established, the parameters of the playing field defined. What he believes he's making clear are the boundaries of his involvement, the very grammar of their encounter. Certain lovers will later reproach him for holding back, for not pursuing a relationship with them, for being self-contained and unable to loosen up. At which point Berengo will remind them of what he said, of the way he denied the possibility of a love story from the very beginning. It is all, as far as he can tell, rather explicit. These statements are usually hyperbolic, and his lovers often confess, some time later, that they did indeed treat them as hyperbole, that they hadn't taken them literally, even though they were key to their relationship. In this case, the abuse Berengo refers to in his original statement finds a form in their relationship: he and Vera develop a habit of engaging in Greco-Roman wrestling during their lovemaking.

In January 2011, their relationship is blossoming, though it is not without its conflicts, which are usually resolved through wrestling matches that take place on the floor. Vera often wins. She is very strong, particularly when she is angry. Nico finds himself smothered by her hair, by her muscles, her body parts piling themselves onto him like rugs (dusty rugs, when Nico forgets to vacuum and their naked bodies roll around in hair and ash and crumbs and boogers and shreds of Kleenex). Vera fights

Berengo because she is jealous of a British cook, another prominent member of the Corte Amorosa in the winter of 2011. When
Berengo wins, he sits on her face and jacks off as he stares into
her eyes, happy and short of breath. Sometimes, when he feels
his heart skip a beat and when his chest begins to contract, he is
afraid that he won't make it to the end of the match. As he tries
to slow down his breath after a fight, he sometimes manages to
come on her cheek. Vera's skin is very sensitive, and Berengo is
happy knowing that he has caused her a rash that will last until
the following day.

THE BODY
Deformed: six feet tall; nice ass; deflated, wrinkly breasts that col-
lapse when you hold them. Annual Botox injections in the face,
very few wrinkles: a face whose expressiveness is as yet uncom-
promised, thanks to large, dark blue eyes. Long, sturdy legs: "It's
like sticking it up a road," he says, "or into the trunk of a tree.
Her uprightness is the main thing. The roundness you associate
with women—with the egg, the womb, the cocoon—it's lost here;
you enter a vertical space, not a circular one. And her tits make
the whole thing especially absurd: they're empty and ruined,
so you lose that one last element of rotundity. It's like fucking a
man." When he takes her from behind, "you watch her moving
her back like the steel bar that pushes down on the wheel of a
train—the longest back I have ever seen. I pull her hair to hold
her close. Looking at her from behind, as she kneels down, she is
to a woman what a limousine is to a sedan." Her vagina is hard,
though of this Berengo is less sure, because she forces him to
use a condom during intercourse. Vera is very afraid of sexually
transmitted diseases. She is horrified by the idea of the genitals
rubbing up against each other. During their first encounter, she
used the expression "mucosal contact."

Not taking into account the many waitressing jobs she had in
Los Angeles while she was staying at her aunt and uncle's when
her parents were fighting too much, she worked as an intern at
a casting agency (still in Los Angeles), then spent a year at a kibbutz in Israel, came back to study political science at Columbia,
went back to the kibbutz, came back to Columbia for j-school.
After graduating she started traveling around using her father's
money, stringing and writing wire stories she'd try to sell to the
agencies. She started taking pictures while working for the wires
and has now stopped writing. She has been through war, and so
whenever he is with her, what Berengo thinks to himself is: "The
fact that Vera is going out with me means that what she does is
worthless. You can't stare death in the eyes and then fuck me.
I am the Untruth. I am Unimportance. And I'm not even your
husband, in which case at least I'd understand that you needed
stability to compensate for your adventurous lifestyle." Maybe, I
said to him, what she sees in you is a sense of death that's similar
to what she feels when she's actually in the war zone. "That's a
very flattering reading," Berengo said. "But my actual issue is: I
think these photographers are posers. Their entire life is a pose.
They have these conversations where they call each other bro.
They look after each other. They host these beautiful dinners.
There's the one who's great in the kitchen and the one who's really, really terrible, and that's just more reason to love him. You
eat by candlelight. The people there always look like they just got
back from a *Vanity Fair* party that they didn't really care about
going to or from a charity block party in Harlem. Or from Lebanon. They have the same attitude whether they're coming back
from Lebanon or the *Vanity Fair* party: it's hell out there. Their
conversations are uninteresting because they all say the right
things. They're intense. They pick up nice tans while they're out

taking pictures of torn-up bodies and piles of rubble. They dress well. Their coats, their shirts. They get along. Their walnut bread is delicious and homemade. And then when you're busy hating on them, a friend suddenly calls, and you overhear the following exchange: 'Hey, buddy, you dickless cunt,' Vera says. She's calling someone a faggot, then hands the phone over to another photographer who says: 'Hey shithead, two months in the hospital doing nothing, you should be ashamed of yourself!' All those around the table look at each other, sort of uncomfortably. Vera's eyes well up, and she has this angry look on her face. Someone gets up to take the cheese board into the kitchen, all of this in candlelight, by the way, and someone says into the phone: 'No, no, I'll come over myself and stick it up your butt!' When they hang up I find out it was a friend of theirs who lost a leg. I'm not sure where, some war zone. He's gone through surgery over thirty times, and they even removed a flap of skin from his asshole to patch up another hole in his stomach or leg—again, I'm not sure, I didn't totally follow. Talking to each other like that is their code, the way they show their brotherhood: they grieve, and they're brave. And then Vera fucks me, which means her bravery is a pose. She should despise me. I mean, these people make you think that God has to be a hipster, because he allows people like that to see the truth. The affectionate gatherings, the perfect dinners, the perfectly formed sentences about how hard it is, actually, to be there on the front line, but oh the memories. The only possible escape from this is to think that if you fuck me, then maybe you're a fraud. I mean, I'm sorry to go on about this. It's just that they're *real people*."

TASTES
She wears long robes indoors—a look that's subsequently copied and improved on by Nat, another member of the Corte Amorosa.

When she goes out she wears practical clothes that are a bit butch but expensive. She's rarely without her survival pack: folding knife, pumpkin seeds, ultraslim hoodie, K-Way, flashlight, tampons. Expensive bicycle.

PARENTS

Upper West Side Jewish mother, lives alone, three spaniels, a member of a number of charitable organizations, fund-raises for *The Nation*. Her father, a former UN official, is a diplomat currently under investigation in Israel. The parents are separated by two continents, but they're not breaking up.

PRECAUTIONS

"Drink antioxidant kombucha tea. Avoid any contact between the vagina and the penis, not even any pornographic rubbing, which is so on-trend in the U.S., where, as foreplay, the man aggressively strikes the vagina and you get a kind of slapping sound. Condoms are to be worn from the first moment of intercourse, though not during oral sex, which shows that her approach to sex isn't entirely rational."

NIGHT TERRORS

At night, Nico gets restless. In his sleep he experiences something that feels like seeing his father's true face. He says that his father's face—though rarely his mother's— often appears in his mind's eye and that in that moment he feels he can understand it, his real face, as if he were meeting his father for the first time. He suddenly sees his wrinkles, the depth of his cheeks—the whole visage in total clarity as if it were cast in rubber.

Sometimes he dreams about his parents, and he wakes up crying. He dreams that they've "lost their strength" or that they've died. He dreams that he "finally understands them." Then he wakes up, and when he realizes that he's crying he tells himself that by crying for mortality itself, he has finally accomplished his duty as a human being. "The mortality of others generates in them a deep and total melancholy, which they're almost never able to communicate and which you can only access through the intimacy of a dream." Why does he call his parents *others*?

If he has company while he sleeps, the sadness doesn't come. When he falls asleep in a woman's arms he is able to "sense her absolute sanctity, her absolute preciousness." He feels "these really strong outbursts of tenderness, outbursts that won't do me any harm."

When he dines alone he eats too quickly; reclines too far back in his sofa; stains his t-shirts, his sweaters, his button-downs. He's scared that he will begin to choke and die alone on his sofa. The pain he feels under his sternum when he eats too quickly only exacerbates his fear of dying. He is on Facebook constantly but especially during meals.

THE PURCHASE OF THE HOUSE

The house in New York was purchased in 2008. The mortgage signing took place on a cold fall day. Berengo's parents were there and two lawyers.

NICOLA SAW THREE missed calls on his mobile from his father. Nicola was in Rome, in his house in Pigneto, stabbing an icon on his desktop with his pointer. The file contained an audio interview with Lenny Kravitz, which he had recorded the day before and saved on iTunes but couldn't be bothered to transcribe. The ring tone on his iPhone (one of the first iPhones to be spotted in Rome) was set on silent, and he'd left it on the magazine rack next to the bathtub. When he returned to the bathroom—when he worked at home he would pee every half hour (he is de facto incontinent, since he never needs to suppress any of his bodily functions—not urination, or evacuation, or the release of sexual tension accumulated while researching the latest news about Jessica Alba)—he noticed the missed calls and immediately called his father back on Skype. He was deeply distressed. His father answered the phone: "It's nothing, don't worry, good luck with work, goodbye."

"What do you mean 'goodbye,' dad? Tell me what's going on, or I won't be able to do any writing." But his father had already hung up.

The son pleaded with him via text: *Dad, I can't keep working on my piece if you act like this. What's going on? I am worried about you.*

His father called back: "I just wanted to tell you . . . We bought the house. I wanted to speak to you, darling."

"That's great! Dad, are you crying?"

His mother came onto the phone. "No, he isn't crying, *Ciccio*. We bought the house. Are you happy?"

"Mom, he's crying. I know he is. If you're not able to handle the implications of making a grand gesture, then don't make any grand gestures! I'd rather you didn't!"

"What are you talking about, *Ciccio*? Stop this."

"You know what I mean. He gets so upset thinking about the continents, the ocean, time passing, intercontinental flights. I know it and you know it."

"Calm down, Nico."

"Come on, Mom. I love you. Please don't make me worry so much. I have a deadline on this piece."

"Oh, that's great. What's the piece?"

"It's an interview with a singer."

"Oh, that's great. Is he American? When are we coming to New York together?"

"Soon, Mom. Soon."

"Oh, that's great. You'll be able to interview him here next time. Did you interview him over the phone? Is he in Italy? Which singer is it?"

"Lenny Kravitz."

"Oh, is that the black Jew?"

"Yeah, the black Jew. How do you know that? Where did you hear about him?"

"Oh I don't know, *Vanity Fair*? Or maybe *D.*? Were you nice to him?"

"What? Listen. Tell Daddy to stop crying. Otherwise I'll keep worrying about him, and if I'm worrying about him I can't get any work done. I interviewed the guy over the phone."

"I'm telling you, he's not crying. Your English must be so good if you can do an interview over the phone."

"And I'm telling you I know he's crying! Why do you have to lie to me? He's thinking about the house as if it's on a different planet somewhere, as if you can only get to it on a spaceship, like there's no coming back. He's probably thinking about time and doing all the math in his head!" (The reverential fear with which he treats the subjects of time and death kept him back from saying to her that what his father was really doing was calculating how many times he would go there with him before he died.)

"Stop it, *Ciccio*. You're talking nonsense," said his mother, who knew exactly what he was talking about.

"I don't think so. What I need to do right now is focus, and you've gotten me all riled up and angry."

"Don't be angry, love. We're happy; we've just bought the house! Come on, please, don't be angry. You're making Daddy sad."

IL DELICATINO

He is very much his father's son, and he often cries in front of his parents, which causes his mother great distress. When his parents are in New York and he ends up sleeping on the sofa, there is always at least one evening when Nicolino can no longer keep it together. He ends up spending the evening crying in front of them, his seventy-year-old parents, as he tells them about his life in New York. He doesn't manage to say more than "it's very hard" before breaking down, and even that he can barely pronounce, as huge tears roll down his wrinkled, yellowing cheeks.

"It's hard everywhere," responds his mother. Yet she spends the night after each of these crises unable to fall asleep. "I couldn't sleep," she says to her son the following day. "I was too worried." Berengo, meanwhile, spends an hour at the gym after he wakes up, and he always emerges feeling fresh and calm, baffled by his mother's worries about his so-called "physiological breakdowns."

According to his father, Nicolino is a "prophet of our time." His father was a Benedictine monk who quit the convent for love, and he says that Nico has found the only emotional outlook appropriate to a world that is "regulated by secret societies that have managed to impose too much progress, too quickly. Societies that have tried to enforce a world of free exchange and laws that are reasonable in theory, but which in practice are deeply unfair to the very soul itself. We are all forced to consume, and abstinence is no longer a virtue."

Like the son, the father has long been engaged in the project of formulating his own personal interpretation of the Christian faith. "We have to consume all that is consumable, all the products of Western civilizations and those of other civilizations that are now imitating us. We have to consume as we deny the self, as we avoid thinking about the future, because the future is now unthinkable. We have to bring the cycle to a close. It's like knowing how to die."

Nico swears that this is how his father actually he talks, that these are direct quotations. All of this sounds like something Berengo himself would say, and so they could be his father's words, too. (I can't imagine having a conversation like this with anyone, especially not with my father. Not before his strokes, and certainly not after.) According to his mother, this approach is something of a lost cause, and the philosophical understanding between father and son only serves as an impediment to the healthy development of Nicolino. His mother—and Daria and others—calls him "Il Delicatino." But how can a son escape his father's melancholy?

PLAGIO

He always uses the word *plagio*. He says that it means something different from "brainwashing," but I don't think it does. *Plagio*, he says, has a more intimate connotation—it's less cultlike. He describes a number of relationships that matter to him with the word *plagio*. Daria has been *plagiata* by Gustavo Tullio. Nico, in turn, has been *plagiato* by Daria. He explains that the Italian tradition of kids forming very steady couples from the age of sixteen throughout their youth—until the age of, say, twenty-six or thirty—is the implicit explanation for most of the psychological breakdowns experienced later in life by many members of the bourgeoisie. By getting engaged at such a young age, a boy never learns to be on his own. The *fidanzatini in casa* maintain very strong relationships throughout college, usually with the support of their parents, which leads to a pattern of domination: the stronger personalities over the weaker ones. This, he says, impedes the full psychological development of male Italians. "It's like a *fontanelle* that never closes."

"THE RESURRECTION OF THINGS"

"If the spirit can be resurrected, then the body can also be resurrected, because here I am missing Daria, who is in another continent, and my body perceives the ocean between Rome and New York much more than my mind does. Which must mean the body retains important memories and also deserves to be resurrected.

"And the fact that I am here in this room, which contains these books, which are important to me, and especially this black Lack bookshelf in three units, which means so much to me because I bought it with my parents at the Ikea in Red Hook. We went by bus one day in winter, and we ordered home delivery, and we were there waiting for them when they came, and we assembled them together sitting on the wooden floor in an apartment on the eighth floor of a building so far from our dear ones, so far from our Rome, our Milan, finding ourselves, our aging bodies the core of a family destined not to breed. What did we see when we looked at each other? We were so far away now from the places that had turned us into a family for the first time, thirty-six years ago. The scene was captured in a photo taken by a relative in the clinic where I was born. And the fact that I am here, in this room, with this three-unit bookshelf that means so much to me makes it really hard to believe that there isn't a resurrection of things, too."

CAREER

In 1997, Nico moves back to Rome.

In the aughts, blogs begin to emerge as a competitive force, a challenge to the magazines. He starts a blog and develops a following. He is hated, and his posts are reposted. He can't stand all the hating. He tries to write novels and stories, but he stops because of something Flannery O'Connor may have said, maybe in a book of essays: "You're really not required to write, there's never going to be a shortage of writers anyway."

In 2009, he moves to New York because he can't stand the haters. He was already spending more and more time in New York, in the isolation of his parents' apartment. He gets a media visa.

GONZO BORGHESE: EXTRACTS FROM BERENGO'S INTERVIEWS WITH WRITERS, THEOLOGIANS, ACTORS, AND MUSICIANS

_____ is a gay artist who wears a leather jacket and a neckerchief and stares directly into my face every five minutes. The only thing he seems to care about during our conversation is that my respect for his artistic vocation is genuine and appropriately scaled. I tell him it would have never occurred to me to question it.

AT THE END of the day, though _____ and _____ are two men in their fifties, and each of them manages to keep his distance from me in his own way.

312

HOW DEEPLY SHOULD we commit to interviewing the great personalities of our time? How much of our hearts should we invest in it? Do you want us to take you seriously, or just to say: "Heeeeeey, so, what's the deal with this greeeaaaat recoooord? Tell us everything?" I want to be able to talk about intellectual honesty with _____, about mental and physical illness. I want to be able to speak the truth, whereas he—I believe this completely—is bound by professional secrecy. He can't tell his PR people that he said too much.

I HAVE SO many memories of _____ that I am suddenly moved to tears as I walk through the snow, skidding onto the frozen sidewalks, on my way to hear _____ and to interview _____ and _____ at the Gramercy Park Hotel in New York.

YOU REALLY MADE it with your first _____, but how was it when the _____ phenomenon blew over?

THANK YOU FOR taking my question seriously. I was thinking—perhaps this isn't actually a question—but I couldn't fail to notice that everyone on the Internet seems to be freaking out about certain psychological issues of yours . . . Listening to you just now I was thinking that here is this person who is taking my serious question seriously, here is someone who knows what it means to suffer. Because when you're suffering in your mind the problem of what is good, of how to do good, becomes a very serious issue. So this question—about how to do good, how to give to others . . . you end up thinking about these things at night, during your night terrors. You can't sleep, and you just want to be sure that life has some value . . . well . . . now I've said all this, and I don't think I should actually put it in my piece but . . . "I think you should, actually."

THE FAME OF OTHERS

Berengo spends hours sitting in hotels, waiting to interview singers, and he feels wealthy and unproductive. These great, expensive hotels he hangs out in feel like home. Expensive hotels remind him of his parents, of what it's like as a child to be in a hotel with your parents. He doesn't even need to buy the magazines that publish the few articles he writes, a maximum of two per month. He is paid between €200 and €300 per article. "I would have to do six per month to earn the equivalent of what my father gives me. And I'm one of the best. (I think I'm the best.)"

SELF-ENDORSEMENT / LACK OF INCOME / LIFE AS A DADDY'S BOY

He meets up with famous people and tries to understand how fame has affected their lives.

"You go in, and they give you an iPod. You listen to the album, the new album, which hasn't been released yet. It's a hesitant album—you can tell it was made by a star who is unsure if they'll go on being a star or not, whether they'll make a comeback or fade away. You listen to the songs, and you wonder if they've lost the fight. You hope the artist will make it; you hope it works it out for him. Lenny Kravitz is roaming around the room holding out his laptop, trying to connect to the wi-fi so he can see how many views his new video has on YouTube. He's shorter than you think. The artist is tired and kind and twitchy. They've made it, and now they face the problem of having to account for it. Maybe they act tough for the camera but not for the interviewer. 'Can we start with the first question? What's the first question? Can we start from the first question?' As if they're in a trance."

NEW YORK, VISA, DETACHMENT FROM THE WORKING WORLD, METAPHYSICAL CONSUMERISM

When he set up his blog to post his articles and email himself links, trackbacks, and random mentions, any comment would get on his nerves. Everyone always seemed to misunderstand him. He was always being discussed as a powerful man taking advantage of his position. "Does that make me the bad guy?" "Am I the bad guy?" He turned off the comments. On another blog, someone called him a coward for removing the comments.

He often went to New York to stay with friends who worked for *Vice*, who were part of an extended network of Italian photographers. When he was in New York he accepted assignments to interview residents or visiting artists. When he was in New York he felt far enough from home to be able to spend less time online, googling his own name only rarely.

He met a lawyer and sorted out his visa.

He took the blog offline. He deleted Facebook. He kept Twitter but unfollowed anyone who wasn't hugely popular. He didn't want to work as much anymore; all he wanted was to be supported financially, so that he could be free to consume.

Now he is unable to earn money. He feels that he deserves a €5000-a-month lifestyle, but writing thirty articles a month doesn't seem feasible (€200 euros per article on average—a tenth of what we pay for them here). Why not write them in English? I asked him. He said that here journalism is the real deal, and he's too old to learn how to write a good piece.

(His mother is also unable to earn any money. She used to get offered good journalistic gigs all the time, thanks to her family connections—ask again about the idea of the *raccomandazione*—but she would always push back: "If you think someone put in a good word for me, think again. I'd rather get no work at all than get it like this." She's had a long *militanza* at *il manifesto*, the Communist newspaper for which Daria will later write, totally coincidentally.)

CLASS STRUGGLE IN POP-CULTURE JOURNALISM

"Paying for my own flights is the basis of my career. No one can compete with me. Not only am I the best pop journalist in Italy, but I also have enough money to pay for my business trips. The only issue is that I am my only reader: only somebody who lives my lifestyle can understand the importance of interviewing Katy Perry at the Greenwich Hotel, while her husband wanders off past the reception and into the area reserved for singers' husbands."

LOVE

He likes to be held and have his qualities listed aloud to him. Berengo in Daria's arms, in bed, on a Saturday afternoon in winter, looking up at her as she lists his good qualities: "Can you tell me my good qualities? Do you love me? Why do you like me? No, just the good qualities, not the flaws."

Berengo has advanced beyond the inherited bourgeois notion that the world is composed of goods that can be consumed peacefully and pleasurably and renewed at will, according to the material needs of man. He has entered a stage he calls "the metaphysical consumer." He sees physical goods as dull, heavy entities that occupy the border between life and death. The existence of physical goods seems an absurdity—they are, he thinks, a kind of offering from the dead to the living—a token delivered to us by inventors, creators, and previous users. It's as if the dead had covered the world in statues, outside and in their homes, and now those statues are cities populated by the living. "Cities are dollhouses built by the dead when they were alive, and now we occupy them." Or, more prosaically, they are objects that have been left behind. All of these objects would have disappeared into another dimension if human beings had held them in their hands as they passed away.

If all of this is right—if it's so spot on—then why is it so boring to take notes on it?

I'm reluctant to admit that I might be wasting my time taking these notes.

FATHER AND SON, REDUX

The father believes that the world is going to end in 2012. He was persuaded by the idea of the "end of architecture", because he thinks that human life can't survive where architecture can't prosper. Architecture knows that the world is about to end, and this is why it allows chaotic matter to proliferate: halogen life preserved inside shopping malls, their fragments assembled without purpose or order. Architecture has sensed the end of the world.

In our times, according to Nico's father, it's pointless to seek out a progressive or an alternative lifestyle. He thinks: the reason why my son is so upset about the possibility that these buildings could exist without people—and he is telling us this—is that this will never happen, because it is all going to end in 2012, all of it at once. The end of architecture is proof that the most profound, useful, and organic of the human arts has prefigured the arrival of the end and has ceased to evolve autonomously, independently. Berengo is so close to his father that he is able to convey these statements word for word.

His father wouldn't mind if his son worked a little more because it would make his mother worry less, but he can see where Nico is coming from. Since he moved to New York, Nico stopped working almost entirely. He spends most of his time introducing people to one another, using his extensive network of contacts to help out his friends and acquaintances. To his father, this new behavior is proof of an enlightened, Franciscan path, a path that pushes his son to dedicate his life to others and humbly reject all personal ambition.

The son salutes the role of consumerism in the end of the world: let's consume all there is left to consume. "Before the wi-fi radiation kills us all."

BULLSHIT.

His father handles the bank transfers—€2,500 a month into his son's account—and all the taxes.

NOW THAT HE'S INSURED, HE'S NO LONGER ABLE TO TAKE WORK SERIOUSLY.

- Life insurance
- Health insurance
- Private pension

His parents pay in the neighborhood of €10,000 a year to cover all three. "Why should I be expected to earn a salary if my parents are doing so well that they're already providing for my old age?"

BERENGO AND ME

He is a cold and childish man. He's loving and intense, and he's doesn't do much with his time. He has no steady relationships. He seems incapable of building anything. He is paralyzed by complexity and criticism, especially of his loved ones. I experience the exotic thrill of finding my Oblomov. Some days I revel in his frenzied apathy. He's my Stranger.

We met in 2008, at a party at Gary Shteyngart's apartment. We sat on two stools Gary had bought at an auction that had once belonged to James Brown. (It was the night the DFW news broke. That may be why we bonded immediately. I had started teaching at Columbia, and I remember feeling awful, thinking about how Dave was going to become God.)

"You never let your characters just fuck. You never have them enjoy it and just leave it at that. There's a conflict or anxiety or regret every fucking time! It's like you don't know that there's actual pleasure in the world. It's really puritanical."

Also: "How come in *Godspeed* the bad news always breaks after someone fucks someone they aren't supposed to? Like, Dad was supposed to pick up the kids after school, but he was late because he was banging his lover, so the kids go home on a friend's helicopter and they die. Then people write about the helicopter metaphor, and they don't even notice the function of pleasure in your work.

My take on this is: "You don't solve loneliness with pleasure."

"*HOW CAN YOU* believe you're speaking to 'human beings' with your books, to real people, if a European who reads them has to put aside everything he knows about pleasure in order to adhere to the abstract ethics of your cosmos?"

And all I can think about is I should really spend a summer in Italy: the Magna Graecia, the Roman ideal of *societas*, villas filled with friends of friends of friends.

INTERESTING ITALIAN SLANG

Svarioni: A combination of anxiety attacks, panic attacks, and fear of death.
Insicurezzine: Berengo's petty insecurities.

SEXUAL IDEOLOGY

The problem with sex, he says, is that it's associated with time rather than with space. You have sex during a period of time. It's an event, so it can't help but take on an aspect of causality—of cause and effect. "Sex happens when you go after it, and you obtain it. And then you obtain it, and it's over. Satisfaction. But for me sex isn't time; it's space. If it's a place, we can inhabit it with no purpose. Aristotle, right? Scrap the *causa efficiente* and pick the *causa formale*. We can inhabit sex without having to leave sex after the drive is satisfied.

(This is BS. Should I point out all the reasons why I think it's BS? Don't I just enjoy writing all this down? Is that enough?)

"If you give in to the tyranny of linear time—and this is the case with all your Puritanical redemption narrative shit—you get into this need to give ourselves moral goals we have to reach through sex, and . . . I don't know, it's a slippery slope, man. You think you're different than the bros in the YouPorn videos, but you're the same. You're using your partner as a means to reach your ethical goals. My ideal is to inhabit sex completely, to empty it of purpose."

THEORY OF SWALLOWING

Above all, Daria's mythical blow jobs. Apparently she's relentless, and she swallows in such a way that he can doze off while he's being catered to. He says he doesn't need to go the bathroom and rinse. So he basically faints: he's stoned, he's already lying in bed, and after he comes he passes out.

His theory of swallowing is that it extinguishes a fire that, unattended to, can transform itself into more human life. Swallowing eats that fire whole.

What is she like, really? Is she a fiction? "My wife doesn't swallow," I tell him, and this feels so strange to say. And writing it down is even stranger: it feels like an endeavor totally different from my writing, from my *literature*.

BARBRA

One of Berengo's lovers. In 2010 she wanted them to be in a relationship, but he wasn't interested. He had given her much thought. Twenty-eight years old, American, born and bred in Chicago. She had fallen in love with Nicola after spending two weeks in his apartment in New York while looking for a room in Brooklyn. The girl had brought a touch of grace to the house: she decorated and cleaned, bought fresh flowers. She encouraged him to drink boiled ginger root. Nicola was going through one of those phases where he felt like he needed to find a proper girl-friend, and Barbra was everything he might want. But when she left his apartment and moved into a room in Brooklyn, Nicola realized that he didn't love her.

Barbra's plan was to be an artist in Williamsburg. Nicola thought you were only allowed to "have a plan" before you turned twenty-five. By twenty-five you had to know whether you could make it or not. She avoided the subject, but she didn't look like she was rich enough to be able to afford avoiding the subject. These might have been overly cold calculations—and it's true that many of his friends and acquaintances thought that Nico was cold when it came to evaluating partners—but they made Nico stop loving her. He couldn't imagine a future with her. (Which brought closure to yet another, febrile foray in search of Mrs. Berengo. Finding Mrs. Berengo is an impossible task—one of Zeno's paradoxes— because of his relationship with Daria, who is ever present, despite being on the other side of the Atlantic.)

But Barbra got in touch with him again. Nico agreed to go to dinner and accepted her invitation to come back to her apart-ment. He knew he couldn't resist her, and something told him he couldn't follow the impulse and just get laid and judge later. (He has never told me the obvious: that he was terrified that sex Barbra might take him somewhere.) So right there and then, he came up with a funny game: in order to discover the final piece that would explain why their relationship wasn't meant to be, he would only let her kiss him if she paid him. The girl said she had no money: all she had was the $11 in her wallet, and she couldn't use her debit card, because everything was allocated for her rent and her bills. Or so she said. Nicola had no way of checking. Barbra started to tease him with her mouth. She was dressed in black and had great breasts: they looked dreamy when she stood upright, as if pinned onto her chest by invisible hooks, mature but firm, with great, pale nipples. But when she lay down, they parted and fell to the sides, disrupting the overall vision.

She sat directly in front of him, her eyes roaming around the room but always wandering back to him. She smelled of seductive Indian flavors, which burned off candles she had placed around the room as well as the rough sticks of incense scattered on the table. Nicola thought he was about to give in, and so he said he didn't want to kiss her at all. She had to pay him. They had a discussion right then, in the middle of a Brian Eno song, the incense smoke mingling with the soft, warm light from three lamps hidden somewhere in the room. A heavy snowstorm hissed outside. Barbra bought a half-hour of kisses with five, damp one-dollar bills. When their time was up, Nico asked for three more dollars if she wanted to carry on. The banknotes were still cold and wet from dinner. By this point Berengo was ready to explode, because Barbra had been rubbing her breasts against his nose and chest between kisses. She could feel he needed to come, and they laughed together, realizing that the stopwatch on his iPhone was about to run out. The ad hoc gigolo told her that she could buy herself the right to give him a blow job for just five dollars. She responded—cheekily, logically, obviously—that he was the one who had to pay. She thought she could turn the game around in her favor, that he would pay her back the money, so that balance would be restored. (They had had dinner in a sad, empty Indian restaurant on a street that was clearing out due to the coming storm. The Indian waiters stayed glued to the new, fifty-something-inch flat screen TV, which ran a story of a gruesome murder that had occurred somewhere in Queens. All the waiters carried white napkins on their left arms, and the utter uselessness of those napkins had irritated Berengo so much that the feeling still haunted him during this exchange of money and kisses. They were supposed to become boyfriend and girlfriend, but he already knew they wouldn't.) Here, Nicola showed off his rigor—or his cruelty.

"You're the one who has to pay, because you're the one who wants to make me come."

"But you're dying to come."

"Think about it: you want to make me come more than I want it."

"I only have three dollars left. And you're the one who should pay."

He suggested to her that she invest her last three dollars in another half-hour of kissing on the bed. He put the money in his pocket. "Come on," she said, "let's make love." The timer was running and Barbra was hoping—or losing hope—that passion would put an end to that game. It was still snowing, and it was past one o'clock. When the alarm went off for the third time, Nicola got up and said goodbye. His soul hurt, and so did his crotch, but as he walked down the narrow stairwell he was convinced that giving up on pleasure had been the right thing to do. He had shown her that their relationship was not meant to be.

The following day, Barbra wrote to him to say that she had felt humiliated and that she couldn't afford to spend the last of her money on giving him head.

Berengo: "Surely that wasn't all the money you had." He apologized for sounding patronizing, admitted that what she was saying sounded reasonable. "However," he added, "I'm confused as to whether paying me money was a moral issue to you or a financial one. You're confusing me. I'm sorry, but I'm just trying to explain my point of view. I realize I'm not being very clear. I'm sorry I couldn't give you what you wanted."

THE PROGRESS OF CONVERSATIONS AT NICOLA BERENGO'S PARTIES

It's impossible to join in on any of the conversations that take place at Berengo's apartment. The language of these conversations—Italian or English—is immaterial. The key is the code: everyone who speaks is so well versed and proficient in it that it forms a dense cloud of text. One evening I take notes on all the topics discussed: the ethics of taking pictures of skaters who then end up dying of drug-related deaths, Jap rock, Shibuya-kei, Pizzicato Five, Jerry Seinfeld, Ricky Gervais, *Parks and Recreation*, Louis CK "talking about shit and niggers as if they were one and the same thing" followed by endless singalongs of "We're so good at television," Grand Billiards, Filipinos, Bill Simmons, "Oklahoma City is like *The Wire*: Durant is Avon, Westbrook is Stringer Bell," Fujiya and Miyagi, Neu!, Can, Happy Mondays, Stereolab, Simon Reynolds, The Mighty Boosh, Dexys Midnight Runners, a friend who is posing for *Jacques* and who has already posed for *Jalouse*, Lil Wayne, Weezy, Purple drank, "Is Tyler, The Creator a hoax?" "Russell Simmons meets Rick Rubin and wonders how he could possibly be white," Comme des Garçons, Number Nine, Prada, Issey Miyake.

CLASSIC BERENGO

"Only by consuming can I leave a written, recorded trace of my uniqueness. I'm the only person in the world to have bought 'Spin the Bottle' by Juliana Hatfield at 6:01 p.m. on a January afternoon. As I watched *Forgetting Sarah Marshall* at 5:13 p.m. that day I thought about how girls today seem more sincere than they used to. Winona Ryder was our nineties-era model of sincerity, and she turned out not to have been that sincere after all, what with her being a kleptomaniac. Winona blasted onto the alternative scene with *Reality Bites,* a fake or half-true movie that we watched as though it was fully true, and every love story any of us had, or any of us attempted, had to be on par with Ethan Hawke and Winona's. That's why I downloaded the prettiest song from its soundtrack, the song by Juliana Hatfield, who was the perfect woman for the real greats in my generation. She was petite, modest, weak-haired, but she still was the girlfriend of the prettiest singer, Evan Dando. I downloaded the song because Cugino Hitler stole my iPod, so now that 140GB of music were gone, I was paying $1.29 for a single song.

"A messiah who is unaware of the subtle difference between conceiving of Winona as a generational idol and Juliana as a more authentic version, who is unaware of the consequences all this would have. The entire meaning of sexual intercourse would be skewed for me, would be full of huge mistakes, and the messiah would never be able to save me. What would he save me from? He wouldn't *know* what he'd be saving me from. From the sick idealism that made Juliana Hatfield a crucial presence in my life, that made me think of Winona as a real-life person? This is just off the top of my head.

A list of famous people Jesus definitely knows?"

METAPHYSICAL CONSUMERISM

"Ideas are so important for man, yet they occupy no space. Man turns ideas into things that will occupy space. Man wants every idea, every thought, to be realized, to be made into things, until the world is crammed and saturated. Recycling makes no sense.

"Every idea has to be transformed into matter, so that the world is filled with ideas, so that the weight of human ideas on the universe will be such that any idea, in a given region of the universe, will beat matter. What do I mean by 'ideas'? Bands' posters; Roberto Saviano, Lady Gaga, cardboard cutouts of Obama; the confusing paper containers yogurt cups are sold in now; the packaging on remote-controlled cars; the milky-white of little Apple boxes. Ideas suffer until the minute they become matter; until that moment they're unfulfilled. To witness the continuous incarnation of ideas is a pleasure and a mission. Man gets no credit for saving his little corner of the universe."

(If you say so.)

(No, really, we meet, and he preaches and ad-libs. I don't mind letting people talk, but I feel he needs some kind of intervention.)

CLASS STRUGGLE

"This Latino cashier in a Park Slope supermarket threw all this shade at me because I was buying condoms."

SALON

"Marcello" aspires to be the Italian Kanye West, a racist Kanye who raps in English about the cruel and unfair destiny of not being able to make tons of money just because he's Italian. A neo-Socialist Fascist. "Represent for the internationally wealthy, the porn flick healthy." He might get an internship at RAI because he's connected.

I like Cugino Hitler better. He shot a video for *Vice*, a collage of all the videos published by the newspaper *La Repubblica* where you can see people dying. It's called *Education*. For his current project, he hands out t-shirts with his nickname on them to people dying of cancer. He had a show of his photography titled "We're shouting because we're pouring vodka on our eyes."

HEY, JAMES MURPHY!

Maybe a cycle of stories. *Decameron*. Try different routes. Existential porn? Anti-Nicholson Baker. Can I get enough material? Short, Boccaccio-like stories. Berengo is obsessed with Boccaccio: "Sex, illnesses, money, aging, death, pleasure, eating, idioms."

Follow Barth? Pursue his path toward anonymity as a practitioner of non-Puritan American writing?

(Addendum: These were obviously ridiculous observations, but something must be admitted: I HAVE NEVER ENJOYED LIFE, and fame makes no sense if it produces such boredom. I wanted to have a renaissance man for a friend, but a renaissance man or a douche bag? He broke up with me. And I still can't gauge if he was just a frat boy after all or something more.)

NICO AND I BROKE UP!

He got pissed on Saturday, while we were having lunch. Two days later, the doorman lets me up because he knows me by now. Elevator, buzzer. NMB waits and then gets close to the door. I hear the peephole swing open.

"Throw away *my* notes! Give them to me! You can't keep your notes on me!"

"I promise, brother, I'll delete them, trust me."

"Okay. Throw away the notes, and don't write about me ever again."

"Will you open the door, man? C'mon. Please."

(But if I am to be honest with myself—as honest as Montaigne—the sudden realization that I won't need to deal with these notes anymore, won't need to figure out what they mean, is somewhat a relief. I've learned some things, and it'll end up somewhere, in some form, but it's liberating not to have to hold myself accountable to Il Delicatino.

HOW HE GOT PARANOID

He was trying to get me and Gustavo to talk about his sex life. It was very conscious. He wanted us to blame him for something. He wanted to connect the two of us, so that we'd form a big, shaming combo. Maybe his bigot friend really was trying to shame him, and it's true that I might have treaded more carefully, but boy, I can't face that kind of paranoid momentum.

I'm disgusted by these two grown-up men, these two men who resemble teenage versions of themselves when they get together. And I hate that Nico thinks Gustavo is his friend. I wonder if this is a peculiarly Italian thing, considering these wholly toxic, ancient relationships worthy of preservation.

The irony is if my late-night phone call hadn't woken Gustavo up in Nico's room, he might not have found out that Berengo was sleeping around.

So now it feels unfair and unethical to get a story out of this. It seems to belong to Berengo. (Also, I don't do this kind of overtly personal shit. Also, it's about an erection I got from a twenty-year-old.)

At least it's in the third person.

JM, CUGINO HITLER, "Marcello," and Anna are at a party in Bushwick. The apartment is huge. It belongs to someone in the *Vice* clique. A friend of a friend of Anna's was asked to take photos for a new Ray-Ban campaign. She has gathered a large group of scenesters together: they'll be the crowd dancing around a female model wearing Ray-Bans. They're supposed to start dancing when the DJ gives the cue, but the rest of the time they can hang out and drink. The dancing is intermittent and occasional; it's less a party than a quantum event. The lights go on, then they go off again.

Anna keeps James company throughout the shoot. She says she's "refusing" to dance or to allow herself to be photographed. "Losers . . ." she says of everyone and no one in particular. The party sucks, she says, and the people are lame.

[Will I ever learn Italian? Will I ever be able to write a short story in Italian the way "Marcello" wants to rap in American English?]

The hollow white picture frame has been a Ray-Ban signifier for some time now, though I realize this only when I see the model holding it in front of her ear as they shoot. She also passes it around the room. If you're handsome, or if you're dressed in some interesting or noticeably strange way, they take a picture of you, too, and put it up online. JM is recognized and photographed by a well-read photographer who revels in the singular oddity of JM's presence.

[Berengo would be proud that I'm acknowledging my fame here, that I'm finding a way to write without the usual puritanical denial. The ideas of younger men feel so true, so right. So now there's a picture of me with my Wayfarers on, framed by the iconic white frame. I hope Franzen never sees it.]

After the shoot, a band takes the stage. Their faces are young and virginal, Anna says. They look like farmers. She says all Americans are farmers. James says that this is a belief of Berengo's and that she's only quoting him. Berengo also treats him like a farmer.

Anna says, "*Grazie al cazzo*," which means that that is so obviously true that he should feel ashamed for bringing it up. She makes James feel dumb and young. [Rudeness in another language is so inspiring! Even if in your own language it's just bad and ineffective. Also, I'm trying to cut down on "he said" and "she said," because according to Berengo, Italian literature has been screwed by an endless flood of American novels in translation where we keep she-saiding and he-saiding. We never travel down winding roads to tell our stories, so now our empire has ruined not just their culture but their language, too, like GMOs drifting through the air all the way into remote countrysides. Ask Canobbio at Einaudi Publishing if that's true. I know I should ask Daria.]

As the shoot winds down, Anna begins to dance, and she keeps going through the band's set: an uninspired performance but just the right amount of wallpaper for a party like this. She loves playing the part of attractive girl who's somewhat perversely, even violently shy. This is her niche. She's been shouting in JM's ear the whole night. She has this tender, manic way of going on and on about how everyone here is "rotten to their core and they're all pretending they don't care, but they do, oh they care so much." [I've never been this close to a girl. Not since my two girls left home for college. I guess I have to let them be in college and be whatever they want to be without giving it much thought.] He was thinking of his daughters, of the fact that they were in college and Anna wasn't. The college years are not really a phase in the lives of these Italian expats. All of them seem at once younger and older than their American peers. [They have no plan, and yet they still seem to accomplish more, though Berengo maintains that they won't, that it can't last.] Anna calls the tall DJ an ignorant poser, then approaches him and repeats her accusation. They hug. She comes back to James, who shouts in her ears: "Maybe you care too much, too? Why do you care? Leave them alone!"

[She gets anxious gauging the level of people's commitment to the party, their involvement in the scene. I think this is crazy, but I find myself taken by her total concern. Everything she does is an act, and there's nothing real about her, but she also feels so close, and she's so affectionate. Every scenester seems to respect her, even though she "hates" all of them. What can this mean? What do these emotions add up to, and where are they located, and how do I process them? Does this feeling (this lack of feeling?) allow her to experience reality in a different way? Is any of this literary, or is my note taking condescending? After my "breakup" with Berengo, I think I sort of know what I'd love to write about—these kids? I'm using the fake interrogative form—the up-talk—just like my kids would.]

Now James and Anna are sitting on the couch. She is upset. She says she's only here because "Marcello" and Cugino Hitler begged her to come. And she has also come for James, she says. His jaw drops as he hears this. Throughout the shoot she has stayed with him and has shown no interest in the many young men or young women milling about. There were boys who took off their shirts to shower in beer and pose for dumb photos, but they had no effect, and when two young Italian men offered her the white frame, she turned them down cold.

When she tries to leave the party, the young men force her to stay put, keeping her down on the couch with JM, who then gets up and tries out some dance moves. He stays close to the couch and keeps an eye on her. She sits straight and unmoving, her hands on her knees, and the men hover around her. JM comes back over and tells the boys to go try harassing some men, because harassing women isn't in fashion anymore. He squirms at his own quip, at the effort exerted.

A minute later, JM is back on the couch with Anna. Their knees rub together.

"Why aren't all young men like you?"

James has found a folded-over piece of paper stuck in the couch. It lists all the pictures and poses the producer needed tonight. It represents the matrix of party photography, and while the logic is straightforward enough, James can't help but think of it as a major historical discovery, a cultural breakthrough: *(1) someone showing a tattoo, (4) two girls, piggyback, (5) fish face, (8) someone doing a handstand . . .*

Every picture you see on social networks has a name, then— it's a catalogue! All the poses have a name.

Cugino Hitler, Anna, and "Marcello" begin playing with the list, while James picks up the phone to tell Berengo he's found the Magna Carta of hipster aesthetics. Anna is dancing. It's two a.m., James's wife is in Akron with the girls, he is sweating in a checkered shirt. (The flannel shirt is back in fashion, so he's slipped back into the zeitgeist with his old clothes.) Berengo isn't picking up the phone. James quits trying and shouts, "Anna!"

333

Anna hears him, comes back, a dumb smile on her face, leans over him, hugs him, and starts crying. She has nothing under her Godardesque striped shirt, her hard braless breasts (between a B and a C cup) vaguely shaped like those of his female relatives. Anna sits on his lap. She presses her breast against his chest. (Berengo once said, "She's the sort of *figa* who is so *figa* that she can't hide it, so she'll fuck anybody and not care." Berengo has slept with her. "It's easier for her to sleep with anybody than deny herself all the time." Since she has no confidence issues, when she's not down to fuck she shuts down entirely. So what now? I mean, tonight?)

"It's a nightmare, *zio* James, a nightmare," she says as she rubs her cheek and her chest against him, weeping. "I hate this city."

James tries to soothe her, reads her the list. He's being fatherly, but he's keeping her close because he wants her to keep rubbing against him. The list doesn't seem to soothe her; it only makes her angrier. "I hate these people. It's all written down on this piece of paper, and it's all true. It's all fake!" Her face is red. James has never seen anyone turn this red, this splotchy. It seems like half the capillaries have burst. Is it possible, JM wonders, to feel such strong emotions because of one party? Does she feel that the people here are keeping her from becoming something she wants to become? It feels as though they're denying her some basic liberty, some right. But what is it, exactly? This war she's waged against God knows what indignity makes her look ridiculous and weak and fluid—all this pressing up against him, all this leaning.

Anna seems to be in the middle of a crisis, and now she's kissing and nibbling on his ear. JM can't pull his ear away even if it hurts.

Anna gets up and asks JM to read the items on the list aloud, so she can act them out.

(5) She sucks in the insides of her check and puffs out her lips [so much flesh, it's overflowing].

(1) She pulls up her t-shirt and flashes a tit to show a tattoo of a candle on her rib cage.

(26) She rushes to a table and gets some peanuts, which she then throws to people.

(8) As she attempts a headstand on the floor, her t-shirt falls to her neck, and her belly and then her breasts are exposed. James reaches the point in the list where a couple is supposed to kiss, and he skips it, though she manages to read it over his shoulder. A whiff of melancholy, then the sudden feeling that he's wearing boxers.

The game ends, and Anna is back on his lap to tell him about a dream she had a couple of months ago in which a gypsy stopped to talk to her and Berengo. She had two strips of toilet paper—one that she'd used to wipe her vagina, the other her ass—and said, "I have nothing, but I have this, and so I preach the Gospel." In the dream Berengo was chatting up the gypsy, and he and Anna weren't able to get to an appointment they had—they were supposed to paint a wall. "It was a wall where they were pulling out these kittens from between the bricks." Then she confesses that she's lying, at least in part. The gypsy is from Berengo's dream, and the kittens are from hers.

Now she stands up and pushes him violently, so he sits back down on the couch, right at the moment when he was trying to gather the strength to stand up and kiss her. She leaves without saying goodbye. James hangs back, upset with a hard-on, until "Marcello" and Hitler come over to him and sit on either side to have a talk.

Hitler asks James to write a profile of "Marcello."

"Marcello" tells him, "Will you leave us alone you piece of shit?"

Now he and JM are alone, and he begins a monologue about

cultural relevance that makes JM ill. "I'm rich, but rich Italian *uguale* no bling, don't count. I make my English worse so I sound like a slave . . . My hunger is for big audience . . . The problem is irrelevance," which James records on his iPhone. In that squeaky voice, all the inanity and grandeur and fascism and the end of a generation and maybe a country whose . . .

RAY-BAN PICS TO-DO LIST

1. someone showing a tattoo
2. knuckles
3. drawing on the wall
4. two girls, piggyback
5. fish face
6. band playing in the kitchen
7. crowd surging/freight elevator
8. someone doing a handstand
9/10. 2 shots: girl and boy swap clothing
11. couple kissing in bathroom
12. dance party in the freight elevator
14. legs in the frame
15. someone holding it up and getting confetti thrown in
17. someone putting on a guy
18. someone putting his or her arms around someone but too tall out of frame
20. people dancing on table
21. someone dancing on table
22. someone shaving his head
23. Ron holding a puppy
23. fake fight
24. wide shots and close-ups of the band

25. someone wrapped in toilet paper
26. food fight
27. someone doing a heart sign with his hands
28. a guy without his shirt
29. picture of Nicky
30. sticking out your tongue
31. someone pouring a drink into someone else's mouth

MARCELLO'S LATE-NIGHT RANT AT THE RAY-BAN PARTY

I'm crazy mad, James man, crazy mad. I talk to my italo-americano bitch lawyer from Long Island today. Big office Midtown, big window with a view. A view of old skyscrapers, old copies of *The New Yorker* in waiting room. Twenty floor. Visa-denying bitch. I have need of visa. She deny visa. I can't live *senza* visa. Not Visa the credit card; I have credit card. I'm flush and have credit-visa. I mean ID visa, *visto, visa lasciapassare* to live in America. Today Long Island lawyer bitch, the bitch my friend and manager advice that I visit, she change idea. The prostitute. How can I make record if bitch don't give me visa? She change idea, she change what she say to me, no, she change what she say to my friend manager about my possibility of have a visa. I think you see the game I play here.

You prize-winning taker of sensible notes: all start with the notes. You take bad notes; you fuck process.

She say this winter American authorities spy that too many Italians obtain visa and now I can't have sponsor for visa at fake company that a friend of my manager invented to get visa for talent artists like me.

I want to make it U.S. hip-hop and not in Italian hip-hop because Italian hip-hop have no relevance. Better talk like Jamaican. Better sound poor. All money my rich father spend on my English school with English teachers since I had six years, I stick those money in my father's culo and bring back my English to basic English, and I am poser of poor-sounding Italo-American–sounding Italian that make me next big thing in America instead of another Lil Wayne record with electric guitar.

I speak child English and try rhymes.

I want to make it big, so I make my English bad so I can sound poor like Weezy and seem that I come from idealized Italo-American slum and seem that my polo shirt is heartbreaking because it's sign that I rise from the ghetto. But you and I know I am not ghetto, not inside not outside; I am all money. I have money like Lil Wayne's daughter have money.

I look exotic, but I in reality speak English like sons of ambassadors, those sons of ambassadors so black they're invisible, from French-speaking country, from civilized third world country. I am like them.

I am "Marcello," like the late great Marcello Mastroianni, the man who beds your sisters and girls, the man who has a flow, the man in the unforgettable roles as an Italian representative of universal appeal and undying relevance. I'm rich, but rich Italian uguale no bling, don't count. I make my English worse so I sound like a slave, and you digs me, for I'm fast and schemey and I use the tropes like make your head pop with my 9 millimeters I don't really own but have money my Daddy money to buy a hundred Uzi and kill your whole ghetto.

And you love me, for I'm simple and next-big-thingy already and have hunger for relevance, like handicapped underprivi-ledged kids from Odd Future Wolf Gang have hunger for relevance. Me: same hunger, no fake psycho issues. Me: honest. But like them I serve the White Man with passion: they do advertisement for Supreme; I come to New York with my rich money and buy Supreme t-shirts. Only I am white, and the Man, the Power, the Man is my Supreme Dad and all my butt surfing is bound to serve the glory of the Man my father. Father, Money, America, Glory, Polo.

I escape from the former civilization, Italy, the world-famous country of Vinny and Pauly D and The Sitch and of orgy and of binge drinking underage by American students and marveling at the Colosseo.

I grow up listening to white/black conspiracy of The Special, Two-Tone sound, and the white/black conspiracy of Rick Rubin and Russell Simmons sound. After that, I find euro-trance and start produce hip-hop dance records for Italia, but not, no, Italia is no relevance, so am here to impose my will via the inner beauty of English as second language for the poor of the land, the sad-eyed nations of other planets coming to take New York and ask the mayor for a section of the island they can call Little Country of Origin.

Ex romanità, former empire, and I produce tracks for Italian distinguished hip-hop scene but have never rapped before. I don't waste songwriting skill for small Italian audience.

My hunger is for big audience.

The lonely hunger of the man already rich that resonates all the same in the poor man's heart.

I'm young and hood in my striped polo, and no one can beats me for I have history, I stay in school, I take the cocaine and shoot the girls with porn iPhone like in Italian songs.

I come to New York and have no hood, no projects, just I'm cool. When I come to New York I sleep at my manager's apartment. He want to make something new of me. House high-rise very expensive in Williamsburg on the river, kicking all the poor away, soon kicking the Hasids away, kicking the brothers away 'cause we want the new okay neighborhood all for us. We live here, I and manager.

My manager love cock, but he promise he not butt surfing in my presence. He nose like I nose. We do. I promise my mom I never become gay in pursuit of career. But bashing gays is good career move. Young people love the easy predigested scandal. Because it's a thing we do together. We organize the layers of fun.

That's why I see potential of inspiring heartbreak in my friendship with homosexual manager from repressed Italy. He repressed. Big time repressed. Orphan, too. He more heartbreaking than me; he success story. We fuck you up with cry for our story, especially his. Read gossip magazine and find out if he fuck me.

Have not decided which hos I want yet. Only thinking of developing my tear-inducing, scrappy flow.

If sucking manager's cock is needed I ask my mom she does the cock sucking. Rich woman must know how to, no? even if she have back problems? Sucking cock for rising from misery is more typically black problems but she got back problems.

See? I make joke, maybe I be comic. Immigrant comic.

The problem is irrelevance. Is losing sleep over irrelevance. I will fuck Italo-American lawyer because her typical Italian inability to do right.

If I don't get visa my life is useless; have to spend rest of days taking ketamine to fight the feeling.

Case *popolari* = not the projects. Projects = MIT-like research and development of arts. Case *Popolari* = delusional people.

I wanna lose my Italian 'cause talk Italian only makes you sleep with Italians or with American tourist in Italy, but not make you relevant unless you fuck daughter of big CEO of music business under the Colosseum in a dream and then in the dream he makes your dream come true.

Me, no Baywatch bagnino, no operaio, no Pasolini butt seller.

Me no want to lose my hair but accept my macho legacy. My hair already thinning. Me skinny rich but balding because macho legacy. Me Italian for real. No Vinny. No Sitch. Me hundred percent Italian. Even Fascist.

All must converge. Money my father earn through hard work as lawyer. Me, too, lawyer. Me twenty-five. Me laureate in law. Will I ever be lawyer or will I be hip-hop sensation with simple accento and tear-jerking rhymes about hunger for success? Everybody digs "Marcello."

All the money the piccola imprenditoria italiana gave to my father for their lawsuits and their gestione del personale, I spend in cab rides and cranberry crap at the Jane Hotel, and Coogi puttane in Miu Miu sandals. I buy mocassinos and moccaccinos to hos and they blow me.

See new collection of Miu Miu sandals? Fashioned like slaves of ancient Rome, slaves for my pleasure. All must converge.

We use Italian accents to impress people, like young good-looking Albanesi in the bars of Stazione Termini in remote Roma, the city that I don't love and that won't give me nothing except my money.

Problem is this is not supermoney like, I don't know, Britney Spears money: our money is only family money. It is just a lot of money.

My father money are lazy money: money that buy irrelevance, and this means a life of ketamina.

Look, James, look at me. Take the notes. Take the good notes is half the work.

We the posers at the opening, we open the fancy store and buy ourselves all the merch, all the clothes, and then them niggers kill us because we want to die. But we die here and you call the Italian parliament and give the news that we die because irrelevance.